DAVID IRELAND was born in 1927 on a kitchen table in Lakemba in south-western Sydney. He lived in many places and worked at many jobs, including greenskeeper, factory hand, and for an extended period in an oil refinery, before he became a full-time writer.

Ireland started out writing poetry and drama but then turned to fiction. His first novel, *The Chantic Bird*, was published in 1968. In the next decade he published five further novels, three of which won the Miles Franklin Award: *The Unknown Industrial Prisoner*, *The Glass Canoe* and *A Woman of the Future*.

David Ireland was made a member of the Order of Australia in 1981. In 1985 he received the Australian Literature Society Gold Medal for his novel *Archimedes and the Seagle*.

David Ireland lives in New South Wales.

KATE JENNINGS is a poet, essayist, short-story writer and novelist. Her novels, *Snake* and *Moral Hazard*, were *New York Times* Notable Books of the Year. She has won the Australian Literature Society Gold Medal and the Christina Stead Prize for Fiction. Born in rural New South Wales, she has lived in New York since 1979. Her most recent book is *Trouble: Evolution of a Radical*.

ALSO BY DAVID IRELAND

The Chantic Bird
The Unknown Industrial Prisoner
The Glass Canoe
The Flesheaters
Burn
City of Women
Archimedes and the Seagle
Bloodfather
The Chosen

A Woman of the Future
David Ireland

Text Publishing Melbourne Australia

textclassics.com.au
textpublishing.com.au

The Text Publishing Company
Swann House
22 William Street
Melbourne Victoria 3000
Australia

First published in the US by George Braziller Inc. 1979
First published in Australia by Allen Lane 1979
This edition published by The Text Publishing Company 2012

Cover design by WH Chong
Page design by Text
Typeset by Midland Typesetters

Printed in Australia by Griffin Press, an Accredited ISO AS/NZS 14001:2004
Environmental Management System printer

Primary print ISBN: 9781922079824
Ebook ISBN: 9781922148025
Author: Ireland, David, 1927-
Title: A woman of the future / by David Ireland;
introduction by Kate Jennings.
Series: Text classics.
Other Authors/Contributors: Jennings, Kate.
Dewey Number: A823.3

CONTENTS

Am I Perhaps Australia?
by Kate Jennings

'LITERARY sewage…A dreadful sex-ridden fantasy…doomed to oblivion.' Harsh. But that's how Colin Roderick, a judge of the 1979 Miles Franklin Literary Award, described David Ireland's *A Woman of the Future*. The other judges demurred and gave Ireland the prize anyway. Cue the literary-world kerfuffle!

Roderick was disturbed by the forthright sex in the book—sex that is particularly jolting because it's from the uncensorious point of view of a child bent on discovering life's secrets. And she begins her candid explorations with her father's genitals. In truth, the sex *is* confronting, but it's supposed to be. Discovery of sex varies, but adolescents think about it at first furtively and obsessively, and then, most likely, enthusiastically.

The child is Alethea Hunt, one of the most singular female characters in fiction. Dorothy Hewett acknowledged Ireland's achievement, calling it 'extraordinary'. You won't forget in-your-face, kiss-my-arse Alethea in a hurry: 'I was born a person, not a limp babybag with suet brain,' she tells us in one of her early journal entries. This fully formed brain allows her to chronicle her babyhood and childhood as well as adolescence.

·She isn't pleasant. Too abrasive, assertive: 'My attitudes hardened, my ambitions were forming, as vague as they might be. I would be as good as any man; as brave, as strong, as ruthless, as independent, as benevolently contemptuous of others.' Too intent on winning, attaining greatness: 'Even at that age I knew the Halls of Failure were full.' Too intent on demolishing lies, constructing truths: Australians 'have no dream, just a national sleep'.

One of my favourite parts from her babyhood is when Alethea—a name derived from the Greek word for truth—tells the reader that her mother, who uses the excuse of writing to retreat into not just a room but a world of her own, has 'advanced ideas', which 'often led to simple opposites'. Instead of dressing her baby girl in pink, she dresses her in blue: 'Mother thought that by taking the word, which represented a thing, and twisting the word, she was twisting a thing. Throwing out pink booties and substituting blue was overturning generations of sexist child rearing. It was a new beginning. The past was abolished.'

If only. Ireland predicted some things accurately—his characters have multicultural names, and everyone at school receives awards regardless of performance—but he could not have foretold the hordes of little missies dressed from top to toe in retrograde Disney pink that honks *feminine!* When I fret about this development, a friend reassures me by predicting that this generation of girls will be the next wave of radical feminists. They certainly have something to kick against: nauseating clothes as well as rights that are patently fragile. Men still run the world.

David Ireland wrote this novel at the end of the 1970s, coming off the heyday of the women's liberation movement. We protested customs such as pink or blue bonnets and booties on babies to designate their gender, and using the word 'girl' to describe a woman of any age. Small beer you might think against, say, equal pay and control over our bodies, but we believed that words use us as much as we use words. Ditto colours. Feminism might be a yawn today, but back then it was startling, table-turning.

Ireland was thinking his way into a woman's mind at a time when not only all these ideas were fresh but when fiction was markedly more adventurous and unafraid of offending. The result is gutting, combustive. Stopped me cold. Time and again I found myself rereading a paragraph: Oh my! Did he really write what I think he wrote? John Leonard, a highly regarded New York critic, was also bowled over by the novel. He confessed that *A Woman of the Future* made him feel provincial.

Alethea isn't just exploring sex and a corollary, what makes the opposite sex tick, but also the shape of society. Men: Stupid and undeserving users of women. Society: Unfair. Social structure is a preoccupation of Ireland's, as it was in the decade when he wrote this novel. We brimmed with ideologies, the rosy and the rancid. In this novel's future, society culls itself, the best and brightest becoming the Serving Class and the rest, the Frees. By calling themselves servants, the upper class can lord it over the masses, a clever sleight of hand borrowed from Dostoyevsky. More importantly, they have work with which to occupy themselves; the underclass have to spend their time with 'the trivialities of freedom'. This was before computers came along to disenfranchise unskilled workers and reality television plumbed new depths of trivia.

Alethea doesn't dismiss *all* men: her mother is drifting jellyfish-like in her writing, so her father is her mother, and she loves both of them. Comically, he's an actor, dying early in a recurring piece of theatre in which his body is then 'investigated'. Alethea's subsequent conduct is not without precedent. The play lasts all day and has given him a bad back. Touches like this are typical of Ireland's humour. When Alethea first surreptitiously examines her father's genitals, while he is sleeping, she frightens herself and runs back to her room to read Jane Austen: '*Oh, cried Elizabeth, I am excessively diverted. But it is so strange.*' In her next attempt, less inhibited, she has the thought that she was 'sorry to be getting near the end of Jane Austen'. Never was Austen put to such wicked use.

A Woman of the Future is an impossible book to summarise. And Alethea's pushy, dissecting mind doesn't make for easy reading. The novel is all threepenny bits, no plum pudding. That is, despite succulent sentences, no comfort. It's *wild*, an amalgam of reality and flights of fancy. A cabinet of curiosities and, like any such cabinets, best examined slowly. Some objects will charm, others disgust. Indeed, one way to be designated a Free is to become a grotesque worthy of being preserved in formaldehyde. These folk grow appendages such as coffins and cannons or sprout coins on their faces and vulvas under their arms. One takes root if he stands still. Another attaches herself to anyone she touches.

Ever more intense and irrepressible, Alethea progresses from seeing no reason why she shouldn't be generous with her body to being gang-raped to falling in love, which she calls her 'first sickness' because it drains her of will and energy. At which point she doesn't become a grotesque; she changes completely. Earlier she had wished that she were 'a long, fierce snake living a private life on the edge between bush and desert, and my world plain to me and not puzzling at all'. She goes one better in her evolution, and the story heads inland, to the misunderstood middle of Australia, to vast red-dirt country. Her high-school certificate results are a final barb in a novel full of them.

Colin Roderick was right about one thing. *A Woman of the Future* might have won the Miles Franklin, the third awarded to Ireland, but after a blaze of sales it slipped into oblivion, as did Ireland's career, with publishers turning down his recent books. Arguably, the novel would never see the light of day were it submitted for publication now. Partly because of the queasy-making sex and partly because of its hybrid form; it's a platypus of a novel, a curiosity in itself.

And then there is the matter of Alethea's likeability, not a small one for publishers who are forced to judge writers only by the sales of their last book. I can report being asked by editors to make thorny characters nicer, give them more soul, be less intense, so as not to alienate potential readers. Check out what happens to books 'without visible means of support' in Ireland's imagined future. A belly laugh if it weren't true. Critical acclaim, poor commercial success: bonfire.

Still, I was surprised—given his impressive if knotty body of work—to find that David Ireland had been written out of Australian literary history and omitted from the mammoth PEN Macquarie anthology published in 2009. (I have the same distinction. An exclusive club.) Vogues come and go, times change, posterity is fickle. Listened to any Dory Previn lately?

All the same, no wonder Alethea was never seen again, not in the empty interior nor at the crowded edges of the continent. Given the treatment handed out to her creator, she probably left the country.

A Woman of the Future

EDITORS' NOTE

These notebooks, diaries and papers were found among the effects of Alethea Hunt, and are reproduced by kind permission of her father. We publish them without alteration. Many of the pages contain no hint of the date of writing, but we believe, from the handwriting, that those dealing with her childhood and infancy, and some of the explanatory and reflective pages, were written after she began to find evidence of her change.

Some papers had the year of her age on them and were arranged in chronological order. Where she left headings we have shown them; where not, we have used the first phrase or so of her notes. We have no idea of where she wanted to insert her various general remarks, so we have placed them throughout in the order in which she left them.

Mother's stomach bellied out like a sail. Young, she was unable to say no to anyone who asked her to make love. Her reasons for her behavior were all her own; never, after she'd had me did she allow another man to enter her: my birth was her real marriage. And when I was six, she shut herself away entirely.

It happened in the Chalet, on a ski holiday. Perhaps the cold weather. She knew she had probably made a mistake with her contraceptive, but went ahead, alive to the risk. They did it quickly, against a wall. She had known him years before; it hadn't been a grand passion, more like a baby grand.

I think she half wanted to have a baby.

My mother thought standing up could make it all right, less likely to be productive; gravity might prevent the little wrigglers from getting at her egg.

I may not have been Boyce Hart's little swimmer: I may have been father's. After all, they were married; they'd been having intercourse regularly and often, including one before breakfast that day, and one after Boyce—that is, after lunch.

The upshot is, I don't know who I am. Of course I know I'm me, I mean I don't know the exact name of my father. Having narrowed the field to two is something, I suppose.

It only took a minute or two, nine months before I was born. Two stolen minutes against the wall of the gear room! I know lust means never having to say I love you, but my mother said he seemed uneasy, on edge, playing his role as if he expected someone to trump it.

He came quickly, and released her. She took his handkerchief, wiped herself down there and gave it back to Boyce.

She walked back along the corridor with the polished timber and stood in the door of the lounge and smiled into the room, radiating a look that would have gone well as dessert after a magnificent meal. A trickle started between her legs.

Boyce folded the handkerchief with the leaked semen, pocketed it and went down the back stairs and out into the cold air and stood looking down the snow-covered valley. Once he shivered, suddenly lonely. His past was before him like a beacon; he would keep going in that direction and call it the future.

And then it was father's turn. That radiant smile decided him. He jumped to his feet proudly, turned her round in the doorway and hurried her off to their room where he laid her down with love. She used her panties for another surreptitious wipe.

She confirmed her mistake with the contraceptive when she checked, late at night. All this was common knowledge in my family: mother told him later, and me much later; she didn't know I was listening: common knowledge, that is, until the censorship clamped down and they wouldn't talk.

I daresay happiness is possible, with a little shutting of the eyes. Anyway, it was two chances to one in father's favor.

FATHER'S WEDDING SONG
Here I am, standing in the aisle
Waiting for her to stand by me.
From a long way she comes,
On her face is the swelling that shows
The face of her child-to-be.
I see its features: it is not like me.
Will I wait and let myself
Be married, or will I –
Will I run now?
Will it be
Just a little like me?

My father didn't write that: I did.

I imagined the act of love between them their first time; before ever I saw them doing it; the first time after I was born; and always the other picture, indistinct and alternating, of two people present at my conception, and my mother the constant one.

I'd like her to have had time to look forward—at the marriage ceremony—to her baby. Perhaps she did, as she looked in at the church to check that father was there, ready to be joined in holy padlock.

6

I showed the verse to him when I was sixteen. He congratulated me. He always congratulates me, no matter what I do.

"Did you feel that at the time?" I asked. (If only I could go back, now, and have him refather me.)

"A little. Maybe. I don't remember." And later, as he was putting the dried dishes away up into the cupboards with the cobalt blue doors and the pretty shelves, "I did realize, standing there, that there was still time."

My father wasn't the sort of man to exaggerate his love.

"But you were brought up not to run away?" We all had the idea our parents were "brought up," instead of, like us, being allowed to do as we liked, and that this was why they were different.

"No. That was my own idea," he answered splendidly, and I kissed him below the ear on the edge of his jaw, where he liked me to. He got impatient if you tried to kiss him more on the round, plump part of his cheek, and waggled his head as if he had been a pilot trying to see ahead, steering his vehicle in a blinding storm and plagued by females shaped like large insects.

Things I Remember from the Womb

Several smells. Including one that, ever since, I have not been able to find repugnant.

Intestinal solos, melodies you sometimes hear with your head on a stomach. And in the distance sometimes when I move, the music humans made with their technology of wood, metal, air, precise measurements and stretched things.

Kicking to push myself round. And using my elbows to turn slightly when I got bored with being where I was. It was pleasant to be anchored, and to find there was a limit to how far I could turn in any direction. It felt safe.

Sometimes a push in the back and my head being knocked. Softly, of course. Cushioned. I think the lack of this occasional push toward the end had something to do with my stirring to get out.

A lovely jogging feeling; up and down, side to side. All my life it's been such a temptation to let myself be carried.

The difference between daylight and dark. Perhaps I was helped in this by the inert posture of my host's sleep. I observed no hours, woke any time I pleased. I got a smug pleasure from getting a response to frenzied activity I put on after we had both been still for a long time. I jumped and flailed about, and she sat up and called and I felt her alarm.

I never regarded myself as one person with her; I didn't really consider that we inhabited the one space. The part of her that I occupied I considered my own domain.

I was getting my arms in the way of my head, making the whole operation dangerous and somehow fucking everything up. My head felt tight, something gripped it fiercely and would not let me go.

My parents didn't seem to realize I was trying to supply something I thought they should have supplied, something they should have done, or said to me.

I know I would have responded to a few directions, but they didn't seem to think I was a party to the birth: I was a splinter to come out, and was only me when they saw me.

I was a three-hour labor. By rights mother should have loved me madly, softly, gratefully till she died.

They did it on the kitchen table. When the doctor came they had already got my head round and into position. They were surprised to see the caul on my head, which was patched and marked with uterine material, like a small spotted cub, Doctor Lal said.

So began my aloneness, my separateness from others. Wednesday's child has far to go, they say.

A Note

I can't very well tell anyone this is a diary, it's mostly papers I've kept, and things I'm remembering here in a terrible hurry, but if I manage to finish enough of it before my hand can no longer hold a pen, perhaps father will try to get it published.

If people somewhere down the slope of the future read it, it may help them if I start with a note about the sort of society in which people like me are possible.

Here goes:

The common people have become redundant, though that word is never used. The serving classes study them, describe them; produce, provide and prescribe for them; analyze, diagnose, manage the machines that have replaced them as labor units; allowing them the dignity of life, costing that as an expense against the State; granting them the luxury of reproduction.

The social classes have been reduced to two: Serving Class and Free; the battle between the two was decided when one class took Dostoyevsky's advice and, tongue in cheek, became servants in order to be leaders. But of course they weren't princes of ancient lineage: they were the bourgeois, who flourish in a meritocracy.

At the end of school years the grading system diverts a small stream of young people toward the class of professionals, those named the Servants of Society. The rest are Free Citizens, proletariat. The trivial occupations of freedom are their whole life. They see the divisions of society, they see the success of others, they see their own failure; the seeing begins to interact with the seen, the eye with the object: aberrations blossom.

My Father is an Actor

My father was given the news of my arrival during a performance, and he was so excited he told the audience during one of his many curtain calls. Although he was the dead body on stage for most of the performance, he was one of the most popular players. He died beautifully, was dissected, and parts shown amongst the audience.

Later he stood in the foyer, laughing and smiling, and moved through the press of people to the entrance, where there were three steps down to the street, still smiling and talking. When my father smiled, the whole of his face lit up, even his ears. He was the center, briefly—for he wanted to get away to the house where I was born—of the well-wishers, and since in those days it was only possible to get large crowds into the city in the daytime, he was coming out of the theatre in the peak traffic hour of five o'clock.

A demonstration of grotesquely changed women was going past, marching ten abreast. He was smiling as he made to leave the theatre crowd, smiling as he turned to face the demonstrators, wondering who it was this time. Banners were approaching, he delayed a little to see them, waiting for a slogan in which the cause was mentioned.

He was still smiling as a group of demonstrators detached from the main body and ran over screaming. He hesitated, not knowing if they recognized him and were wanting a word with him, or autographs.

"It's no laughing matter!" One small red-haired girl screamed. Her face was worked into a plasticine mask of hate, and she kicked him. He hardly had time to lift the injured shin to give it a cuddle when the rest descended on him, knocked him to the grey-black bitumen and kicked him with great enthusiasm and some precision. In a crisis the best protection is often plain cowardice: he stayed down, curled up.

It was a long time, perhaps the best part of half a minute before some of the theater staff rushed over to see what was going on. The hand-shaking public stayed out of it.

"What's going on?" they asked. Carefully, for the ferocious women were not likely to care what else they kicked.

"He was laughing!" they screamed. "As we marched past!" and carried on as before.

Since it was a money demonstration, not merely a parade, and since money is what government is about, there were plenty of police in attendance, shepherding them. One officer left his bike and pushed enough women aside to show his uniform. The few punches he got were inexpert and glanced off his ample ribs; he stood over my father, and recognized him.

"Bayard Hunt!" he exclaimed. "The actor!" He was obviously about to go on and talk about the performance he'd seen: every man, woman and child in the country had seen it at least once. *Changes* was deservedly famous, a blend of despairing philosophy, mindless optimism, and violent sexual action—but my father cut him short with a groan.

"What did you do?" the officer said good-naturedly to the public figure.

"Smiling as I came out, that's all," said father.

"Dangerous to laugh," said the cop wisely. "Specially women. Surveys show—"

"I know the surveys. I was talking to fans, and trying to get away. Of course I was smiling. I got news of my baby. Baby girl. Born during the performance."

The policeman helped him to his cycle, put him on the pillion and roared off toward the parking station.

On the wall of an old building a night painter had written:

Consume
Be Silent
Die!

The lettering was many years old. Once it had meant something.

Above, the upturned bowl of sky—blue, uncracked—taunted him and all who crawl on earth's surface with what is eternal.

He told me later he was thinking that the silent majority is better silent; when they talk their voice is the voice of children: pathetically innocent, or cranky, uninformed and spiteful; there could be among them some fool with a weapon, who wanted to make history.

The powerful Japanese bike stopped at the entrance to the station, and father, who had been thinking of some reward for the officer, fished some complimentary tickets from his pocket. He had about twenty, kept together with a rubber band. He intended to peel off a few, perhaps half a dozen. As he got them out he had mentally reduced his gift to two when he was so overwhelmed by the meanness of what he was doing that he handed the whole packet to the officer.

Foreheads Have Bled Where No Wounds Were

Mister Parkes, guest attendant at the parking station, was solicitous when he saw my father's blackening and nearly shut eye—and the

11

abrasions on his face where shoes had marked his forehead and cheeks and neck. Both ears bled.

"Mister Hunt? You OK?" And when father hesitated, not having any lines ready, Parkes said, "They had a hard job killing you off today." And stood back, head to one side, a dog waiting for a reward.

"I don't blame you. It must be tough getting the chop every day of your life, when it's coming to us all whether or no." And fingered his hole, a little down from his left clavicle. He didn't care whether he got an answer; his hole was his life, his inner life, far beyond the reach of whether an employer chose to use his talents for directing vehicles to one parking floor or another. To be fair to his employers, they often gave him the chance of standing on different floors.

His hole was an entry mark. He could put his finger in. There was no exit mark. Nothing had been discovered in him. All the tests had been tried. There was nothing in him, but that didn't take away the hole.

He hadn't given up X-rays. He was always about to go for another. No medicines, probings, dietings could heal the hole.

In some people it was the eyes or ears that interacted with the chemical environment on the planet to form unusual growths or manifestations, so he slept with his eyes bandaged and his ears stopped with earplugs. Nothing affected his hole, perhaps it wasn't eyes or ears that caused the infiltration. He tried to form an association for those suffering from unexplained entries or invasions, but no one came.

"A demonstration ran over me," said my father. He had a permanent parking spot, and was soon on his way to see his beautiful daughter.

The attendant didn't hear a word, his mind was in his hole, but the look he gave father in that brief moment was the same as father always got from Frees: What you are I can never be; what I am, no one wants to be.

Church Hill lies on one of many rounded, eroded hills extending north from the shallow depression containing Shoppingtown,

Cheapley, the Mead, and on down the river. Father had thirty kilometers to drive, each way, each day. It was May 28; father and I were soon to meet each other.

Birth of the Woman of the Future

My head was out, part of the caul on my head like a cap, a lei of pubic hair round my neck. They laughed. "Isn't it funny!" Notice the "it." I felt cold. It was the air of this planet. My mouth, my eyes, my scalp were unbearably cold. I say unbearable, though I bore it.

Then helplessness as my arms were pinned to my sides by the muscles of mother's vagina. A little further and I whipped up my right arm. It gave me comfort to have it near my face, a protection. When both were up I felt defended, and relaxed a bit. At one stage I was out, from the hips up, arms waving jerkily in tight arcs, like a boxer, with fists.

When they got me out of there they didn't cut the cord right away and maybe it was just as well. My first breath of air was like breathing fire. It was like the "lungs on fire" feeling you have when you are suddenly called on to run a long way in an emergency when you are out of condition. Yet the air was cold.

After my cord had stopped pulsing and they cut it, they put me on mother's stomach. She touched me—first my face, my arms and legs, then all over my body. I fancy I shivered. It must have been then they put me in warm water. My hands and feet uncurled and curled. Mother never tired of telling me how she couldn't take her eyes from the sight of my hands and feet curling and uncurling, clenching and relaxing, constantly moving.

"Its eyes are open!" they exclaimed. There's that "it" again.

And all the time looking round, my eyes as far open as I could manage them. How I loved my bath! I splashed. Mother played with my feet. I was gurgling.

Father took my head, molding it in cupped hands as if it were a lump of dough. It had become elongated on the way through.

And then, they said, I began to grin. No one referred to it as smiling. Always grinning.

"It was such a wide grin," my father said. He was the first man to see my nakedness. "It began slowly, then got wider until it seemed to fill your whole face. And not a yell out of you, just your legs kicking, hands clenching, and this grin. Oh, and the eyes; the eyes all the time. Open and looking. And every time something moved, your eyes caught it. We put you down on the leopard skin, and you loved it."

It would be boring for me to go on to tell you that I had no problems with taking food, with constipation, with toilet training, with sleeping. Or that I never cried. I suppose you're annoyed already.

The Beginning of My End

When they got me out of there and separated me from the entire past of the race, I was the end of a long chain of biological possibilities.

The me that might have been any other thing, that might have been some marvelous mixture so far unknown, that had hesitated so long on the edge of becoming, that might have put off existence for another thousand generations, had been forced to arrive.

My brief flowering had begun.

She Bled a Lot

To this day I have it on my conscience that mother lost a lot of her blood having me. Not that I saw the blood. I wonder what effect that might have had on me, particularly, as I have often imagined, if the world outside us is not outside. If the world is part of us, and perceived events and objects interact with one's brain, then the eye is in chemical conjunction with the object. Seeing: a chemical process! (I wonder if there's anything in it.)

14

A Baby Born

I was born a person, not just a limp babybag with suet brain. I had grown and listened in my fluid bath to the sounds of the world that came near mother's abdomen. I had some idea of the alternation of light and dark, noise and quiet, and linked light with noise, quiet with darkness.

I was born with desires, with a personality make-up that was clear, with drives discoverable to any organism or machine that knew what to look for.

I was born with equipment that I have had all my life—abilities and capacity to absorb from my society things that will build on what I started with—so that others can not avoid calling me "intelligent" and "able", and those with less speed and facility in gathering and adding to themselves cannot avoid looking up to me.

I was a human from the moment I first spied daylight.

The table I was born on is still honored above all other tables by my father, who sits and eats his food at it every day.

The Babwe doll I was given, that wets and expresses tears and can be milked by her own tiny baby, is still on the mantelpiece father made.

My father allowed me full humanity from the first day. I was the only girl I knew to have been loved by her father and close to him in the sense that he did everything for me, just the same as mother did. I had a real father, he thought I was beautiful.

Change

I was young when I first saw the ways people change. I trace it to the time when I was put down on my back in the blue bassinette and left to watch the world.

Objects change. Our ceiling, for instance. Sometimes it got higher, and when dark, quite low.

But also my cord. The cord on which were threaded my small plastic ducks came down in an arc from the eyelet at one side of my container. And it wasn't straight! I had seen the angles of my room, the straight lines of the ceiling aiming inexorably at the corners where they met the straight lines up from somewhere below eye level. But the cord was curved. Curved most when strung with nothing but also curved when it carried one duck. When father moved the yellow duck along, the shape of the cord changed and the curve was less one side and more the other. When the yellow, blue, green, pink and white ducks were threaded on the cord, I looked carefully to find the small amount of curve that must remain in each section of cord. (You will understand the great pressure on me to look for curves in all cases, after I had found them in some.)

Father believed I should have lots to look at; I was accordingly put into the largest room. No one thought to tell him that the objects seen so early have a great bearing on how one sees later. And what one sees.

To My Reader

I've always liked talking to one person at a time, probably to avoid the charge of seeming different to different people, so I'll address myself to one reader. Not for me the multitudes who relished Sterne nor the hundred Stendhal promised himself, not even the modest five anticipated by the delicate Machado. I am quite satisfied with one: you, my reader. I will be talking always to you and the time will always be now.

Another note on this strange and primitive society of ours:

The people are redundant at a time when the children of the human community are just conscious enough of history to ask: Why are the dinosaurs gone?

Others are undergoing cell changes as a result of consciousness of their own personal history, their profound and private failure, their need for punishment, their obsessive guilt.

We react constantly with the atmosphere and the substances that make up the earth and our bodies, and everywhere we go, even to outer space, we must take this atmosphere and those substances with us. We cannot escape them.

The Room I Lived in Most

The waterdrop machine sprayed its few lamplit drops out toward the collection of figurines and the small settlement of dwarf plants that congregated in pots like an audience round the glass parapet of its upper part. The tiny black earthenware men that sat round their campfire of painted red had their backs splashed by stray drops. Their spears, a millimeter thick, they had firmly in shiny knuckles. When drops fell on their red fire, it became shiny and cheerful. A porcelain willow tree, wet by the drops, had its trunk in human shape.

The leaves of mother's daphne bush were very still. When it was stirred by a breeze from the back door, its astringent perfume snaked through the house.

On the mantelpiece a cigarette lighter, in the form of a brass cannon, stood pointed at the door, and the soldier standing by it melted into it, formed of the same metal. By the cannon was a hand-high stone statue of a boy peeing.

A hole in the timber of the mantel, a hole with neat sides and no outlet on the other face of the timber, hooked my mind. Was it the hole of an animal, and was the animal inside?

A group of porcelain figures that had come down through mother's family and was one of the things she brought to this marriage—to any marriage she had—stood on its green and white base. Children of the Vine: the words etched into the border. Vine leaves sprouted from their ankles, arms, waists.

Porcupine Man, a quilled side-show freak of twisted metal dipped in plastic, sat in a pose of despair, his arms lifted toward something in the sky. He sat near a tiny wooden coffin my father made from unpainted applewood. A curio pipe cut in the figure of a woman had the pipe stem going up into her body. Mother had made two figures in her craft class at high school; painted, glazed and fired them herself. A boy and his sister, hand in hand. To my eyes, so new to the world, their charm, their interest, lay in the way their feet joined the ground, which was an earthenware base common to both. And where their hands touched, their flesh flowed together. I always wanted to see the joins. Where did one end and the other begin?

There were little animal figures, too. A cat, a pig, and a shiny horse—but the horse was broken. Part of its head had cracked and come away, showing the white china underneath. Yet it still stood, one foreleg raised, pawing the ground. The piece lay on the mantel beside it, and before I was two, father had mended the horse's head.

For hours every day, day after day, for many months I lay on my back looking up at these objects, my eyes running over every curve, every detail, clinging to their surfaces; I moved my head and found they looked slightly different. I went to sleep looking at them; I woke, and there they were.

My parents watched me look from object to object, and said I was remarkable. They noted my expressions, exclaimed when they changed, and marveled at my intelligence. I heard them congratulate each other on the brilliant future that lay ahead of me. I would be famous. No superlative was too extravagant for them.

Up a Gum Tree

My father had always wanted to put his baby in a tree, to hang there in a sort of sling. He rigged a hammock with a stretching piece each end and a baby blanket sewn both sides to the two ropes, and laid me in it.

I have always liked the underview of trees. With a slight effort of memory—how does one exercise one's memory?—I can see tree branches moving across my field of vision, the blue of sky with the fuzziness of white at its edges, and fingerings of fine cloud at the sides of the picture. Sometimes I can see the converging lines of the hammock ropes, going away.

When I was older he made it into a swinging seat; my legs went through one side, and I held on to the front bar of the seat. Father pushed me.

Later still, he converted it to a swing, just like those in the park. He used to swing there when he was thinking.

We had a cocky in a cage on the back patio. His name was Pretty Cocky. Father used to talk to it.

In those days time was unnoticeable, like air to the lungs.

At Six Months

Father photographed me bare-bottomed on the leopard skin in the lounge room—I was six months old. I was raised on my elbows, my head held up, my legs straight out behind me, my bottom high. Very jaunty indeed. My hair was a cloud of white that fluffed out, like Einstein's or Leopold Stokowski.

(What will happen to my memories when I'm no longer here?)

One thing about visitors I didn't like. They had expressions on their faces as if they were saying: It can't talk so it can't think. And looked down on me from higher than they really were.

The First Mirror

I remember the first time I caught sight of myself in a mirror. I lay on my back and mother was bending over me, her finger touching the suspended plastic ducks with the satin finish. The afternoon sun slanted in through the windows and must have caught her eyes at a tangent, for there, in the patch of light at the center of her two eyes, was a tiny scene. She stayed, still and smiling, looking right into my eyes and I into hers. I moved my right arm up toward the row of pierced ducks. My eyes caught a movement in mother's right eye. I moved again, and again I caught the movement. I looked into her other eye and moved my arm: I saw a tiny white thing move on mother's eyeball. I looked closer. I moved my head in case another position would give me a better look. I saw a movement. I checked it in the other eye. It was a sort of face. I wanted to say something, I made a sound. I saw the mouth move. Her face was very close. I smiled, and the face smiled back at me.

I relaxed back into my soft pillow. I was there. In mother's eyes.

Her Fingers Touching Me

My mother loved me.

She played with me as I lay on the table after my bath, and I loved that. I enjoyed lying on my back with my knees drawn up and arms moving around, head turning from side to side, from one ear to the other, while she tickled me. I don't mean that my head flopped from side to side, merely that the back of my head made it difficult for me to look straight up with my head vertical. I still am rather pointed at that part of my head, a pointedness relieved only by two smaller lumps further down at the back, closer to my neck. My mother called them my combative bumps when I held food in my mouth without letting it go down. When she finally had to put her hand under my chin and catch the finely-mixed mess, there was a look about her that meant that without the modern books on child care, I might have got an ancient box on the ears or a smacked botty.

The tickling I remember still. It has bored every male I knew for any length of time, for my demands always included being touched. I called it touching, or stroking, but to me it was tickling. When they touched or stroked, under directions, very softly, then more softly still, more slowly and gently, they were tickling, just like mother did.

"You laughed, and waved your arms, and your little toes and fingers curled and uncurled all the time. Never still," she told me later.

And to others, "Such a lovely baby, she was. Never cried. Never made a fuss. Beautiful. SSSShh, she's listening, the little bugger."

I enjoyed the touch of her hands so much. Why would she never keep touching me as long as I wanted her to? Was there some correct time that she observed and I was ignorant of and so wrong about? Certainly I was a mere baby, but I was the one that knew how I felt and if I felt I needed and wanted more, who can say I was wrong?

I was lying on a table on soft towels, being touched and fondled by a mother who released on to me all the affection of which she was capable. I lay looking up, my arms and legs spread and

20

waving, her fingers touching me on every part of my white and pink skin. Every part. I know that I played up when she stopped, and controlled her to the extent that her goodwill allowed her to give me five or six repeats, which gradually got down to three or four, one or two, then at about two years she must have thought I was too old to be tickled.

Cold and Blue

Mother's advanced ideas often led to simple opposites. The old custom was pink for girls and blue for boys, so I was dressed from my birth onward in blue.

I never liked blue. I found it cool and depressing. Even now, whenever I see blue, I see grey in it, and something of ice.

Mother thought that by taking the word, which represented a thing, and twisting the word, she was twisting the thing. Throwing out pink booties and substituting blue was overturning generations of sexist child-rearing. It was a new beginning. The past was abolished.

It gave warm ladies the horrors.

Mother kept all my clothes right from the first pair of booties and the bunny rugs relatives and neighbors gave her for me.

At first, having far too many, she thought she'd keep them for other children, but as the years passed and more cupboards were filled with bibs, nighties, pajamas, jumpers, shoes not worn out, shirts, she simply found more space, put the cast-offs away, and forgot them.

She could as little throw out an article of clothing as a word. And she kept every word.

Toilet Training

My chamberpot was blue. When I sat on it, my weight closed a switch and connected the battery. It was ON. When a cascade of pee or pooh hit the bottom surface, "Greensleeves" played.

"I want to go and do ice cream," I used to say, when I found it brought on laughter among parents and neighbors. Ice cream and gelati vans used "Greensleeves" as a Pied Piper tune.

"We'll have to change the tune," father said, wiping his eyes. He was emotional, and loved to laugh.

I had my own jokes with them, too, that started when mother was a little too insistent that she knew better than I did when I needed to go. I took a heavy book in with me, put it on the side of the seat so that it connected the battery, and there was a space left into which I could lob peas and other harmless things that kept the music alive.

"Bullets, that's what she's doing," mother said. "I wonder what she ate." She was always ready with stories about picking them out of my bottom—small, pale yellow and ochre, pellets like marbles—when I had been constipated, and would release these bulletins to whomever happened to be near. I was embarrassed and had no weapon against her.

"Bullets?" said my father.

"Yes. Listen, snatches of music. She's doings bullets."

"Smart kid. Because I can see—" He was too good a sport to finish. He could see me behind the Chinese lantern bush, on tiptoe on the spare concrete blocks he'd made for some unfinished project, aiming missiles in at the window.

The hose was best. After the first deluge, which alarmed them, I got the adjustment right, and the drips made it a happy, musical house, and my mother as content as if she were doing it.

Once I left it on, it must have been hours, and mother was happy all that time, doing her notes, smiling, pleased, and she kissed me when I came in the house, not realizing that I had come in from outside and the music still going. Father had the job of dealing with the flooded toilet when he came home from acting.

Two and a Half

I was two years and half a year. My father was walking along holding my hand, which was raised high above my head. It's not a comfortable way to walk.

I had this thought come into me. I can still see the street with the paling fence alongside us and trees—oleanders, I think—coming over the top of the fence and brushing Daddy's shoulder. I had the thought then, and didn't think anymore about for a while. Then when we were sitting in this place, this big hall with the interesting roof and someone was talking, I remembered it.

I had seen the ground and the fence and the trees, the cars, dogs, people gardening, kids playing, clouds fluffy in the evening sky, and I thought of myself walking and my tall father, and it seemed to me that everything was joined to everything else. Fences, trees, people, houses, flowers, dogs, cars: all belonged to the whole picture, all together.

Later, as I grew, I never was without that feeling: that all things hang together, they connect by uncountable strings, good and bad together, the whole earth. It was as if I saw the particularity of all things, plus their necessary connection.

Later still, I extended that opinion, to cover all acts people were capable of, to all the odd things I saw.

Simple Prayers

Father started me on:

> "*Gentle Jesus meek and mild*
> *Look upon a little child*
> *Pity my simplicity ...*"

and at the table it was:

> "*Be present at our table Lord*
> *Be here and everywhere adored*
> *These mercies bless. ...*"

and so on. Everyone knows them.

> "*Matthew Mark Luke and John*
> *Bless the bed that I lie on.*"

23

But never at any age did I wish for a handsome prince to carry me off to his rich palace.

I'll Kill You

At three I used to threaten kids and anyone who displeased me, however slightly, with death. I'll kill you, my father will kill you, the police will come and kill you; pure, childlike, naked promises.

But when Uncle John died—I can barely remember him: I think perhaps the memories I *do* have of him are the shadows and hints left over from descriptions of him that I heard then and later, and that I fleshed out with a fuller body in my head, to make him visible to myself and give him an identity—when he died, my father saw my puzzlement and gave me a fairy story to tell to myself.

"He's a nice old man that used to lift you up and say how pretty you were, and he got sick and died and went up to heaven in the sky, and that's him now up there shining and twinkling like a star."

It side-tracked me from asking how he died and whether someone killed him, which was what interested me.

A Hard Job

Mother gazed impatiently and wistfully at the blue potty, secure in the knowledge that I was not being conditioned by pink to wifehood and mother-business. Underneath, the receptacle was in position, but there was no music. It was empty.

They had been supervising me for a long time, and still my bowels had not moved an inch. I gazed, fascinated at their concern. Father marched up and down the hall and in and out of the little room where I squatted, knees apart, leaning on my elbows.

"E-vac-u-cate. E-vac-u-ate," my father chanted in the accents of a Dalek. He had a metronome on his head—bought in advance for my piano lessons—ticking aggressively. He had it clapped on his head with one hand and in the other an old spear-gun held at the ready like a rifle.

24

From being interested, I became amused, then absorbed. I would have continued to refuse duty out of curiosity but my mother lost all patience and came in and abused my father so politely, so cuttingly, so put-downingly, for showing me a martial example and probably turning me toward violence and murder, that to pay her back I shit myself. The material came out in a funnel-shaped spurt and covered the whole inside of the lower receptable. "Greensleeves" started with a clash and sounded loudly as it always did when the batteries were fresh. There were some lumps the color of golden clay, hard and nearly exactly round, like marbles. They were first out, they had stoppered my works.

As I got older, they got more brown, and I insisted on being allowed to do it all myself.

"I want to do it mine self," I said. "Nobody helping me."

Ping!

In our house there was no such thing as a locked door. Mother and father showered in full view. When my father dried himself with one foot on the bath edge, I was fascinated, repelled, and fascinated again by the huge scrotum hanging down and the penis resting on it, not quite hanging down vertically. There were long, wild-looking hairs on the scrotum-bag, sticking out at right angles, some of them, others lying down and then shooting out at an angle like you first imagine a space vehicle taking off.

When he put his foot down and stood up to dry his head and chest, keeping himself erect, I got in close there and watched the long thing swing.

It was irresistible. I got my front finger, curled it up and let it go, like you flick at a piece of paper on the kitchen table, or a dead insect.

Plip! went my finger, and knocked the head of it sideways so it swung back and forward as if it had jelly inside.

"Hey!" commented my father. "What's going on down there?"

He reared back a bit, but there wasn't very far to go, and he was still wet. I advanced on it with my finger curled threateningly, and looking up at him. He yelled, pretending to be afraid.

As I plipped it again, I said, "Ping!"

He went round later telling mother about the Ping. I heard him telling visitors for months about his daughter's Ping habit. He was very proud of me and my finger and my Ping.

I never forgot the long hairs on father's scrotum. The white hairs among the darker ones—they were a lighter brown than the hair on his head—seemed much thicker than the dark hairs. Also I couldn't see why they were so far apart; like an afterthought on a bald carry-bag.

My own hair had changed from white to a little on the tawny side of straw-colored. My eyes were sometimes grey, but mostly green-over-grey.

The Preservation of Memories

My mother never would change anything. If the ornaments you saw on the mantelpiece over the dummy fireplace were several vases, three pictures, a pot plant with a plastic creeper growing and hanging over the side for half a meter—it had to be washed from time to time of the dust it accumulated, but it hardly faded—and an urn with the ashes of a relative, you could be sure they had always been there.

The photos were very old. They had rested on her mother's mantelpiece once and before that on grandmother's dressing table. There was even a picture, high on the wall of the lounge, of the room in Islington where grandmother was born. We were all born in rooms; my father was a kitchen table birth.

In a picture frame was a facsimile of Jane Austen's handwriting, and a real life page of grandmother's mother's writing; faded now from black to a washed-out licorice color, so that the marks of the nib, which had spread on the downstrokes, were the most definite marks. I knew it off my heart, and later thought the sloping, graceful writing far more elegant than the modified cursive we had to do at school.

One of the photographs was of my mother's grandfather on her father's side, a Grossman, and the urn contained his ashes. He was a military man, and the photo showed him standing with great dignity beside a piece of furniture, an ornate sofa with a hand-carved cedar back. The urn stood beside the photograph. The sofa stood in mother's parents' house.

That Word

My father made out small cards and printed in large letters on them the names of objects round us in the house and outside. Fence, carpet, table, tree, wall, gate, leopard, piano, butter, vase, knife, plate, concrete, window, stove—had their cards stuck on or nailed. Getting used to the words and how they looked helped me when I got to school. I had no trouble with spelling because I reconstructed the words as my eyes remembered them, not bothering about rules.

I was shown off to all our relations. Isn't she bright? they said. Mother said: "She's a genius. Look at that forehead. There's greatness in that brow."

Father wouldn't say that word, and looked as if mother was exaggerating mildly, but he nodded.

People in People

At three I liked making a trampoline of father's stomach, jumping up and down. But the thing I loved best was to stand on him, pull up my legs suddenly and land on him on my bottom.

I think he was rather proud of being able to withstand my weight in front of visitors. And when I ran at him, head down, and collided with him again and again, never grizzling or being in pain, he was as proud of me as if I'd been a footballer.

At three and a half—I remember it because from the age of two and a half when my mother referred to me in extravagant terms in front of neighbors or relatives and to what I was like at one and a half, I could never be quite sure I understood what the half meant, and I always remember not being sure—I heard the mysterious words, God is in man. Already I knew from the way they spoke that man could mean any of us, even small girls. But where was God? Was He in places where I had a pain? Was He where I usually felt nothing, such as in my head?

At four I began my childhood habit of embracing. I ran up to people, flung my arms round them and hugged on tight. I don't know that it did a great deal for them, but it was a great thing for me. Perhaps it was much the same as others yawning or stretching—it was a relief for highly compressed feelings. I stopped when I was six.

> "My arms can't hold you, but
> You're in my heart
> Part of me is you
> Can't you see, oh
> It's so difficult to love."

Father sang it as he worked round the house. Usually the words said themselves in my head and I didn't listen, but sometimes I stopped doing something and wondered if people borrowed parts of each other. And if God was in people, did the doctor find Him when she operated?

Behold the Lamb of God

Religion gives stability: it has you saying the same words all your life. But my parents weren't religious, they went to church when I came along just to let me know churches were there, and it was OK to go along to sit in them if you felt like it. I had seen a woolly lamb in one of my picture books, its fluffiness, its capacity to spring about lightly, the pretty sight it made all snowy on a green page.

There I was listening to a preacher talking familiarly of the Lamb of God. I didn't get the implication of the use to which the lamb was put. The wisdom of cutting a lamb's throat for the spiritual health of the people had not been explained. I knew nothing of the Lamb pointing the way to death, of the Lamb being a sacrifice, an inducement to a savage god to show mercy to a weak and credulous people, as we learned later in Primary.

As the preacher's voice rose and her face became more piercing, so that it seemed she wanted to get down off her perch and shake us in her exasperation and urgency, I got more and more restless, and began to make disturbances, until they took me out.

Outside, old Mister Scully waited in a heap. He was the keeper of the door, handing out hymn books, and was taken ill that very Sunday. He was coughing too much to stay inside. I saw a complicated diagram in blue, of veins on the old man's ankle.

This was the church where I heard about God being in man.

They took him home but he was still very sick and the ambulance came for him at four.

I asked where they were taking him.

"To a convalescent home, Al," father said.

"What does it mean to convalescent?"

"Convalesce. Mister Scully will convalesce."

"What does it mean?"

"Convalesce means get better."

"Oh, good. When will he get back?"

"He'll never be back, darling," my father said kindly, looking at me as if I was sick. I mean a loving look, sympathy.

"Where's he going? Why can't he come back? We'll have no old people at all if he doesn't come back!" I said. Mister Scully was the only person you could rely on to see in his garden if you went for a walk. Everyone else was inside, or gone out.

"I don't think he'll be back. I think he's going to die."

"Die? You said it meant get better!"

"Well, they use it sort of to be kind to the old people."

"Kind? To die them?"

"The name, Al. They give them hope that they'll get better."

"Do they tell them they're going to get better?"

"No. The name does that for them. They say nothing. They let them think because it's that sort of place, that's what'll happen. It's to keep them cheerful."

"Would they cry if they knew?"

"No. They're too old to cry."

"And they'll never come back?"

"Never."

"That's the end?"

"The end."

"Is it dark there?"

"Nothing but dark."

I kept quiet for a while. There were two large tears, one either side of my face, the right one further down than the left side one, about on the round part of my cheek, in no hurry. Then I said, "Will we get another old man round the district?"

"I hope so." He looked at me. "I certainly hope so."

"And I can take round things—flowers, and scones?"

"You bet you can, darling." And he lifted me up, his big arms around me, and my face was pressed into his shirt near the shoulder.

Already I was thinking of Mister Scully's destination—a place no path leaves, immersed in a dark no light can touch.

The Long Distance Lecturer

No matter where you were in Shoppingtown he seemed to be looking at you. He sat in a window, his head slightly on one side, but looking straight ahead, talking. Relayed to the shoppers and outside to the street, his voice came at the level of conversation.

Kids talked back at him, but he couldn't hear. His friends communicated with him on bits of paper: Time For Lunch, and Do you want to use the Toilet.

His name was Doctor Buckman, and he was going for the world record at lecturing. The subject "The end of the world." He started before I was born.

For his record he had to beat thirty years and ninety-eight days, set in Los Angeles by a Professor Kingsley, who died in mid-sentence, his topic "The rights of man." The rules were they had to begin at nine every morning and go to five in the afternoon, they had to stay in the same place and keep to the same subject.

Kingsley died when his heart blocked, Daddy told me, and stopped beating; earlier record holders had given up, been shot, strayed off the topic, gone mad, developed throat cancer.

Around the world there were others going for the record; it was a matter of having judges on hand to keep track of them, ready to disqualify offenders against the rules, and to coordinate the performances of those who were newly started and those who stopped. People bet on the result. Doctor Buckman failed when he chose to retire from the Servants' ranks.

He had charts, books, maps, and a large black moustache and beard. I stood in front of him on the first day and pointed at it, asking what it was. It was a moustache, darling, they said. My Mummy's got one of those down there, I said. It can't be one of those, they said. Well, it's the same color hair, I said.

Changes

My father had been dying on stage for years. *Changes* was the longest running play in the history of the theatre. It had been going long before I was born, and there was a constant demand for seats. Everyone has heard of *Changes*. Not only is it the longest running show, but the longest in running time. At six hours, with rests and lunch breaks and discussion and participation pauses, it takes an entire day. Factory staffs, office staffs, people working in the new labor-intensive industries, don't have to conceal their delinquency by pleading a "sickie." Managements have long regarded the play as therapy, helpful—necessary, even—for the re-creation of good attitudes at the work place. *Changes* had come into its own.

Father died at the 243rd minute, and was dead on stage for the rest of the working day. When I was little he hadn't developed the stiffness that he later suffered from—and still has—that affected his lower back, left side.

You might think it was a sleep break for him, but there was a lot more to it than that. Being dead throughout the greater part of the play, he was still subject to all sorts of investigation. His body was exhibited dozens of times; the audience, in the participation episodes, handled it to feel the appropriate stiffening and relaxing. Then there was an autopsy and bits of him went on display on microscope slides for cell examination, pictures of the corpse in all stages of undress were taken on stage, enlarged and displayed. Some were distributed to the audience. It was calculated that everyone in Australia had at least one picture of part of his body, or one tissue slide. (Pretending, of course.)

There were doze breaks for the audience. At the rear of the theatre were living quarters for the actors. My father lived in a flat there before he was married.

Sometimes, at home in Heisenberg Close, my mother and father would say, "Don't you wish we could be back there with the cast?" And they'd look at me. I was the stumbling block. Other kids allowed themselves to be tranquilized, so they could stay with actor parents, but I wouldn't.

The neighbors didn't treat me with envy. They didn't care that he had a part in *Changes*, he was just a neighbor.

Grow Your Own

It was the sort of spring that's nothing more than a few new leaves on an old tree.

Mister Cowan, in Edison Avenue, noticed a swelling in his side, then a thickening, a lump; the skin broke one Saturday afternoon as he was discontentedly looking out at the spring yard that needed attention, and scratching his side. What appeared—he didn't look at it until he was in the garage messing about with the mower unused since autumn—was an unpainted piece of smooth wood.

"I've never even been inside an undertaker's workshop," he explained to his wife. Mrs. Cowan was an attractive woman, though not to him.

The unpainted end of a coffin grew slowly outward from his side. Beveled edges, beautifully made, ready for varnishing. He sat watching it, couldn't see it growing, but from morning to night there was a visible difference. He insisted death was not an obsession with him.

After his natural interest in it, such as you might have in an outstanding pimple, he was ashamed. This was a difference that would set him apart from everyone, and though he was pleasantly aware of differences between him and other men, to his advantage— he could see them himself, they were obvious—this was a difference that climbed to another degree of difference. He cut it off.

Whittling it with a penknife caused him no pain, though he was wary of the blind feeling it gave him when he twisted it to one side against the flesh with the pressure of his blade.

He cut it to skin level, put his shirt back over it, and got on with his work at the shop. In addition to the newspapers, he had gifts, toys, wool and knitting patterns. The magazines made the money, and the nearby school made stationery worthwhile. He had plenty to do, but it was mostly automatic. Once you slip a paper bag on something, take the money and make up change, there's not much to think about. He thought of his coffin, he thought a lot, but as with these thoughts and being the man he was, he didn't get far. Each time it protruded far enough to bother him, he cut it off. Not that he didn't get to like it: he did. He sandpapered it to make it smooth, blowing the sawdust carefully away at first, then later gathering it in a paper bag.

(An observer from a strange place might have noticed that these growths and changes, though they provoked some interest, produced no wonder.)

Many times he cut it off, each time leaving it a little bigger before he brought himself to do it. Not once did it hurt. As far as he could see the sawdust was genuine sawdust.

I was still four. I only heard about it, until hearing father telling my mother about this manifestation of novelty in the neighborhood, I asked to see it.

Saturday I was taken in the car to a back street where it was possible to park, and my father and I walked to the shop.

Mister Cowan didn't let me see it. He showed my father the respect due to a famous actor, but looked very possessive when my request was whispered to him.

33

After the word of his coffin had been abroad in the district for some months it leaked to the metropolitan news machine.

People took up the debate. Nonsense, that sort of outgrowth does not exist; that sort of thing can't exist; more exotic things are happening to people in other cities: these were some of the things said by the people, who had a great voice in the news in those days.

"You are the outgrowth on that coffin," said a wise correspondent to the morning papers.

Mister Cowan retreated into himself and refused to talk about it. The difference between him and other people was becoming precious to him. There were news agents in every suburb, but none with a cell change like his.

It wasn't necessary for him to get fired or resign: his wife could do the work in the shop. Since it wasn't productive, but merely a form of booster pump to force manufactured products out along the finer capillaries of the suburbs, far from the centers of making, his shop and the work it entailed were outside the scope of the Serving Class: he was a prole.

The Creative Proletariat

In the westernized world for many decades no new political ideas have come; present ideologies are those based on nineteenth-century theories, altered and patched to suit circumstances and problems, contradictions and failures; revised ad infinitum.

In Europe, it is true, those aged and tyrannical and still ambitious old courtesans—communism and marxism—are being passionately embraced with more fervor than ever before, precisely as they are on the point of death. Perhaps it is a religious ardor.

There still exist also the intellectually limp, but cunning and adaptable traditional ways which are not political theories at all but derisive names given by their more earnest opponents.

Into this empty space events have pushed their way. Work has become the desirable and rewarded occupation of an elite. The concerns of the proletariat have forever changed.

The Free can be idle if they wish, or can fill the hosts of supportive positions that grow up round the fringes of a complicated society.

Nothing time-consuming is despised: the consumption of time is the chief object of mock-work done by the free; as consumers of time they are safely occupied until they safely die.

In earlier times they would have been called unemployed, their condition a matter of shame to themselves and reproach to their society.

Now the stigma of having no profession is officially abolished, abject poverty done away with. It is as if the proles, having escaped poverty, have become creative, as early political idealists prophesied: creative in finding mildly useful work; or creative deep within their own cells.

Once, some thought the need to produce alienates the passion to create. But now, when the passion to produce is alienated, there is a need to create.

Or is the promise of freedom too much to resist? Do they change, to be sure of grasping freedom?

My Noticeable Lack of Penis Envy

I didn't meet penis envy until I was five. I picked it up from a visitor, shouting to make herself heard at one of father's Friday night parties.

I went round chanting, "Penisenvy! Penisenvy!" until they took notice of me. The grown-ups were amused, and wanted me to go on chanting. But mother, as usual those days, was direct and efficient.

"Shut up, darling," she counseled above the din. Small people were out.

I followed father into the bathroom and as he was doing wee I stood there, my head on a level with it, and flicked at it.

I hit it, and said, "Ping!" But the wee went spraying from side to side onto the tiles, and he didn't laugh. When he'd finished, he didn't like it when I tapped it from side to side with both hands, either.

I didn't touch the big fat bag hanging behind it, with the hairs sticking out. It looked too funny. (Once when he was sitting in a chair with nothing on and the long thick hose thing was over to one side, I saw the big bag move within itself. Parts went further away from other parts, then moved closer. The hose thing moved, too. Do you know what I mean? It can turn its head from side to side, slightly, and come forward and go back as if it's a tortoise head going back into its shell. But it never goes right back.)

"She certainly seems to have none," auntie said. I knew she meant penisenvy. They looked at each other's faces.

"She has a definite penis interest," said my father mildly, lifting me up into his arms.

The rest of what I heard was only word-fragments, murmured by adults.

Origins

Mrs. Bassett, who lived in Faraday Place, had a lump on her stomach. A very big lump.

"What's that lump on the lady?" I asked father.

"I think that's a baby," I was told.

"I can't see it, is it inside her or is it under her dress?"

"Inside her, darling."

"Did she swallow it?" I asked.

"No, Mister Bassett put it in her."

"How did he get it in?"

"Well, it was very small then."

"It's grown a lot, hasn't it?"

"Yes, by the time it's ready to come out it will be a full-size baby."

"Will it cry?"

"All babies cry, except you, darling."

"Where does it come out?"

"Down there."

"Where? Here?

"Yes, darling."

"Do they wash it?"

"Straightaway. As soon as it comes out."

"That's good. Otherwise it would smell, wouldn't it?"

"I suppose so," he said doubtfully. I could see I had puzzled him. It was much later that I realized where he meant. I thought he meant it came out of the bottom.

It was at this time I heard mother and father talking about when I came to be started. I'd gone to bed and been tucked in: they talked in the lounge room. I'm not sure I remember if father raised his voice, but I'm sure mother raised hers. What I heard then was confirmed much later by something I read for myself.

School

At five, life spreads out so broadly and stretches so far.

We'd passed the school often in the car, and there was plenty of talk about my going to school, talk that increased as my parents seemed to be urging me to say I wanted to go to school, talk that meant nothing to me. I had to go sometime, I knew that.

One day I went along with my father to enroll. Mother got exemption from most trips if she was busy writing. Father had the understudy take his role.

When the time came for father to leave, I waved to him where he stood outside the fence, put my schoolbag in the room they had shown me, and went outside to look over the other kids.

There were several I knew from round about, but the most interesting were a group of larger kids that were sprinkled round playing in unattached ways. I wanted them.

Boys

I was introduced to boys on my second day. When the teacher on playground duty was looking the other way, our gang cascaded out of the white-lined area, past the grey lunch forms, over to the Corner to watch the big children. The Corner was where I found out what boys were.

37

As we looked round, five heads at different levels, a boy face confronted us.

"Girls," he said, and his mouth went down at both ends and up on each side, just in from the end; it was an expression of distaste I had seen before only when Odia Watson said the word Communist. She lived opposite, lower than us, and she pronounced it "Commonist."

That boy face told us we were lower than insects. Not that we were upset: we were stronger than that; we could have stared at him if we wanted to and he would have curled up and died.

It was not that boy that showed us boys; other girls could look at us even worse: it was the Corner-game.

The face went, the cries of the playground sounded louder, but nothing prepared us for what came next. Kids older than us, with license to go into the bigger section where the six- and seven-year big kids played, passed round us with only a scornful look—but they ran into the Corner-game. One at a time, boys ran full pelt on a signal from another that meant the coast was clear of teachers; it didn't mean there was no one coming round the corner. They weren't allowed to let the runner know if there was or wasn't someone coming: the runner had to go as close to the corner as he could. If no one was coming, he hit no one. If there was, he did. The lookout warned if a teacher was in sight.

We rounded the corner. I was first, with the others in a loose wedge behind me. A boy hit me practically everywhere all at once. I was hurled back against the others, but didn't hit the asphalt. Nor did I ever hit the asphalt.

We went away, back to our section. This was something to think about. The others gabbled complaints, but I thought alone.

The Corner-game was unreasonable. The boys were unreasonable to charge round a blind corner not knowing what they were going to encounter. Yet they were doing it. That was what I couldn't understand. At home if a thing was unreasonable, it was unreasonable. You didn't do it again, or if you did, you laughed at yourself. Yet I could understand the Corner-game. I could feel the joy of the full pelt run, the fierceness, the savage knowledge that some unwary kid was going to feel your full weight suddenly and be borne to the ground underneath his conqueror.

38

And neither you nor he knew who it would be. It was a wild world of chance. Anything could happen. There may be someone there to hit or no one. You were no longer ruled by "I should" but by "I will." And it was that part that fascinated my mind.

> *I'm the king of the castle*
> *And you're the dirty rascal.*

How Did These Monstrosities Filter into Time?
Mister Cowan's coffin grew, like grass and all living things grew, with no relenting; it thrust itself, as all other things thrust themselves, on the uncomplaining world.

He decided, after many times of shaving it off and smoothing the end, and accidents in which he irritated and cut his own flesh, to leave it grow.

He kept to the back of the shop, and as it became so heavy that it threatened to break off chunks of him, he rested it on a chair beside him, so the end could rest on it and not tear the flesh out of his side.

"Are you sure it doesn't hurt?" his wife asked.

"No feeling at all," he said.

After the first week resting it on the chair she didn't ask anymore. He just seemed to sit there, thinking.

Sex was out of the question. Mrs. Cowan thought, in the first week, a little guiltily, that perhaps she ought to relieve her husband's sexual feelings in some way that she had heard of but never done, but somehow the subject didn't come up. He didn't say anything, and she felt she might have the effect of spurring him to do things he didn't have energy for.

Little Boys' Dicks
I was six, and in the playground we found that the minor difference we knew to exist between us and boys, was not at all minor to them.

Little boys' dicks seemed to be the constant concern of little boys. They spoke about them to each other, they fiddled and scratched, their underpants scrunched them up so they had to put their hands down their fronts like headlong hands plunging into a lucky-dip, they noticed if their friends' dicks were lumpier or sticking further out than usual, they hit each other there in moments of anger—which could come over them with no warning—and they got other kids down and played with theirs and made them cry. (I didn't understand this, I thought playing with them would make them tickle, until I realized that unauthorized use of or access to the dick was a sign of hopeless inferiority on the part of the victim.)

In class Everett Vaux had more latitude to scratch than the other boys, and he used his freedom to the full. The teacher wasn't sure if it was going to grow on to something and she would get the blame if she didn't allow him movement.

> *What are little boys made of?*
> *Snaps and snails and puppy-dogs' tails.*
> *What are little girls made of?*
> *Sugar and spice and all things nice.*

He May Have Been She

My dolls were mostly boys; I had Katherine and Sylvia and Deirdre, but I was most motherly with Bradley, Timmy, Duke and Colin. Colin was the beautiful one. His skin was so fine it rippled in the wind. They were all provided with proper penial attachments, that is, a penis and testicles, which I made them wash as often as their faces. I couldn't get little nuts the right shape for their testicles, so I used dried peas which you could feel with your fingers moving about in their little under-bags behind the penis.

I daresay there was one main difference between my playing with dolls and, say, Susan Haynes's playing with dolls: she had mostly girls, and did all the work herself. I was more like their platoon commander.

If I accidentally hit them there and they doubled up in pain, I always apologized beautifully.

My favorite girl doll was Deirdre. It is my recollection that I christened her, though I have a faint doubt-shadow. She had a receptacle for tears, and I loved to see her sorrowing.

Teddy had no name. Just Teddy. He was born with short brownish fur, that felt rough at first, if you were a stranger, then when you knew him you realized it wasn't rough at all, it was just the way he was. His arms moved up and down, he could put them round a person's neck.

He had nothing to do his wee-wees out of: I asked at the shop where he was born, but the girl only laughed at me.

I called him Teddy, but he may have been she.

A Marriage of No Importance

Bradley had married Sylvia before they were half through their teens, then had affairs with Katherine and some of the straw offspring belonging to Graham Lasseter down the street. He was to be married to Graham's Marmaduke, because they both got on better with other boys rather than girls.

In ordinary life, as they came out of their solitude when I got home from school, they played a lot together and I enjoyed doing with them the experimenting that I imagined boys did with each other when they were alone, without girls watching or grown-ups.

They played with each other's bodies, naturally, and it was in such circumstances that I first realized the need for genital equipment for Bradley and the others. Colin had everything.

Bradley and Marmaduke were married in the back garden, and their honeymoon began on the grass right away since I had been called for tea and they had to get a move on.

> Here comes the bride
> Fair, fat and wide.

41

Nothing Was as They Told Me

They told me I would love the surf. My first visit to the sea I had firmly in my mind, "I will love the sea." And I didn't. It was very cold. True, I soon forgot it and began to play violently, all the more violently for the first cold shock, and paid back my father for his laughing splashes by splashing him when his body had been out of the water for a while and the sun had warmed him. He leaped in the air, and the water took his breath away. I laughed, and he did. (I had noticed, before, that if you laugh after doing something regarded as naughty, or aggressive, the laugh makes it a joke. He'd done it to me often enough, specially when I was quiet and he thought I needed "bringing out.") I learned to love the water later, on my own.

They told me I would love the teacher. The truth is, I learned to manipulate the teacher just as I could feel her manipulating me, and influencing my behavior. But I never loved her. When I found that certain things I did made her show public favor for me, I began to learn my place in the world; but the familiarity—the power, dare I say it—of influencing her by what I did, gave me a superiority that, for me, cut out love.

They told me I would love pumpkin and carrots. "The red vegetables are necessary, too," my mother said—absently, a point I didn't miss. They weren't red, they were orange. And I was not going to like them. I loved potatoes, for some reason, and when my father mashed pumpkin and carrots in with them, they were spoiled, on principle. On the other hand, they didn't serve me marrow, and chokoes, which I loved as soon as I put them in my mouth and they squidged up into smooth bits and slid down my red lane on a smear of butter.

I was told that getting things would soon pall. It never did.

I was told that winning wasn't the main thing: the game itself was. I'm tempted to leave it like that, so you can see the idiocy of it. I grew to like most games, but who can say it was the game itself I liked, for I won at almost everything I did? I was luckier than some—actually than all the rest—in that I was good at everything. I was like that from the start, and never failed at any game I attempted. But the winning! If it isn't the only thing, who can

42

remember what the others are? I never reached the point that the casual, the sickly, the halfhearted reach, where after a win or two they lose the taste for winning. It never left me.

The Lord loveth a cheerful loser, my father freely adapted an old saying, wasting his breath. "Yes, Daddy." Parents spend such a lot of time digging for the correct response that they usually don't hang about to see if the later actions line up with the response. I said "Yes," but went ahead savagely, relentlessly, fiercely, confidently, to win—at lessons, in the playground, in the group. They must have hated me.

Playing with myself was going to be a disappointment, they warned, and a source of shame. It never has been. One thing about masturbation: you don't have to wait for anyone. Don't forget that the thing that is supposed to be better—others playing with you—is often wide of the mark. What an apt phrase!

And the beauties of reserve. Stand back and let others go first. This was one of my mother's bits of advice. It was supposed to give you a glow that others of discernment could see. I did once or twice, but never again. It was an empty thing. If a volunteer was wanted for anything, I was that one. A message to the headmistress—who'll stand up and make a speech of welcome—who can tell me a piece of overseas news right now and give its background—who will help me with this experiment—anything: I was first on my feet.

Winning wasn't important? Even at that age I knew the Hall of Failure was always full.

When they told me of things to come, what to expect in the future, they were never exact. Perhaps they feared I couldn't follow their detailed descriptions and would get flummoxed; but from as early as I can remember I was quite willing to listen to the most involved instructions—I always remembered them when the time came, but nothing was as they told me. The game's the thing—what nonsense!

The only difficulty I had in my first year at school was that I got *b* and *d* back to front. I was embarrassed when Mrs. Molong pointed it out, and never made such a mistake again.

These are all stories bearing on my years of life. Bearing on, not following a timetable. There *was* no timetable. Sometimes at six I was a grandmother.

You try and bring back your life, get it all back the way it came: you can't do it. No more than you can tip up a bucket of apples and have them roll all over the ground, then get them back in the same order. And they don't come marked with numbers, as years do. Even years don't come in the right order. Not even when you're living them.

Maybe if you kept a record all the time of what happened . . . But then there'd be no time to *do* anything. Recording isn't living. But how can you? Who knows what's going on all the time? What's your stomach doing? What are the nerves in the left corner of your mouth up to? Where's your digestion at? What was your recording center recording when you were reading these words?

Who says I was never a grandmother? What about the time my father came home and didn't exactly burst into tears, but started slowly, like something heavy starting to move, then rolling down hill, picking up speed until people no longer try to stop it, they just get out of the way, and watch.

"How can I go on making a living out of acting a dead man?" he said when he took a break in the sobbing. Mother comforted him, monosyllabically, then got it all down in her notebook. At least I assumed that's what she was doing.

I sat back, tearless, nodding now and then. In that family, at that moment, I was grandmother. When they stopped their fuss, they would turn to me to see what I had to say, and I would say something that would either fix everything or start the whole business off again. A perfect grandmother.

This year my mother shut herself away and did nothing but write. She had a peephole set in the door to her room to make sure she didn't want to see visitors. If, as usual, she wanted to be busy with her notes, the word came out that she was sick or busy.

How she got on when I was at school I don't know. Maybe the front door was shut, and they got no answer.

Once we'd had a knocker, but mother hated it. She hated being summoned by anyone with strength enough to hit it against the timber of the door, and campaigned for a new door. She settled for one of those acid-proof (why acid?) door covers, that made the door proof against burglars. The one she wanted was covered with a lumpy decoration, I think it was a wild relief depicting some young artist's brainscan; the point was that there was no place on it where you could knock hard without injuring your knuckles. If you were careful you could manage a one finger tap, but hard knocking seemed to jar the fine bones of your fingers.

From inside the house, the knocking sounds that penetrated were humble indeed.

So. Mother took her rings off, put them away, and stayed at her desk. Her love, which until then had been to me like a beacon filling the days and nights with bright warm light, switched off. Was I too boisterous; too like a boy for mother?

Her retreat into her own world was not understood by the neighbors: anything out of the ordinary was to them madness. They had no conception of eccentricity, or the freedom to be different without a class change.

I thought it was because she had discovered she was not beautiful.

Not Exactly Lying

Midget was the worst boy in the school. He rang the bell when it wasn't supposed to be rung. He stuffed up the bubblers in the wash shed with paper and chewing gum.

For a change he'd climb the big trees in the playground and wouldn't come down. No use anyone trying to get up there after him, he was the best climber in the school, he was the best climber anyone had ever seen. When the kids took home stories about Midget, fathers would say, "I could climb trees like that when I was a boy," but then they'd ask again how far the first branch was off the ground and they'd begin to look doubtful, then they'd end

45

up trying to say Midget couldn't have climbed that tree anyway. As if Midget threatened their whole boyhood, their whole treasure of a past.

Midget grabbed the tree, hugged it and dug in. Then it was just a matter of how high. He always beat the teachers. When they got the fire brigade once, he climbed down just as they were coming in the schoolgate.

He put dud refills in kids' pens. He pulled hair. He ran around corners and tripped people. When they ganged up on him and cornered him, he suddenly ran at them, bent over double like a cannonball, and burst through their legs. Everyone was taller than Midget.

One day at assembly there was a visitor. I think she was probably around nineteen or seventeen, it was hard to judge when you're six. She was the world record holder for the fifteen hundred meters. Swimming. She was tanned, her legs glowed golden, she was pretty, her hair bleached by sun and the chlorine of pools, she caused the teachers, male and female, to gape. She came to say a few words to the school, because she'd been there when she was a kid. Midget was in the front row. He shouldn't have been, he was in fifth class, and fifth was near the back of the lines.

As she ascended the steps to the platform, she trod too near the edge. A piece of wood came away, and she fell sideways.

Before she hit the ground, Midget was under her. She landed on him and rolled, but didn't hurt herself. She got up and bent down to thank Midget. She had to help him to his feet, his leg hurt. He grinned at her, and we'd never seen him embarrassed before. He was almost shy.

A teacher rushed forward, to try and stop him doing something nasty to the prize visitor, but Midget was too overcome to do anything like that. He went back to the wrong place in the lines, where he could watch her. He watched with his eyes, his ears, his nose, his mouth—which hung open—and his hands. His hands twitched.

There were two big scrapes on his knees, and one hand had a piece of gravel embedded in the round part at the base of his thumb. He didn't notice. When the goddess went, he was still in a daze.

He came in for a lot of congratulations from the teachers. The kids, too. A world champion is a big deal to primary school.

That was Friday. Monday when he came back to school again he was different. He didn't trip people, pull hair, climb trees; he didn't do *anything*. He picked up an exercise book the teacher of KA dropped, he turned up for cricket practice, and when winter came, for football. (Later, in sixth class he represented the state for football.) He was smiled on by teachers, got prizes for sport at speech day (there were no prizes for schoolwork: something about equality. Merit was only rewarded where it mattered.) and was in every way a successful citizen.

The thing I noticed was, he was better thought of than all the kids that had never played up.

(I started this chapter with the words Not Exactly Lying, but in the space between I got lost. All I was going to say was about a habit I had of not saying all the truth. I'd say some of it—the acceptable part—and finish saying the rest in my head. It wasn't *exactly* lying.

Do you think it was? It still troubles me.)

On weekends Midget came back to look at the spot where his goddess fell. Even when he went to high school and came past Primary every day, he looked at that spot. She changed him.

A Hot Bath of Something Nasty

My father denied me nothing, his theory of child-rearing had all faith in the goodness of the child. This was a long way from born in sin and shapen in iniquity, but nothing I did was seen by him in such a graceless light.

He hated wasting water, consciously a member of a dry continent, but when mother insisted on my bath being full of warm, comforting water, he did nothing against her wish.

Surrounded by the sensual warm, I would lie in the bath with only my chin above water. Mother came in if I seemed to be taking

47

too much time. I suspect she didn't want me to start playing with myself too early. They both seemed to love drying me with towels taller than I was.

Naive, childlike, trusting, I was soon lying warm in bed. In summer, only a sheet was necessary, in winter, a blanket. Always these were crisp, spotless, and smelled of the sun in which they'd dried.

Light came through the crack at the edge of the closed door, which they would open when they both went to bed so I could run in and be comforted on their bed if the dark or ghosts troubled me. Nothing troubled me, but I ran in, anyway.

Suddenly one night I was shoved back from the edge of sleep by the sound of voices. It took only a moment's orientation to know they weren't ordinary voices. My parents were shouting. Accusations clattered back and forth, distrust and anger, they were yelling at the tops of their voices.

I huddled at first under the sheet, worried. I thought I should get up, run in to them and separate them. Then I thought—maybe they're rehearsing something, she's helping him with his lines.

Again I sank into fear and the deep thought that my parents were deadly enemies who managed to hide their enmity while I was awake, but whose hate was so great that sometimes it must overwhelm their good intentions. I waited for murder to happen, then must have drifted off.

Some time later I woke fully and told myself it was all a dream. The house was quiet. I didn't go out to see, just lay there, waiting for more shouts. They didn't come. It was a dream.

In the morning I couldn't be sure. Yet they might have been rehearsing after all. I didn't feel like asking. Sometimes when I ask questions I see a sudden expression in their eyes, as if I was something that fell into their wineglass.

One of Father's Sayings
"Don't be afraid to take a risk. For something you believe in, risk everything." And he went on, as if quoting: "To the dangerous

48

element submit yourself, and with the exertions of your hands and feet make the deep deep sea of life keep you up."

I think it came from the play he's in. I went out and told Pretty Cocky. Somehow that took the pressure off me.

In the backyard several jasmine blossoms collapsed and fell to the ground.

Old Mac

Old Mac in happier days had been a slaughterman at the abattoirs. Albert James Conachy McCarthy was his full name.

He often took walks down into the reserve, the valley beside the old creek that he had known as far back as his boyhood. Once he walked everywhere in this "bush," as he still called it, but the building of houses on a few blocks thirty years before trimmed his walk of some of its extent; in the next ten years a lot more bush was covered with the smooth plots that had houses supported on their thin carpety grass. It was hard to resist the feeling that the ground was not so much cleared and smoothed, as that the new plots with their borders and paths and shrubs had been laid down on the old bush soil, for there was no resemblance between the latter state and their untouched, blackboy-spear, mossed rock, twisted scribbly-gum former existence.

Old Mac always wore a hat. If he lifted the hat forward and sideways to his right you could see a patch of old, greying timber set into his head, like a weathered tree stump. He had no conversation, but neither did he smoke.

Talking to my father one afternoon—his walks round what used to be his bush so sadly circumscribed that he had to walk on roads for a mile before he got to the easement opposite and could make for the remaining trees and battle his way through the horrors of unbridled privet—Old Mac said, "This world could support constant rain." Out of the blue. "Sunshowers'd be nice."

My father agreed. The stump showed under the side of the old felt hat. "The sort of clouds where the sun comes through, most. Warm. Wet, too." The grass below us was biscuit-dry. The trees limply stirred their tops. A leaf fell, spinning.

49

The whole district heard about it when a shoot appeared below the inset dry timber part, where the living bark rolled like a thick firm porridge over the hard dead wood that greyed and split. Some variety of spiritual rain had watered him from within and powered the small pale green shoot that showed between the hairs of his head.

Old Mac makes me think of bones, old campfires, flints.

What Causes Such Changes?

Opinions vary:
1. Events or ideas not assimilated in a time of rapid change.
2. Fragmentation of personality following on the fragmentation of society.
3. Preoccupations of the person, obsessions.
4. The shaping power of society.
5. We shape ourselves.
6. The body's interaction with the eco-system.
7. Genetic manipulation by the professional class.
8. Ineffective social adjustment.
9. The stars.
10. Guilt at failure, and craving for punishment.
11. People treated as objects becoming objects.
12. The chemistry of sight.
13. The chemical nature of time.

Some Boys Have Thick Skin And You Can't Get Through

He was a nice shape for a boy, and he had a skin nothing could get through. It didn't look thick on the outside, since it was shiny and smooth and took a tan, but it reached right inside and wrapped round his bones. Crying Clive was always crying. His parents couldn't get through to him. If a hand covered his mouth, the sounds poured through the fingers. They began everyday after breakfast to thrash him, and continued on into the day. His cries went straight to the hearts of strangers. We were four houses away and could hear him clearly, but when you got used to the crying it went on without you noticing. My parents had lost the art of hearing poor Clive; even when he ran his voice up to a top note they gave no sign they'd heard. Once, father said, "A kind man is one who never hits a child except in retaliation." That was all.

Sometimes it was eight hours a day. The education authorities had got used to Clive's absences; they knew it was impossible to get through to him. Pills didn't work, but then prescribing a pill is often no more than helplessness and ignorance hiding behind weird handwriting.

He was twelve then, and they'd been thrashing him solidly for six years. At the age of six he changed from being a nice little boy to a roaring uncontrollable something-else. Not that the treatment diminished the roars, the roars went on the same. But they had hope that the treatment would begin to help them control him. At night I used to laugh at this—I thought of him being thrashed until he was old enough to take the stick off his mother, then off his father, and going his own way, roaring through the world. His father took time off from his work as Voting Behavior Sampler and Opinion Poll Designer to help Mum with the treatment. She had to take strong powders to combat the headaches she got from having to administer the thrashing. But she kept in good general physical condition.

Crying Clive, I guessed, had no him inside the thick skin. There was only bone inside, nothing to hurt. No actual flesh. That makes the whole thing take on a better complexion, doesn't it?

Perhaps when he died surgeons would pick into his body looking for reasons.

Obedience Training

The Vaux children had to have special consideration at school. There were lots of times in class when we were expected to keep perfectly still. Little boys were still given encouraging nods—and gold stars stuck on their foreheads—for sitting up straightest. But this enforced slowing down of our natural activity was neatly dodged by the

Vauxs. If they stopped too long in one place their toes grew to the ground.

Everett Vaux was in my class. Arabella Vaux was older and in 1K, Miss King's class. We envied their freedom to move around while we were given obedience training. Everett's freedom especially suited him; he liked to sit straight up for a very short time, then get up and move, break into a trot, dart around, sit, then jump up again. We looked at his freedom with longing. Our freedom from his dangerous condition made us liable to the confinement of silence and enforced stillness.

Father wouldn't believe that we still had to do this; he thought that since he'd had to when he was a child, it was a harmful or at least old-fashioned oppression and would now be gone. All I could do was say it was so, we did it, and he could come and see for himself. Actually this last wasn't true. If a visitor came, any visitor, there was no way our class could be said to go on in the usual way. The teacher super-kindly said, "Now feel free to draw in your books, or read your reader, or practice your writing. But no running around, and talk as little as possible while your visitor is here." And that was what happened when the headmistress came, or a parent, but not while we were alone with her.

What is it that runs, but never walks?

When Screaming Last in the Neighborhood Flourished And Bloomed

I didn't notice Clive until I was in my sixth year, and when it dawned on me that no one ought to be screaming, they couldn't stop me crying in sympathy. I could hear his screams in my ears late at night, long after his parents had finished for the day.

I took only the usual few weeks to lose my hearing for Clive-cries, but the time it took was full of voluptuous misery. I cried and cried, nothing would pacify me. My father got through to me with his tenderness, and with sweets, but it made little difference to the length of time I cried.

That such cruelty could be in the world, near me, when I was so happy and comfortable . . .

"You mustn't think of it as cruelty," my mother said. "Think of it as treatment they have to give that poor boy, and you won't feel nearly so bad about it."

"Can't Daddy do anything about it? Can't he stop them?"

"People can't mix in other people's business," she said.

And father said, "The people of the world aren't our family, darling. They're not your brothers and sisters."

When I got over it and no longer noticed Crying Clive's anguish, I didn't reproach myself. Was I healthy?

In the middle of a rowdy game on our front lawn he could sometimes be heard, a bagpipelike wail in the distance, there and not there, coming and going on the wind.

Amid cries of:

> *"Giddy giddy gout*
> *Your shirt's hanging out*
> *Five miles in and ten miles out!"*

it was even funny, and we all stopped and laughed.

But later I began to resent his screams and wished I could do something to make him stop.

If he was hurt bad enough, perhaps.

Mister Inman, Tea-Boy

Over the years, a snout appeared on the old man's face. The shape of bluntness had always been there. Then the nose flattened, and the nostrils seemed to shift: instead of facing down they looked forward. Long hairs came from them—perhaps in real pigs the snuffling round on the ground and in troughs wears away the nostril hairs—the hairs came out boldly and curled round once they were outside. They were thick and shiny, and several were thick and silver.

53

On weekends he tended banks of pigface that grew lustily in the yellow clay and managed to strangle even the couch grass that intruded on its empire. Pigface needed no tending, my father said.

At mealtimes his children put out his food, and as he made a sudden heavy run at the small trough containing his chop and vegetables, they played the hose over him.

"He's very dirty if you don't hose him down," his eldest son explained, and thoughtfully played a jet on the parental snout to wash away gravy. But even their faces had a certain bluntness.

Their lodger brought out the footbath, scented with disinfectant.

"For the footrot," she said confidentially to the passersby.

Lady Inman was a very clean individual; she seemed unaware that she lived with pigs and potential pigs.

To be fair, though, most men work when they can and are plain: he was just plainer than most.

It's No Secret These Days

It's no secret these days that lots of people have the beginnings of animal features; those who feel they are free of this hazard often speculate on the faces round them, and speak not always kindly of those who may turn out at any time to be more plainly animals than the rest of us are.

Look around. One sees snouts, beaks, huge thin flapping ears, the long sad muzzles of horses, deer and collie dogs; the short rounded mouths of snakes, the tentative noses of mice and bandicoots, the placid features of cats, the fat buffoonery of the hippo, the spread limbs and sinister aspect of spiders.

Some Frees think they may have been like these people in the last birth before this, or that the rest of us may end up perhaps as real animals in the next rebirth.

When Mister Cowan's Coffin Grew

When Mister Cowan's coffin grew to its full length, after months of sitting in the back of the shop with it supported on a chair, it came to an end and fell off. There was a raw pink rectangular patch where the coffin finished; it soon faded and became much like the surrounding skin.

He waited for another lump to appear, for the skin to break, for the planed bare timber to show, but nothing came. He would have settled for anything: a china cabinet, a bar. Nothing. After six months nothing.

He decided to use the coffin himself, taking it rather as a joke at first, then getting seriously involved in preparing it.

There were no books on coffin preparation outside the industry itself, and like anyone, he'd always had his doubts about the solidity, the waterproof qualities, the lasting strength of the rather light-looking timber that one can see at a funeral where the square deal shows through the scratches, and the patches of rosewood or mahogany varnish knocked off in the hustle and bustle of the mortician's workroom. Some even look as if they've been used over and over, as why shouldn't they be?

He decided on proofing it against damp, lining it with lead, putting pictures in it, some of his treasures, keepsakes, sentimental items . . . He began to serve again in the shop, using all his spare time for the preparation and care of the one thing that he had produced, all by himself, in his life.

His wife didn't interfere. She began taking sessions with a healer, not being able to afford a psychiatrist.

The Grading Gate

Change was confined to proles. Change transformed a pro to a prole. A change in childhood was an instant, permanent demarcation. Some who at the end of schooling were graded Free citizens never changed at all; their failure was obvious: it was their own selves, the way they were formed in the womb. To be fair, some late starters were admitted at a mature age.

To the Serving Class, the professionals, who loved peace and order and the continuance of things as they were too much to talk publicly about the less fortunate, the changes were always and only a signal of failure. Servants of Society could retire at any age, but few did.

For those who failed the Grading, failure reached deep into their bodies; either to the cells themselves, which grew confused, their recognition systems faltering and forming, in a panic, some strange new thing; or to the heavy knob of conviction inside them that they were *as* they were and *where* they were in society for the term of their natural lives.

But none of these things should be surprising in classes of individuals within a society, who are being turned over like sods by the plough, products of processes they cannot control, at the mercy of processes they can never understand.

Someone Always Tries to Stop a Suicide

Marie-Louise and I looked like religious symbols standing on the eastern cliffs of Australia with the sun behind us. We held our arms out straight beside us, and our shadows on the afternoon sea were two crosses. They reached a fishing boat bobbing up and down in large waves that played with it as with a toy.

We'd got tired of playing on the grass in sight of the adults and decided to climb the hill to the cliffs and the Gap. We picked up stones and tried to throw them in the sea.

"It's no use." Marie-Louise was my friend from school. She lived in Malthus Parade. Her parents and mine were having a picnic at Watson's Bay.

"They're only hitting the rocks," I said, confident rocks couldn't be hurt. Did we want to hurt the sea or its neat waves?

Boats far out went north and south. Some yachts and fishing craft on our left were entering and leaving the Heads. The Gap was a steep amphitheatre hacked clumsily by the sea out of the cliffs. Spoil was tumbled at the base, there was no order, no regular tiers of seats.

Marie-Louise and I stood at the guard fence, arms down, no longer symbols. Hypnotized by the rhythm and voice of water.

A voice said to us from a distance, "Girls, wouldn't you like to go and find your Mummy and Daddy?" We looked at each other.

We felt strange being taken for sisters. I wondered what Marie-Louise thought of me as a sister. We stayed like that for a while, thinking.

"It's getting late," the woman said. We said nothing, just dreamed away.

"They might worry if you're not there." And she smiled at us.

We'd been smiled at by pros, smiles meant nothing to us. Teachers, parents, faces trying to sell something—we could resist the world. Besides, we didn't have to be polite to strangers if our parents weren't around.

"I think you'd better go."

We were the only people there. We looked softly away, admiring an old tired boat on the edge of the world. It looked rusty and slow, staying afloat was an effort, it was low in the water; far, far out.

Next time we looked, the woman had climbed between the rails of the fence and stood on the sun-warm rock. She didn't look at us. We watched with interest. Maybe she was after one of the tiny flowers that grew between the cracks of the rock. Maybe she was a spy for a foreign power about to send a signal and she wanted us out of the way but it was the deadline for the signal and she had to take the risk of us handing her over to the authorities and being the cause of her execution. Maybe she was one of our spies. A double agent, even.

They were barefoot. That's why we didn't hear them, I guess. Three boys, at the railing where she'd been standing. If she wanted to get back she'd have to get past them. I wondered if women spies had guns. If so, where would she hide it?

"Hey, Missus!" one of the boys yelled. She didn't look round. The three boys didn't like her not looking round. It was as if she thought their voices meant nothing and the three of them didn't exist. Perhaps the gun was in her handbag.

"Maybe she can't move."

"Rooted to the spot."

"Ought to be rooted."

"Seized up."

"The old gear box clapped out." They were much older than us.

"Hey, para!" Para was the word for paraplegic. Kids shouted it at football matches if someone missed the ball, or just for the sound of it. The other word like para was spaso, short for spastic.

"Para!" they yelled.

"Get on with the act," one advised.

"The show must go on!"

"It's got stage fright."

"Gunna walk on the water, lady?"

"Yeah, she's women's lib. Wants to be JC."

"The para needs a parachute."

"Call Evel Knievel. He had a chute."

"Shoot, baby!"

The woman looked round at last. She had been weeping. She looked at us all for a long time then looked back at the sea.

She wasn't watching the horizon, she was looking down. She didn't even glance at the ladylike yachts, with the colored spinnakers swelling out in front like maternity dresses that had ventured into blue water.

"What's going to happen?" I whispered to Marie-Louise.

"How would I know?" she said loudly. I was glad she wasn't my sister.

The woman looked around again. The despair on her face looked as if it had been stamped in there with something heavy. It was never going to leave. I felt sorry for her. Uncomfortable. I didn't know why. Were the boys right? Was she going into the water? But there were no steps down. Nothing to hold to.

"This is a lousy show," one boy said.

"The script's up to shit."

"Bloody local content again."

The woman turned again. Her face wet. "Please go away, all of you. Please."

"Balls," said the boys as one.

"Won't you please go," she said to us. "You're girls. Someday—"

We waited, but she wouldn't finish the sentence.

"Listen, lady," one of the boys said. "If you're gunna jump, for Christ's sake jump. We've gotta go. We can't waste time watching nothing."

The woman looked them up and down. That was old-fashioned: it didn't work. "People are allowed to sleep in private. Why won't you let me do this in private?"

"You're not *in* private, you para. We're the public."

"Shouldn't we get someone to help?" I said to Marie-Louise.

"She won't take help from anyone. She's an adult," my friend said. She pronounced it "addult."

"If you don't go now, we're pissing off," one said.

The woman put her hands to her ears. This time she seemed to look at the horizon. I saw a drop fall to the rock, where it soaked in immediately and was gone. The woman took a few clumsy steps, ran to the edge and went over. I like to think she was looking right out to the horizon as she fell, rather than down at a lot of tumbled rocks. She took her handbag, still clutching it.

On the way down she didn't yell or make a fuss. We listened. She didn't make a sound, hitting. But any splat she made wouldn't have carried up to us.

The boys crowded through the fence to see.

"Where's she gone?"

"Can't see hide nor hair of her. Must have bounced back under the foot of the cliff."

"Should have kept her talking and got a photographer."

They looked some more and turned to go.

"If these kids were a bit older we'd have some chicks."

They looked over us with serene contempt. We were so young we didn't count as human.

They went off whistling. The tune they whistled was an advertising jingle for an old brand of cigarettes. The cigarettes were off the market, but the jingle was alive and well in the heads of boys.

Marie-Louise and I enjoyed the afternoon a bit longer and picked two blue flowers growing in a crack in the gold sandstone.

Holding one each, we went back to where the fathers and mothers were talking.

"A lady ran off the edge up there," my friend said, but no one heard.

"She was crying. Three boys gave cheek," I said. They unheard me, too.

Later my father said, as if he had partly heard us but had forgotten who spoke, "Isn't it funny how when people want a place to jump they choose the Gap? Just because it's *the* place and every suicide goes for the high jump there."

"Don't," said my mother. "Kids have ears."

"Well," said father defensively. "It's nothing but rocks. No chance of even landing in the water," and they talked of something else.

Marie-Louise and I ran into the setting sun down to the water's edge. We took our shoes off and paddled in the water. It was very clear. Three gulls held their heads to one side, standing in the shallows, listening to the lost music of the waves.

In the distance the tall buildings of the city stood close together as if they felt cold as the light got weaker.

Once, I said:

> "*Stare, stare, like a bear,*
> *Then you'll know me anywhere.*" To a seagull.

I found a lucky stone, too, and took it home and put it under my pillow.

We got home just on dark, and I had to go outside to bring in my tricycle; I'd left it across near our neighbor's ground. I came back a slightly different way; a black spider hung down below the phone wires just on a level with the top of my head. It did not sway. Not at first. As I moved toward it in the blackness against the tall bushes it began to move. Side to side, a huge blob. Was it warning me to go back? I wouldn't go back. The swaying stopped and, motionless, it was more terrible, hanging there; as if it had climbed out on one of the spokes of the dark wheel of night, in the same way as we were out on one of the bent arms of the galaxy itself.

My father said, looking at mother's bent head, "One day not long ago a man came up from the river out there," and he looked from the window downhill to the creek that wound around between the bottoms of the hills that converged on it. It was a wide creek, no more. Only in the country could a creek which was at the most ten meters wide be considered a river.

"Up from the river carrying a baby in a baby chair. That's it, the baby sitting in the baby chair, he was carrying the lot. No one saw where he took them, but day after day, around half past nine or a quarter to ten in the morning, up he came from a gap in the tea-tree on to the flat where the grass is, near the scout camp, and made his way to the rocks and the steep ground just below the houses on the other side of the street. People all round were looking out for them. The easement nearly opposite was the place between houses that he was looking for and sure enough he came walking up the last steep slope where old Jack mows to keep the fire danger down and so you can see what the kids are up to, and then they walked along the road, round the bend and out of sight. But others round at the outlet of Heisenberg Close saw them cross Newton Crescent, go up Galton Grove, and round Velikovsky Lane to the oval on the hill. And there on the pitch, under the goalposts they watched him with binoculars. He did something to them so you lost sight of them for a while, then the baby appeared again and he nursed it. People like the Maguires went creeping round in their cars. What they found was the whole thing was a blow-up."

"What's a blow-up?" I said.

"He let the air out and put them in his pocket while he made a drink on the barbecue grate, then blew them up again, detached the baby and nursed it. Finally he went back round the streets to the river."

"Did he go toward the Lutherburrows?" I asked. Lil Lutherburrow was in my class. They lived in the bush.

"I don't know where they are these days. But he went off toward the thick bush past the big new bridge."

"He could be one of them."

"I don't know. Anyway no one liked that baby. People tried to prick it. Kids shot BBs at it. Arrows with nailheads in. They didn't get it. It was tough, like life-raft material."

He said nothing, and for once my mother filled in the empty space.

"To the river, you say."

"Not just to. Into."

"He went swimming?" I said.

"Into the river," looking across at me. I had been painting with big round bowls of primary colors on coarse, absorbent paper. The paint ran along the fibers of what had once been wood.

"Into the river. Into the water. Not out again. Into."

My mother shrugged and went on writing. The whole story was a waste of time, to her.

Why Do Fish Swim in the Sea

In my room at school, we had a big poster: Why do fish swim in the sea? Every so often Miss King would take answers to the question. After each answer, no matter how cute or clever or downright cretinous, she gave no indication whether the answer was right. Because it's wet, Because they're hot, Because they haven't learned to walk. She noted the answers in a book, with our names.

Miss King wore a wig. Anthony Curran saw her take it off in the staff room.

There were drawings and paintings and fingerwork, and collages of wool strips on breakfast-cereal-in-paint, and charts and demonstrations of how letters and numbers were written, and saucers in which carrot and onion ends were sprouting in a film of water, and drinking glasses and honey jars and proper vases with flowers in. And sometimes they would have roses.

The roses. Ah . . .

Even at six I devoured with my mind the downy red tightly wrapped buds that held such beauty within them, round them, and made beautiful the patch of painted ledge on which they stood and the window behind them that was slightly dry-misty with the natural accretions of dust and lit by the incoming sun. Something arose in the top and the back of my throat that had to be swallowed when I looked at the bud of a rose, and I held my eyes wider to give more surface area for the small flood of wetness that gathered there so no one would notice it gather at the bottom of my lids.

Red roses. To me, the words themselves are pictures.

Can you, my reader, get a picture in your mind of a small girl standing up with the others, doing the actions, and singing:

"I'm a little teapot, here is my spout,
Fill me up, and pour me out,"

in her first years at school, having turned six, and it's October and a glorious spring after a dry warm winter, looking sideways at roses on the ledge in water in a common glass, and the tears dripping and sliding down her face, some into the corner of her mouth and others dropping and wetting her school tunic? Can you?

Not Exactly Pretty

I saw him once, that was all. I was six, and my mother hadn't mentioned Uncle Rory before.

He was hideously rich, I heard Daddy say. But the sight of him was the thing. If his riches were hideous, his deformity was beautiful to a child avid for newness and variety.

His face was twisted by a muscular disease so that it was longer than proportion would allow, and bent to his left underneath the cheekbones. The mouth was further bent in the same direction, so that it was within fifteen or twenty degrees of being at right angles to his brow line.

His spine had two bends, from another kind of wasting disease. One was near the shoulder blades, and bent him forward as if a hump was forming; the other was where his trouser belt was, and bent him back. He looked from the side as if he was perpetually in two minds as to whether to tie his shoes or rear back in surprise

63

from a sudden attack. Although horribly deformed, these weren't changes: his wealth did not depend on employment.

I never saw him below the waist.

When he left, father said, "The body wears out, Al. With everyone. You, too."

It seemed a funny thing that after all the efforts of chance down so many years to bring me about, I was no sooner in the world than I began to wear out.

"Dying begins now," he repeated.

I looked at myself to see what was wearing out. When I closed my hands there were lots of wrinkles, and when I saw Mrs. Bassett's new baby its feet were quite old, with lines all over them.

Cocky was awfully old, he'd been wearing out for fifty years, father said, but he was still there in his cage.

I tried to teach him "Same to you with knobs on," so he could answer anyone who talked to him, but all he got was "Knobs on, knobs on, knobs on."

I was too young to be sad at the thought of all the future time when the memory of me would inhabit nothing but random breezes.

Word and Object

In the course of *Changes* my father was murdered. Public statements were regularly made that father was not the murderer in the play, but the conjunction of the word "murder" and my father's name and picture were enough to ensure that a significant number of the Free population would turn on him like wild animals, as if he were an animal that must be destroyed. The conjunction of a face and a word. Their disbelief could not be suspended: they had none.

Attackers who had been questioned revealed a depressing similarity of response. "Murderer," they said. "Murder."

Questioned further, they repeated the two words as if they were interchangeable. "Murder, murderer."

Faced with the proposition that my father was an actor, they showed no confusion, merely said firmly, "Murder."

Told that he killed no one but was himself killed, they repeated, "Murder."

Asked why they blamed him if he was murdered, they said, "Murder." And without the slightest change of expression said, "Murderer."

No amount of expostulation made an impression. Expressionlessly, even with a pitying expression, they shook their heads, "Murder."

There was no comprehension that he was acting. Even his repeated death and occasional appearance in the streets did not disturb this opinion.

In their minds he was the one who should be destroyed.

He was unable to get out of the car in any place where large numbers of people might be gathered. He had been beaten up so many times that he had resigned himself to suburban seclusion.

Nonetheless, in spite of the fury of the Frees, his attitude was: I have a country; this is my country—Australia, the great south land. I love my country. And this sentiment was part of my earliest education.

By contrast, among the liberal humanists Internationalism was a cold superior mood, warmed by the glowing words in which its ideal was expressed, but still cold, like a metal. And like metal it was a favorite weapon for bludgeoning the hydra-headed nationalism that sprang up like a weed from the ground. A weed, that is, to its enemies: to those who ate of it, it was wonderfully nourishing; it gave a superhuman strength to those addicted to it.

My father, though his ideas and philosophies were patched together out of bits of dialogue and the more learned theater reviewers' ideas, nevertheless wasn't blind to the picture of a small, weak country professing internationalism, thus stabilizing the great powers in their pride and strength by its effect on that small country's actions. And the effect? To make it choose to keep out of competition, to be mild and good-mannered, to be on good terms with everyone, never to play power politics, never to try to gather its strength and push forward in wealth and power to a more prominent position, as those "emerging" countries did whose memory of subjugation and slavery and the wrong end of empire was so strong that they would risk life and limb and wholesale destruction to get their turn in the ruler's chair. At that stage the impotent cry of Peace meant one obvious thing: the stabilization in pre-eminence of those nations already there, those nations who had never wavered from the extreme, single-minded, aggressive nationalism that had got them where they were. They preached internationalism and peace: they were on top. Peace would keep them there. Internationalism, if it came, would give them first choice of seats at the banquet.

"Liberal-minded people just don't care for their country," my father lamented. "They're a rabble," he said.

Tibby and Tiger

We got them from people in Einstein Crescent. They were both morose, and inclined to long periods thinking. Father never used to call me when they were doing things to each other, but I watched when I came home from school.

Tiger had duplicates of himself running around all over the district, so he wasn't anchored to homosexuality. He was a great jumper, and superficially friendly, but although he would fight when females were in heat, he wasn't a good fighter.

Tibby had longer fur, almost like a Persian, and was a darker homosexual, an exclusive. A baby's foot protruded from underneath his chest. We noticed it growing when he was sitting down alone on a patch of dead couch in early winter and he was licking himself. Perhaps Tiger and he weren't speaking. But there it was, the sole showing through.

We watched while it grew to be a complete foot, then it stopped growing. Tibby wasn't a jumper, like Tiger, who could spring on to two-meter fences, but when aroused he was a fierce fighter. Yet, often he wouldn't eat. He was finicky, and made a fuss over nothing. Sometimes he wouldn't come near us, even me. Yet we'd done nothing to him. During the energy crises he was unbearable.

Tibby licked the foot, but in fights Tiger would go for it and scratch it. Often it had deep scratches, bleeding red blood.

66

(Was it baby blood or cat blood?)

Every morning, if it was fine—or in the wet, in a safe dry corner under the bushes near the cigarette plant—you would find him doing his usual brush-up, cleaning himself, sharpening his claws and cleaning between the toes and fingers, getting his penis out and making it shiny and red, and licking his baby foot. Why does an animal change? Animals are failures to start with.

Cats and dogs rest a lot. Where they come from it must be a shorter day. Ours is too much for them.

Lucky Number Seven

On the day before my seventh birthday I saw my parents doing sex.

She was lying on her back and her legs were drawn up. He was on top of her and I thought: *that* must be heavy. It would be hard for her to escape.

She didn't seem to want to, though. She was yawning. Father was pushing forward, then going back a bit; forward again, and her head moved back against the pillow. That was all I saw.

I wondered if it hurt the part he was pushing against. It seemed a bit rough, yet not very. I went back to bed.

I never saw them do it again. There were many times later when their door was shut and I heard the bed, but I didn't sneak up to look, it didn't seem important enough.

In the morning the rooster next door was blowing his own trumpet, and woke me. The hens, though, were getting on with production.

I don't know why I thought of it like that.

Mother's Love

This is a short interruption while I think of it.
It is about my mother and the fact that she loves.
She is capable of great love, and expresses it.
But she *does* nothing.
She writes of it. (I think.)
She talks of it.

67

She has loving expressions on her face.
Her voice is full of love.
But she *does* nothing.
I wonder if I am being critical without cause.
Am I too practical? Is this why mother has turned away?

My Investigation of Sex-Directed Learning

Little girls are in no position to question the things they're told, or the objects they're given to play with. If you were put into a pink blanket, if pink plastic toys were hung on a string above your eyes, you'd touch them, wouldn't you?

You'd also come to expect to have pink things, and softness.

The advantage I had was that I got any color but pink; and where, in a family of boys and girls, the little jobs that crop up are given out, the manly ones to the boys, the soft jobs to the girls, I got any that were going. I washed dishes. I helped father as he mattocked the backyard, I painted a small piece of wall when he painted, I climbed our trees to escape my mother, taking books and drinks and sandwiches up with me to share with the ants and mosquitoes. I played cricket with father, hard ball and all, and kicked a football with him just as if I were a boy. He was pleased with me.

He told me things like:

> *"The boy stood on the burning deck*
> *Melting with the heat*
> *His piggy eyes were full of tears*
> *And his shoes were full of feet."*

and

> *"Mary felt a little queer*
> *She took some castor oil*
> *And everywhere that Mary went*
> *She fertilized the soil."*

68

Mother didn't know until I recited them in the house.

An Interesting Speculation

Odia Watson lived in one of the houses opposite. She was a huge woman with heavy opinions and strong breasts like muscular footballs. I think her name may not have been Odia: that may have been father's christening.

"No pensions," she said to father, as she borrowed the large scissors. "Pensions, government spending, they're the beginnings of communism."

"Oh dear," said father. I think that's where her name began. "And what about child endowment?"

"Same thing," she said. "Let the government feed you and look after you, and freedom's gone."

She didn't know it, but this was where she had father. He could never make up his mind where the citizens' right to tax money ended and where freedom from bureaucratic control began; all his life, as long as I knew him, he gave out strong opinions on both sides but always hesitated as to where the opposing sides met.

On the other hand, Odia Watson, believer in freedom, called the police on her telephone every time she heard neighbors arguing.

"Every argument is violence. We must have order. Words of conflict are only one step away from blows. We must live in peace with one another, without asking for repressive communist government to step in and give us peace and order."

Every time she heard a child crying, she called the welfare department. She hated cruelty. She was a religious person, attracted by the sort of God that wipes away all tears.

Odia earned her fame in the district, fame that lasted long after the police and the welfare had ceased to answer her urgent calls, with a careless dive into her backyard pool. This pool was placed so that the shallow end was just past the back of the house and the deep end took advantage of the slope of the ground. It still had to be built up from the ground, there was a drop of four meters from the far end of the pool to the rock below. She dived after a run down the yard, aquaplaned half the length before her two bosom-floats would allow her to go below the surface, went under, barely had time to get her prow out, and cannoned into the far end where the concrete was a mere ten centimeters thick. The concrete broke, opened up like a dam wall, and Odia rode the wall of water out into the valley. When the flood passed over her she was pressed, in a surfing position, into the top of a tree. Both arms, both legs, her neck and her waist were caught in forking branches. Her bosoms hung down a long way, out of her costume, swinging like pendulums.

The neighbors speculated for some time on the best method of getting her down.

I Had a Weak Thought

I had a weak thought in the playground. They—the boys—were playing Pushings. Pushings was when two crowds of them ranged up on both sides of a crack in the asphalt of the playground and put their shoulders down like a giant scrum, and pushed.

Perhaps I was feeling gentle that morning. I had been walking along in the sun, keeping away from the Corner, then going toward it, surprised to find no bodies hurtling round it. I had wandered away from the others, who were quarreling and spiteful.

I kept out wide near the Corner. Nothing. No boy was there. Instead, the main playground was packed with them. Suddenly, with no signal that I saw, the ants of this big heap of them formed up into two sides. There was a cry of "Pushings!" and the push began.

In the middle, some went down, some trod on others, but the main lines stayed as they bent forward, shoulder crunching against shoulder, with the ones at the rear bending down, seeing nothing, pushing for their side. The ones in the middle must have been taking a terrible weight.

I stood watching. I don't know how long, perhaps I was in a dream. My eyes saw them as a mass, not as particular ants. I began to think of dresses—such as I'd seen in the shop windows on the weekend when father took me out in the car to the shops—and nice things, and ribbons, and plaits at the side of your head like some kids have, and the dolls my relatives brought for my presents and which my mother put away, and the sewing machine father was teaching me to use (I loved to watch as his big thick finger-ends touched the thin cotton and gently pushed it toward the needle's eye) and pinafores such as the Lutherburrow girls had, and party dresses like the Headen girls wore with their noses in the air, and all the pretty, graceful girlish things.

Then I caught myself. I shook my head. Some of Them came in focus. Barry Lutherburrow, two of the Vauxs, and leaning over the school fence the fifty-nine-year-old idiot son of Mrs. Brown. I had been weak. The shoulder crunches had been a push in the face. I was ashamed.

> See my finger
> See my thumb
> See my fist
> And here it comes!

Don't Touch Me!

Audrey Major who lived in Joule Street had a different problem from the Vaux children. Where their toes grew to the ground, she wasn't allowed to touch others for too long. She and people grew together.

Her mother had the itch, the seven minute itch, and needed people to touch her in places, or to take her clothes off. She got hysterics if no one helped her.

It was a game in the playground, touching Audrey lightly; daring her processes to hold us fast by a finger. She ran away crying: "Don't touch me! I'll tell on you!" So we all chased her.

I never saw anyone joined to her. Perhaps her parents spread a nonstick ointment over her surfaces. But she told of having a doctor separate her from one of her uncles when she was small. Down there, too.

The Scarecrows' Lament for the Wild Birds

Grandfather Grossman was a domestic, ordinary old man, held in subjection by Grandma; he had drinking habits that got in her way when they were much younger, but she had long since curbed him. Now, in their twilight, she hardly ever needed the reins. He went naturally in the direction he had been trained, like a good old carthorse that stops at all the stops he's got used to on his rounds, and if there's a vacant house and no need to stop he'll still stop, indeed insists on stopping, just as he was trained to do, outside every stop on the way.

He'd had work habits that annoyed her, too. On the farm he worked hours she considered far too long, and on household repairs and tasks far too little. She adjusted this balance by a system of rewards and sanctions that Skinner, if he had known, would have adopted immediately.

They lived in a valley, on the MacDonald river. We visited them twice a year. They said I was marvelous.

Father looked sideways at me when grandfather began one of his monologues. "Weaken the tyranny of the family at your own risk," he said, settling his glass one ring further on the shiny table so the new ring linked with the last. "The result will be an increase in the tyranny of the state."

As usual, mother wasn't listening.

I was seven; my father listened and watched; the sun shifted a tiny bit west and the shadow on the carpet approached the east. Soon we would get in the car to go home. A magpie sang its long rubbery notes.

"Collectivization is not for your good and my good but for *our* good." He underlined the word. "And the good, the comfort, the ease of our rulers."

There must have been something safe in my expression; my father relaxed, as he always did. I always watched to see him relax, then listened just as I did before. I needed no special guidance to know how to treat grandfathers. Years before, I had noticed how he couldn't get around as well as mother, let alone father; and as for dashing about quickly, as I did, he simply wasn't in it. A child can see that a person that can't move around quickly is at a serious disadvantage. Even cats and dogs know things like that.

"In 1901 we hadn't looked. In 1975 we hadn't looked for three-quarters of a century. You must look closely at all things. No, *my* Australia exists only in museums. They gave the vote to people who can't be bothered thinking about politics."

When we were climbing, in the car, I looked around and could just see their house with its trees kneeling protectively around it. It looked lovely from a distance.

Once we passed a big paddock, and up in one corner there were lots of gloomy cows.

And in fields where vegetables were planted scarecrows stood up looking sorry for themselves, and lonely. No birds bothered to come and sit on their shoulders. Not even the wild birds that didn't give a damn for anyone.

Freedom

At the local shoppingtown a rival long distance lecturer set up. Professor Henrietta D. Walden II had freedom as her subject and intended to spend alternate years on Freedom From and Freedom To; she was now on Freedom From. Freedom from poverty, from riches, from sickness, from health, from light and darkness, from war and peace, sorrow and joy, miracles, disappointments, frustrations, ignorance and knowledge, hunger and fullness, ambition and sloth, success and failure. She had a board showing the program, her name and degrees, university posts, her publications in learned journals and her two books, and the names and specifications of the two children she had borne into the world.

"New jargon; new bondage," she was saying. "Every new theory oppresses."

Her voice was harsh, and didn't care for its audience, like a prime minister's voice when he has a record majority.

The shoppers had blank faces and moved toward the mouths of shops looking for things to exchange for the money in their pockets, not even conscious the economy was on their shoulders.

The message of Henrietta D. Walden II beat against the shores of their collective mind with all the fury of a caramel milkshake.

My father said, "Freedom's great, for a holiday. You wouldn't want to spend all your life there."

Coming home in the car I thought all the night shadows far too long, but father assured me everything was normal.

Jerusalem the Cocky

To say I was happy as a little girl is perhaps too strong. I was cheerful, lively; I was vigorous. These manifestations of health are often taken for signs of happiness when you're young. You're at the mercy of all sorts of unqualified diagnosticians. But how do you get to be qualified to make a diagnosis about happiness? By being happy?

No, that won't do. You might find out how to play football by watching footballers, but don't ask them how. Words, and people's control of words, can't encompass actions. There's a sort of mystery surrounding actions. Words try; but finally fail and break off, leaving shreds of their flesh. Actions stand entire.

Every morning the world was fresh. The milk came: fresh from the factory. The sun came up fresh on the dew in the cool months, and the grass was fresh. Except for places where it was bent over and crumpled and disappointed looking; you can bet I had been lying and jumping up and down there the day before.

Jerusalem, the cocky, looked very wisely at me, even if I said something to him that didn't require wisdom in reply. He was old, and his name wasn't always Jerusalem. Once he was Pretty Cocky, and he was happy with that name, but I guess that I—I'm ashamed of it now—got tired of having him around.

Maybe it wasn't *that* so much as wanting a different sort of bird, perhaps I wanted a different pet as well as the cats and Pretty Cocky.

The different pet I wanted was a white rabbit.

"When Cocky goes you can have a rabbit," father said. It usually fell to mothers of families to do all the feeding and making sure pets had water in their cages, but since my mother was pretty well taken up with making notes, that work passed along to my father. When work passes along like this, it doesn't get any easier. It grows. The getting of a rabbit seemed like a mountain we all had to cross, on account of the extra work that would have to be passed along. I had to wait for Pretty Cocky to die.

He had no intention of going anywhere. If you opened his cage he didn't escape, just looked at me wisely. (I opened his cage hoping he'd embrace freedom.)

"I'm going to call him Jerusalem," said my father at last. "Because he will not pass away."

One morning we found his feathers, and his yellow crest. The cats had got him in the night. I must have not fastened the catch properly.

The Open Society

Unlike earlier societies, ours had no need of a priestly secrecy. The information on how to run the society and its machines was freely available; examinations were open to all at whatever age. Initial grading could be challenged at any time in a person's life, but there were few later admissions. The point was that no matter how available the information, the knowledge, the circuitry, the logic, the Free Class was unable to grasp it. They simply were not up to it. No matter how the grading tests were changed, the same kind of people succeeded. The justice of the position where the able had entry and others had not, was accepted. It seemed as natural as breathing to reward ability and penalize the less able.

Even as a child I felt it remarkable that they seemed to feel no resentment; neither the Free Citizens, nor the Servants on their behalf. I guess they saw clearly the failure of others and how absurd it made them and so weren't willing to look absurd themselves by objecting to what was inevitable.

It wasn't even a secret that nuclear shelters were available for less than a tenth of the population.

A Family of Idiots

The Lutherburrows might not have been smart, but neither were they soft. They lived in the bush doing no harm to anyone. In tents. When well-meaning people came into the bush to move them out and into the clutches of the mortgage companies, they moved to another part of the bush. If the authorities were stupid enough to descend on them in force, the Lutherburrows told tales to the environmental guerrillas, who manned all entrances to the bush and stopped intruders mucking up the bush tracks with vehicles. The authorities could not conceive of a deputation on foot, they had to come equipped with the might of engines and shiny paintwork, and this cavalcade did no sort of good for the bush tracks that the Lutherburrows traveled on foot. They simply moved away, dug cute dunnies and were so stupid that they didn't mind carrying water by hand. They didn't mind boiling it, they didn't mind getting wet when it rained.

Sometimes they were seen sitting out in the rain, in a circle, as quiet and still as leaves thinking. People took photographs.

They had two dogs, so beautifully trained that they knew when to disappear, and did it quietly. They alerted the family to intruders, usually boys, but it wasn't all that necessary. The Lutherburrow boys were hard as nails, they knew every inch of the bush in the dark, and never hurt the boys badly.

While not one of them was actually mad, the family as a whole was crazy. There were some well-off people in the district who thought they ought to be preserved and not harassed, the Lutherburrows being an example to the rest of us of one of the lost arts of living. They had a word in the ear of the politicians, who spoke to the police, and so it goes.

They stayed.

They were different from us, with our appliances and debts. The old man and the boys had casual jobs, they worked well, they had money enough for clothes and soap and food. That's all they seemed to need.

If civilization tends toward softness in its captives and softness was the enemy, the Lutherburrows had it licked.

When Doctor Wise was called to the Lutherburrows by one of their anonymous friends—they tended to delay calling the doctor to give sickness a chance to develop and when it did, they tended not to call the doctor, to give themselves a chance to get well—people thought he was doing something very like charity, and charity was one thing the authorities had tried to eradicate. The boys of the idiot family always repaid a favor and appeared very early in the morning on the weekend and did the doctor's garden like the fairies. The eldest, Challenger, knew which weeds to leave in, to make the other shrubs and flowers grow better.

That was our lore, at school. Challenger's name got round in circles where there was some reverence for this simple knowledge, and he was in demand to tend garden beds and to give advice. He did what he could, but couldn't keep up with the demand for his talent; as for putting what he knew into words, he was a failure. People didn't understand that you could know something and not be able to use words to encapsulate it.

The idiot family had a natural tact. They never mentioned the name on Doctor Wise's arm. They were the only ones to know his secret, and his status was safe with them.

In raised flesh on the side of his right arm stood part of a name. The letters "r Woodbur" stood up enough to be made out. Was the "r" the end of a first name? Was a "y" or an "n" missing from the surname? Lil told me about it. She trusted me. I suppose when people read this he'll be prosecuted. We went into it all at school in the playground, standing around under the angophoras, watching as the leaf-shadows strayed from here to there in the slight breeze at the treetops that we could not feel on the ground.

The Drunkard

When I took Anthony Simonetta home, his mother was there. He had been sick in class.

I could see her inside the back door bent over the table, head loosely on her arms which lay on the table, flat and uninterested, her face and mouth out a little from the table edge so that when she felt like having a spit, the material went on the floor, not the table.

She came out of her daze a bit later and I heard her give this foolish snuffling laugh, saw the hunching of the shoulders and upper arms, the sinking back into the chair, the lifting of the head, giving her audience a sight of vacant, drunken eyes.

I had never seen a drunk person before.

When I got home mother was sitting perfectly still in her chair, hunched over the desk. As if she had died sitting up. I called, and she began writing. She wasn't drunk and she wasn't dead: she'd been thinking.

They Told Me About the Place of Skulls

Why is a skull such a menacing object? The Place of Skulls, commonly called Golgotha at Sunday School, must surely have been only one, and a tiny one, among all the other places of skulls in the recently ancient world.

But in Sunday School there was a passion for descriptions of the torture and death of Jesus that brought the blood and thorns and whipping right before my eyes. I saw the cruel men putting their backs into the scourging, and the more experienced ones using the wrist artfully, like the boys at school who knew how to hurt, getting the flick of the thong at the end of the stroke and not having to use up energy. I saw the blood run down the Lord's forehead and through his hair down the back of his neck, mixing with the sweat on his shoulders and back. He had a little hair down in the lower part of his back on both sides of his spine, which was indented there and was only a deep channel between the two stiff muscles supporting the back. His waist was covered lower down, preventing my imagining eyes from proceeding further, but in general you could say his back was rather like my father's. Not like Odia Watson's man, who was covered in black hair, front and back.

And which bones did the nails pass between? I touched my own hands, feeling for the most painful spots, wondering. The flesh must be very strong, I thought, to hold together, supporting a man's weight without tearing. If it tore, he'd just slide down to the ground, because the finger bones are separate nearly up to the wrist. But no, there were the feet. How did they get the nails in someone's feet? I felt my own, the bones were quite close together. They must have hammered hard. Did they have hammers like Daddy's hammer? With two flattened bits hooked over on the other side of the head to pull nails out with?

And in the hot sun, with blood running down—why, of course! He'd have fainted after a bit, so maybe he didn't feel it. And if executions were regular things, there were plenty who suffered. I was glad he didn't have his legs broken, like the others. But how did they break legs, at that height, at that angle? With a hammer? Or did they break the leg backwards at the knee, like the terrorists except that they shoot a bullet out through the kneecap from behind. It terrified me, for a little while.

A Vale of Tears

I often wanted to be with people. With anyone, just to keep the aloneness away, the aloneness I first felt when my childish mind grappled with the awful details of the crucifixion. To me it seemed that it was far more terrible to kill a good man than a bad.

And did they really leave him some clothes around that part like the statues show? And how did it stay up? I didn't know whether the Hebrews had belts or not. I knew the Romans did. I knew that when my arms were raised my waist seemed to be thinner, but of course I had hips for things to rest on, and he was a man. Men are thinner there.

These speculations made me sad, and the cruelty involved. I had quite a lot of sadness around that time. Mother said it was a stage.

The Sorrowful Death of the Prince of Glory

It was enough for my father that I had some religious tuition so that I knew at least the names of the officials in our local branch of the world-religion. We were nominally Christians, though all around were Eastern branches, and new-founded religions, which started, dwindled, but rarely disappeared entirely, so that there were, scattered about, many shells of once fashionable sects, still with their faithful few.

Father didn't protest when I wanted to take part in a school production of the Easter play, and came along on the night. I was an angel outside the tomb. But where I should have enjoyed being in the play, since it was a combined effort of Junior Primary, I was more affected by the message of the play.

It struck me that something was wrong in the world if the Prince of Glory had to die. Not that he was said to die for others, but that he died at all. Roger Hardy, two classes above me, was the Prince.

"Were you there when they laid him in the tomb?" the chorus asked us all, and I was so wrapped up in the feel of the thing that in the pause after that haunting question I said in a small voice, "Yes." The whole church turned and looked at me as if I had lied.

My father didn't encourage me to go after that, but he taught me to say:

> Hot cross buns
> Hot cross buns
> One a penny
> Two a penny
> Hot cross buns.

We had them every year at Easter. I had to ask him what a penny was.

My Uncle in the Soil

My uncle Maurice, mother's brother, died years ago at the age of eighteen months of what in those days was called cot death. My father suspected Maurice died because he wasn't fit to live.

"Something wrong, a child that age suddenly dying. Maybe it was one of those kids that just scraped through getting born. There's so many combinations, darling, of sickness and health, of fitness and unfitness, there's bound to be lots that just scrape through and die sooner or later. Maurie was sooner. Others die at eleven, or twenty-five, or forty. There's no natural age to die. He's at rest."

He was calming me. All I could think of was how I had an uncle of eighteen months, who would always be my uncle Maurie, always eighteen months, and here I was: seven.

His grave was the first in line as you turned from the straight-in cemetery road at the fourth row. It was a new cemetery. His memorial plate was set flat in the earth and the grass mown all round. It was an act of faith to believe there were dead people underneath.

Over in the section that wasn't lawn the earth was pastel-colored where the clay—white, grey, pinkish and some lumps almost blue—from deep down, had not been put back first and there wasn't enough brown dirt to cover the clay and it drew your attention because it looked so like a scar, almost violent, and death violent, too. Not peaceful at all.

And all those jars and receptacles on the graves. Were they to catch the tears of the mourners?

My Uncles, In Memory and in the Flesh

All we had were photographs. My uncle Maurice was a fat boy with a pale face, and stood awkwardly hanging on to the seat of a chair. His age when the best photo was taken was thirteen months. The others were baby ones and little-tot-walking photos. I thought about my uncle a lot. Whatever age I attained, he would always be eighteen months. And he was in a place at which one's hitherto mysterious existence after death arrives, continues for a while, then fades. It corresponds to the existence in memory of memorable persons. (And when those who remember die, their last hold on existence is gone.)

If he had grown up to be a man, my uncle Maurice might one day have said, as I heard my uncle Ken say to my father as they were

81

opening beer on the back patio, "There's nothing really—nothing much—" (he looked for a place to throw the rings, then remembered and put them on the table) "to interest a man," he said, and paused. My father lifted his glass, looking at the bubbles on the side of it, and listened. "In a woman," my uncle said. "They don't actually—well, *do* anything; nothing, apart from their basic attractiveness; they sort of play around, they groom themselves in front of mirrors for hours, they check to see their eyelashes are on, their skin is wrinkled, their this is so-and-so and their that is whatsit. There's nothing *in* 'em, *to* 'em."

He saw me listening to him.

"Little people have big ears," he said. And tried to take the edge off his words by holding up his glass and smiling at me. But all I could see were his teeth that were worn down and had brown on them from the time when he used to smoke tobacco. There are two types of people as there are two social classes, and Uncle Ken was a loser.

Not long after this, he began to get pains. Shortly after, he got religion. Their family lived in one of those terrible suburbs where no one speaks the truth.

Death May Come

"Death may come anytime," my father said. "So confront it. After all, what is death?"

I thought it was the end of everything, and inconceivable. In the normal order of things he would die before me, so talking about it showed a certain courage.

He recited:

> *"The crematorium in the sun*
> *Implies that life and death are one.*
> *I wonder what else would be the same*
> *If I gave death another name."*

From my earliest years he threw the word death around; all the other kids I knew were familiar with death and the idea of killing people from very early on, so their fathers probably did much the same.

I didn't know what would be required of me when death came. I thought of it as something that suddenly happens. I didn't know what mine would be like. It was a word that I had to fill with whatever meanings I cared to.

It would bring peace, plenty of it. Forever. Perhaps that's why I don't think too highly of peace before I die.

Did they know the thoughts their words gave rise to in me? Surely not.

My dear parents: may dreams, like sentinels, forever guard your sleep.

The Reverend Buggiar

The Reverend Buhagiar was a visiting preacher who took it on himself to visit the houses where kids dropped attendance at church. His explanation to my father when he was tackled about the words raised up in flesh on his head, was that the words had run through his mind for years and now were manifest in the flesh.

My father looked at him. Was it a joke? There was no way of telling. The Reverend Buhagiar fingered the words. The first two were mere patches, lumps under the surface; "the Cross turns" was the only visible readable phrase.

"What's the whole sentence?" said father. I guess he felt, as I did, that it didn't matter what you asked of a person committed to the truth. Fibs are usually more interesting.

"'Call me when the Cross turns over,' that's the sentence," said the Reverend. His black socks ran smoothly up his ankle and where they stopped there began a marble-white leg, populated by a few weary hairs that pointed this way and that, not like the hairs on the legs of the big high school boys that passed outside our fence. Theirs were thick and black—or blonde or ginger— and seemed to go all the same way as if they'd climbed out of the water and the hairs had dried as they were swept by the current of water.

83

His favorite sermon was on gravity. The force of gravity. Time—or life or love or anything that could be represented by a word that meant lots of things—was earnest, passing by. Too much in life was trivial and unserious.

Everyone—that is, all the kids—called him the Reverend Buggiar.

Rain

> *"Rain rain go away,*
> *Come again another day!"*

sang my father and I as we danced round the lounge room while the rain pelted down. He was teaching me to box. He had big fat boxing gloves on. Mine were smaller, but they still made your arms tired. The venetians were right up so when we stopped for a break we could see the white columns of rain striding across the low ground beneath us falling away to the flat river plain that extended to the hills on the horizon. Rain spattered up from the roofs of the houses on the low side of Heisenberg Close and poured into guttering channels and out into the street.

He had a wonderful ability to enjoy himself and be happy. I wanted to be like him: smiling, alert, strong, attractive.

> *"It's raining, it's pouring*
> *The old man's snoring*
> *Six o'clock in the morning."*

The wind had come up. It beat bitterly on the windows, pushing branches and shrubs against the house. Elsewhere houses were unroofed, and in the morning we heard that another cliff had fallen into the sea, and the land was less. When I went outside after breakfast the only sign of the storm I could see were the many fat diamonds of dew gathered in the hollows of nasturtium leaves.

To My Father I Owe

To my father I owe my ability to organize myself. He allowed me to keep my room shabby and disordered, he was never sarcastic about my rare bursts of energy when I would clean everything up and have it looking like mother's room. But of course she used nothing, only her pen and writing pads, no cosmetics, no perfumes, no aids of any sort. Her room was still as tidy at the end of the week as it was on Sunday when my father did it. And yet, despite him, it smelled of negligence. Only the fine layer of whitish dust over everything was different, and that was unavoidable, unless we'd had air conditioning. My father didn't understand how air conditioners worked, and all he would say was he didn't want to breathe dead air or burn fossil fuels just to avoid the weather.

"Your room has to suit your way of living, darling, not mine," he said. "A child's way of living is not the same as an adult's. I want you to get from your home a personality full up to the brim with deep inner contentment." That's how he talked.

I think he thought that sort of contentment far and away the prime goal of his education of me, as if, having a person full of deep inner contentment, the other goals, concern for others, intellectual achievement, skills of all sorts would flow from it. How that was to happen, how anything much could spring from contentment I do not and did not understand, and later I thanked whatever gods there may be that I had something more powerful pushing me.

He went further. He was like an idealistic teacher, who had great faith in human potential, but in a special direction and one that could not be deduced from his magic contentment. It was that given the right environment people will naturally grow into zestful, positive, living human beings. And his recipe: freedom, love and self-regulation. In its way it was as much magic as thinking that hard work and right living will bring happiness.

Canned Laughter

Mother had a notation that enabled her to write with a sign the expression of a voice word, the lift of an eyebrow, an unusual variation from a person's norm of manner, the feel of the air at the time, her own transitions from one feeling to another, a facial expression and so on. The notation consisted of dashes, stops and curly bits, and I think there were some bits of shorthand thrown in. She called them grammalogs and "my signs."

It was as if a secretary or shorthand-writer had come to a place of business and begun like an automaton to take down everything. Without pay, for she was noncommercial.

She washed obsessively, and father often seemed unhappy at what he took to be guilt behind this washing. "Guilt is washing your underwear after one wearing and your hands before you touch anything," he said anxiously if mother got up in the middle of dinner and went to wash. I thought she might simply like the feel of water on her skin.

He was convinced she had nothing to be guilty about. He told me so a lot.

Mother—original, inspired, peculiar mother—heard nothing; she listened to a prompter no one else could hear.

She had been, before she married my father, a Canned Laughter Adjuster. She was good at her job, the family said, and hovered over her laughter tapes during recording sessions—even live ones—like a sort of angel.

When the laughter level fell below required figures consistently during a live performance, her machine augmented the audience appreciation. I daresay the audience thought others in the auditorium, over there somewhere, were doing the extra laughing and chuckling, even the odd frantic whistle of manic enjoyment, despite all the evidence that their environment was managed.

She used the name Joy, then. Now it was Mara, from the same root as Mary. Bitter.

I heard mother say one day, "I love you so much when you seem to want me," to my father, and I puzzled about it.

I hadn't read about love—real love—only about Alice. And it was in the spirit of Alice that I took these words; they were a puzzle, and it was open to everyone to work it out if they could.

I would have thought, knowing my pets, that you loved something whatever it did, no matter what, and only pulled your love in a bit if the loved one did annoying things, and then only in words. You fed and cuddled them anyway. Hoping, I suppose, that their behavior would return to what was reasonable.

One night, after tea, I was doing a drawing of the backyard; I was going to take it to school to show the teacher. I was best in the class at drawing—my work was always shown around. I looked up once to say something, but I stopped: I saw father looking over at mother—bent over her notebooks—looking helplessly at her, and in each of his eyes there was a big unshed tear. I looked quickly back to my work in case he saw me see them fall down his cheeks.

I daresay it's fair to say that each human unit sees herself as the center of the universe, and that center is a convention, like any other position; rather like the "position" of an electron.

Yes, each unit-human is like an empty spot, round which all else spins on long, fine threads.

Mother's Praise

I guess mother's calling me unique and cleverer than other kids and beautiful and brilliant, meant to me that however different from others I felt, I was perfectly right the way I was.

The constant admiration made me complacent. I wasn't threatened by the difference of other people. I saw their failure, but it didn't apply to me. I was what a girl ought to be.

Maybe every mother should tell her child she's beautiful and clever and has great advantages over other kids. Then the kids can adjust as quickly and tidily as I did to the strangeness of others.

The necklace of praise she ornamented me with could easily become a noose if she made it too strong or spectacular.

I wonder if she did?

I guess I am a little frightened of her.

Not That She Refused To Work

Not that she refused to work, but my father treated the place as his house, and liked to keep an eye on the carpets, the state of the walls, the way the furniture was placed, the amount of light in the rooms. He could do electrical things and paint and cook. He was a competent wife.

When mother was reminded that something needed doing, one of the few simple things father thought she ought to do just to have a minimum interest in the home, she'd say "Of course, darling," but an old, starving, one-legged arthritic Eskimo in the Arctic could have got to the workface far quicker.

Deep in her eyes was a vast room of papers, and tables to write on. Did mother come from another planet?

Social Justice

Pros never allow themselves to be heard in public discussing proles, but the private pro word for proles is the Id. I overheard this word at our place; it was spoken by one of father's friends, a judge. It is pronounced with overtones of respect, as for a satanist of the psyche. But of course Id means Idiots, those who let themselves be organized and ordered and ruled, and do nothing. The doing nothing charge is particularly cruel, since by their place in society, which in turn is determined by their constitution and ability, they are not allowed or qualified to *do* anything, except what they find on the fringes of productive work. (Tribal pottery therapist, anger perception adviser, cemetery patrol team member, meteorite recovery programmer: that sort of thing.)

Judge Lorenz came to our place every few months and father always said something about him when he was gone.

"A judge is a person who when you say, you had measles thirty years ago asks How many? and prove it," he once said after they'd been arguing and he thought his friend was too pernickety.

Some time later he said, "A judge is a fool like you but smart enough to be sitting up there in that big chair." It was when the visits were getting fewer.

But when Judge Lorenz hadn't been for a year he said of him bitterly, "A dumb animal can sit in a chair and look all the more grave and dignified for a sheepskin draped over its skull. But when it barks or brays you know it is judging some poor unfortunate."

Another friend of father's had been jailed for a long time by the judge for trying to conceal a change in a professional. He was a doctor, and tried to cover up with plastic surgery a phrase against society that appeared in raised letters on the poor pro's forehead. It was "freedom without justice."

The judge was one of those Servants of Society whose pride in themselves and their position was as bright and cold as Sirius seems.

In That Nest Sits the Nameless Bird

I was eight, and called into the backyard next door to watch a hen laying an egg. I was given the egg, took it home, broke it against the side of a pan, I watched it cook, I ate it—all in half an hour. My father meant well, I'm sure, and it didn't do me any harm, but the looming thought behind this contrived sequence was what hung about in my mind. What *was* its significance? Father didn't say. He wanted me to get the connections, and I did, but I could just as well have pieced it all together from the breakfast table backward to the hen, some other time and months apart.

Why, then? What he gave me was this one-two-three performance, with an unexplained lesson; the abiding thing is the almost mechanical transformation of one thing into another. One minute the egg is part of the hen, next I am eating it, spread out and scrambled, yellow on a plate.

I can't explain what such neat, step-by-step changes mean to me.

Boof Not Biff

When Jerusalem the cocky died, instead of a rabbit Daddy got me a large modern Labrador, suspicious and moody. He resented the presence of others on the planet, and even barked at us when we came home, as if we were strangers. His name was Trotsky, because he never moved faster than a walk. We tried to calm him down and cheer him up with Valium and whiskey, but he became addicted and needed more of each all the time. Finally we gave him both together.

He was assassinated one morning in a stupor by the car of a radical biologist who lived in Einstein Crescent, who apologized with a smile, said it was an accident, and presented me with a large mongrel, the sort of dog that's full grown early—in parts. He had a big head, prominent hindquarters and a dip in the middle. He looked as if he'd been ridden mercilessly by an aggressive and hefty toddler.

Daddy didn't ever know that the man laughed with his friends and told the story energetically and was applauded for getting rid of a useless mutt. The Dog was christened Boof, short for Boofhead, and we saw no reason to change it.

Boof could do nothing right.

One day I was swimming with other kids in one of the chain of bush pools, the sort which, when they're deep, have cold spots. The cold got me, my legs cramped, I began to sink and the fronds of something underwater brushing my legs added to my alarm. I sank again while the other kids looked on, interested.

Boof didn't look on. He sprang off our diving rock about a meter above the pool, swam toward me and grabbed a bit of shoulder strap in his teeth and tugged with his head enough to make sure I stayed on the surface. Then he set sail with me for the bank, where I found a footing. I sat on a rock and used both hands to straighten out my legs.

The other kids said: "What's the matter with you?"

Boof shook himself thoroughly, standing right next to me. I didn't have the heart to rouse on him.

When I got home I told the story. "I'm going to change his name to Biff," I said. "Hey, Biff!"

Boof growled. I tried several times. "Biff."

He growled at me, he showed his teeth.

"Boof?" I said. He wagged his tail, glad to have cleared that up.

After that it hurt every time I called him Boof, short for Boofhead.

Maybe Father Would Have Liked a Boy

Not that he ever let me know by the smallest thing that I wasn't just what he ordered, but he did make me a slingshot. He said slingshot was American, and catapult or shanghai was the right word. He used a forking branch of the old pittosporum; I watched him trim down the bark and make it even with a sharp knife, then tie rubbers to it from the bladder of an old basketball, with a soft leather part to hold the stone.

He told me it was illegal and not to shoot it out in the street. After lots of shots at the fence, and a carton, and a target hanging from the lowest branch of the box tree, I needed a more interesting target. I spread some crumbs right up the backyard and waited inside the garage back door. A mynah hopped down and his mate stayed up on the clothes hoist. I went to fire. Then the eater flew up to the hoist and the other one landed. Just then a peewit swooped into the yard and I pulled back the rubbers and let it go. The marble—I'd run out of stones and used some marbles I'd won off the boys down the end of the street—hit the peewit in the chest. It must have been a fluke.

I ran out from the garage and over to where he lay on his back.

"Why have you killed me?" he said.

"You're not dead. Get up."

"I'm dead. You shouldn't have done it. I've got a young family."

He died.

I had a few more shots, mostly at the trunks of trees, but I lost interest. I put the catapult away, hanging it on a nail in the garage wall.

Composition: Rain

I was walking home in the rain and a sudden trickle of water went down my collar. It continued down my back, tickling me as it went. It went down my side, down my leg and into my rain boot. It started tickling my foot. I lifted my foot up, took my rain boot and sock off and dried it. When I got home, I told Mum and Dad. They laughed, too.

Others Exist

The deliberate creation of a universe is a chancy thing. To shape one's own universe and then one's place in it, in decision, action and suffering, is a labor that, if it did not come apparently automatically to us, would be more than we could—I nearly put "dare to do" but a better word is: accomplish. For many of the things we are doing when we grow ourselves and erect our world are done while we are dreaming, or asleep, or thinking of anything but what we are about. For if we thought of what we are about we would be building something else: we and our world are outside ourselves, and the building and growing operation is how we grow onto the world: excrescences, products, leaves of a tree, proliferations of a culture.

There is a good case for saying, then, that others are really there. Around us. And that they exist. We don't wholly create them. Though they often think they created us, and therefore can take us out when they like; waste us, perhaps, like spoiled ingredients or leftovers.

Let's get to the point. Everything I wanted, at eight years, they well may have wanted. All I thought of as mine by right, they might, too. All I reached after, they may have wanted.

What was I to do about this? Stop? Hesitate? Or point all my efforts to being first there.

Sometimes when I am trying to manipulate words into a position where they mean what I mean, the words become soft like putty; spreading, sticking, crumbling: like an idiot's.

An Ascending Person

Mother wrote everything down. Everything that happened to her. She wrote down this dream.

92

In the middle of the night she was in a room high up in a high-rise building. At the first door was a band of young men and girls dressed in harlequin suits; sometimes laughing, sometimes shouting and threatening, they alternately joked and banged on the door and milled around outside. Mother knew if they got inside they would attack violently and perhaps kill.

Perhaps? She was sure they were after blood and corpses.

Where was father? She somehow got outside without letting them in, and joined the killers, trying to act as they did, and be one of them. After a while they got suspicious of her and began to look menacing.

Father was sometimes there—he would appear in the middle of a group—and again he would be gone, yet she felt he was around somewhere all the time, though she lost sight of him, and despite appearances, she was safe. Maybe she wouldn't be killed.

This was her harlequin dream, she had the same dream at least once a week. When she was at the table for breakfast I could tell when she'd had the dream: there was a frown on her forehead, sketched in by a vertical line above the left side of her nose and a slanting line veering out above the right side.

"The harlequin dream, Mara?" I said cheekily.

"Please call me mother."

"Yes, mother." I had a mouth of cornflakes. "Yes mother. Smother. Smother."

This annoyed her. She wrote down her annoyance, and the surrounding feelings, and how I looked and how father looked and her tone of voice and father's tone of voice. (I assumed this was what she wrote.)

Father's tone of voice? He hadn't said a word.

That didn't bother mother. She knew the tone of voice he was *about* to use.

My mother was beautiful to everyone she met. I don't mean she had a beautiful face, nor a beautiful nature. Her face was real, and it radiated her closed-in, heedless, absorbed nature wherever she was, and people found that beautiful.

There was great power in the emotions inside her, I can tell you.

When I was older, her affection, her conviction all those years that I was something special, had worked on me so much that whenever I ascended to the top of a flight of steps—in the open, say, like at the Opera House or the Town Hall—I felt like a returned wanderer home clad in the glory of destruction, holy with the death I had trailed behind me, standing tall for all those I had put down. I was a hero, a wonder, the greatest girl in the world.

This feeling of being an ascending person, one who would necessarily climb higher than others and look down, was there even when I had to ascend the school steps at assembly in front of the whole school to be reprimanded.

I didn't hear the headmaster, I was searching with my eyes among the ranks of kids for Sarah Sarau, who had reported me. She said I was tormenting her. All I did was say to her "Know what? You're mad and I'm not" in the playground and when she said "What's the time?" before we went in after lunch I said "Time all dogs were dead. Feeling sick?" Perfectly normal playground talk.

> Tell tale tit
> Tongue shall be split
> Every dog in Church Hill
> Shall have a little bit.

Reasons Why Mother Cannot Be Interrupted:

Mother is having a cuddle.

Mother is eating.

Mother is on the toilet.

Mother is concentrating.

Mother has a headache.

Mother is having a shower.

Mother is putting on her face.

Mother is taking off her clothes.

Mother's trying on her new dress.

Mother's teeth hurt.

Mother is in a bad temper.

Mother has a poisoned finger from a bindi.

Mother is writing.

Mother is talking to herself.

Mother is making birds' nests.

Mother is composing a Rondo for string and hairpins.

Mother is limbering up for the fencing season.

Mother is talking to a wallaby.

Mother thinks it is Walpurgis-night.

Mother has shriveled up to nothing.

Mother is studying metapolitics.

Mother is preparing a paper for a conference against low-cost technology.

Mother is pulling a hair from her head: if it curls she will know she is jealous.

Fading Echoes of the Boy That Cried

The cruelty of the world made less impression on me as I became part of the cruelty. I grew up, I became acclimatized.

The cruelty that Crying Clive introduced me to lived on as echoes that bounced off episodes in my life. If you imagine a body moving through a stationary landscape with each episode a rock or solid object, then you have a picture of the way I felt, moving through my life. (Not that I'm sure it was I that moved.)

The way the people lived who made the clothes I wore, the food I ate; these things occurred to me occasionally. (Don't you like that—occasionally? Luxurious, isn't it?) And when I heard of price rises and pay rises, and saw the free persons' costs and pitiful expenditures itemized to the last cent in public, I looked for the costs and expenses of the professionals to be shown in public. I didn't see them.

Waste. Profit and theft. Unkindness, killing. These aroused small sighs. Quite small. Tiny, in fact. Even the meanness of copyright and patents aroused only small reflexes.

But a window on the world of cruelty and callous disregard for the existence of others was opened for me by poor Clive.

The Dog Family

We were in the car, winding along the expressway, and pulled over to the verge. Daddy said he wanted to put up the car bonnet, and when we stopped, that's what he did. He left it propped up.

By chance there sat below us a lovely panorama of waterways and darkly green bush, thickly growing to the water's edge.

Out of propriety, I think, we stayed in the car. The traffic near us was fast. And when I say near, I mean about two meters from the side of our car. No stopping, the green sign said.

On the other side of our road, at a lower level, the returning half of the expressway had a similar verge, where tame grass grew quietly and would no doubt be mown by Main Roads workmen when it began to look ambitious.

Father and mother gazed round at the view. I watched idly the zipping traffic on the returning highway. As the vehicles passed, I kept my eyes fixed on one spot and the blurs had a hypnotic effect. Not unpleasant.

A lull in that traffic unsettled me, and I noticed a car slow down. Nothing either way in sight. From it were pitched four or five things that skidded and tumbled over and over. The car revved its engine and was off like mad. The tumbling objects consisted of a lady dog and four small puppies.

The people who dropped this live litter hadn't been fussy where they did it; the mother dog had three lanes to cross to get her family to safety. Safety was the far edge of the expressway, where grass gave way to the surrounding bush. Maybe there would be water, and if she got them to a house hidden in the bush, well, maybe . . .

She picked up one puppy and tried for the far side. But an overtaking car got one of her back legs. She yelped and dropped the baby, then quickly picked it up again and made it to the opposite verge. She tried to will the baby to stay there, then limped back with her crushed leg lifted, to reach the others.

"Al," said mother, probably wanting to point out something. Then she saw the horror show I was watching, and fell silent. (I saw a poem lately about the wild beauty of a street accident, but this was different.)

"Al," said my father absently. "Answer your mother." He thought he might be having a mild disciplinary problem with me.

He saw the dog family, then.

It took him only a few seconds to take in what was happening, jump out of the car, close the bonnet and drive back into the traffic.

In that time Mother Dog had taken another of her babies across the three lanes, the rescued one had wandered back on to the roadway and been stamped flat, and while she was taking the second, the third stumbled on to the fast lane and was pasted. She looked back and took the second far off the verge into the edge of the trees and started back for the fourth.

We were out of sight then.

Several times on the trip we were in the middle lane passing a large load on our left while another huge vehicle overtook us. Looking up at the height and size of the trucks on both sides, I looked at my mother and my father and the interior of our car with its fragile roof that my father—at home—forbade me from climbing on, and I thought of how close the traffic was to its neighbors, and how easy a collision must be, and how miraculous it was that there were so few. Perhaps I could make a composition out of it for school.

We cut the outing short. The sandwiches weren't as good as father's food usually was, the Esky hadn't kept the drinks cold enough, the car wasn't running smoothly enough, and the view wasn't as good as it had been.

When we got back to the place, the dog family was gone. Well, dead. One small flat shape was in the fast lane, a large and a small were in the middle lane, and the first one to be flattened was in the far lane.

There was no way of missing them. I saw it coming, my mother did, and my father said, "I can't swerve, I can't swerve," in a high voice as we saw the cars in front go over all four and as we in our car ran over the bodies of the mother and her fourth baby in the middle lane. As the ker-thump of the front and rear wheels sounded I brought up the half sandwich I'd eaten, plus the cornflakes I'd had for breakfast. Oh yes, and the three slices of tinned peach father had put on the cornflakes before pouring the milk.

The peaches came out in lumps, still the same bright orange.

"I'm sorry," my father muttered to no one in particular. He didn't know what to say. Shortly after, he wound his window down more, and my mother did the same. I suppose they thought they'd leave the smell in the back with me, but you know cars. It was everywhere. Mother got us to stop off the expressway, and they tried to clean up the mess.

I was useless. I couldn't get out of my mind the sight of the limping mother trying to save the baby dogs with her last effort. I can see even now the four flat shapes pasted on the roadway. I can still feel the double thump as we rode over the poor lady dog.

Night, and as he kissed me goodnight, father said, "Don't forget the other one, darling. The little one in the bush didn't get run over."

That was something. But in the night I was wakened by the tailend of a nightmare. I saw the whole thing again, this time the motherless puppy struggling helpless through the bush and I stumbling in the dark after it, calling, "Here, pup! Here, pup!"

After trying to go back to sleep again to bring the dream to a happier conclusion, I lay awake for hours.

When I went back to sleep all I could dream of was standing still in the blackness of the bush willing the pup to find its way back to the road. I willed it to sit patiently by the verge so passersby could see it, not to take any steps on to the road, and preferably fifty meters past the skins—they would be flat by then: no ker-thump—so a kind-hearted motorist would see what had happened and stop to pick it up, traffic permitting.

When I had adjusted all the conditions for the safe return to a civilized home for the puppy, I woke. Immediately I remembered that the puppy hadn't been seen as we passed the spot, that it was miles from the smallest township, and I began to cry. It seemed to me then that all the sorrow in the world was concentrated in that small bundle of fur. I imagined lifting it in my arms, its little stomach bulging, and all its bones soft under its fur.

"Make it safe," I whispered, but I didn't know who I was whispering to.

The following night I dreamed of them again, but this time all were alive and they were mine and I had them on my bed and I fell asleep stroking the littlest one, then the others in turn, then the mother with warm eyes.

The Man From the River

The man who disappeared into the creek with his blow-up baby in its baby chair came back on the King's Birthday that year, at eleven in the morning. This time he ascended to our street, the first above the bushland reserve, and carried floppy plastic bundles that he took round the streets until he found undeveloped ground, where he blew up his house and bed and chairs and settled down there.

Kids shot at him with guns, but didn't collapse his constructs. Father said they were made of self-healing plastic. He was there until the beginning of July. We didn't have a community in any ancient sense of the word, but bit by bit, information was passed around. It was mother's birthday before we heard that the blow-up man had gone. He deflated his house, went back to the creek and disappeared.

The Wandering Crowd

They had never been along our street, never even within sound of our place. We'd heard of them occasionally in the next suburb.

It was Sunday, I was standing around while my father did things in the rockery bordering the front of our place. I called it helping.

The sound came from several valleys away, it rose and fell; it was the sound of an unknown beast. Round that way the streets were bitumen and the footpaths concrete. The tramp of feet was the dominant sound of the beast, and mixed with it a low sound, the sum of many voices. Every few minutes, the voices were raised in what was a howl and a roar from the distance, but which we knew, from others, was shouts and angry bellowing.

Most of the time they walked, and when police came they crowded on to footpaths, but the police didn't often worry them. It would have been a twenty-four hour a day job, and everyone had a relative in the crowd.

I watched in the direction of the fitful din. I saw it turn a corner a kilometer away, and go up a steep hill obscured by houses. By the time the leaders disappeared, the sound came to us of the beast with a thousand heads and no brain. My father, though he was stooping over some tufts of grass—or valuable plants—straightened and stood, as if he'd heard it a fraction before I did.

It went away for minutes, then it must have turned along the highway and passed some cross streets which channeled the sound toward us, for a great tumult hit us for several seconds, then was cut off. The highway was level at that place, and shortly I heard the sound of running feet on concrete, like gunfire.

"Dreadful sound," father said.

I was listening.

"Can we take the car and go to watch?" I asked after a bit.

"No use. They're on the highway. You never know where they'll turn off."

"I've never seen them," I said wistfully.

"Keep it like that. When they turn they're likely to charge. Sometimes that crowd grows to ten thousand. Ten thousand directions average out into something like a liquid, with density and viscosity, pouring through the streets." That's how he spoke, sometimes.

Another time he defended them, saying the description of the wandering crowd as superfit idiots was unjust; in this mood he allowed them some individuality.

"Some run for philosophical reasons," he said. "Some see themselves as joggernauts. Most are filling time, killing time. It's an outlet for the Frees. Some do it for the knee rot or the calf slump."

Looking back now I think they were running in fear of time.

A Man in Malthus Parade

A Mister Amundsen, descendant of the explorer, had joined the wandering crowd when he was younger and been caught up in its depredations. In those days the crowd did bad things; it was common for them to go through shopping centers and lay waste anything in their path. Amundsen had been a leader then, for a brief six months. He lost his speed and his originality, and one day the crowd kept going straight when he'd turned off. He noticed the different direction of sound, and joined in the back of the crowd. A month later he retired.

After that he put on so much weight that he lost all thought of going back to wandering. He developed a bear-like shamble, with head inclined; his shaggy auburn hair spread all over his body, thick on his chest and back and thighs, but it was rubbed off his kneecaps by his working trousers and only grew again in summer when he went about in shorts.

He became more bear-like, his employer moved him away from the public view at first, then when people sought him out to look at him, moved him back to the enquiry counter. It was a timber yard, and apart from contractors, they supplied weekend carpenters with the pine that grew like a weed through the land.

Harold, one of his sons, was in the same year as I was. He had to repeat first class.

Diggers

The Australian digger had been given a new meaning by the system of declaring areas free for archæological investigation. People were digging everywhere. Holes appeared in the city, holes not meant for the foundations of buildings; building sites were invaded at weekends by people licensed to dig. Everywhere, Australians were digging, searching for evidence of the past.

In the ground that swept away below our street, and formed a valley with only one side, people were dotted about. It seemed they preferred to dig in places where they thought no one had been. Students used core methods, others gelignite. Dogs stood around, puzzled, children enjoyed the play with dirt, while the serious business went on of looking for the past.

(Wouldn't it be good if humans took the next step, and tried hard to think with goodwill of the future of the race?)

In the old days of what was called full employment, work had become a ritual observance, so that one's energy was taken up mostly with one's weekend relaxation and the re-creation of the body, and very little with work, which was often little more than a matter of reacting, recognition and habit, and doing the damned thing as quickly as possible to get away from it.

Now, of course, the emphasis has shifted. Work, so long despised, is become a privilege; people scratch their heads for something useful to do.

Moses Betts and Ermelinda

I took Ermelinda Betts home on Monday when she fainted in the schoolyard. They allowed her to rest in the teachers' room, then when she got up she caused such a noise in class that they got rid of her, giving her to me to take home. She lived in Newton Crescent.

Her father was working in the front garden, picking out small plants that didn't fit his idea of flowers. He looked at me with two round eyes that blobbed at me from the muzzle of a bulldog, then waddled toward his daughter, caught her by the shoulder and—I thought—was about to hit her. He didn't, but all the while he held her he seemed to be torn between violence and moderation, holding her hard enough to make her cry out, but not yet hitting her with his outstretched other hand. He didn't seem able to let her go.

I pulled her other arm, intending to take her inside to her mother. I was supposed to get a piece of paper signed to say Ermelinda had been delivered and received, then I could go back to school. I pulled her, sensing her father had finished with her and was not going to punish her by hitting. He was playing, surely. I pulled, and pulled, then suddenly his hand slipped from her shoulder and I had Ermelinda, but some of her dress stayed in the bulldog's hand.

I took her with me to her mother.

102

"A bulldog outside did that," I said, to get Ermelinda off the hook with her mother.

Her mother made no sign that she understood. She looked sad, and signed the paper, and gave me a slice of bread spread with hundreds and thousands.

Ermelinda Betts always helped hurt things, the more so if they were little. Once she chased a hurt bird for three hours before she caught it and ministered to it. She fixed it up, exhaustion and all. Animals too large seemed to lack the necessary cuteness for her; those too small, such as insects, weren't large enough for her affection to be given full play.

If a bird, an ideal size, was hurt too badly to be helped back to normal flying, she put it to sleep. Kids who lived near Einstein Crescent had stories about her wielding the spade or Moses Betts's pruning shears to stamp the suffering mercifully out of a crippled mynah or shot sparrow.

"Watch out for Mister Betts!" called Ermelinda, as I left, skirting the bulldog, who looked after me with his nose wrinkled in the air.

"Yes," said the mother half-heartedly. "Don't speak to him."

I knew more than that. If you spoke to Moses Betts, and he spoke in a certain way back to you, cuts would appear. Bruises. Once he wounded a salesman at a distance with a look. If he spoke with a fierce emphasis, a jerk of the head, a viciousness, he could cut.

A hole appeared in the side of his maths teacher's neck the first time he used this power, which he hadn't known he possessed. The maths teacher was rushed off to the staff room, the kids were searched—but Moses Betts was not uncovered.

If he wasn't feeling well, all he could produce was a scratch. No stray cats or dogs lasted long near his house.

His power didn't work on his family, but when he abused himself for some mistake or stupidity, as some do, it worked on him. His face was pocked with old scars from self-criticism and annoyance.

Testicles

The day I saw Challenger Lutherburrow come down hard on the bar of his friend Gay Donohue's bike, was a clear, grass-smelling day. There had been rain; it had run off our blocks onto the nature strip running by our rockery, where water lay in pools, unmoving.

He lay in agony in the still small puddles, both hands between his legs. His first yells were brief, the pain took his breath away, he said.

Why do boys' bicycles have a bar, when they have testicles to come down on—and girls' bikes have no bar? I wonder if they really hurt that much or if males can't take pain as well as we can.

> *Poor old Challenger's dead*
> *He died last night in bed*
> *Put him in the coffin*
> *He fell through the bottom.*

Two Compositions

1. My Best Friend

My best friend is Glenda Rabic because she is so friendly and she talks about interesting things all the time.

Glenda and I like each other, so I asked Glenda to come to my place, and she did and we had a wonderful time climbing trees, playing hide and seek and eating cookies too.

Sometimes we make daisy-chains, they're so big that we can hardly carry them or put them round our necks. Glenda and I are very good friends.

Glenda and I wished we lived together.

2. School Inspector

One day at school when we were at our desks, the teacher said, "Now listen children Mister Worth is coming to our class next, so I want your very best manners, especially you Neil Catt and Wayne Overton because Mister Worth is very important."

That moment Mrs. Grantham the headmistress opened the door and showed Mister Worth the way. We showed him our books and we did some plays for him and he talked a lot about Queens and Kings and Princesses and Princes and castles.

Mister Worth is a very kind and busy man, we liked it very much at school that day.

None of these things happened: I made them up. The names, too. I didn't have a best friend. Actually I didn't get on really well with anyone, but I wasn't unhappy. I knew I was different.

Sir Boof

They said at school that animals don't know they're going to die. It wasn't true. One afternoon, after I'd snapped at Boof for jumping up on me, he came round later and said, "I'm not feeling the best lately. Hope you don't mind me making a bit of a fuss when you come home each day, more fuss than I used to. I know I'm sick and one day soon I won't be here among the living. Don't cry. I know I jump up a bit and bark a bit more than I did, but it's just gladness. It's sort of relief that I've lasted another day and here you are home again and you won't be going till next morning. And on Saturday you'll be here two whole days."

Remember when Boof rescued me in the flooded creek, and wouldn't take a more dignified name?

I got round that in a ceremony attended by my father. Mother said she was watching from the dining room where she sat at the table. I lifted up a plastic sword, given me by a relative who thought I was a male child, and knighted Boof.

"I dub thee Sir Boof." And brought it down gently on both Boof's narrow shoulders.

I guess he didn't mind the "Sir," because he didn't growl.

When he went to sleep for the last time, one Friday morning, I had to wait for my father to come home in order to tell him, to ask him if Sir Boof was really dead, and how we should bury him.

The Burial of Sir Boof Hunt, a Good Runner

My father dug the hole at dawn next day. I didn't hear him get up. He came and woke me in my yellow room. I tried to cry when I remembered why he had woken me, but the world itself was yawning, and it was impossible to weep.

Sir Boof was in the laundry, on the cool concrete. I daresay any fleas he had were getting nervy. I had worried, the night before, about flies getting at him, but there were none alive there. Several lay in the sill behind the shut window, legs in the air; when I blew at them they were carried away, they were so light. They must have died a funny sort of death: seeing the big world outside and wondering why they couldn't get past the invisible wall. Actually it wasn't all that invisible; father often forgot details like cleaning windows.

We made a stretcher from two branches of the prunings of the pittosporum that had the worm, and put some old shirts' arms over the branches. It was a good carrier. Sir Boof was quite stiff, and seemed a bit lighter, easier to pick up.

I went first as we carried him, and father behind.

When we reached the corner of the backyard, father said, "Squad halt!" When I looked round, I found he was more upset than I was. Perhaps it was because of me.

We put down the body beside the open grave, chocolate brown and moist. A worm showed a shiny part of itself, about a centimeter, where it curved over and pointed down into the earth again. More of its rings showed, then its tail, and it was gone.

We decided not to put him in the ground just as he was, and wrapped him in the shirts that formed the stretcher, until I decided that wasn't good enough and crept into the house and stole from mother's stock an old baby blanket of mine and wrapped Sir Boof in something that once kept me very warm and comfortable. It was blue, with miniature trains and cowboys in red and orange.

Father was all for leaving him as he lay there at the bottom of the hole, perhaps fearing my reaction when the dirt was put on him, but I wanted to do the whole job in one go, and started to put the dirt over him with my hands.

In all the years of his life, Sir Boof never once ran. I never saw him run, mother and father didn't either. I asked neighbors, but no.

I think, though, that if he had wanted to run, he would have been a good runner.

There was a storm that afternoon. Someone behind the world, over the hill to the west, lit a match that flamed suddenly high into the air. Many seconds later, the noise-crash came like a bomb. Dribbles and threatenings of rain came down, and stopped. Showers fell steadily, fine slanting silver strands against the sun, but only for a minute or two; they eased off, came again, then with a beautiful show of the finest drops drifting down and across and whirling round in a faint breeze, gleaming tiny and lazy with the sunlit trees behind, closed off the performance.

For a few minutes a thin thunder sounded far off on the rim of the world where the grey sky came down like a lid. Then that, too, stopped.

I shivered as the sun came full on the yard. I opened the screen door and stood on the patio in the sun, warm. The mound marking Sir Boof's bed was dark with wet. He would never wait for me out the front as I walked round the bend home from school, and it hit me then, after the rain, and I cried.

"Will Sir Boof go to heaven, Daddy?"

"Heaven! Good God! Where did you get that idea? What do you mean: heaven?" father said in a rush. He knew perfectly well.

"Where God is."

"Which God?"

"Well," I said, doubtfully now, "which God do you believe in?" I hadn't counted on getting a lecture, but one was coming.

"Gods are different, from person to person," father said. "Mine was created by me. Each has his own. Some are born with the individual, they are attributes of that person. Gods are sometimes born, sometimes made, sometimes patched together from shreds of other people's gods. Gods are property." He took a breath, and said more slowly, "Maybe they were the first property."

"Do they all live in heaven?" I persisted.

Father looked at me as if I was a cheeky little girl.

Composition: My Mother

My mother is a nice kind and good looking mother. She has glasses brown eyes and black hair and likes waves in her hair. She is a writer.

My mother is married to an actor.

She is good at the housework, does all the washing and all the cleaning and all the cooking.

My mother buys wool to make jumpers and cardigans and socks and trousers.

She has a lot of money and she is a good mother.

I like my mother.

And the teacher wrote in red letters beneath: "Alethea, you are good like your mother." But she must have known about mother: everyone did. Actually, I *do* like mother, but I can't say straight out that I love her, like I love father.

Even when she scratches herself, I like her . . . (She does it in such a way that she looks as if she can't see herself doing it, and wants not to notice.)

Also, she doesn't seem to get around the house so often now with no clothes, but that may be because of me. I'm nine now.

I like mother best of all when she's dressed up. She has smart shoes which cost a lot of money and beautiful dresses, but the most wonderful thing my mother wears is her leopard skin coat. My father said if anyone asked, it was made from a leopard that was bred specially for coats, not a wild one that someone shot in the jungle or trapped and later stuck a needle into.

Mother looks like a princess in the leopard coat; looking at her makes me feel proud she is my mother, not someone else's. I wish she dressed up more often.

Alicia

My mother was born in the year that the first generation of great human devices were exploded against humans.

In the back of her first photo album, the one she had when she was a young girl, I found colored pictures of Great Men of History: generals like Montgomery, Rommel, Alexander; Winston Churchill during wartime; religious leaders; Caesar, and that sort of person.

I tried to find out why she kept the pictures, but she was her usual evasive self, covering her dodging and weaving with words, words. Until I gave up and told her she might as well shut up, since I was no longer listening.

(But you had to be severe with mother or you'd be there for ages, suffocating under a flood of words.)

At nine I was beginning to be powerful; feeling that pride, that aggressiveness that was to set me apart from others.

I feel sure mother wanted a boy. Yet in her album there was one photo of a beautiful young girl, dark, and on the back of it was the word Alicia. She had a Spanish look, and smiled out from the glossy surface like a princess.

I think mother was in love with Alicia when she was young. Perhaps she never really wanted to be a mother.

Why Do. Fish Swim in the Sea?

Regularly we had to write answers; these are some:

Because that's the law of the sea.
Because they can't do anything else.
They're not smart enough to think of other things to do.
Because anyone that didn't swim would be unpopular.

Miss King didn't indicate whether she was pleased with our answers; we kept on thinking, often giving answers others had given, but she didn't even tell us then what the right answer was.

It irritated me that no one was either right or wrong.

109

Last in Lousy!

You could play it anywhere. Going in to school, into the school shop, the library, to the sports oval, the swimming pool. Or it could be Last out Lousy, Last up, Last down, anything. People still play it when they're old. I've heard men running up the steps of a pub saying it, people leaving work and hurrying home saying it. Long after they've stopped playing hopscotch.

In fourth class it was specially popular. "Last out, lousy!" It was the end of the day, just after three, and the whole class barged for the door, bags burst open in the crush, kids were trodden on, the door was kid-jammed and only the first few got out; the rest were trying to pull themselves, their legs, bags, books out past the rest. It was best to say it and dive for the door yourself, not wait for someone else to start it. That way you got out safely and could look back and laugh. They always rose to the challenge.

> *What's your name?*
> *Baby Jane.*
> *Where do you live?*
> *Cauliflower Lane.*
> *What's your number?*
> *Cucumber.*
> *What's your address?*
> *Watercress.*

The Female Christ

I was in the Scripture class at school. It was Wednesday. The man sent along by the authorities was telling us as well as he could while the kids played up, about the Jesus of the Bible. (He didn't like it the week before when after he said "Amen" I said "Gesundheit.")

While he was running through the Sermon on the Mount, turning the other cheek, forgiving people seventy times seven and allowing the soldiers to whip him, I had my brilliant idea. Christ was a woman!

This seemed such a good idea that I wrote it down. I remembered his forty-day fast—what was that but the ultimate crash diet? I wrote my idea on a piece of paper and passed it to the boy sitting next to me. He read it without interest, but passed it on. That paper went from desk to desk and shortly the man saw it. He let it go for a while, then as the kids paid even less attention to him, he went after the paper. He was comical, chasing up the aisles while the paper went across the aisles. He had no hope and had to stop, puffing. He walked as if he had nails driven through his feet.

"Children! Now I'm trying to bring you the message of comfort and hope that is the Christian message." And puffed some more.

Why bring children comfort? That was the last thing we needed, healthy animals that we were. And hope?

"Now I want you to give me that piece of paper," and he fixed us, all thirty-five of us—two kids were away—with his eyes as if he could perform this miracle by an act of will. His will over ours.

I decided to feed it to him. I stood up. "The paper, please, children," I said, looking straight forward and standing rigid.

Someone passed it along. Still rigid, I put the paper in front of me and let him take it. He read it. "JC was a lady."

"Who wrote this?"

"I did."

"Oh. Well, at least you're honest."

But the others spoiled it. More stood up. "No, sir. I did it. She's just being a hero. She's protecting me," came from all sides. The man got miserable, facing a classful of rigid, forward-facing kids.

"I give up," he said. And gathered his things. "I'll report this," he said as he left.

"What about the seventy times seven?" I yelled after him.

The trouble is in the normal way of things, kids can't speak up to adults.

You know you're you, you know you're the same person as the big person you'll be some day when these wrinklies are old and you are king; but they don't seem to know it and wouldn't accept it if you spoke as you feel; that is, as the adult you really already are, in those little clothes and small body.

He was a meek man, and had to suffer for the others that we couldn't trample on.

> *What's better than heaven?*
> *Nothing's better than heaven;*
> *Jam tarts are better than nothing:*
> *Therefore jam tarts are better than heaven.*

The Terrible Knee Crunch

Players stood face to face; they could nominate whether they were receiver or giver, or both could be givers. They then pushed their knees forward into collision so the kneecaps smacked together. They could have one knee or both. Anyone cheating was punished, unless he was too big; and some of the class six boys were as big as some men.

If you hit the opponent's knee just to the side, the inside of the knee, and slid off it, there was an area of vulnerable nerves that, when hit, could keep the loser out of the game for a week. Big boys limping were given cheek by anyone who judged they could get away if chased. Some of the injured were glad to get back into class after playtime, never mind the teachers' voices edged with spite, or the dull anger so many of them displayed.

Girls' Games Are Different

There was Sir. We got a stocking from Mum or the leg of a panty hose, put an old tennis ball into the foot, tied a knot and held it by the end. You stood hitting the ball against a wall. One hand had to be free all the time. The ball could bounce against the wall at eleven o'clock, one o'clock, seven, six and four; you could even bend over and bounce it over your head.

The rhyme had the words, "Please sir," and then we had different words, according to who was near us in the playground. Like, "Take me home, sir; Put me to bed, sir; Cover me up, sir; Kiss me goodnight, sir; Close the door, sir; Take my clothes off, sir;" and so on. If a good-looking teacher was on playground duty we'd have lots of looks at him, getting the joy of saying the words and thinking he was Sir and putting us to bed and so on.

It was a lot of fun.

It wasn't much like the Corner-game or knee crunch, though, and often I used to be looking at their games when I was supposed to be listening to Kara Mitchell telling me secrets about Sandra Cunningham or Rachel Masselos or Miss Scanlon, who had everyone talking about her because different people dropped her off at school every morning, and all kissed her passionately, men and ladies.

The Value of Being One of the Recorders of Your Time

It's funny to think that writing this puts me in a direct though distant line with the scribes of the ancient world, who used to write down the quantities of grain and slaves in stock, and later as civilization got underway, the amount of money owing; and in line with the kids of ancient Egypt who wrote their homework on clay tablets, the Greeks and their Mediterranean neighbors who did the same, down through the times when religious men were the only ones to value book learning and the art of writing. Others in the same line are the archaeologists who'll come after us.

I was an archaeologist once. We went in, us kids, to an old house in Cheapley set well back from the road, backing on to bush. It was empty, the developers had got the people out. The old place had once been the only house in about two hundred hectares of bush. Now it was the only house of grace and shade among two thousand houses of brick and paint and wrought iron fences and concrete driveways and variegated pittosporums and broom and castor oil plants and all the rest. Except that the old house had the fragrant pittosporums that bloomed in October—three of them—and jacarandas ten meters high and bottlebrush trees and eucalypts and looked like a mountain cottage. A bulldozer stood in the garden.

We got in, and I found a piece of paper. Maybe a writer had lived there, or the son of a writer, or a promising young Australian writer, aged fifty.

It said,

> "I try to make use of the world
> but
> you can never use it to the full.
> Hardly even grasp it.
> You have to let it flash by
> made up of innumerable moments
> and later try to recall one.
> What about the world
> when you're not looking
> and the parts we've
> missed?
> It's hopeless trying
> to do more than attend
> to a few single moments."

The ash-pickers of the future, when they come across bits of paper like that, may find out where we went wrong.

I put it in my sleeve, took it home and buried it in an old cigar tin, a thin flat one, at the corner of the house, the corner where no drain pipes come down. I put a stone on it. It was a time capsule.

Looking west from our place were blue mountains and their cliffs of air that I had seen from the car. It was a windy day, above us were windblown, threadbare clouds, and the wind beneath those clouds was green. In a hundred years would there still be such things, and a girl of nine watching? A girl like me?

When Men Were Working in the Street

When men were working in the street digging deep trenches for the sewerage, they used to speak to us kids as we passed to and from school. They were rough-looking, much more rough than any of the men round about when they changed into their weekend clothes to do the grass. Much rougher. Their hairy legs were hairier, their backs browner, they had tattoos. One had tattoos all down his back and front and arms and on the tops of his legs.

I used to wonder if he had them under his shorts. Shorts was all he wore when the sun was out.

"You got a big sister, kid?" they'd call out.

The second day I said "Yes." I'd love to have had a big sister. Sometimes, anyway.

"What's she like?" said one.

"Has she got good legs?"

"Big boobs?" said one, drawing curves with his hands. "And a shape like this?"

"Better than that," I said, and shook my head.

"Does she have a suntan?"

"Yes."

"Where does it stop? Do you see her in the shower? Does she sunbake out in the yard?"

"Yes, on the edge of the pool." That was naughty. We didn't have a pool; my father wouldn't have one no matter how I pleaded.

"Does the tan stop here?" the man said, putting a finger below his navel.

"It goes all over," I said, realizing I'd most likely be trapped on specifics if I was trapped at all.

"Can I come and wash her back in the bath?" an older one said.

"No, but that one can," I said, pointing to a handsome young one that hadn't said anything.

Those men were a different species from my father. They really fitted doing the work they did, standing in the bottom of trenches, working big yellow machines and graders. Maybe they *had* to be different, to do that work. Maybe their difference had sorted them out into that trench.

115

"Have you got a brother too?" said a big fierce man.

"Yes."

"What's he like?" said the same man.

"Like him," I said, pointing to the one I liked.

They all whistled, except my favorite. I think he was blushing, but I couldn't be sure. One of them tipped him under the chin and called him a name. It sounded like Linda.

As I passed the Goughs' house I heard Robert Gough doing his piano practice. He was playing a Beethoven sonatina, and the notes came clearly to me. I stopped to listen, it sounded so clever. Not a wrong note. I wished I could play better than Robert Gough.

Mister Ackhurst's Fragmentation

It wasn't really leprosy, it didn't affect the way people bought their fruit and their vegetables.

"It's noncontagious," he told the locals who still bought from his corner shop despite the few extra cents on everything.

And it wasn't real leprosy. It was just that bits fell off.

"No germs," he said cheerfully, as a new customer eyed his hands. He still had the index finger of his right hand and the middle finger of his left. He also had most of his right ear and almost all his nose.

The bits that fell off didn't cause bleeding, and that was what caused him to run the gauntlet of the hospital, knowing he might be kept there if they ran tests that kept him out of the shop, but at the same time having an appreciation of the fact that there might really be something tragically wrong with him.

The bits that fell off—they fell apart too. Not that many bits had fallen off and much of the time it was when he was in bed. When the lobe of his left ear parted company with the rest, it was in the shop and three customers saw it. Luckily, it fell to pieces quickly on the floor, and he was able to stamp on it and grind the powdered ear into the rest of the dust and the cracks in the timber floor before the customers had a chance to complain.

His name was up on the side of the building; in the old times he owned the whole block of four shops—chemist, fruit shop, milk bar and barber's. The paint had faded and rain had washed most of it off, but the name could still be made out. I used to wonder if it would all be gone at the same time as Mister Ackhurst's last bits disintegrated.

Aspects of Family Life

Mother kept her eyes on her plate. She ate a lot and always praised father's cooking lavishly. When she went to put sugar in her tea she seemed fascinated by the sharp white crystals, and I wondered if she would ever let them drop in. She took milk, too: her tea had to look like a lightly muddy river.

She made a lot of noise eating, and was the only woman I know that broke wind unself-consciously, like a man.

If she suddenly ate something and no one else was eating, she'd turn and look at you. You got the full blast of the sound, and you knew she was looking straight at you. It was a funny feeling.

Every time, every single time I looked up at her when she did that, she said, "I love you." In a most accusing way. "But I love you," as if after impressing *that* on you she ought to be able to do what she liked. It didn't even sound sincere.

"You love everything, Mother," I said with all the knowledge of nine years on the planet.

She looked at me as if I'd tried to hurt her, then wrote the whole thing down. I think she did: I'm not sure. At least she doesn't shout—she never shouts—or slobber on the floor.

Father had come home from dying on stage and seemed pleased to be cooking. In the colder months he was beginning to get a stiffness down one side. Sometimes he said it was arthritis, sometimes he said it was nothing. Cooking warmed him up after the day's work.

"I love chicken," she said, apparently to tease me. Her mouth dripped with oil and one white piece of chicken flesh stuck out of one corner of her mouth. Her lips sucked at the leg of the bird, the flesh slipped clean off the bird's bone like a sock, and she laid the leg bone delicately down at the side of her plate. I was amazed.

117

She took her partial denture out. "I like the butter and oil washing over me gums," she said.

"Through the lips and round the gums,
Look out stomach, here it comes!" said father cheerfully.

What had got into mother? She wasn't supposed to make jokes. Was it possible I did not correctly assess the mental life of my own parents?

Sometimes I wish she would sit silent; brood, remember. But she is ceaselessly active. She is invulnerable. Nothing can scratch the surface of her soul.

Today I found a piece of paper with these lines on it in handwriting that looked like mother's, but more vigorous. Perhaps she was younger then.

> *My life was closed before its end*
> *When neither I could see;*
> *I wandered in a foolish land*
> *Beside a ghostly sea.*
>
> *All memories my mind commands*
> *I give the vagrant breeze;*
> *Few things are treacherous as sands*
> *Beside imagined seas.*

I kept it so I could try to understand it, but I kept it so long that I felt guilty about giving it back. Then I just forgot. What had happened to her when she was young? I would wait and ask her when I was older.

I Worried

I worried about my mother and father.

She was undoubtedly mad.

Equally surely, she was full of love for my father, since she kept saying so.

118

Here was my problem:

Was the expression of love from my mother—if she was mad—as valuable as if it came from some other person whose worth and sanity could be seen by all?

If it was worth anything, was it worth what it was because of her? Or as existing in its own right as love?

If it was worth nothing, did that matter? Did love, any love, exist in itself and for itself, as light blessing a dark place? Was it a stray fruit of the earth, the earth or loam of the human mass, that poked up out of its human humus, to bloom and live a while and die like anything else, with no more justification than a flower on a mountain ledge never seen by any eye that knew it as a flower?

Why did I think of worth? Perhaps the problem was in me.

I worried about my father and mother and about me, and like most problems, it went round and round, like a merry-go-round. You could get off at one place, then get on again and off at another place, but it still went round and didn't go away.

The Life-Sharpener

The life-sharpener had his stall set up in the shoppingtown. Father took me in on a late shopping night simply to see the people and what went on. Being at school we knew very little of what the people did who had got out of the childhood machine.

There were about forty people meditating in a half circle round him.

"The diminishing point; the mass, the position which decreases until the mind, in following it, is left suspended on nothing; follow it into nothingness, allow your mind to play, to dance on nothing, to be independent, dependent on nothing; a floating self sensitive to the least touch of the Eternal."

The meditators solemnly, with eyes closed, concentrated to purge their minds, diminish their consciousness, and all the while the shoppers hurried or lounged around, feet shuffling, babies and children crying and yelling, sucking lollies, being slapped mercilessly by women dying to get a look at the goodies in the shops, dying to be rid of the kids.

My father was watching me.

"It works," he said.

"How?" I asked.

"If they believe and make an effort, they will contact something, whatever it is. Even if it's their own brains talking back to them when they're in a receptive state, ready to be obedient, they're sure to hear something that will help them."

"All of them?"

"A few. A few," he amended judiciously.

Somehow the sight of those people ignoring all else round them annoyed me; I wanted to go and shake them, I wanted to pull their gaze away from themselves on to the world of objects round them. I daresay I wanted to be a tyrant and tell them exactly what they should do.

On the way home we passed school, where the two pruned and leafless plane trees lifted their knobby fists; whether at the sky or at each other, I could not tell.

On the Geography Table

On the geography table there was a relief map of the country built up from clay and plasticine; it showed the great mountain range that cut the coastal fringe from the interior, on the east. It showed rivers, and all the other ranges. I kept looking at it after 4W had gone out to playlunch.

I was fascinated by the flat middle of the country, and without quite thinking what I was doing I lifted the bottle of water from the nearby nature table and let it spill on to the flat and arid center of Australia, where it spread and formed a pool. I hadn't noticed, but the bottle had in it the tadpoles collected by Stewart Regan and his mates; they swam painfully around and wriggled in the very shallow lake I had made. I say shallow and it was, but the size of it! Again without thinking too much of it I got up some of the water with the mouth of the empty clay jar and my lake shrank to the size of a rather fatter Lake Baikal, which we'd had in geography last week when someone asked which was the largest freshwater lake in the world.

A teacher saw me from one of the windows on to the corridor, and I was sent to the headmaster for a talking-to.

When I told father he said, "That was a great fuss just for putting water into the dead heart, darling."

I had to stand in front of the class and tell what I'd done and apologize and explain why what I'd done was wrong.

I had to make it all up. I couldn't see why it was so wrong. But I did it well: I was a fair liar and a natural hypocrite.

I Was Dying to Play With the Boys

One day in the vacant block of land I picked up the long iron bar the boys were using to show their strength—they tossed it two-handed over their shoulders—and hurled it like a javelin. The tip hit a boulder, slid off, the shaft of the javelin came down on the rock and the whole thing bounced up and forward and took a paling off the fence of the next house.

The boys tried to protect me in their fashion, from the opprobrium my action attracted, by insisting I did it. I confessed readily, and wasn't believed. The boys' parents were complained to and wanted to believe the boys did it and I couldn't have.

I kept owning up. The boys got sick of me.

"We'd be better off taking the belting than with her following us around," I heard them say.

They took the belting. I waited for them after school next day but they went the long way round. I went home and lay in the hammock and looked up at the few clouds stitched in place high up in the blue. Over toward the horizon were white cloud-towers, and behind them ice-mountains of cloud. I fancied I could feel the world turning.

I went inside and practiced Clementi, glumly.

Be Merry, My Friends

When we heard that Mister Randall was to come to live in Dalton Walk it was news. Up to then the oldest man in the district after Mister Scully went was Mister Bell, and he went jogging every morning. The oldest lady was Mrs. Kentwell, and she still played tennis and worked on the stalls at the church, the tuckshop at school, and gave out leaflets at the schoolgate on election days. Practically everyone else was young, and kids didn't like them.

Mister Randall was really old. He just sat there, but that was what we wanted. Every time we went round, if it was a nice day, we knew he'd be sitting out front. That's if we got there before five o'clock.

The day he came, fourteen of the kids in my class turned out in cars and on foot to see him. I took round a plate of scones, father wouldn't let me take anything more than that, he said they might think we thought they were poor.

Apart from my class, there were kids from all the other classes in the school. The lady, Mrs. Sheedy, came out and didn't know what to do. She asked us not to make a noise or he would have to go in, so we just hung over the fence and watched him. Dead still and silent. He didn't seem to mind.

Griselda Cadbury broke the silence. She would.

"Are you very old, Mister Randall?"

"Not as old as I will be," he said with a nod of his head.

"Can you get out of that chair?" asked a boy from fourth class.

"Watch," said Mister Randall. And he got up and went over to the flower beds with the Shasta daisies and lupins and Lilliput zinnias and bent down and began to weed them of very small green weeds. You'd hardly bother. He bothered.

The lady came out after about ten minutes and said it was nice of us to call, and she couldn't ask us all in, but perhaps we could come a few at a time in future. There were cakes, scones, fruit, and parcels wrapped up so you couldn't see what people had brought him. Mrs. Sheedy picked them up. She was smiling at first, but by the time she turned to go back into the house she was crying. But not making a crying noise. Just tears.

Of the inhabitants round about, some were pros; none harmed them, just as the previous "rich" lived here and there, unmolested among the poor.

> *Whenever you see the hearse go by,*
> *And think to yourself that you're going to die*
> *Be merry, my friends, be merry.*

We never said that poem in Dalton Walk, only where it didn't really matter.

A Natural

At nine, in fourth class, Everett Vaux had an unexpected dividend from his disability. He'd always had to keep on the move, since his toes wanted to take root and grow and to get out of holding the markers for the half-kilometer run as he did in previous years for the older boys, he went in the race himself. He wasn't strictly allowed to be in it, it was only for fifth and sixth class boys, but he made a fuss at the start and shouted about his roots and he'd be growing if he didn't do something quickly, and the teacher in charge, more concerned to be seen to be not having a fuss at his end of things, hissed at him, "OK, you little bastard, run and be buggared." They were free with their abuse at Church Hill Public.

He ran out in front of the other eighteen inside the first thirty meters and had fifty meters on the field at the end of the first lap. He didn't slow as much as a meter but kept on running easily and pulled up without breathing hard, a hundred meters ahead of the next boy. The school had found a runner, and immediately entered him in the zone athletics carnival.

He was left to walk away alone. No one congratulated him. He'd always been different.

> *Where've you been, Everett?*
> *There and back to see how far it is.*
> *Who with?*
> *Me, myself and I.*
> *Where's your sister?*
> *In her skin.*

123

If you yelled before you were hurt, you were out. That was the rule of Befores.

They held a big stick or a rock over your hand, which you held, knuckles up, on the asphalt, and brought it down hard, pretending to crush the hand.

A centimeter above the hand they stopped, usually. There was the odd accident which we all knew was more than an accident: it was to make us believe in the power of the threat, and the bigger boys made sure there was a slip often enough.

The Befores game worked beautifully with my fellow females, and that was part of its purpose. They—the boys—felt they were so different, they wanted us to feel they were different, and more powerful, and always to be feared; they were preparing us to fear them and be nudged into position easily when they and we were grown into adults, and out of the machine of childhood.

> *Cowardy, cowardy custard*
> *Can't eat mustard.*

Love

Today I saved the Sunday boy. I only ever see him on Sundays when he goes to church and comes home past our house; I think he lives down in Pascal Place. With me helping him, he just managed to get past two savage girls who attacked him in the waste land where the big pipes are for the drainage. I held them off while he ran down the street. I hope he makes it next week, I can't be out helping people all the time.

It was a quiet day and I stayed inside, reading.

I found out just how it is that babies and love are made. The female opens herself and the male puts part of him into her. It is much the same sort of thing I saw father doing with mother on the bed on the day before my seventh birthday.

As I was looking at the series of pictures that showed the male and female right from undressing their bodies until it was finished, I was filled with such a warm feeling—like a tide of soft liquid feelings of love—that I couldn't help saying to myself how beautiful it was, and how wonderful to have that to look forward to. I wonder when it will happen to me.

I found the book in the high part of the bookshelves. I stood on a chair.

There was dust on the top shelf. I disturbed some, and it settled back down. Perhaps the same dust was here in this room—getting disturbed, then settling again—right from its beginning.

Seventeen Years Underground

I was amazed when I learned from father at breakfast that some of the cicadas that entertained us in the hot weather had been in the ground for up to seventeen years before their brief entry into the daylight world from their round holes in the ground, to fly about and be caught by children or birds and fill the air well on into the night with their steady machine-buzz.

Seventeen years; a short time flying; then nothing. Bare husks clinging to trees was all that remained of their larval stage, brown and light as feathers, then when they were dying and dead they too became light as their chrysalis, their overcoat, and ceased to be. They passed on the future to others.

What a length of time to be a possibility!

I think now how much better not to be born, but to remain a possibility. To have emerged when I did was not just the beginning for me. I was like the cicada: emergence into the breathing world of daylight was the beginning of my end.

When I think thoughts like this my food begins to have no flavor.

Revenge of the Slaughtered and Sliced

On our West Australian weeping peppermint, the lowest, widest branch relaxed softly at the ends and fine leaves hung down to my face. A growth on the thinnest piece of branch fascinated me. It was no more than a swelling at first, thickening into a bulb-like growth about ten centimeters from the tip. The growth took the color of the brown pieces of tree where the sap no longer traveled, for they were dead: a darker, stringy brown.

With that growth in my eyes, I looked for others every time I went near that tree. It was in the far corner of our yard and the cricket ball rolled up that far when I made a big hit.

Other trees had thickened growths. I saw leaves with knobby, fibrous lumps in their middles. Not the lumps that meant a burrowing or house-building insect, but a lump that was part of the flesh of the tree.

The red-flowering gum out the front had lots. Its leaves, too, were often misshapen. And the pittosporum, too, with its infected, wavy leaves, and its borers that suddenly came into the light at a joint of the tree and the rest of the branch first died, then hung down and grew brown, waiting for a wind to blow it off and away.

I took some to school for the nature table. In fact I took a project of them, so many that the teacher made a fuss of it. I did the same thing with various grasses that I found in the paddocks down from the other side of the road: one for branches, one for leaves, one for grasses.

I wondered if there were other deformities in the things we ate.

"Do the people at the slaughteryards look specially for lumps in the animals they cut up?" I asked father.

"Of course they do," he said. I knew he didn't know.

"I mean, in the muscles themselves. Inside," I persisted.

My mother told me not to make people sick. No one knew, in our family.

It was disappointing, but there was some satisfaction in my having thought of it, when they hadn't.

I think people could consider more closely the animals in abattoirs. When their heads are off and their bodies drained of blood and they're split up the middle, does anyone have a look for tumors? Well, do they?

126

Are you sure? Or do you just leave it to some Free on the spot who is lucky to have that job?

How does anyone know that cancers in animals won't spread into the bloodstreams of us that eat their bodies? Cancers on their eyelids, round their eyes and eyeballs, can be seen by the growers of the meat, and I guess they do something about it, but I don't know what.

But cancers and tumors within the muscles, attaching to arteries; the bits of lung, the cancerous liver, the kidneys with tumors inside: who looks for them? Does anyone actually know that animal cancers can be cooked and eaten and are a help to good health?

And all you vegetarians, don't laugh. Trees get tumors; so do their leaves; so do grasses. Are there any in wheat? Beans? Peanuts? Cancer in carrots? Cabbage carcinoma? How about the grains that go to make your breakfast cereals? What do you know of them? Or do you leave all that to the authorities?

Humans love to have their revenge: wouldn't it be understandable if sheep had their throats slit, cattle stunned and pigs left hanging screaming, all with the knowledge that they would have a little revenge on their consumers?

And in the killing, who knows if there is or there isn't a death change, a chemical suffusion through the meat in the instant of death, a compound of fear, that takes its toll of the eater?

(I wonder if they have satellites in outer space monitoring our thoughts.)

Thoughts You Never Have Again

Kids have plenty of thoughts, but not always the words to dress them up in. They stay, the undressed ones, in you somewhere, then maybe you remember them later. I'm remembering now a thought I had when I was ten. It floated round in my head, but never got said.

The thought is this: Everyone is unique and important. And every thing is, too. Yet without any single thing or person the world still goes. The planet still drives on round its circuit. The machines that serve us, drive on through the night, unresting. Yet when you look back to each single thing the world can do without, you are faced with the conviction that it *is* important. And nothing like it—or like that person—has ever existed.

Maybe the word I've left out is "now." Maybe everything is unique and important now.

It's not much of a thought to bring back from childhood, but it's a genuine thought, and when I was young it was one I often had, without putting it into words.

I guess that's one for the scientists, having a thought for so many years. I bet they don't know where it hides, or if it's there for all those years as a bundle of words, or some other thing—chemicals maybe—waiting to be reconstituted.

But the good thing is, though we don't know where the thought is, we have it. Unaware of the process involved, I lay in my bed all those years ago, listening to the sound of the wind in the electricity wires and thinking of the creek muttering and clinking at the bottom of our valley and how the creek was the brother I never had.

But thoughts you never have again: are they still in there somewhere?

We Had a Zoo Excursion

I loved the deer. Their yard wasn't big, and they seemed to crowd together a lot of the time, but I liked their dappled backs, fine legs, their sensitive noses, big eyes, the quick movements they made, the lovely soft curve of their throats.

The lions were limp and lazy, the tiger neurotic, walking round his yard in endless ellipses, the panther seemed like a theatrical animal with its light green eyes, but the leopard looked at me. She looked at me with a sarcastic pair of eyes, and even turning she looked at me from the corner of one eye. I thought she was saying we had secrets, she and I. She was the nearest one, in appearance and mood (on a far larger scale, of course), to the cats I knew from Heisenberg Close. It was noticeable that the keepers had taken more precautions with her than with the other cats; they knew she could jump high and climb practically anywhere. I loved climbing too.

I went home with the aquarium fish swimming in my memory; the brilliant birds making short flights in my eyes; the proud, tenacious, clever leopard in my heart.

Next Day At School

It was the first time we'd been invited to do a composition on just anything. I sat at my desk and tried to think, but nothing came. What? What? I dare say I ought to have thoughts, but after all, who was I? It seemed in those moments that I was only a short step away from being a toddler and a baby, with father taking photographs of me on the leopard skin rug. The rug. The rug? The leopard skin—the leopard!

Once upon a time that leopard skin had a leopard in it, a real live animal that hunted, and though not as fast as a cheetah, was much stronger, and able to take its prey up into the branches of trees.

I didn't know all that then. I wrote about a gentle leopard that loved to walk to school on a path that led between the tall silent trees of the forest, across a wooden bridge, and up a hill to the school with the shady trees and the grass trying to grow near the flagpole and a big bronze bell hung in the playground, and at the end of the day went home to a nice mother leopard and waited for father leopard to come home from the theatre.

Celts Never Forget

The Campbells were subject to a specific and original disability, and in the school it was referred to as McDonald's Revenge.

Acky Campbell had a bulge below his belt for months in fourth grade, and it was only at swimming that anyone discovered what it was. Astrid Wagner raced along from the end of the dressing sheds at the pool and told us Acky had something red coming out of his stomach.

"His guts are coming out," she said. "Sticking out of his guts."

Several of the girls, like Clandra Webb, said bullshit, but it was sufficiently likely for the rest of us to listen.

"How red is it?"

"Pinky red. Sort of shiny."

"Bullshit," said Griselda Cadbury.

"Bum," said Rebecca Shatley.

"Knackers," said Aysha Kemal.

"Knickers, knockers and knackers," added Emma Castleford. My friends Shanthi and Chrismi didn't use those words. I was glad they weren't there.

"Show me," I said to Wagner.

She ran back to the end of the sheds, climbed up on the seats, then higher on the clothes hooks to look over the top of the brick wall.

Acky was drying himself, and kept himself turned to the wall, away from the other boys. He was turned at right angles to us. Some of his guts were indeed outside his abdomen. I couldn't tell what it was. In class next day I asked Miss Mullock about the organs of the lower stomach and what they looked like. I caught her give a sudden look toward Acky, and I knew his parents had set it up with her to protect him. It was going to be hard to get any angle or crack in the defense to get at Acky, and after I'd thought about it, I suppose I was glad. He was a snivelly kid then, the sort that never seems to notice the rounded end of the greeny-yellow blob of snot that came down out of his nostrils in fits and starts, sometimes disappearing back inside when he took a breath, other times hanging desperately out near his top lip and getting thinner in the middle. Once you got over the horror of the slime, it was interesting.

I held him with a knee and my left hand against the brick wall of the toilets, and squeezed his appendage once myself, but he didn't yell. He watched me to see if I was going to tell anyone, and was glad to be released.

Joy of Flying

I have told you how my mother insisted on my beauty, my health, how bright and clever I was. How I could do anything: I had only to try. All success could be mine, I could do whatever I wanted. All I had to do was choose.

Choose . . .

Never mind that I didn't believe it completely. (And yet I did.) Her outrageous enthusiasm contaminated me with a recurring emotion that carried me up above the heads of all around me. I was a higher being than other children, other races; higher than all who lived before.

There was great power in the emotion that got into me, enough to carry people who have it off the spot where they stand and transport them some distance away—to triumph, to revolution, to lovers; perhaps to disgrace.

Stirring music sounded within my tunic-covered breast. And I could fly. I flew off the top of the assembly steps. I had to go up before the whole school and be punished for bullying. Acky Campbell had complained.

The power in my mother's emotion worked against the usual force of gravity, filled me like a wind, and carried me off into the air. I didn't need to listen to the stupid headmaster or look at the stupid teachers or the stupid kids.

From a standing position all I need to do is lift my arms and bring them down hard on to the resisting air, which then lifts me up. A few more flaps and with my head leaning forward and body nearly straight up and down, I move off through the air, above their heads.

Way above. But:

> The higher up the mountain
> The greener grows the grass
> The higher up the monkey climbs
> The more he shows

And it was cold up there. Cold as Calvary after closing time. Never mind. If I was different I had to endure the difference.

The Thieving, Murderous Sea

I got a lot of appreciation when I drew a picture in Craft of a phrase the teacher used in social science.

"On the edge of affluence," she had said, and I drew that.

A fertile land extended back from the cliff edge, it was green with living things, colored with the many shapes of life. At the edge, the brink was sheer. Rocks had tumbled down and smashed to pieces at the bottom, and the roaring surf and breakers crashing on the rocks were specked with blood. Pieces of limbs rose and fell on the waves and the mouths of fish and sharks were full. The sea of poverty and defeat lay under the green and pleasant land, and bit by bit, rock by rock, the sea was reducing affluence to its level.

I was congratulated. It was hung on the wall. Miss Mullock said I had vision. Father kissed me with pleasure when I told him, and praised my originality.

To tell the truth, I didn't know what it meant. If it meant anything. Though now I think about it a little more it does remind me of a thought that has chased through my mind in such a way that I've sort of seen the thought but never had the words to catch it in. And the thought? It occurred to me when the teacher spoke of the sea ebbing. It's the land that's ebbing, not the sea. Ebbing continually.

Changes

My father had one of the curiosities made available by an economy that left no stone unturned in its search for the new, the original, the weird. It was a small book made from a collection of his family photographs, rather like the flip-through books in which sporting figures demonstrate cricket shots or football maneuvers. This flip-through book showed my father's progress from babyhood. You flipped the leaves of the book and his face and body changed before your eyes. Very quickly, too. It was funny at first.

When you looked, though, at an adolescent picture, then at a recent one, reduced photographically to a common size, it was hard to see why he had changed so much. Of course I knew why—it was the chemical effect of the years. But really, why *those* changes? And if you went right back to his wizened little old face at three days old and compared it with his face at eleven or nineteen or thirty—the change was not a fraction less than astounding.

There were other compilations which showed the whole process from the cell division to the foetus to baby to toddler to schoolchild, adolescent, young person, adult, right through to old age and finally to the repose of the face in death. These were made up from many contributors and were used for instruction purposes. From time to time bans were placed on books showing the deterioration after death through to final decomposition and skeletal appearance, according to whether death was considered taboo at the time or a proper subject for public scrutiny.

Our Culture

Around the large shoppingtown center a few kilometers away, was a lot of Australia's culture: car cleaning, car tinkering, car selling, car insurance, life assurances, printing, young girls in ballet tights, wealthy shift-workers, big plumbers, the knighted rich, knighted public servants, the subservient poor, working-class conservatives, fugitive policemen trying for a lower profile behind a mower, convalescent home chains, enlightened prisons where labor was cheap and laundry mass-processed, electronic engineers, cosmetologists, ambitious music teachers, towing engineers, automotive suppliers, hairpiece designers, swimming pool repairers, pizza huts, real estate agents, packaging manufacturers, riding schools for young ladies, steakhouse proprietors, taverns, boatmakers, panelbeaters, nurseries, optometrists, finance consultants, drug suppliers, professional games players, pigeon fanciers, unreliable actors, racing touts, mechanics, brick cleaners, park watchers, environmental midwives, auctioneers, thieves, butchers, nurses, bricklayers, clerks and carpenters, managers and married men, cashiers and cooks, builders and typists, limb fitters, waste analysts, industrial spies, thought detectives, behavior modifiers, shading off into the growing limbo of the token job and the supported poor.

> Catch a falling leaf
> And make a wish.

Hope was catered for: lotteries proliferated, attractive new multiple choice betting opportunities expanded to fill, as they opened, the gaps in the employment structure.

Stuart Regan

Stuart Regan was the best at Knuckles. The boys put their fists out and took turns in bashing each other's knuckles with closed fists. The one that didn't give in, won.

Stuart Regan brought a green frog to school. It had been raining a lot and he'd found the frog climbing up his front window that began at veranda level. He put it in the coat Miss Mullock left folded over her chair while she walked around the room looking over our shoulders at the work we did. There were frogs made of cut-out paper on the windows of the infants' room. I could see them. I was finished my composition, but you weren't supposed to be idly looking around. They didn't explain why not.

The bell went. She didn't want to let us go. It was playlunch time. We waited, not wanting to get up until she put her coat on. She bent to pick it up, straightened, teasing us unknowingly, bent again and in one movement—perhaps because we were all attention, not all half on our feet waiting to dive for the door—slung it round her shoulders as if she was acting one of the ladies from the age of old movies and set sail for the door. Disappointingly, she went through it with no screech. We waited.

Our reward came a few seconds later as she was twenty meters up the corridor where the main door led to the playground. She stood in the doorway screaming, shaking the wretched coat out from her extended arms, too fearful of drycleaning bills to let it fall completely, holding the frog at arms-length. It sat on the coat clinging to it, looking over its shoulder at her.

"Grwalp!" it said hoarsely, gutteral as a comic German. It jumped on to her shoulder.

She dropped the lot and ran out into the playground. Kids scattered like tenpins before her. She stopped at the fence under the shade of the big tree. It was an angophora. And drew breath.

134

Equality

For a while we had the open classroom in fifth. Mondays we worked out what we expected to do during that week, then were free to go and do it. I finished my maths quickly and had a lie down under the jacaranda tree for a while. The smaller kids that finished quickly had to be on guard they didn't cop a missile while they rested, so usually they went on to do all their assignments, then got together in a defensive gang, and rested in turns. The vicious ones, the ones that never got anything finished, could be held at bay that way.

All the week's work could be finished by lunchtime Tuesday: the quota was geared to the slow. We had culturally uplifting things to do such as talk, rest, get together for games: anything we liked.

One of the teachers noticed this after six weeks, so the quick ones—my group—were taken in with the sixth. They folded up the dividing doors and made room for us, and we listened to what the sixth was being taught. They didn't have the open classroom so it was a case of sitting in rows or groups round separate tables. When we found how interesting it was, we sucked everything in in large lumps. The enterprise lasted three weeks; the kids of the sixth complained, and a pressure group of powerful mothers put a stop to it. Their case was: where were the higher classes for *their* kids to learn from? The next stop was high school, so the ideal of fairness won: there was no advantage for them, so we couldn't have any. We loved it for three weeks. It was better than the nitty old stuff we had in fifth, which was so much like fourth that it was no effort. Once writing the answers was done, everything was done.

We were lucky to get a chance at the open class: the lower kids didn't; they had too many stupid boys, who mucked up as soon as they got a bit of freedom, and spoiled it for the rest. Some girls copied the boys, and smashed other kids' rulers and tore books and made it impossible to work; they helped fix it for the classes beneath, so they'd never get the chance at the open method.

Sometimes they broke up a good group and put each one with a group of duller children, but Miss Mullock didn't agree with this, and left our group alone. I just happened to be friends with other girls around the same level in schoolwork.

Without Chrismi, or Shanthi, someone a bit smart, there was no one to keep you on your toes, there was no rivalry. It was something we needed. Every time we talked together there was a sort of skirmish, friendly of course, because we were all each other's best friends, but it was rivalry and we loved it. We sort of sharpened ourselves on each other so that when other kids came up against us they encountered very sharp tongues and minds indeed, and kept away.

> Don't care was made to care
> Don't care was whipped
> Long ago.

Conversation with Father

I had asked him things like why people get poisoned when poison bottles have labels, why people become criminals when police exist. I've written down as much as I can remember of what he said.

"There are wealthy lords of industry whose income in the safe-making game depends on the persistence and ingenuity of the safe-breaker. A myriad middle-class minds on the law game, are supported by the humble breaker of the law. Wealth is fairly certain at one end of the game and prison, disgrace and humiliation at the other. But the one depends as much on the other as the batsman depends on the bowler to make a game of cricket. Like Communists depend on Conservatives for their effect."

"Your friends are mostly Labor, aren't they?" I asked, just to be contributing. "Aren't they opposite to Conservative?"

"Labor has no understanding of the Right, darling. Conservatives understand Communists very well, and vice versa, just as the old aristocracy and the dregs understood each other better than the middle classes understood either: they're similar predators, only their coats are different. But the Left is lonely, and has no claws. And it does not know that Communists are not Labor."

"Why do you vote for them, then, if they're not so smart?"

"I think a government should act like the head of a family. Society is a family, with its members not all the same age or with the same abilities or enjoying the same state of health. The youngest, the oldest, the sick and the poor should be looked after first, then the rest in ascending order of physical and financial health and competence. Hunger, homelessness, disease and ignorance should be attended to first as a civilized duty. Of all things in the world, people are the most precious, and preserving them, we preserve the human race. And I haven't even mentioned the rights of man, and freedom and enterprise, and the relations of property. Perhaps I will when you're older." (Actually he hadn't mentioned money, either. I thought that was the main thing, from listening to the news.)

"Is that what Labor's about?"

"I think so."

"Why don't they ever get in?"

"Well, I'm not sure, but maybe people like the head of their family to be more fatherly than motherly. They can often talk Mum into going easy on them, but they have less confidence in her for that reason."

"If they got in, would a Free get your job at the theatre?"

"Al, the acting ranks are open to all: if someone else, even a Free, can act better, they get my job. But I *did* qualify, and it might be hard for a Free."

"You'd think they'd like to try," I said. "And have a better life."

"Don't forget. We in the Serving Class don't really have a life. We have no experiences you could reminisce about, nothing interesting or exciting, no picaresque adventures, no entertainment during our daily lives, only out of hours; while Frees can do this and that, go here and there, laugh and yarn all day or just sit out in the sun. Even our holidays are not anything more than a decent reward for our talent and responsibilities. Of the classes, ours has no stories, yarns, adventures, dangers, and less and less interest in our lives as we serve more. It's status, not interest and adventure and carefree laughter, for us."

The Decline and Fall of Children

Discussing the motion of the bodies of children falling in Toongabbee Creek after heavy floodrain can be academic. Discussed by heated parents looking to hit something that can't hit back, it can be more than academic.

"These Leatherbarrows, it's their fault. It's what they've done to the banks, the course of the creek, the noise they make, their dogs scare the children and when they run away naturally they fall in the water." There were plenty of reasons why the local residents were enraged by the Lutherburrows. Even their name was distorted in the general anger at those who didn't pay rates or look for credit.

Chlorine Lutherburrow (they got her name in the hardware shop window) made eighteen rescues near Rutherford Road bridge when the creek was brown and wide and rushing. Privet had taken over the banks, grown from cuttings thrown out as rubbish along with the myriad seeds householders hated. Privet made the bush wretched, but no one thought to root it out or stop tipping it. Banks of clean sand, friendly greyed rocks, were precious and were places for the dipping of meat on bits of string into the water, for eels to surface and snap at it, and in small pools for crayfish to wander crookedly near.

Some boys fell regularly into the water, and got cut on branches and rocks. Some boys, a little older, would go there specially to be rescued by Chlorine Lutherburrow. She went in after them and when they were out and drying would still clasp them to her chest. It was the same general size and shape as the rest of the big girls, but there was something different about the way she pressed them to her.

Chlorine was three years older than Lil. The family went on rescuing kids and not resenting the nasty parents of the kids. Lil was particularly fond of forgiving people. I'd have thought better of her if forgiveness came harder. She was noted for the sweet-faced smile and implacable affection.

In the evenings I often thought of their family and how down the hill the dark bush welcomed the night.

My Pony Was Red Again and Again

Father gave me a lovely surprise for my eleventh birthday: a pony. Actually I got him back at the start of the May holidays and by the twenty-eighth I'd been riding him for a couple of weeks.

We kept him out at Kellyville in a well-disposed paddock. He was stolen twice, but always came back even though he was, apart from his loyalty and his love for me, an ordinary hack.

I had often thought as I walked him along the dirt roads and felt him react to the things about him, that he was possessed by a sort of ghost. He would make an unauthorized stop to listen to an Indian mynah, or a lizard's nervous scurry over dry leaves would bring his head round and his steps toward the lizard's hiding place. He didn't seem to want to interfere with the creatures, he was simply interested. He stood there, often with me trying to get his head round, looking down at another Australian nonhuman. Interested: that was it, exactly.

When he began to steal for me, that was going too far.

At first it was small things. He could jump the paddock fence, and did so when he felt like it. (He would never take the fence with me up.) He stole from picnickers, I think. When we went to his paddock during the week, I'd be presented with a radio, a hat, a shirt—things he could get in his teeth.

He showed his affection for me by rubbing his soft lips into the angle of my neck and shoulder.

The day came when he was so irritated by my rejection of his presents and all the head-shaking we went on with when we saw his crimes, that he threw me. I was so angry I could have ground him to pieces so that his bones were powder. The family was there, and some friends who'd come along to have a picnic and watch my father's little girl. My father jumped up, made sure I was unhurt, and went after the pony with a rifle he kept in the car, and shot him through the side of the head. With the sound of the shot some of my anger dissolved and I felt easier.

Down fell the pony with a horrible groan, sideways. Last of all, his head hit the ground. I rushed over, his eyes were open, a great red patch of gore and smashed bone looked up at me. I cried.

(Hypocrite!) My father was instantly apologetic. The eyes of the red pony blinked, he struggled to his feet, the red disappeared inside his soft coat, and the bullet plopped back out of his head and fell on the grass.

I mounted him and again he threw me. Again he was shot, in anger. On the disappearance of anger, he revived. This happened three times.

By the third time, my red pony knew I would never let him die. Never again did he venture to throw me.

We planned to keep his coat long in the winter. There was a lot of frost out that way.

Not many other kids had horses. I felt pretty lucky, and asked father whether we had a lot more money than other people.

"Not a lot more," he said. "A bit more. Once, a while ago, it was a statutory requirement that our class had to be given no more than equal pay. Equal to the class of Frees, that is."

"Did we *take* more?"

"It was necessary to add an allowance for skill and responsibility and extra expenses incurred in the line of work: new study courses, equipment, and so on. Basically, though, it's still the same: equal pay for all, plus an allowance for the Serving Class. They call it the Service margin. The margin is bigger than the base rate, now."

> One fine day in the middle of the night
> Two dead men got up to fight
> Back to back they faced each other
> Drew their swords and shot each other ...

My Father

It has been a long time since I heard my parents talk about the question that hangs over my birth. I think mother must have made a fuss about discussing it in front of me. The only clue I have is part of a phone conversation I heard my father having in which he used the name Hart; the words he said were, "Hart's gone. He was last heard of heading toward the forest country south of the Horn of Africa," and he saw me, and whether it mattered or not, he said Hart's name no more.

But what if this mystery had been invented to throw me off the scent? What if my origins were quite different, so different that it was better for me not to know? However mysterious, I wanted to know the truth. Even if I came from some place other than this planet: even if my origins were nonhuman—and I was some kind of god.

One night I woke up from a dream, full of fear and unimaginable pain, convinced that home, for me, is not here.

I asked father, "Where did I really come from?"

"I don't want you talking any more of these ridiculous things!" His voice was loud. He spoke quickly, as in thunder.

Someone Lower

I was eleven in sixth grade. A little younger than the rest of the kids, and a lot bigger, though I wasn't as fat as Keith Maxinou or Virginia Yuen.

The furniture of our room had changed from charts with easy writing and spelling, to graphs of coal production and oil and mineral reserve guesstimates and population densities. One thing didn't change from room to room in our school: the poster with the words WHY DO FISH SWIM IN THE SEA?

We were now doing essays, quite long ones, to answer the question. I often asked my father, but he didn't know why. It was a mystery still. Dozens of times he was on the point of going to the school, even phoning from the theatre, but it was too inconvenient. His working day coincided with the school's, and he never really had time to spare.

"Because it's handy" won the booby prize of fifth, and the surprise of the year was that it was Lil Lutherburrow that wrote it. She never had much to say at school, at least that got noticed in class. We accused her of having her father do it, but our collective parents, liberal souls all, wouldn't have it.

141

"People like that can't come up with original ideas," Mrs. Cadbury said. Her daughter Griselda was in our class.

Even kids down in third grade had opinions on the Luther-burrows, even ones with changes. All felt they were above someone, at least.

Lil had a big friendly face, and her long straight hair like a downpour.

Pity

Narelle Duncan came out in sixth grade with part of the map of New Zealand's south island on her right cheek. Her father, a Servant, could afford to have doctors treat her with hormones to try with hair to cover the map, but she was too young for this work. Surgery did no good: with her parents' permission a small incision was made on the Mount Cook area, as an experiment, but after the scab peeled and the scar diminished, Mount Cook re-asserted itself.

She was no good at geography, so we in sixth grade didn't have the satisfaction of saying she was obsessed. Her mother, though, thought it was a judgment, and said special prayers eleven times a day. Narelle was eleven. She intended to make it twelve times when Narelle was twelve.

By comparison, those of us with no changes, and with full expectation of a meritorious passage through the grading gate, were living within our little lives as comfortably as when we were in our mothers.

We used to call her Narelle Dunnycan, but after her change we took pity on her.

I Like Myself

At eleven I looked at myself down there for the first time. It's one thing to see yourself in a mirror standing up, either in the bathroom, in your bedroom or in the change rooms on sports day. It's quite another to shut the door and hold a hand mirror up to yourself with your legs tucked up, and suddenly to see the folds and wet lips. And a bit further down, the anus.

The anus was rarely mentioned among the kids, as such, only in talk like "up your bum," or "get your arse over here."

It had lines radiating from the circumference of the pinky-brown part, inward to—to what? To nothing. The muscles kept the hole closed. If you opened it out to one side with your finger the radiating lines dipped in and disappeared at a slightly different length from what they were before.

I faced my bottom toward the window to get a better light, but I didn't feel like continuing to look at it. I pulled my pants up.

It was rather indefinite. I mean where did it begin and above all where did it end? Also, it was an exit, yet it looked so much like a mouth, and a mouth sucks when it puckers. But it whistles too.

As I bent forward to get up I caught a frail odor that must have hung there before I covered myself, and was now gradually rising, being warm. It was my odor. I liked it.

Next morning when I woke, I felt, for some reason, fully equal to the morning.

The Hill Children

The Hill children lived out past the monastery on the other side of Hanging Hill, in the last vineyard left within a hundred kilometers of the city. There was no actual Hill family: the Hill children were kids who lived on that hill, for down past the edge of the vineyard there were houses, little fibro cottages and mock weatherboard places where the hill descended into the valley and the winter nights accumulated heavy cold air that felt like a fog to walk through.

All the children on that side of the hill had vines which, when allowed to come to fruit, produced a wine like no other.

The children had for a while been victim of a disappearing disease—they had been abducted by profit-makers who wanted desperately to bring out an original vintage—until they received a dispensation from the authorities to have their own school. It was dangerous for them to go into the world, the world wanted to make something of them. And at school some of the other kids got them at the beginning of the year, at the end of January; some held them down while others plucked them, at each grape a scream.

The beginning of the grape-growing area was hidden by a huge trick picture of houses and streets, barred by yellow street barriers, as if council workmen were tearing up the street. In front of the houses were pictures to show fields and grapes continuous with the fields beside them and behind.

The usual growth was from the legs and arms. I particularly liked it when the vines were beginning to sprout. I think there is nothing so lively as the fresh green of innocent plants pushing out into the light with the energy of life behind them. Ah, the buds and baby leaves and miracles of spring.

Bottled, it was called Child-Wine. Armed security guards protected the Hill children everywhere. They always went round together. Scientists came and studied them. They lived like royalty. But at night the children's vines entwined, fighting each other. They had to be patiently disentangled in the morning.

Spiros Kyprianou

He was frightened of mirrors. A tidy boy; more brown than fair, more small than big, more timid than forward, more mid-class than bright; neat, good on little details like drawing red lines under the titles of his work and in the margin and keen on tiny drawings to illustrate the geography or history he was doing. He even drew little diagrams in his number book, and colored them in: little pictures of the problems. You know the sort of thing: tanks emptying, areas of fields—he drew in the trees and animals—and piles of shot.

He was very tidy.

I slipped and fell on him one Friday afternoon leaping for the gate on the way out. There was a patch of gravel shading into sand on the asphalt surface. I hit the edge of the gravel and skidded on to the sand, was airborne briefly, then landed on Spiros. He skidded on his belly, and got up, and I waited, prepared to dispense a brief word of thanks, or to strike like the taipan if it was cheek and dirty words he had ready.

Instead, when he saw me his eyes rounded and something suspiciously like my dog Boof's look crept into his eyes. From that moment, he *was* my dog. I used to whistle and click my fingers at him, and he would come running.

I found I could look straight ahead and see sideways at the same time. I could look straight at the school bell, with Spiros over on my right; when I whistled him I could see him stop and come toward me. (When I extended my arms sideways and waggled my fingers I could see both sets of fingers—still looking straight ahead!)

He was only a medium sort of boy, but advanced in his capacity to love. (You mustn't think I was unable to distinguish at that age between those boys who wanted to look and touch and master me, from the few who might some day be capable of the rarer feat of love.)

For an English Expression assignment he included the lines:

> "A beautiful girl is like a tree in Spring,
> A bird in the sky, free of the earth.
> A beautiful girl is a gift of God."

He didn't leave it at that. He titled it "The Beautiful Alethea Hunt."

The teacher was so taken with it that he had it read out to the class by the best reader. Me. Luckily, we all made such a rout of the English class that the kids thought I just stuck my own name in for the hell of it. When the teacher pointed out that I hadn't invented anything, I could have died.

Spiros was pink-cheeked and black-haired and spoke nicely, and it was predicted that he would play five-eighth for high school by year nine or ten, but he had this open sincerity when it came to me. He worshipped me in the playground and in class, and followed me with his eyes when I dashed into the girls' wash sheds.

His devotion, after boring, amusing and irritating me, began to affect me. I thought of him at night, I wondered where he was when I lost sight of him in the playground. I felt peculiar when he came near me.

In class, we learned that the mutton bird kept up its cycle of flying, mating, nesting, in a huge circle round the rim of the Pacific. An enormous merry-go-round. It didn't care that I was being caught up in feelings that I didn't understand.

In English, the teacher blithely went ahead with an inspiring lesson on working for the world and earning undying fame for oneself, but when I looked around innocently to see if Spiros was watching me and found that his warm eyes were like suns big enough to swallow me, I shivered. And shivered at night in my bed, thinking over what was happening and what was to happen in the future.

Next thing I knew, he had written a composition about me. It was called "My Close Friend."

But I wasn't. He was the friendly one.

My friend has a striking appearance with a longish face and angel-shaped head. Her nose protrudes like a freckled umbrella sideways in the rain, and her soft green eyes hide under long, tawny lashes.

Her eyebrows are a whitish-golden mixture, scarcely noticeable at first sight, and her long legs carry her to victory in the "zone" sprint championships.

Her house is near an oval where she trains with her father spring and summer, but in the autumn and winter she plays touch football with the children from the next street.

She is eleven years old and is always top of the class and best at everything, even singing. She has a quiet and soft emotional character which she hides behind her brains. She is a lone wolf who asks help from no one.

As suddenly as I had slipped and fallen on Spiros, I got sick of having him round me. He liked me: so what? I told him to keep out of my way and look at someone else with those brown eyes of his.

> *Brown eyes, pickle pies*
> *Blue eyes, beauty*

Green eyes, greedy guts
Grey eyes, duty.

I Resented Having to Feed That Horse

That afternoon I had to feed the horse, and after that, Daddy had to shoot him. I was tired of having a horse. We'd tried to get rid of it many times, I hated being tied to it. I'm grateful that at last his resurrection failed him.

I'd taken the initiative of putting a mattock and shovel in the boot of the car, all that remained when Belle was shot was to put in a few minutes pleading with Daddy, then we could get on with it. I dearly wanted to dig a hole for old Belle.

Belle was short for Bellerophon. It had another connotation too. (He was a homosexual.)

Belle, despite his many brushes with death, still maintained the usual animal stolidity when the gun barrel pointed at his brains, which hid modestly under his skull, which in turn hid decently under soft brown fur.

When father had blown his brains out and he'd fallen, we dug the hole.

I know what you're thinking; why not dig the hole first, then bring the horse over to fall in it. We tried that. The paddock was studded with the scars of many holes, but as sure as we dug the hole and tried to get Belle anywhere near it, we couldn't. You'd think a nag with so little teachability that you could shoot it any time you liked would also be dull enough to be led over to his grave and shot conveniently beside it. Not Belle.

Yet he didn't mind the gun pointing at him.

The hole was five feet deep, and it wasn't till we'd got the earth in around him and heaped on his legs that we really believed he wasn't going to wake up healed, and step with dignity out of the hole.

I know the desire for revenge is a bad thing, but with all my differences from other people I am still human, and need to be able to pay back aggression, insults and blows. And that horse did throw me. How could I forget that?

147

When I got home I cried wholeheartedly. I guess the hardest hearts squeeze out the biggest tears.

The Authorities Tested Us

The tests they came to do on us from their education headquarters in the city were attempts to find clues to the potential within us. Even the slow ones, those who couldn't string their words together with any sureness of arriving at the end of a declaration without loose words left over like spare nuts and bolts, must have been considered to contain some of that precious ore, since they were tested just as often as I was.

It could be that the more medically aligned tests were for some sort of genetic variation that they hoped to discover in me. (And the others.) They took smears; oral, anal, genital, and when we were eleven, a small piece of tissue from the side of a finger; they took it away in a separate marked glass container as big as a twenty cent coin.

Sometimes I think: If I could wake tomorrow and be a little girl again. But this is today and I am here: there's no going back. Cruel time carries me forward to meet whatever is waiting. Whether I'm ready or not.

Composition: Deserted Wilderness

The warm October sunlight bathed my weary head and the gentle swaying of the train was making me ever so tired, though I had never been tired before in my life. Suddenly the train came to an abrupt halt and jerked me into the world of reality. Smiling, I thought about all the things that must have happened in the two years I had been away. The train would not stop much longer, I made my way to the door. My foot slipped on some food that a careless passenger had dropped. My head swam as I went flying through the door onto the cement platform. The last thing I felt before I merged into total unconsciousness was a searing scorching pain across my forehead. My mind drifted into oblivion, and I followed.

Dazed, I sat upright, or what I thought was upright. My first reaction was total amazement. I had a dull recollection of flying through the carriage door and the impact of the cement could still be felt—everywhere! As if I landed on everything I had!—Yet I saw no platform, and no sign of a station. Stretching out to the horizon in all directions was complete waste land desert. The dull bronzed yellow of sand met my gaze in all directions, there was nothing to be seen or heard. Only total silence and desolation. I looked up. The blaze of sun penetrated my body and the harsh heat flooded me. I was tired, so tired. Once more, oblivion . . .

I awoke refreshed in close, utter darkness which was not only the absence of light but the tangible presence and body of dark. The silence was intense. I tried to remember: I couldn't. Thoughts swirled about in my head like a gargle. My eyes grew accustomed to the darkness, and I made out the horizon. It was so peaceful sitting down all alone as gradually a gentle light bathed my form. I could see something illuminated by the soft dawn light. I ran toward it, filled with gratitude and enthusiasm. I stopped. I could see I didn't have to run. It was coming toward me! It was the beast of the desert, spotted and tawny like a leopard.

It is much nearer now. Its eyes look through me. Its jaws are open wide.

The End

One of the Boys from Another Country

One of the boys from another country, Rinalde Dalneri, had paper growing out of him. An irregular sheet came from his side where the ribs make ripples under his left arm. It was paper, all right, but flesh-paper, like skin. I mentioned it at home, and father asked, smiling, if Rinalde was going to make lampshades of it, and I made the mistake of asking Rinalde. He didn't speak to me again.

Words grew on the paper as it came out, unknown words in a strange tongue. A teacher he trusted was always going to find out what language the words were, but never did; instead, he dropped guesses that it might be Basque, or Sanskrit.

We told him they were filthy words. (As if words could be filthy.) But he didn't like being teased, and kept to himself. When he went to sport he always appeared with the flesh-paper trimmed to skin level.

I tried to make it up to him, simply because I was curious and I didn't like to accumulate enemies by accident, and he wasn't really a nasty boy. He got embarrassed when I apologized, so I talked quickly about Mario Fattoretto, one of the kids who'd been at Primary in the class below, and had just died with blood cancer.

As I went away he said, with a look of regret that I cannot forget, "Thanks. You're trying to be nice, I know, but it's me that's the failure. You'll never fail."

I didn't know what to say. The sadness in his eyes was more than sadness at his change: it had something to do with me. Then it occurred to me that he could never hope to have one of *us*. As a real friend, anyway.

I told Father about him, and tried to explain.

"You didn't tell him he was a failure, did you?" he asked.

"No."

He seemed relieved.

"None of *us* ever say publicly that they are failures. They look at themselves and conclude they are failures, since they don't get through the grading and they become different. We never make fun of them."

"It isn't necessary?" I asked.

He looked sideways at me, perhaps thinking I was trying for sarcasm. My face was as pure as I could make it.

"Well, I daresay—"

"But why do they change?"

"People lose some things and gain others. I think you'll find as you go through life that they, the Frees, regard what happens to them as a type of justice. I know they often lose their humanity *because* they have lost, but after they have safely failed, they gain other things."

"But don't *we* label them failures because they change?"

150

"Never in public. And it's good policy never to talk about them to other Servers, because you never know when you're going to change. Or when *they* are."

I thought about it after dinner, and decided that I didn't think people unfortunate enough to belong to the Free class should feel there is any stigma attached to failure. After all, personal growth is a greater thing than poverty.

Could it be that the difference between achievers and those who fail is some kind of difference in the individual attitude to originality, to difference itself, to standing out from the crowd? Those who fall back to the majority, are they cowed by life, are they cowed into conforming to what is, thus losing their chance to step out into confidence, into the work of the world, into fierce competition with the best of humankind?

Even so, surely it could be possible for some among them to perform acts of heroism, even to die for others.

The Coming of the Janicskas

The coming of the Janicskas next door was a great change for me. I had been used to noting the differences between the households of my friends, but I knew that when I visited them I was the stranger who might have changed things and that when I wasn't there everything might well have been different. The point is that in those houses the mothers did most of the arranging and organizing and giving orders and driving people round, but in our house father did everything. Maybe in my friends' houses their fathers kept a polite silence while I was there, but maybe not.

Mister Janicska fitted exactly the collective impressions these fathers made on me. It was my first feel of that joy that comes over you when your prejudgments are confirmed.

He was optimistic and slightly crooked—he would say something that wasn't the exact truth if he wanted to get something done now—he was often elated and cheerful, brutal and active; he had a lot of personal initiative, but he was inclined to be hasty.

Mrs. Janicska was bigger than he was, but still his follower. He was quicker, he was louder, he was readier with an alternative if she backed him into a corner; and it was he who cheered her up, not she him.

She was inclined to be pessimistic and a little helpless. I could never decide if it was from laziness, remembering mother and my opinion of *her,* or lack of go. She seemed depressed even when she wasn't; but she was kind even when she shouldn't have been. For instance to that Greg Grayling who knocked all the little kids over and laughed. She was thoughtful and considerate, and she considered and thought a lot, but you could never tell if maybe she wasn't perhaps just a little tired and her passivity was just that she was about to go to sleep.

"How did he get to be boss of their family?" I asked father.

"I guess that's rooted in history," my father said, smiling.

"I guess he's the man and away at work a lot and less visible than Mrs. Janicska so his authority seems greater," he went on, treating me seriously.

"Did he just get married and there he was: boss?" I said.

"Some people when they pair up work out like that. Don't forget that she looks after those four kids very well," he added.

"Michael says his father says she's too sympathetic, and they've got to learn to do things for themselves," I said, quoting Mike. I'd seen him trying to get his mother to show him how to cut the edges with the garden mower, and his father had come out and sent her inside and taken Mike by the ear and said, "Find out yourself."

"When I was a boy it was a case of, if you want sympathy, see Mum," my father said. "Dad used to listen, but only a little. If he thought you were after sympathy he'd send you out to do some job for him. Mum was the one to fix up cuts and bruises. She'd never let me leave the house without my breakfast." His eyes were remembering.

I think he thought from my questions that I was missing the thing he couldn't give me: brothers and sisters. Mother wouldn't have any more kids, not even adopted. She had to be free to do her writing, and she had given time to me, a few years, and that was enough. She'd had to catch up that time, and that was sacrifice enough.

It was Sunday, and father gave me all his time. He didn't even look round for a new play to read so he could enjoy the pleasure of thinking what might have been or might still be.

The way it turned out, he made sure I pursued the subject until I'd worked out this big family thing—the unfamiliar spectacle of a mother being an old-fashioned mum and the father an untamed male, instead of a reclusive mother and a housebroken father who did all the work.

When Phillip Janicska came home with a black eye after school, and played around in the yard to keep out of range of Mum's heavy sympathy and was seen by Dad—the moment he saw a slightly averted face he noticed something was wrong—Dad went up to him in his hearty way and began to teach him something about keeping his "right" up.

"Keep it up, son. Keep it up."

"But my arm gets tired, Dad," said Phillip.

"Tired be buggared," said Dad. "Keep it up. See?" And that was an explanation of how his own hand happened to sneak past Phillip's guard and tap his chin. He kept his hands open, though.

"Best you learn to fight, son." But his mother had heard. I watched through a crack in the grey palings.

"I don't want him taught to fight! Fighting is rough and brutal and wrong!" And she came sailing out.

"You have to protect yourself in this world."

"I want him to keep away from rough boys," Mum said.

Phillip could see me, so I went and sat on the patio and listened.

"And try not to grizzle when you get hit," added Dad.

Mum didn't hear that. She was off at a tangent.

"And don't forget tomorrow. You can't go to football until you finish your music practice."

Dad let it lie there, and when things were quiet, said, "If you're beaten, and get upset, try and get over it by yourself. You get better quicker that way."

Mum heard. "You come to your mother, Phillip. Mother knows best."

"Above all, don't come crying to me, specially when I'm busy." And he grabbed Phillip and playfully lifted him up, turned him like a catherine wheel and set him down vigorously on the grass. Mum said "EEE!"

When Michael spoke to his parents about the latest thing the kids were sniffing to give themselves a kick, Mum said, "It should be banned!"

Dad said, "No, son. I wouldn't sniff that if I were you. Likely to make your reflexes slow, you'll never get in the representative team then. Sure, others do these things, but *you* don't have to be stupid."

Mum said, "If it was up to me I'd make a law about that."

Michael, who scored a major proportion of his football team's points each week, was trying out an idea on his father before he put it into practice in the game. He wasn't even going to tell the coach—or the other kids—until he found if it worked. He ran into the usual split in parental advice.

Mum said, "But you can't do that! That's not football!"

Dad said, "If he wants to do that and there's no rule against it—let him! He didn't make the rules. Let the referee blow the whistle if he doesn't like it."

"You should conform to the traditions of the game, Michael."

"You play the whistle, son."

Phillip, two years younger, had climbed the box tree and was taking timber up in order to make a treehouse. We called it a "cubby."

Mum got on to him as soon as she looked up from the kitchen sink.

"Phillip!" You could hear it miles. She dashed out and stood at the foot of the tree.

"Why did you climb that tree and upset the bird's nest?" There *was* a bird's nest there, and he *did* upset it, but it was the only climbable tree.

154

"That was thoughtless, very thoughtless. What if you were a bird? Put yourself in its place!" Phillip tried to, silent and frowning with concentration, wondering if he really had to come down out of the tree.

Dad saw it. "Damn it, darling. He's just trying to set up a cubby in the fork of a tree! If you're always telling him not to do this and not to do that he'll never do anything."

"That's all right. I want him to be a good, kind boy. Doing things all the time can be a very thoughtless activity." Mum eventually went away, and the cubby got started. I think she was resigned to the fact that it would be built. She was always fighting rearguard actions.

Her next complaint was that Dad was on his back under the car while Phillip was up the tree trying to manhandle planks and manage hammer and nails, spilling them, going back down, climbing back up.

"Aren't you going to help him with the cubby in the tree?"

"Leave him alone, darling. I'll have a look at it later, and if it's not safe I'll tell him. He's got to do things for himself."

The third Sunday in a row Mum was on some sort of high. She rode in to the attack again and again. It was the last of my tuition Sundays and taught me more about traditional families than I wanted to know.

It started quietly. Mum said mildly to Dad as he was dismantling the pool pump, "Can't you stay home a bit more during the week?" He went to meetings of this and that, and was always available to work late at the office.

He'd pinched his finger and dropped a washer down into the body of the pump. It wasn't the best time to grill him.

"I'm busy all week earning money for you to spend. And when I stay home you want to go out shopping and spend more, or spend it at restaurants or shows. I'm chasing my tail." He'd got her off the subject, he thought, but she picked him up on the money issue.

"Well, I need more money. I need it—we need it—for extra lessons for Greg. He shows real promise on the piano, Miss Matthews says. We should get him now, while he's keen."

Miss Matthews was the local teacher. Delrene wanted him sent to the music Conservatorium several times a week. Dad could see the end of sport for Greg coming, since artistic pursuits had nearly lost Michael and might lose Phillip. He knew they'd drop music when they were older, anyway. They were just ordinary kids.

"I'm not giving you money for that. No way."

"But you must. We need it."

"No." And that was that. She said nothing for a while, but later came out with a mug of coffee for him.

"The lawn needs cutting," she said reflectively. It was almost a reflex action, that remark.

"There's painting needs doing," she added.

"I'll get round to it." And that's all she got out of him until some school friends of Greg's got there with their horses and ponies. I looked over the fence when I got the first sniff of horse.

Greg ran out, admiring. His best friend got off his horse and invited Greg to get on. They showed him the right side to mount.

Dad got into the act, pleased. You can't be saving money and working every angle to get ahead as an executive and still spend money on horses; he was pleased Greg was getting a chance to taste the pleasure of riding someone else's toy.

"Jump into the saddle, son," he said to Greg. Mum loomed.

"There's a proper way to ride a horse. It's not fair to the horse to have inexperienced people on his back." It was a mare. "I think he should go to a riding school and learn about horses, where to ride them, who to go with, how to groom it. He should think about these things first and plan ahead now, and maybe we can get him—"

Dad saw it coming and headed her off at the pass. "Just jump in the saddle, son. Once you're there, stay there. That's all there is to it."

Eventually all the kids left, tailing the uneasy but enchanted Greg clinging to the gentle mare, and the others on their ponies. They used the footpaths, the nature strips, the traffic was dangerous.

Mum took the opportunity of their absence to sit down while Dad pottered, as she thought of it, and got into his ear. I didn't feel a bit guilty, listening.

"We should talk of their future, John."

"Sure we should. They're doing OK at school, aren't they?"

"I'm worried that Michael might have attempted more than he can do."

"Good on him. He's a good boy. That's the sort of son to have."

"Be serious. Don't you think he ought to take, say, photography and art instead of two foreign languages?"

"Damn it, Del! I want him educated. If he doesn't come into the business with me, at least he can go into law, or engineering, or medicine."

"I still think he may be attempting too much."

"That's what makes a man a man."

"Don't you think *he* should be given the choice?" She knew this was a good thing to say: Dad loved free choice, especially if his customers freely chose *his* goods.

"Sure he should be given a choice. Where is he? I want to talk to him, man to man."

I didn't need to listen anymore after that.

But as we sat inside, having some of father's yummy chocolate biscuits, father suddenly said, "What way do you think they vote?"

I didn't know, but "don't know" wasn't much of an answer for father, so I said, thinking of the stereotypes we'd been given at school, "Well, the chances are the woman is conservative and the man votes for the left."

"You're not right," he said gently. "From all they've said, he's conservative and she's labor. Work it out, and let me know how I know."

He'd been listening, too. I nearly said to him, "Isn't it fascinating hearing how a real family goes on," when I caught myself and stopped in time. I didn't want him thinking I thought we weren't a proper family.

157

Next evening, after I'd been given a horrible load of homework and was having a bad time getting on with it, father looked up from his paper. He fixed me with a solemn gaze and said in what I can only call a profound voice: "There is now only one way for freedom to go, and that's inside. Pulling your borders back, your defenses, your gun-emplacements of the mind, and withdrawing your forces inside your own mind, that's the new freedom." He put the paper down on the table, gently, not blaming the paper. "In spite of the labors and the dangers and martyrdoms of the past, it's come to this again as it always does. But it's a step on the way, a wave on the graph of change. It will happen again, and the appearance and the feel of freedom will happen again. And the dark nights of the mind and the body when knocks on doors will herald partings, these will recur. All of them. We will never be rid of them, nor rid of the recurrent change and the pattern of now more, now less freedom. And always we must put forth an effort to get as much as we can, to restore the balance against the days when we lose and lose and lose.

"That is what is meant by the duty of being human."

What had happened?

I waited. My eyes said: I'm listening.

He gazed into the distance, his eyes alighting on the top of the piano, near the metronome. He picked up the paper.

I was determined to wait. So was my homework. I lifted my pen. He put the paper down.

"They won't leave you alone, Al. Restrictions, restrictions." He pointed at the paper. "Investment restrictions, health restrictions, parking restrictions—they want us all to become what statistics say we should be."

I pointed to the paper: Is that what's biting you?

"Yes," he said in a grumpy voice, interpreting my sign. "They've closed off another street. It was my favorite short cut. Now I have to stick to the highway with the solid line of vehicles."

I could have kissed him. Such portentous affairs, such fuss! Instead, I said nothing and returned to my books. A man like my

158

father deserved respect from his child—a man who fell deep into one love like a grave.

No One Knew What He Had

Peter Jessup kept apart from everyone, he didn't play with the other boys, he didn't go swimming and always stayed dressed. Even his family had never seen him undressed since he was nine.

From his sister we learned that when he went into the bathroom or the lavatory he took all his clothes with him, stuffed up the keyholes, locked the door, and in his bedroom he puttied the unevenness of the windows and doors and got his father to put new, blurry glass in his window on the world. No one knew what he had. He locked everything up inside him.

The Difference

I noticed in other people's houses that girls were expected by their mothers to be little ladies, as if nothing had happened, nothing had changed, as if time hadn't passed for a century. Mothers, despite their pride in girls' athletics and debating, wanted a girl to sit down immediately after training or a good game of chasings and be cool and elegant, not sprawling limbs in all directions comfortably. You could almost hear the impatience during a backyard karate practice, with legs and feet flying out and upwards, and short, vigorous movements being made that had no reference to cooking, sewing, and the nurture of infants. You could see their minds churning and fighting it, wanting and pressing their daughters into the mold they knew was safe and unalarming.

The boys were let run wild. When they were brought home by the law or parents summoned to the supermarket, they'd shake their heads, give the boys a number of hits, and look proud. Boys will be boys, they said.

I guess boys had freedom from birth, where girls were looked at, fussed over, talked at, and in general circumscribed by attention that clung like sticky lines in a web.

Basically they wanted us to be passive, and look nice, like fruit on a shelf waiting for a buyer. Packaged goods. And the boys were allowed, encouraged, to be violent, and of our crowd I was the only one who'd been given a taste for it and the only one to know what an addiction it was.

The difference was not their penis. Let me make that clear. In any sort of combat the penis and its backing group were a serious disadvantage. (Perhaps males had to develop muscles in order to protect it.)

No. The difference was the freedom they were allowed.

Everett Vaux

Everett Vaux was eleven, too. In this, his last year of primary school, he was known throughout the metropolitan area as an athlete; he was near sub-adult times in every running event and still had to shift his feet about in class and the playground and still had permission to get up from his desk any time he liked on his own claim that he was starting to put out tendrils.

He was a pretty boy, with a beautiful slim figure and streamlined limbs, but already the signs of his constant effort were showing, and those signs were round his eyes and beneath his ankles.

Ankles, reader? Ankles?

Yes. The lines on the top of his feet, where the flexing of his feet on their ankle-pivots happened most often, and under the inside of his arches, where the vertical lines are that look so like worry lines, were plentiful.

His eyes showed most strain. All the children in school except the Lutherburrows had dark lines under their eyes, but the Lutherburrows went to bed just after sundown. Everett had fine lines at the sides and underneath his bottom lids, and if you got up close to him he looked, in that one part of his face, like an aging man. If you looked into his eyes, they were cheerful, merry even. But if you looked at the lines and took in the eyes with the peripheral part of your sight, he looked sad.

And grey hair, at eleven. Sometimes I saw him sitting with his feet off the ground, his arms clasped round his knees, a long way from the other kids, looking up at the sky. As if he'd asked a question and was waiting for the answer.

Or looking away from the planet to a better placé, turning his mind toward that better place—trying to eat that distant heaven with his eyes.

What Is Greatness?

I think the thought that really drove me on, was that I wanted to be able to do anything they could do. Males. Their example was held up to me all the time, whatever I read; the records for this, that, and the other were held by them; women's records were lesser imitations. Why shouldn't it be the case that whatever they could do, I could do?

Most of such activities were trivial, it's true, and a sensible person wouldn't have wasted the time thinking them up, let alone the effort of doing them. But trivial as they were, they had become erected into a body of activities established by custom and hallowed in the recording.

After all, it is possible to look at most things and say: this is trivial. You could review a person's whole life and say the same thing. In so many millions of lives nothing happens. They breathe, and occasionally move; eat, sleep, their blood circulates, they appear to observe objects around them, and suddenly they move no more, and as you watch, decay and disappear, blown away by gusts of wind that wouldn't have moved them before.

What isn't trivial? Greatness? What is greatness? Power, strength, goodness, beauty, originality, dignity, judgment?

I suppose mother's choice of words had spoken to the pride that filled me, yet when I could not answer such questions as these I began to despise myself. If the word meant so much to me, why was everything not plain?

If I did something no male had ever done—or female either—would that be greatness?

The Purpose of School

Our teachers thought we were there to learn things and to relate to the community and to each other, and they were right. But relate: that's a word and a half. One teacher wanted us to be open, not just in open classrooms, but *open*: to be honest, to show emotion, not be afraid of opening up to others.

He didn't know what we already knew: that we weren't there to learn to be "with" our fellow kids, we were there to master them. Mastering our environment, our fellows, our teachers, our parents—that was us. Whoever showed emotion left a nice big gap in her defenses—a sharp word could fly, straight as an arrow, into that weak bosom. Whoever was honest left himself at the mercy of the rest of us; honesty was another floodgate—not to let things out, but to let missiles in. Any kid that was open and confessed to something, had to wear that thing round her neck forever. Just like my father still remembered the kid at his school who confided to him that he shoved bits of stuff up his bum. My father told me he never let on to the other kids, but he always pretended he was going to, and he could get that kid to do anything he wanted. He mastered his environment.

Kids that were open and honest like that wouldn't hesitate to give all their guts to anyone wanting to put them in a databank; they wouldn't even ask who had access to the information.

When they tried to get our group to break up according to the different interests we had, we developed the same interests. Once you let them break you up as children they can do it even easier later when you're grown-ups, because then you don't even have the shared community of school.

People Who Love Me

I like them very much. I know the theories; others can do as they like and why should it concern me; but it always affects me that people are fond of me and show me love: I find them better people, in a way; they have a better sense of humor than others. As a matter of fact, that sort of person laughs so much more than anyone else I know. Even in their poverty or their idiocy at school work, they laugh. I laugh at them laughing, I have developed a high ability to laugh, so that I can immediately laugh at anyone.

Remember, my reader, before you judge me, that I was always the one that was loved: it can't surprise you that I laughed at people.

But I owed it to those kind, beautiful, gentle people who had a tremendous sense of humor and a great feeling for life and for vitality and strength.

Of all the things I miss now, being loved is the greatest.

Innelda

One dress I loved—it made itself my favorite because it always had older females gushing—was red, with some white and rust and black and gold, and I was only a child. I still can feel my love for the Innelda dress.

Innelda hung inside a special cover to protect her and to keep her separate from other clothes.

I was the only girl that didn't complain when I had to wear the same dress to different birthday parties and school concerts. My father did his reputation in our family no harm when he helped me choose Innelda.

Out of Line

In the lesson on Wednesday where a few religious items were mentioned, the thing that repelled me was a tenet of Christianity.

"You could say its essence is the ability to stand back and let others go first. Blessed are the meek. Turn the other cheek when someone hits you. Do not try to be first all the time, but give your neighbor every chance."

At the age of eleven, I was already out of line with the theoretical basis of Christian civilization. Turning the other cheek did not fit my formula of the world. I rejected it.

Neither could I renounce my own will, which I looked on as my freedom; nor seeking; nor did I have a taste for that peace so prized in the East. Religious virtues sat on me like a drop of water in midsummer.

I Think Constantly of the Perfect Child

Mrs. Brown of Darwin Parade came close to my idea of a Christ-like woman. She was so very *good*. Her fifty-nine-year-old son Bernie was an idiot. He had come from her body in the same way as her other children, none of them idiots as far as the usual tests showed, though sometimes only strangers can tell. She kept him at home with her all his life, he was so different from the ordinary run of children that he was useless in any capacity other than helpless idiot. He was polite, but his politeness was expressed in halting, roaring syllables. He looked normal from a distance, except for an extreme slimness, as if a thirteen year boy was encased in his grey-blue suit; his face, with its glasses, looked human enough from a distance, but close up his mouth sagged into a hideous lower lip that yearly seemed to get bigger, and exposed all his lower teeth as well as his gum and the trench beneath it that ran round the length of his jaw where the lip joined it and carried the clear juices of idiocy round the mucous surfaces, ready to be drawn on, and sucked up, to lubricate other mouth parts. It was strange to have him look at you and not know if he saw you, or come on him thinking and not know if he *could* think.

Mrs. Brown had another child, which issued from her body in another way. This child's arm began to grow forward from a place below her navel. When the fingers appeared she cut its nails regularly; when the hand had grown outward she had to take special precautions not to knock others in queues or shops or knock it on furniture round the house; and of course she washed it religiously.

Nothing that happened to her disturbed the impression of goodness and serenity that she radiated; they were an aura, coming in a steady stream from her.

"She's a saint," father said unequivocally, but I knew that he often gave an opinion right away when he didn't want to be bothered much, so I knew it wasn't meant to be taken as a definition right from the summit of wisdom.

"I wonder if you can feel the same things coming from her if you stand behind her," I said. But he had his head bent over a paperback book of new plays, looking for some play that might take him from the security of *Changes* out into the manly adventure of risk and uncertainty.

I tried it. But it wasn't fair. True, I felt the goodness, and I stood still while I felt the calmness round me like a nice cloud, but I knew her, so it wasn't a proper test.

The arm grew out until there was a length of twenty-five centimeters of it, which included an elbow. The arm stopped growing, the elbow allowed the arm to fold back against her abdomen; there was only a slight lump when it was folded, easily masked by her clothes.

It stayed the same age, always a child's arm. The only distress it caused her was when it straightened out and collided with something in the summer, or when she was warmly dressed and could feel it wanted to straighten out.

Cruel animals that we are, and with the most helpless young; but Mrs. Brown's potential child would be always helpless, always need protection. It would never see out of its warm prison—if indeed there was anything more to it than an arm. It would never have the chance to be cruel.

My Last Composition In Primary: The Letter.
Dear Cornelia,

I am hoping you can come and see our school. I am in the top class in the Primary section in a noiseless schoolroom with our teacher Mister Heathcliff pacing up and down, shouting one minute and laughing the next. Our clock, which Mister Heathcliff bought for seventy cents, will soon register

165

three-twenty pm, which is stampede time. The classroom, one of the oldest in this section of the school, is adorned with plenty of space, unlike other rooms, which have pictures, rolls, boards, nature tables, models, etc. It doesn't even have: Why do fish swim in the sea? We're supposed to know now.

There goes the bell! In a few seconds there is no one at school except the gardener and me. He is a nice man and talks very pleasantly and quite a lot, but that is all right because I am a qualified listener.

The gardener goes home and so do I. There is only mother at home. On the way I stop at the bridge and spit into the water, which breaks my reflection into lots of pieces and makes ripples. The ripples spread out to hit the banks, then bounce back toward the middle again; you can see them, lower and wider than the ripples that come from the middle, crisscrossing and making a pattern that's hard to follow and keep track of.

When I reach home I unpack, clean my shoes and then have a bite to eat and a drink of something.

I am eleven years of age and I have no brothers or sisters.

Next day is just like so many other school days and all are like today.

Yours sincerely,
Alethea Hunt.

> One more day and we will be
> Out of the gates to liberty.
> No more pencils, no more books
> No more teachers' dirty looks.

Extracts From Class Compositions
These brief passages were put in our school magazine:

David Bilbul:

A journey to the Park is a memorable occasion especially when one goes by ferry from Circular Quay. One obtains the feeling of complete tranquillity as one glides over the waters of the harbor and views the Opera House on Bennelong Point on the one hand and the changing skyline of Sydney on the other.

Angela Testoni:

We went through a cave seemingly filled with the whisperings of many people but on second look it was only a cave with water dripping from the roof.

Krismi Choudhury:

A round piece of green glass, smooth and polished by decades of movement in the raging surf, was lying on a rock like the ones upon which it had crashed for such a long time and which had formed the pit-marks on its once gleaming surface. It was so like a marble that I put it in my pocket and I have kept it to this day.

Chinhua M'aksombo:

The gulls were dipping and soaring above the water, watched by the golden sun rising languidly above a jeweled waste of water. The horizon began to form as I watched.

Richard Wansdale:

I never wanted to kill another rabbit again but I knew someone had to kill to provide food for the human race.

Challenger Lutherburrow:

We were in a hurry that night, mum and dad were angry and it was late, so our tea was meager; toast and cheese were the elements.

Autographs

We passed round our autograph books before school broke up. Shanthi Subramanian wrote:

Some write for fortune
Some write for fame

167

> But I write in autograph books
> Just to sign my name.

Sylvia Strickland put:

> By hook or by crook
> I'll be first in this book.

Griselda Cadbury:

> When you get married and have twins
> Don't come to me for safety pins.

Chrismi Thambyrajah:

> Can't think brain numb
> Inspiration won't come
> Can't write bad pen
> Finished now amen.

Angelika Weidemann:

> If this book takes to the track
> Box its ears and send it back.

And I wrote words of similar wisdom in theirs.

High School

Hopscotch, oranges and lemons—with its "Last man's head head head head head (as you waited for the one you wanted) head head OFF!"—skippings, Handies, Sir, the Clue Chase where you put notes down and sent the searchers off to the next point to read the next direction and on until they got to the treasure: all were gone. You don't play hopscotch at High. We stood around talking. There were lots of kids from surrounding suburbs. We got our textbooks and kept an eye out for people we might like to be friends with.

The lavatory set—the ones that got round in groups behind the wash sheds—had already started to form. The toilet block was near the street: sometimes strangers talked to them through the fence. Things passed in and out while no one was looking—no teachers, that is.

The Head was Miss Fish. At assembly in the playground she re-instituted "lines"—standing in lines—and waited for silence and stillness before anything got under way. The first day she waited nine minutes; in the end the kids got tired of standing in the sun and kept quiet just to get inside and sit down. In the corridors you had to give way to teachers—they were privileged traffic. And at intersections of corridors you gave way to the right. All the corridors in the buildings were narrow, and traffic was one-way. You could be fined if you were caught going the wrong way in a one-way corridor. There were special assemblies called and the Riot Act read if there was a logjam at an intersection On Purpose: that was the crime of crimes.

It was easily done. All it needed was a crowd already at the intersection, largely ignoring the keep left rule. With a knot in the center your four groups joined it from the four arms of the intersection; pushing, crowding, keeping up the pressure, being joined at the back by more pushing bodies.

There was a lovely evil feeling about that sort of pushing. You knew the others would never give in or stop pushing, so there was no way you were going to go anywhere, you were just pushing others into others, and the enjoyment of doing something that was nasty, full of malice and energy, and all in such large numbers that you were anonymous and could get away with anything, was so intense that I, for one, got the beginnings of a lively feeling down there, and for a while after I had a kind of pain.

Our second assembly the Fish told us about the things she lived by, called principles.

"I believe in the power of the spirit over things. I believe there are certain principles whose violation makes life not worth living." She took a breath after this, the sort that conceals a wary look around the school to see if enough of us showed signs of following her. "I believe this approach has implications for human personality as a whole throughout the world and that this conviction is rooted in the very core of man's being."

"There is something common to the human spirit, the human species: what Mumford called—'The self that we share with our fellows.' " (Who was Mumford?)

And she introduced us to the school code.

"The School Code, girls and boys. C-O-D-E. Co-operation, Obedience, Dignity, Effort-and-Enthusiasm."

Lessons Where We Sat and Watched

Lessons where we sat and watched the visual aids, told us of the poor of the world, of what humans were and how they behaved, and always, though I didn't make a point of saying anything in class, it struck me that the behavior and the people and the poor were all around us. Outside the school windows, admittedly, there was nothing to be seen but the street up to the traffic artery, and no one walked there. For the space of the intersection vehicles were visible: apart from that, only the odd delivery man or an old person walking could be seen. But the world was there: all we learned about was out there waiting to be seen. But it wasn't to be taken seriously, and that seemed to be the message. We were being taught to take it from the written word or the illuminated picture on the face of a tube. When it was a picture or when it came dressed as a word, it existed. What we saw in the alleys of the city from our parents' cars after dark, and off the highways on weekends had less existence. How would we ever be able to see the world when it was around us, when it supplied no handy pictures or encapsulating words? How could we rely on something inside us to make the connection between the panorama out there, and the reference words and formal pictures we had in stock in our memories beforehand?

Sometimes I caught behind the actions and words of the teachers, and the rituals and routines of the school, hints of a reckless algebra no one knew was there.

I was bewildered. I was upset. I couldn't get to sleep. Instead of counting sheep while I waited to go to sleep, I kissed sheep. My imagination makes me sick at the thought.

Back into my imagination I go, head down, ruthless, and mark out the sheep in black. Hundreds of them; it takes me ages; but in black I mark them all out.

I mark them out in the cuts the butcher will make, but stop short of making the first cut. To grip the sheep between my knees and have it twist and squirm between my thighs while I pull its head back with my left hand and pierce its throat with the knife is momentarily beyond me. And to push—or is it pull?—the knife so that the throat is slit like a letter, that too is beyond me. And to have the sheep's blood all over me as it gushes and squirts and squishes underfoot, that is beyond me.

And to peel the woolly coat back from the ankles and off the shoulders and find it stick at the head, hands and feet so that I am compelled to cut them off to take the coat right off, that is beyond me.

Everything is beyond me, but imagination.

Imagination takes everything in its stride. Before I go to sleep I begin to shoot my beloved pony. Again and again. The side of its soft head blows out, and its legs fail under it. It collides with the earth in a disgusting heap and I wait for the miracle of imagination that will stop its blood pumping out, that will pull its shattered bone and arteries back together and fill its heart with strong red blood and set it on its feet again so that its wonderfully soft eyes look at me and its chin rests on my shoulder in that way it has as it comes up to me from behind, breathing in my ear.

Just when I was considering whether to make myself tired enough for sleeping, by imagining the map of the world with mountains, rivers and coasts, towns, boundaries, seas, and whether four colors were all that were necessary to show the joining of any states of different political shades, I fell asleep.

An Experiment

My first experience of saying in a strong voice: "Come here!" to a male was illuminating. It was Wim van Heeren, and he turned, startled, then came toward me obediently, as if fulfilling a duty. What to do with him? He looked like a dog.

"I want you to find out when the bus leaves on Wednesday for basketball," I said, fixing my gaze in the center of his nose.

He turned and went away toward the administration office, and I went over toward the edge of the playing fields. I didn't see him again that day, but my experiment had worked: I had ordered and someone had obeyed.

I looked over to the horizon at the distant vertebrae of the land, called hills, and it seemed pleasant that the land was prone while I stood upright.

Behind Many Things

Behind many things father said to me—in the house; when he was off-guard; talking off the top of his head—I thought I detected a connection he made between moral and emotional matters. That perhaps being unhappy caused one to be immoral in action. And of course happiness arises from within, so one's internal balance becomes the spring of everything. Or did he mean being unhappy was immoral?

Is there any truth in this? (Don't forget these are notes, merely; you have work to do, my reader.)

The Compassionate Crane

In the mountains where we went for a short trip in the car we stopped near shops away from the towns.

"I'll get something to eat," father announced, and mother didn't object. The air was cool and felt crisp in your nose. He looked at some old people sitting on a seat as he went into the shop, then stopped and talked to them on the way back.

He talked, listened; listened, talked. He handed over the things he'd bought, to the old folks. He came back to explain until mother reminded him he'd brought nothing back. He went away again with an unfamiliar misery in his eyes.

In the car he said, "Poor old devils. Don't know where they are. Inspection on today, so they're paid to get out of the way. Too scared even to tell me the name of the institution. Dozens of them walking around lost in the mountains because the place is overcrowded according to official geriatric specifications. They haven't even got money for a pie." He drove away, we began to enjoy driving and looking and getting out of the car at lookouts and eating our snacks in the air that was so cool and clean you felt it was washing your face.

Coming back near where we'd seen the aged wanderers, we saw a tall, kindly crane moving toward a house that was obviously going to be moved away on a large truck. At a side window we saw movement.

Father stopped the car and we looked. Movements inside.

"Some of the oldies have taken refuge in there!" I said.

"We'd better do something," said father.

As he got out of the car the crane moved near the house like the tall bird it was named for, slowly. Then stopped as if it detected life, another brain in there.

We ran to the house and the crane saw us, stopping. A shout was raised.

Father banged on the door, two old hobo-men ran out the back. Others were inside. They weren't institution people at all, but derelicts. One old lady lay on a bed, paralyzed. The four others looked dumbly at us as if we had guns. They did not move. The crane driver came and got his lunch to share with them. My father had tears in his eyes. He called a taxi and paid for it to take them back where they belonged. Which was nowhere.

The cab driver knew. He was a local. He let them out on the other side of town.

I asked father why they were homeless when there was money available for all. He explained that some people were so rooted in the old ways that they could not be persuaded to apply for free money: they were ashamed to, and would rather have nothing and pay to the full the penalty for their failure in not being born with the abilities required to survive.

It was weird, somehow. No one else minded.

When we got home that night we were in time to see Mister Grech—the juvenile alcoholics notifier—come home, drunk again. I didn't have a clear idea of what drunk was, so I looked as attentively as I could to his antics. I'd seen people staggering on late shopping nights and clumsy at our parties, and Mrs. Simonetta, but I was young enough to think that anyone might stagger any time he felt like it.

Mister Grech, trumpeting like an elephant on mash and water, made it through the two trees that served as the entrance to his driveway—we had no gates or front fences in Heisenberg Close—breaking bushes, falling to his knees, falling sideways, falling over backwards, but in general going forward.

It was funny.

"The ochna's gone," said father. Mother took a brief look, then turned to her notes.

"We'll hear it if he buries himself in the holly."

I watched. Mother went ahead, hearing nothing.

The variegated pittosporum suffered a broken left wing, the Geraldton wax bent over without breaking, the Christmas bush was thick-trunked and pushed him off, he reeled over to embrace the bottle-brush tree. From there he did an erratic dance from acacia to melaleuca—father called them like a race commentator—and subsided into the grevillea. Second last of all he broke down to the ground the spider flower he'd not long before got from the bush and tenderly planted.

Then when he should have chosen either to go round the back of the house or make for the front door, he hesitated. That was too much: the holly tree reached forward and made him fall backwards. Mister Grech fell back into it and turned round, within its embrace, to get a footing and rise to a humanoid position.

"Wait for it," said father. I waited. It wasn't until he was half-way to the front door that Mister Grech let out a fine collection of piercing roars. They lasted until his wife pulled him inside the door and slammed it, taking a quick look around and spotting us.

"Ah," said father, with satisfaction. "Not a bad voice. Projects well."

Sex Education at School

Sex Education was a thorough book, a great seller and the most popular manual of its time. It became a standard work through its popularity. It was what my parents read, and I'd had a look at it when I was nine. Now we had it at school, and as well as that I read it when I came home from school of an afternoon, sitting rapt in description of tender acts that I couldn't quite imagine. Did my father really—intentionally, deliberately—get his penis to enlarge, take it to mother and tell her he wanted the "sexual relief" the book described? I had heard kids say at school, imitating their Dads: "Here, Mum, cop this!" (Other fathers apparently confused wives with mothers.)

I knew animals had only set times to do it. The thing that lay unanswered in my mind was: why are humans so different that they can do it anytime, constantly, needing only opportunity?

Well, not really. I could feel *in* me, though I hadn't even had a bleed, the answer. And my answer was: female animals got so much less pleasure in it because they couldn't face the person who wanted their body, who wanted to pour hot kisses into their mouths and sperm into their body. Human animals got the pleasure of being front to front.

The manual told me about love. None of the stories of the girls at school did, and none of the words overheard from the boys, or the actions of the big kids who picked up their girlfriends in cars at three-fifteen. Or the poem about the vicar's daughter, where she's covered in white stuff.

But how did father get his penis to enlarge. Was it thought? Did he concentrate? Was it the sight of mother, or the thought of her, or because he was her husband and he *had* to?

I wondered whether I should ask them to show me how it was done.

And how did you know the sperm was in you? Body temperature is a constant. Their penis, their sperm, would be the same temperature as your vagina. Allowing for varying states of health, there would only be a differential temperature of a degree or two. It didn't strike me as anything spectacular.

I looked with a new interest at the boys in the school playground after the sex lessons. Imagine them having so many millions of spermatozoa to put into a woman at the one time. They—humans—were incredibly fertile. And I was part of this and, at twelve, not far from experiencing it.

I wondered how much of it came in one go; would it fill you up? I mean are there buckets of it? A cupful? Does it make a lump in your abdomen. But no, it's a form of liquid, I think, from the way the teacher was talking. But if so, why doesn't it all pour out when you stand upright? And also, do you have to lie down with your head below your feet to keep it in if you want to have a baby?

How much did it really take to fill you up?

I thought, as I went to sleep that night, of father's penis lengthening and going in search of mother. And at the same time mother's words like wraiths streamed from her collected notebooks and entered his brain, eating him alive.

The Feet of Angela Blunt

On the harbor excursion I had been sitting in one of the long seats with a view over the ferry's rail. Angela Blunt sat above me.

I knew she liked me, she was always looking at me. Her feet fitted between my shoulders, on the top of the back of the slatted seat. It was perfectly natural that, out of consideration, she should take off her sandals so that her left foot could somehow curl round my shoulder. From time to time it passed lightly over the top hem of my tunic and I felt the whispering touch of it so very gently on the skin of my neck where it led toward my back. At such times I looked round carefully, but she didn't seem to be looking when my head turned.

After the lunch and the note-taking the kids were spread out a little more, and on the journey back I was caressed by two

Blunt feet. They were very pretty, small and hardly veined, and since she was an indoor person, white. Several blue veins under the skin branched down toward her toes after they crossed the high bone on her instep, reappearing dimly under the skin like the random veins in marble.

Once I casually leaned my arm back, and the feet didn't go away. With a further, still casual, movement my hand touched one and rested on it as if I was unaware. I left it there for a minute or two. I think I could feel her breathing, all the way up from the foot, just by the contact of my first two fingers with that affectionate piece of her.

A week later she sent me violets. I knew, though there was no note with the card. Perhaps she expected me to know and to do something about it. I did nothing.

Often in the playground I felt her looking at me, but when I turned—naturally; at ease; doing something else; in command of the situation—she was always looking a little to one side of me. And never met my eyes. It must have been a test, and I failed.

The Vegetables

In Church Hill High School we got the idiots again, after being free of them for the last of primary school. They mucked up constantly to give themselves an excuse for not having sufficient brains to do the work. We called them "vegies"—vegetables.

The trouble was, their attitude was catching. It became the thing to do as little work as you could get away with. I found myself doing two hours homework and saying I did five minutes, just to be thought normal.

Take the Money and Run

Part of the face of an old coin appeared on Drago Bulatovic's skin, halfway up his right arm and on the inside, just where the division is between the outer line of hairs and the smooth inside-of-the-arm skin.

What date would it be? Everyone was interested.

As more of it appeared, we saw it was old for this country, where history is spread so thinly on the ground. The tails side was outward, so all we had to look at for a few months was GEOR-GIVS V D.G.BRITT: OMN: REX F.D. IND: IMP and the old king's head.

Then Drago was kidnapped. Right there after school. It made headlines.

Three weeks later he was returned, the penny still where it had been. Fear inhibited its growth; the men had felt the bottom edge of the coin and satisfied themselves its growth stopped at the skinline.

But their first instincts were right. When it grew again, and finally fell off, it was that rarest of Australian coins: a depression penny, 1930.

Another one appeared. Drago was guarded every day at school and at home. His family got notes to say he'd be killed if he produced any more 1930 coins. A supply would kill the demand.

The next two were 1952, very common. He wasn't harmed, and his family were ten thousand dollars better off.

Kids like Drago had been born apparently equal, but the underlying and innate defeat had shown itself.

Other kids were taken away from school when their personal growths became visible, and allowed to have as much time off as they wanted. Mostly they were glad to get back into the company of other kids, but of course, although those of us with no differences didn't at all mind playing and mixing with them, there was a social division into those who may end up in the Serving Class, and those who never would.

Drago and his family didn't care about social divisions: they had the money, the only safe thing.

As Good As Any Male

My attitudes hardened, my ambitions were forming, however vague they might be. I would be as good as any man: as brave, as strong, as ruthless, as independent, as benevolently contemptuous of others.

I invented the Super Jump, and kids from the streets around competed to beat me at it.

It was in a large English oak in the paddock past the end of the street, which used to be a dairy; the tree once shaded the backyard of the dairyman's house, but now the house was gone, and the small square of land had been kept for a playground. The Super Jump was from one branch to another, and these were rather special branches: they radiated out from the central trunk, gradually getting further away from each other. They were almost level in height.

I started by doing it myself, then showing other kids after school.

Only one of the boys could do it first time, and he was a little shrimp who only hung on because he was so light. They all started from the place I did, and couldn't hang on. I was already as strong as boys! They all thought—all of them, big and small, weak and strong—that the weakest of *them* could start from my best effort! They didn't, and couldn't, and they went away swearing and never referring to the Super Jump again.

I didn't miss the lesson contained in their way of learning what I showed them: their arrogance, their confidence, in dismissing defeat from their minds. Because it was a female that won, the contest wasn't worth competing in.

I don't deny my own confidence that I would be as good as any male. The next step to consider was their arrogance; their unreasoning, their unthinking, their bashing-their-heads-against-a-brick-wall persistence, confidence, optimism in the other things they did. For somewhere in there was their secret, the secret that made miserable little boys think they could compete with a large, well-built, athletic girl and start, and expect to progress from, *her maximum mark*!

The Shrimp Who Dared

The shrimp who dared to try my best jump on his first go—and who succeeded—stayed in my thoughts while I got my jumps to a distance where none of the kids around about could reach. He was small, and dark, with brown eyes that seemed to dart at you. Hopeless at schoolwork, yet lively and likeable, like an active small dog. His name was Ahmet Mehmet.

It happened one Friday night when I had to go to bed early to get up at dawn next day for a trip with father. I lay on my bed looking out across the shallow valley that went down to the smaller creek, rose again, dotted with houses, to the steep street that climbed up to the main highway. The clothes I had on were loose and fell about my limbs as if they liked me in a casual way, and my skin seemed a little tight for the blood and the life bottled up inside me.

Without intending it my hands wandered over the smooth tanned parts of my legs that were within easy reach. It was as if another person caressed me. I didn't watch my hands' progress over the territory of my self, preferring to be surprised, feeling the new sensations my fingers were generating. New sensations? I remembered dimly, without knowing it, that these were the feelings my mother's touches had given me when I was small. What I was doing was finding what feelings I liked and where one had to touch to produce them.

The tips of my fingers were the most effective tools for enjoyment of my self. The ecstasy I had been given by these touches when I was a baby was completed now, the time was bridged, by my ecstasy now; something in me was being fulfilled.

Should I have made a study of the reactions of the different topographical features of my body to the fingertip stimulus . . . maybe my mother had such feelings and her endless notes were records of ecstasy?

It was my first orgasm. Ahmet Mehmet did it: they were his fingertips. The question I didn't face then was: why the shrimp?

I think now it was because even then I went for someone I could manipulate, while having *some* little respect for him.

No one knows how it is going to be with someone you can't control, in a situation not familiar, but I daresay I will experience that in the future.

And I Often Did

From masturbation I turned briefly to history.

The Heroes of the World's Wars became one of my favorites. It was a big, comfortable book. I read in my room, on the lounge, at the dining room table, or outside, sitting in the box tree.

Greatness, Hitler's for so long undiscovered manuscript, was another favorite, alongside *The Prince,* which I liked only because Hitler had it by his bed: the minute instructions bored me.

The Book of the Great, by one of the factions in the education departments of the land that once had an ascendency, was wider in its scope. Its makers had varying ideas of greatness. There were famous physicians, discoverers, artists, scientists, load-bearers, rescuers, self-sacrificers; all the way from Jesus to Leonardo to Einstein.

The actual nuts and bolts of history, what happened when and what else was going on, in streets and homes and villages, I had no great interest in. Just the personages.

It was possible to perform my new trick in bed or in the toilet, but there was something sneaky about those places and for a thorough masturbation I preferred to do it in the back of the car as it stood safely garaged, and I often did.

At school I heard boys declaiming an old rhyme that made me annoyed:

> Under the spreading chestnut tree
> The village smithy stands
> Amusing himself and abusing himself
> By making a cunt of his hands.

Why didn't girls have a verse about it too?

Great Men

Around my room I had pictures of great men from history:
   Alfred burning the cakes
   Caesar crossing the Rubicon
   Drake finishing his game of bowls

Stanley meeting Livingstone
Galileo forced to recant
Newton under the apple tree
Watt watching the kettle boil
Hannibal crossing the Alps
Nelson's death
Christ hanging and Barabbas watching
Diogenes in his barrel
The death of Socrates
Horatio on his bridge
Lars Porsena with his hand in the flames
Divico's Victory
Washington at the Delaware.

I had copied from paintings, drawing first in pencil, and painting them with poster colors. My Divico's Victory with the yoked captives stretching their necks forward for the sword won a prize at school, largely, I think, because the teachers had never heard of him. I got him from one of father's old Latin books: Latin had disappeared from schools like ours.

They hung round my room like trophies, the first thing I saw each morning. They were all males, but I didn't mind. The lessons they taught were for me, too.

Now that I am a traveler leaving the cold shores of my old self for a shore I do not know, what were those lessons and what have they done for me?

They stand there on my wall as invitations to immortality, the magic, the life still glowing from those names, called to me, saying that somewhere in the world or in my mind there was something I could attempt that might preserve my name from the usual obliteration death meant for the ordinary person.

Mother's Day

Father got mother up at seven, insisted that she have some breakfast, then after reminding me that my sandwiches were in the fridge, drove off to act all day.

Mother had little to say until I went to school, then was free to do as she liked till the afternoon, when I'd come home after sport or basketball practice or choir or orchestra and help myself to cakes or fruit and have a look inside the stove or behind the door where father kept his list of what he intended having for dinner. He always bought a supply of biscuits and cakes, so if I didn't gobble the lot in one afternoon I could eke out three or four each day. He delighted in telling me that the biscuits I liked were ones he had liked when he was a boy; that so little had changed.

Of an afternoon mother might be out where the sun came in at the back of the house, with a pile of paper and her large notebooks.

When she used the large notebooks, the size of diaries, she got through perhaps fifteen pages a day. Thinking and writing, head down, eyes far away, hunched, or up getting coffee in her brown mug or getting disgusted with that and having coffee in the white china teacups with the wildflower pattern.

When father came in he always went to where she was and bent over to kiss her. Mostly it was the wrong time for mother to be kissed, but we got used to that, father and I: mother was known to be impatient of interruptions and we accepted her as she was, once we knew she wasn't going to change.

She would come to the table for dinner, since they had worked it out between them that a combined dinner would be good for me. She contributed little to the talk. Father always had some little story to tell of the day's performance, and when he obviously had nothing new he continued the saga of his fellow performers and how they got on together. It was like a family serial.

How my parents got on at night I never knew. Since the time I saw them when I was seven I've not been curious about that part of their life.

Mother's face had been fashionable when she was young; a sort of country plainness round the mouth and chin, a forehead that looked noble with the hair drawn tightly back, and quiet eyes that misled. You would not have been surprised if she had come into the house with a pail of milk warm from the cow; your surprise would have come when she failed to give you any.

183

Mother forgets things.

She rarely forgets her notebooks and papers, but here is one fragment she left around:

> Our first kiss is both near and far, my breast
> Has lain by the breasts of my beloved in sleep;
> So let us both tread softly, for it is
> Our dreams that pave the ground beneath our feet.

I wonder if that Alicia in the photo album was the beloved of mother's verse. After all, you only have to pronounce Alicia the Spanish way and you have Alethea.

Back Seat of the Car

Reading in the car after lunch on Saturday, I dozed off. It wasn't a day that I'd masturbated—those days became alive with meaning and I was lifted up above people and suburbs.

I dreamed I was a woman, the first woman in recorded history to become stronger than all men. I could run faster, jump farther, throw farther, lift more, fight better, wrestle more powerfully, than any man. I was also smart to look at; not for me the huge hips and pendulous melons of earth mothers: I was incredibly tall and strong, with small athletic breasts that didn't flop around and get in my way, and hips that allowed my muscles to move freely; I could wear clothes that made me look relaxed and easy: a living statue of speed, strength and intelligence.

I inhabited cities, knew and fought with powerful humans, not all of them men; I won power over my contemporaries; my intellect cut through problems, erected new understanding; my eyes directed a beam of mysterious power that illuminated and conquered and charmed; I was older, but not too old. I had a quality that others were tempted to call greatness.

I was awakened by my father hitting the hose against the garage door. Perhaps he suspected the use I made of the back seat.

My dreams of greatness vanished in the effort of picking up my book from the floor of the car.

A Precaution

After the birth film at school I invented what I thought was a good exercise for the muscles around delivery time, and did it along with my sport training. I had no yen for babies, and maybe I would never need it, but I considered it was better to be prepared for the rigors of motherhood than adopt a feminist stance from girlhood, only to find I wanted a baby later and was totally unprepared.

This was the exercise: With both feet flat on the floor, let yourself down into a deep squat, and begin to walk across the room, down the steps and all around the lawn.

I did it for two weeks, then somehow forgot all about it.

My Reading

I had read *Lorna Doone, Black Beauty, Seven Little Australians, An Old-fashioned Girl, Little Women, In Regions of Perpetual Snow, The Swiss Family Robinson, Robinson Crusoe, The Water Babies, The Black Cloud, The Weapon Shops of Isher, David Copperfield* and lots of Dickens, *The Soten Monoplane, The Magic Pudding,* eighteen Charlie Brown books, Conan Doyle, twenty-two *How and Why* books, my *Children's Encyclopaedia,* the *Encyclopaedia of Wild Life, Lamb's Tales,* by the time I was ten.

It's hard to describe the reading of my eleventh and twelfth years, since I read again and again the books I liked, and my new reading was mainly science fiction, together with the novels that my father had in his shelves. And school library books, of course, with lots of writers of my own country, because we had to do a certain number of Australian books for our Library mark.

Also I began to take an interest in father's newspaper and his regular magazines. From them I learned, little by little, that we in Australia are not as distant as we think from the rage of history.

English Expression: How Women Became Weaker Than the Enemy, by Alethea Hunt

Before the seven sages, some women were weak and some strong, some men were strong and some weak, some women as big as men and some men small as women.

And men said, "These creatures think they're the bosses and indispensable and they try all the time to tell us we need sex and babies. They grab the lead every time they're given half a chance. We can't have proper respect and tradition and precedent while they have a big voice in our affairs. We need a division between us."

And other men said, "What is the answer to this problem of the equality of women?"

And one of the smaller ones said, "Specialization."

And the rest said, "What's that, Shrimp?"

And the smaller man said, "Let us erect a barrier between men and women. Let us go for small women, let us choose hairless women" (for in those days men and women were equally hairy)—"and we will breed specialization, for they will stay here and have babies and we will stand apart and go and hunt, and make weapons, and return with large food, and they will stay and work round the camp in their spare time from feeding the children, and we will praise their differences and their hairlessness. And we will create Beauty."

"What's that?" other men said.

"That's the difference between us. We will breed for it, and the big women that hit me and kick me will be tamed by having no mates, and they will be ashamed, and will no longer be competition for you big ones and we will arrange the daily affairs of the tribe among ourselves, without them, and us smaller men will do as you say and the women will do as we all say."

The big men saw the advantage of this, and the small men saw that even they would have some people under them, and everyone agreed. And women became smaller and hairless and "beautiful" and rituals started and legend and precedent and laws and religion. And they called it a step on the way to civilization.

The teachers passed this effort round to each other, and praised me. It got into the school magazine.

It's very pleasant to be praised, and there's something extra special about feeling that you can do things better than others can.

Males

Their hands are quite different from ours, I've noticed. Some I like the look of, being clean and large and powerful in appearance, but the ones that I suspect are really the most powerful, the thick ones with big veins and no grace, I don't like at all.

Still, I suppose women have always said that they must accept men as they are, and habit is strong. Either accept them or ignore them, I'm not sure which I mean.

And their limbs . . . And the hairiness . . .

I don't know if ever I'll be able to accept them.

Sometimes when I'm thinking of these differences and resenting them; and of the incomprehensibility of males as a whole, I think: if only I were a long, fierce snake, living a private life on the edge between bush and desert, and my world plain to me and not puzzling at all.

Palpable Eyes

Today I found what I've thought for a long time: I'm a better climber than any of the boys round here. I don't mean I can climb higher, because some of the small boys can get up on branches much too thin for me. I mean I can climb quicker, and I can climb carrying a weight.

They wouldn't have let me play with them, but since they were building a tree house and they had to get up some rolls of old carpet to put on the floor and I volunteered to do it, they let me. When I had taken up all the things, I went on up to the top of the tree, taking with me a piece of colored cloth. I tied the cloth to the last branch that went straight up, as a flag for them. They didn't say much when I got down, and I could feel the antagonism on the back of my neck and down my spine.

Incidentally, why do they take such an interest in looking up my legs? I could understand a glance as natural curiosity, but they dropped everything to look, all the time I was up the tree. I had pants on. There was nothing to see. Are they simply of low intelligence, that their attention can be fixed on something they can neither see nor do anything about even if they could?

Shortly after, a short active boy climbed carefully up and moved the flag a meter higher. They watched me when I left; I could feel their eyes.

There Was an Old Bayard Taylor Translation

There was an old Bayard Taylor translation of *Faust Part I* at one end of father's bookshelves, wedged between *Good Housekeeping* and *The Idiot*. From its small pages and tiny printing I learned a lesson Goethe didn't intend.

Faust was given supernatural powers, with one condition attached to the bargain. What did he do with the gift of supernatural powers? He gave some accidental acquaintances free wine, conjured music from nothing, had a barrel fly through the air, made flames appear: party tricks.

Even Frankenstein used the dead to raise the dead and bring them to life; to construct new life, instead of trying to discover the secret of invisibility. Dracula wanted long life with no dying and used the powers of darkness to enslave the living, but at least he was desperate and trying to survive.

To Alethea Hunt, Faust was a fraud. Tricks, bargains, supernatural help don't add up to human greatness. I wanted to read of greatness. In that moment I felt greatness meant that life is not enough.

I put the book down.

I was standing, I think, in my usual spellbound fashion, eyes wide open, mouth slightly open, looking out of our large front window, and mother said, as she unfailingly did when she saw me like this, "Dreamer. Always dreaming. What are you dreaming about now? Stop dreaming. Get and do something useful." And she went back to her writing, with complete absorption.

She didn't know that when I was like that the world stopped. She didn't know that my eyes were wide open and motionless because the narrow cone of the world that was in my field of vision was melting and evaporating; the evaporating parts rising as a sort of gas labeled with the names of the things they had been, and wafting toward me and entering me; and the melting objects came as fluid and entered directly into some part of me that conducted them right to my innermost parts. Where I would never lose them, always remember their taste. (But what would happen to my memories when I died?)

As for the people I happened to be looking at when such spells came over me, I am convinced that the "them" I received in those moments was the essence of the persons, an essence perhaps unknown to any other persons, and not well known to themselves.

Father walked in the back door. I picked up *Faust* again. I couldn't shake off my trance-like state and didn't feel like explanations. It was an effort to hold the book, but I held it before me, not seeing it.

"That's a book, darling," he said.

I must have looked stupid, to him. I hadn't opened it. He looked at the spine.

"Ah, Faust," he said approvingly. And launched into a speech. Just what I needed.

"Immortality, or life after the ending of the world, began in man's mind as an ambition, a greed, a craving for more, after man invented weapons and gradually realized the difference between him and animals in general, and after he spoke a language that he found was growing, and could say much more than animals could say to one another."

He always forgot birds. "And birds," he added. Fish never got a mention.

"And feeling so superior. So superior." And he stopped, thinking. It was one of father's beliefs that humans weren't so superior.

I still couldn't move. I clutched *Faust* out before me, my eyes locked open. How could he? He thought *Faust* was about immortality: I thought it was about power. If only he'd stayed outside. I wanted to experience to the full my apprehension of the twin trees in our front yard near the letterbox; their soft bark, small leaves, what it must be like to stand there day and night, in all weathers, helpless to avoid insects, birds, humans; to be there, there, until death.

Yes, I was right: just to live is not enough.

Mister Small

The man who delivered milk in our street was known for his cannon. Every week he filed it down where it emerged from his lower chest, so he wouldn't have so much weight to carry. Plenty of people encouraged him to let it grow, but he steadfastly refused, he cared nothing for the foundry date of the cannon or its history. Historians were always trying to arrange for his expenses and wages to be paid while the cannon grew out of him; they hated the idea that they would never see the inscription on its manufacturing plate. But he didn't like the idea that a ton of cannon might one day be protruding from him, or that he might be stuck on the end of it. He thought of the cannon as his, not as belonging to history.

The Smalls owned dairies once in eight suburbs, and since the value of land increased, they had released five of them to development; our milkman saw himself as a milkman for the rest of his life, and didn't want to retire. He took to bringing sons and nephews along with him, riding shotgun to guard against academic kidnap, but the historians made no illegal attempts on his freedom.

Often I was tempted to get up early and wait for him one rainy, stormy day and call out, "What about the lightning?" and really scare him. But when it came to the point I didn't, I practically always had to be woken up by father (still warm from their bed).

My mother loved.

All sorts of mothers are remembered for all sorts of crazy things. Some grown men are proud of the way Mum used to knock them from one end of the house to the other.

"Had a punch like Les Darcy. Lifted me off the ground," they'll say.

Some mothers talk all day, some work like Trojans, some drink or play up or dream. My mother loved. She loved everything. She told me so.

When my mother loved me; you know, turned the love-ray on me; I could go missing from it and the love didn't miss me; she didn't miss me; the love poured out whatever I did, wherever I went. It was as if once the love had been started, I wasn't necessary.

What did she love? Everything.

Did she love rocks and birds and dead wood and plastic? She did. Did she love sunshine and rain, war and peace, sickness and health? Yes.

She could be hungry, deprived, abused, unloved, but still she loved.

Whom did she love? Everyone.

How can there exist in our world someone who can love everyone and everything?

Did she love Clag paste, IXL jam, Twinings tea, saucepans and socks? Yes.

Did she love wooden desks, leaves of trees, concrete steps, electricity wires, old newspapers, typewriter covers, string bags, camera tripods, tubes of plastic glue, large paper bags, colored umbrellas, roomy slacks, high shoes, birdlime-spattered statues, department stores, the grey timber of wharves, the little waves at the top of the tide?

She loved all these. And more than these, her love went through obstructions, rayed out and embraced all that was, all that had existence.

She told me so.

I saw no sign of this great love. No sign, that is, in action; no practical sign. The nuts and bolts area of love was, you might say, not greatly to the fore.

I don't think she loved father, though he loved her. (No one had ever treated father badly, so I suppose it was easy for him to treat mother well.)

(I remember once he was referring with affection to something she said years before.

"But don't you remember? You said—'You're the only man I ever knew that could run to four in an hour—'" Four what? They didn't say.

"I was joking," mother said shortly.

"But don't you remember?"

"No."

"You really don't?"

"It didn't happen," said mother, putting an end to talk.)

Yet she loved *me* when I was small. I have a wealth of mother-memories; she was round me, over me, everywhere there was her smile, her face, huge on my horizon, noting everything I did, touching and teaching me continually.

When did she do her notes when I was a baby? That's a question.

It must be because of what she did once, that I grew up feeling that mother *was* love. How then, at twelve, could I say that I saw not the slightest sign of her great capacity for love? The very word love in connection with her was continually reinforced by father; he was the one who said the word. All my mother had left of this great love was the look she turned on you. There was no mistaking love in her great dark eyes as they rounded, fixing on you, and the gleam of reflected light on her iris fixed you—more, even than her velvet black pupils did—and somehow something in you was sucked toward her, toward the depths in those eyes, and you felt the first enveloping swirls of the power she had to project the feeling of love.

I suppose that *could* be one of the nuts and bolts of love. Why am I so hard on her?

The Fat Lady's Story

When she was on the lavatory I picked up one of the notes that snowed her table, and returned it later.

Fat Lady in George Street. 1.51 pm

Paddles. (then a gap) fatty approaches. Flapping legs all of a piece with stubby feet. Black coat, white fatshoes, balding. To have less. Hairy cover of the head. Head to foot ____ shortly, receding feet, receding life, hair energy, breath, all receding. Baptist church with brick fence ____ as it always did. Gestetner fiercens in the sun, fire texture bricks heating towards the north. ____ s northern, lady southens in a shallow curve. Do you or I or anyone know what makes the gooseflesh southward go? Those fat feet have plunked down one after the other chasing kids and grabbing pots boiling over. All for others. Yet if they're kids and family, it's not so much others. And if it's sick neighbors it's not others or work for any others it's not others. Others are not others. There are no people who can be thought of as others. All people are us. This fat woman my sister. The warm fence an old friend. The plaque outside Gestetner building a memorial to one of my brothers in bronze. The sun himself brought life to all of us. Dear dear sun. Lovely ugly shoes that carry cracked feet hurrying to serve others. They should be kissed. Where they slop over the edge of her shoes.

The paper was yellowed like old newspaper. There was nothing to tell what year it was. The dashes were bits of words I couldn't make out. It may have been last week or years ago when she, too, was twelve. I have no explanation. I cannot understand my mother.

My father had few close friends. But now and then he would meet people who obviously wanted to make friends, and, unaccountably, he would be the one to forget to return a call.

I tackled him about it.

"I cannot allow myself to stay in the company of people from whom I can get nothing," he said.

Why not? He was an actor, not a banker, accountant, businessman.

"My hold on my own identity is so loose, so slippery—and I don't really know what it is I am holding—that I feel if people get too close to me I may somehow melt into them or become them in some way so that I, whoever I am, may disappear. If my image of them gets too near me, if it takes up too much of my mental screen, I fear that my own outlines may blur and I won't know where I am."

The sincerity in his voice had to satisfy me. I don't understand father all that well. I went out into the garden and found a ladybird on a leaf of the jasmine.

> *Ladybird ladybird, fly away home*
> *Your house is on fire, your children are gone.*

The sun felt faintly friendly. What did father ever actually *get* from other people? He never seemed to suffer from the trivial restlessness other husbands showed, but perhaps he had a deep need for change—having learned this house, this wife, this situation so thoroughly that it began to seem not quite true—and something was blocking him, something inside him.

Why Do Men Like Girls?

I asked my mother why men liked girls, at a time when I was sure she wasn't thinking of her notes.

When I was a year or two younger the stock answer seemed to be that they're pretty, or strong, or good at lessons or they speak nicely, answers tailored to remedy specific disabilities in the child asking the question.

But for some time I'd had an agreement—not *exactly* that, since it was something *I'd* laid down: whether she would agree to it was another matter—that she would answer me as if I wasn't a child.

She looked at me, turning her head slowly in my direction, picking me up in her visual field while her head was still turned well away and keeping her eyes glued on my face while her head completed its arc toward me. It was an uncanny performance; rather the sort of skill you would expect in good sportspeople, used to keeping their eyes on the ball, or good hunters keeping their eyes on the quarry.

"It's something unexplainable."

I waited. So did she.

"That isn't much, is it?" I said.

"It's their one great disadvantage."

I could see there could be disadvantages in liking.

"It's their hormones," she added.

Each time, between each oracular sentence, a pause.

"It's a trap females lay. Like perfume, or a trail of goodies."

Another pause. Any talk from me, would have given her an excuse to pick on something I said, and sidetrack me.

"Because they're so bloody stupid," impatiently, and she turned away to her writing.

I went away to my room to practice saying No to mean Yes, as Aysha Kemal said *she* did.

I didn't have my heart in it: I was too much caught up in why men liked girls.

Why did the pelican stand on one leg?

Rosemary McDevitt

As we started to bud in the region of the chest and some began to bear a different fruit elsewhere every four weeks, the boys seemed

195

to want more than ever to play with us in the playground. They had always run around corners and tried to push us over or generally thump us, but now the out-of-class activities were more violent. Nothing they did hurt me. I was stronger than most of the boys, and much bigger.

Rosemary would never join in. One single touch up the leg would give her hysterics.

She was pretty, attractive, intelligent. When one boy ran up behind her in the paddock on the way home from school and lifted the back of her school skirt high up her back, she reared like a horse, sprang into the air, and when she hit the ground she broke her arm.

She didn't know it was broken until several days later, when the swelling didn't go down. Her parents didn't like X-rays, so she wasn't sent for one straight away.

Other times she dislocated her shoulder and chipped her right elbow in violent reactions from boys putting their hands up her dress when she wasn't expecting it, or reaching up softly and tugging at her pants, or brushing against her in the crowded playground and getting a poor little nipple between finger and thumb.

Rosemary kept up a sort of allegiance to an honorable way of behaving. She never told on the boys, just blew up internally, and fell over or banged against something.

Her reactions were so exaggerated a copy of ours that we enjoyed having her with us. She made us feel better about the sudden alarm of feeling the pencil stuck up between the cheeks of our bottoms from between the slats of our chairs.

The boys went to great lengths to get other kids blamed. One had an extended radio aerial so he could reach Rosemary from several desks away. Marie-Louise gave her hell with bits of string dangling softly on her legs.

She was so sensitive she felt the fingers of the sun, and the wind's cool lips.

For fun we ganged up on Rosemary one day. I grabbed her from behind, she couldn't move. Sherry Porter grabbed her legs, Serena Small lifted her skirt. Griselda Cadbury and Gloriana Doig approached Rosemary's thighs with slow fingers.

I say approached, for Rosemary's fright was mostly in the anticipation.

Rosemary screamed. We gagged her. Raina White held the gag in and the noise was reduced.

Griselda and Gloriana gave her the tickles from the backs of her ankles up to her bottom seam—it was a bluish pink with small flowers embroidered on the edges.

Would she come? Would she merely go off her head?

It was the last time we ganged up on Rosemary. She slumped, and we couldn't bring her round. We laid her down, arranged her uniform and left. She didn't report us.

Her full name was Rosemary Simone McDevitt. I looked it up in father's book of names. Rosemary means Mary's Rose. Simone means Heard by the Lord. In protecting her rose she certainly could have been, if we hadn't gagged her. He might have told her what McDevitt means.

Certainly her future was ahead, waiting for her to catch up; it spoke the language of pain.

Empty Bodies

The antiwork lobby that tried in class to muck up the whole operation were the ones that got nothing out of the system; no success, no pats on the head, no prizes. They reminded me of the old peasants in English history that touched the forelock and said:

> Lord bless the squire and his relations
> And keep us in our proper stations;

except they were trying to ensure that none of the rest of us got above *our* proper stations. (No one told me this; it's my own opinion, so don't blame father: education is training to win, to leave the losers behind.)

> Q: What gets bigger the more you take from it?
> A: A hole in the ground.

197

Ignorance does, too.

Sometimes I imagined I was hundreds of meters high in the air, looking down; all I could see moving were the bodies of school-children walking in the grounds: empty bodies.

The Tit Clash

The tit clash was a horrifying invasion of privacy; it was a sudden demoralization, a personal shock; a triumph of male over female.

They had to get their arms wide and bring their hands together quickly enough to take the girl by surprise, on the outside of the left and right breasts. In the same movement you clashed them together, trying to get the nipples to meet.

In a good tit clash the nipples never met: instead, there was a satisfying sound of flesh, the inside flesh of each breast clashing together. So there were three sounds:

1. The sound of the hands on the outer edges of the breasts.
2. The sound of the tit clash.
3. The sound of the outbreath of air from the victim's lungs.

We were aged twelve, in our group; we had no tits to speak of. Just the same, boys came round and tried to do it to us. Bigger boys looked down on us younger girls and wouldn't be seen dead trying to give our little pimples a tit clash, but boys in first and second year attempted the impossible.

For such imps, there was a range of reprisals. Bear in mind that while they were tit clashing their hands were together and in front of them—their sides and lower fronts were completely unprotected. You should have seen them spring back in fear when the area round their penis was attacked, and the little treasure bag in which they carried, as in a mobile factory, their dubious gifts to the future.

The One Tit Crunch

The one tit crunch was more of a hit and run attack. They kept the palm of one hand flat and crunched one breast quick against the rib cage. It was less spectacular than the tit clash, but more painful.

I do not relate these clashes and crunches as a spectator; I was both cruncher and clasher, though I didn't invent the game.

Boys and girls could play, it made you wary and prepared to defend yourself. Whoever stopped and talked to you, even if only to jeer or stir you up, was a likely attacker, or recipient, of a tit clash or a one tit crunch. If it was a male person, you were under immediate threat because of your possession of female sex organs. This threat was better countered first than dumbly awaited.

> *How many balls of string*
> *Does it take*
> *To reach the moon?*

I guess it depends on how big those balls are.

Pistol Shots

Marie-Louise Fienberg was her full name. Like the rest, we were sometimes whispering together, friends for a day, and sometimes talking about each other, apart in different groups: enemies for a day. She cared for nobody and nothing, and I admired her.

In our school play, *The Duel*, she had to pause, listen, and say "Hark, I hear the pistol shots." She rehearsed unwillingly and always in a dead voice, but Plumpton, the teacher, said that would have to do.

On the night, Marie-Louise struck a pose, listened, and declaimed loudly, "Hark, I hear the shostal pits." That was wrong. Her mouth formed "shit." Her face screwed up, remembering. She remembered all right: she was acting. Spoiling the play.

"Hark, I hear the shistal pots."

Audibly she said, "Oh Christ."

She gave it a third try, and roared, "Hark, I hear the postal shits!"

Laughter filled the hall.

The failed actress waited for a break in the noise and said clearly, "Oh fuck it," and paused dramatically. "Ladies and gentlemen, this is my exit, and the end of my stage career." And walked off stage and down to where her parents sat. They tried to get her to go away, out of sight, but she wouldn't. She beamed and pointed at her Mum and Dad as if to say "I'm with them." Nothing embarrassed Marie-Louise.

Her Dad, Ezra Fienberg the newsagent, had the wound of a bullet below his right shoulder, a bullet wound that didn't heal. The sign of its going in was plain, but there was no place to show where it came out. No X-ray plate showed the bullet, though he'd had more than half a dozen done.

Was it made of plastic? people said. They knew from recent wars that plastic fragments don't show on X-rays.

No, there was no plastic bullet in there, just an inward-lipped hole that didn't bleed.

He was proud of it, and it brought business his way. He had a double reason for pleasure. I daresay it was one of the peculiarities of our suburb that he didn't say how the hole was made, and no one asked. Everyone was different, everyone was separate; there was no community shoulder to cry on.

The Great Banded Bosom-Fly

Outside our classroom the hill sloped down toward Hunter's Creek. Slim trees stood straight, birds sang loudly. We watched out the windows when we could. Some birds were bullies, some sneak thieves, some tried to boss the others, but couldn't get them to obey.

Playtime, lunchtime, and sometimes for lessons we sat outside. Delivery men came into the school in their handy, well-used and often grimy vehicles. We—around eight of us in our gang—used to wonder aloud about the equipment they carried under the zips of their trousers. Were they just as handy, well-used and grimy as their vehicles?

For most of us it wasn't till a year or two later that we realized what care they took with their personal equipment; just how clean, pink, scrubbed and shiny—on the horn—they really were. Well-used, too. *And* handy.

Let us return to our lessons in the lovely shade of the smooth-barked erect eucalypts that mostly had only a small crown of foliage above all that length of smooth pale trunk.

Marie-Louise is drawing. I am beginning the set essay, "Tigers of the Sea."

I glanced across at her work. She drew two large breasts that sprouted wings and trailed a thick body crossed laterally with stripes, like a hornet. Underneath she wrote, "The Great Banded Bosom-Fly."

"What about 'Tigers of the Sea'?" I said. She was supposed to do the essay too. "You pick *your* fucking nose, I'll pick mine," she said rudely. . . . *fucking* nose?

Plumpton cheered up when she saw my essay. She put it aside to read to the class. Leafing though the pile she passed the bosom-fly, unsigned, and came to Marie-Louise's "Tigers of the Sea." We were reading something while the teacher looked through the essays. As I watched her face I knew ML had done it again. We called her ML to save time.

"Do you really think, Fienberg, that any body of sailors that ever inhabited the globe and sailed the seven seas could possibly fight—never mind fight well, but fight at all—with names on the bows of their boats—"

"Ships," corrected Fienberg.

"Ships, then, and on their lifeboats and equipment—"

"Get to the point, Plumpton."

"Respect, Fienberg. *Mrs.* Plumpton."

"Never mind the self-pity. Call me *Miss* Fienberg."

"All right, Marie-Louise. All right. You tell me how men could fight for their country in ships with names like Vulnerable, Movable, Vincible, Domitable, Fatigable? And this? The frigate Pitiful!"

"Frigate, yes," repeated ML.

"Frigate indeed," added Plumpton. "Well, Miss Admiral Fienberg?"

"Think back a bit, my dear respected Mrs. Plumpton. I wouldn't lay this on you without good historical backing. Remember the Old Contemptibles?"

She remembered. The class waited, yawning delicately on the brink of sleep.

"Their enemies christened them that. And they wore it. Insisted on it. Did they fight lousy?"

"Lousily. It's an adverb."

"Same thing. So why shouldn't sailors have a sense of humor?"

"Don't be impertinent."

"I think it's pertinent," said ML. Plumpton was pleased she knew the word.

Plumpton looked back at ML's essay.

"You have imagination, Fienberg. Ships that move on the sea, over it, under it. You can't have things like that."

"The creatives put imagination into words; scientists then know what to invent. Buck Rogers . . . Leonardo."

Plumpton screwed her nose. "Straight off the sci-fi shows, Fienberg. But these places: Tokyo, Alabama; Budapest, Illinois; Berlin, Saskatchewan. Are you making fun of the Americans again? And I suppose this is yours too?" She held up the bosom-fly. "May I ask what this is?

"The great banded bosom-fly," orated ML. Plumpton showed it round.

"Go on, Fienberg. Explain. We'll wait."

Marie-Louise began to sing:

> *"Jesu lover of my soul,*
> *Let me to thy bosom-fly."*

"That'll do, Fienberg. We get the idea."

She liked Marie-Louise. Liked her a lot. Often we noticed her looking at ML in the playground, if you can imagine a wistfully predatory look

I can.

One Good Feature

None of the rest of us thought it was much of a poem, but the English master, Mister Jagarnath, had a very high opinion of it, and put it in the school magazine.

Here it is:

I am the sister of a motor mechanic.
I am the daughter of a bush carpenter.
Maybe I will marry a plumber
And be the mother of a civil engineer.

When the magazine came out, with the poem proudly at the bottom of a page on the basketball team, she bore her poem proudly home and showed it to the Lutherburrow family, several of whom could read.

The poems *we* wrote were far more inwardly directed.

Lil had one good feature. Her fingers, from where they joined her hand, down to the nails, were a milky color tinged with pink. But already the dark hairs were hinting on the backs of the third joints, as they were apparent on her forearms and shouting on her shanks, between ankle and calf. I hoped she would keep one good feature when she was grown-up and hairy.

The Thoughts of Mukami

Zekia Mukami played soccer in one of the school teams, and cricket in summer, and had no fights in the playground; he was aloof, self-possessed and looked superior.

One day his superior expression cracked, and his aloofness was abandoned and the anger in him came out with a rush. It was after the social science class; we had been discussing antidiscrimination laws of the past.

"You can't see you are insulting the people you make laws to protect!" he shouted in the playground at a group of us, as if history were in the present tense.

"You are saying they're helpless! But I tell you this: the black races have no intention of passing antidiscrimination laws to protect whites when they get in front of the whites! There are no gentlemanly feelings then! When the black races hold the whip firmly, they will give it to the inferior whites, I can tell you. One day, my father says, the white man will be the colored world's Jew! Whites are animals, they are degenerate, my father says!"

We didn't know what to say. I'd heard father talk of the recurring speculation about the white races being overwhelmed by the colored, and the colored having no love for the white, and when I mentioned it to him that evening, he said, "The world's Jew, eh?" And nodded his head, but didn't say any more. I guess he was getting his opinions in order, or thinking about it.

Zekia Mukami hated us. For him, history wasn't past at all: the hundreds of years of crimes against blacks were against him, and they were now. The rage of history was on our doorstep.

Zekia was a very good boxer. I was one of four girls who were allowed to box at school, but although we sometimes fought boys, we didn't box with Zekia.

Nipple-Napping

It wasn't a special game like the one tit crunch or the tit clash— anyone did it, including much bigger girls; especially the gang-girls of year eleven and year twelve, big-thighed bruisers who intimidated shopkeepers and received warnings from the police not to go round in large groups on late-shopping nights.

Anyone could be a nipple-napper. You simply made a sudden grab for the edge of the breast, and since the fashions made the nipple conspicuous, it was rarely that you grabbed the wrong place. The best method of escape was movement. If you saw a female walking along and suddenly making a waltz step sideways, you could bet she'd evaded a nipple-napper.

It wasn't completely one-sided: we did the same to boys. Theirs were harder to grab hold of.

One of the boys that gave the best reaction to nipple-napping was Anthony Yuen.

His nipple was hard to find for the first two terms of high school, but it grew with constant attention, and became as big and outstanding as most of the girls'. He squawked every time, and went round clutching it, swollen and painful.

Anthony had deer-like features. A few meters away, he would turn his head, and stay still, not so much watching you, as regarding. His thin shanks narrowed to fine ankles. He would stand still, for a long time perfectly still, then canter off, gently, lightly, a few meters, then if any threat or alarm disturbed him he was off like a shot, lightly, on his toes, his legs twinkling as if they had no weight. Or he would stop, and turn again, twitch his ears together, and sometimes one at a time, then if any nipple-napper appeared, he broke into an immediate gallop. He would dash right on into the playing field until he was nearly a hundred meters away, then partly turn, watching, perfectly still again, ready for flight.

If he'd been nipple-napped, he would be holding his chest with one narrow hand that was as close to the fine bones of a paw as you'd want to see.

Always the one nipple, the left one. The big one.

I could make him run just by looking at it hard.

Buck was our name for him. His parents thought of him as Anthony, which was absurd.

Once I saw him backed against a wall. His eyes were stark, but something looked out. Something; and I had thought that place was empty.

Coming Ready or Not

Fulvia Strickland had an older sister and knew more than we did about boys. We gathered round in the playground, eager to learn.

"When they're about to blow," Fulvia told us, "that's when you've got the power. They know if you wriggle free or pull away they get nothing. But that's when you're liable to get hurt. They hang on real tight so you can't dislodge 'em. Animal reflex."

"How can you tell when it's happening?"

"They start to get very sincere—facial expression, hard muscles, more powerful thrusts—"

"What sort of thrusts?"

"Back and forward. They're not going anywhere, but they go back nearly to take it out, then jam it in as far as it will go."

"But their bones must stop it—"

"Naturally. There's nowhere to go, but they take it very seriously. Ever seen dogs?"

"Yes, horses too," I said. "But it never seems to take long."

"Listen, kid." She was forgetting we were the same age. "Some of the older ones, they know how to hold it, they'll stay in all day. The only way to get round it is to relax, but even then your skin gets so tired of being jammed between their bone and yours that you wish you had a gun to put 'em out of their misery. Say, that *would* be an experience!" She was lost briefly in her own dreams, and we looked at each other, and away.

We all knew of Stuart Regan after school beating the other boys in a race to get it to come, and I looked at the faces of the other girls. Were they scared? Were they thinking privately that if they got part of a boy in they could control the rest of him, and wondering if it was true? And were they wondering if it was true that some could shoot it so hard that you could feel it hit the sides, or bounce off the back wall?

The Social Science Class
"Australia has an empty belly," said jolly Mister Chandragar. "Look at the map and you will see that the ocean and the coastal strip contain emptiness. That is the first impression Australia makes. When you get to know it, it is strange how that motif repeats itself. No ghosts, all is plain and above-board, you see. Not even a bunyip. . . ."

He began to laugh.

"Supposed to be a bunyip!" he spluttered over a pile of our exercise books. "A bunyip."

"And what happens?" he asked rhetorically.

"No blooming bunyip!" he squealed. For some minutes he was out of action.

We didn't understand why he laughed but we knew he was laughing at us. Whatever emptiness the land had, we were born to: we shared it.

It was soon the end of the period, and when the siren went we rushed for the door, and he gathered up his papers and things, but couldn't resist shouting after us, "Not even a blooming haunted house! No jolly bunyip! No jolly ghosts! Jolly nothing!"

The next time we had Mister Chandragar he was more serious. He was still on his favorite topic, though, and we had to wear it.

"Australia does as the world does, it sits on the comfortable coast of life, where its settled nature is steeped in the past. The future is the greatest problem. The future is at the center of Australia's problems."

It made a big impression on me, for of all things the future was the most mysterious, the most inviting. And the idea of a useless existence, dragging on till I was old and worn out, repugnant as it was to me, seemed to apply to my country as well. What a future it would be for the land of my birth if Frees and Servants of Society could both be living their lives so that no day is futile and no hour bored!

The Apple Time Bomb

On the way home from school my case was light, and I felt like running. As I passed the shops at a run I lifted an apple from a stand outside the greengrocer's shop and kept going. A few dogs came out to bark at me when I went past their houses, but these encounters came to nothing.

I showed it to my father.

"Why a Democrat?" he said. "You'll have a mouth full of skin—in your teeth, everywhere. They're only good for transporting. They're good travelers, they're so tough."

I put it in a drawer where some of my winter things were kept. The thing about winter clothes is that a lot of them never get worn. You always think you're going to need warm things in the cold weather, but you never do. There might be a few cold days, but that's about it.

I put the apple at the back of the drawer and forgot it. As I got into bed it occurred to me that no one even saw me take it. But lying there waiting for sleep to come I thought: some people are ordinary and have ordinary desires and ordinary rights, but the extraordinary have a right to transgress with impunity.

That wiped the apple off my conscience as if it had never been.

Dizzy

We had a craze for a while, us girls, saying "I love you" to each other as if we were beginning a romance. From there it developed into saying "I love you" in as many different ways as we could think of.

We didn't necessarily do it with the idea of practicing for males later on. Though I daresay it would come in handy, because though we expected nothing much from them, they, romantic creatures, expected of us something comparable to what they saw on their screens and in their magazines, the poses and mouthings of trained actors.

I could say "I love you" hatefully, casually, sincerely, belligerently, laughingly, at the top of my voice, commercially, stupidly, in a sneaky whisper, derisively, lovingly, commandingly.

Has anyone said to you: "I love you," commandingly?

Another thing we did was look in each other's eyes for as long as we could, and no wavering, then when you got dizzy with keeping it up for minutes and minutes, you said: "I love you!" This combination of dizziness and emotional declaration was overpowering, and once Angelika Wiedemann and Jessica Spruiyt nearly fainted doing it.

Yet another game within our group was to ignore boys; a later variation was: first one to show she likes a boy is out.

> *What are big boys made of?*
> *Dead dogs' guts and dead cats' eyes*
> *Scab and pus custard*
> *Green snot pies.*

Why Do Fish Swim in the Sea?

"Why do plants live?" I asked my father.

He looked at me, wanting to get on with reading a play he'd love to have acted in, but not wanting to refuse his daughter.

"You've done biology. Tell me why they live."

He'd misunderstood.

"I mean, they don't go anywhere, do they? If they're alive in some garden of eden and there's no one there to pick the fruit, what do they do with it? A tree doesn't eat the fruit itself."

"I think I know what you mean. But you're thinking from within your present circumstances. You're in a human-centered world; you think the trees are too."

"Yes, but they were here before man. What did they do with their fruit? What did it do for them? I mean, what did it actually do?"

"Put seeds back into the ground, darling."

Oh. What an idiot I was. But what about the flesh of the apple? Double idiot. Of course, the flesh of the apple was nothing to the tree; it was just the seed-case. We merely happened to find it delicious.

"Didn't they give you that in biology?"

"I remember now. Seed-cases. It just didn't make an impression then, until I thought of it myself. When I'm told, things a᷊ further away than if I see and feel them."

But if that was the case with apples and plums and tʰ what about us? Was there no actual purpose in the outer us? Was it all just a seed-case to drop seeds into the ground? Were we all here just in order to go on being here?

The phone rang. It was Rosemary. The wandering crowd had been up her street, and I had to listen for twenty minutes solid. After being awful to her at school, I felt I owed her something.

Stacks on the Mill

One mad day in spring someone yelled "Stacks on the mill!" Six or seven kids had been playing some game and had all fallen over in a heap, laughing helplessly. "Stacks on the mill!" The yell was taken up. Kids swarmed to the spot. Hundreds. "More on still!" And the heap grew rapidly, spreading wide, and kids climbed on kids, were pushed over, and more came for the magic moment of standing upright on all those bodies, to call: "I'm the king of the castle! And you're the dirty rascals!"

The teachers had to pull the top ones off to rescue the kids on the bottom of the stack. We didn't mean it to get savage, it just turned out that way. I know when I ran in and jumped from about three meters onto the backs below me I felt a great joy, a sort of jaw-firming joy, as my feet landed on flesh, and I took care to press down as hard as I could, taking my eyes off just exactly who it was down there under me—I didn't want to know—but trying to be heavier than I was to put more pressure on the anonymous squodge that was rightly beneath me.

It was an exhilarating feeling, one that you allow yourself rarely and only a bit at a time, rationing it. It was a recognizable me enjoying the oppression I was part of, but I had stripped away other parts of me that normally didn't let me do this. But it was me all right.

My mouth was smaller and tighter, my eyes squenched up so as only to see that object I had in view, the backs and awkwardly crushed legs and arms beneath me. That was it: beneath me!

If I could, I would in that moment have crushed those other stupidly existing semihumans to a porridge.

For one second of a fearful joy or escape from pain
I'd smash them down and if they rose I'd smash again.

The teachers came in a body, making a concerted rush to this heap of writhing animals. I was still pulling others down on me to make more weight for those beneath when the teachers were pulling us off. Miss Goff and I had a tugging match with Lewis Manotta. I had his arm. She won, but only because Mister Sanders came and pressed a knuckle into the back of my hand, on the nerve.

Inflatable Man

In October the man came again from the river.

Just as before he came up on the grass paddock and made his way slowly up to the road, where dogs barked at him. They were sleepy dogs, and there were plenty of children around, since it was Saturday morning, to take their attention and wake them at odd times with play and yelling, so the man didn't get bitten.

I watched as he got to the road, looked back at the river, then walked slowly along Heisenberg Close on his way to the sports oval on the hill. When he stood on the eastern end of the playing fields near the creek, he took out something to eat and while he was chewing, a blow-up object came from him. Don't ask me where, none of us knew what he looked like close up. (There were stories of kids going to look at him, who came back saying that when they got where they thought they could see him he was still as far away as he had been in the first place.)

A chair grew out, and inflated. A small table came. Then a continuous sheet, which he took with him as he walked round in a circle and let fall to the grass where it stuck. It then became a tent that he zipped from the top down to the grass level. A door was set in, with a small handle.

I went around the street and looked at his tent from several points. Perhaps it was true that it looked the same from any angle, but there was a sort of pushing-you-away feeling about the whole thing that killed your curiosity. Persistence died when you got too close. I gave it up, and went home, accompanied by a peculiar feeling that somehow it was good to go away. As if something spoke directly into my mind, bypassing eyes and ears.

Do you ever have the feeling that the ground is a thin shell, with caverns below?

The Vulva Surprised

Under her arms Rosemary McDevitt developed a tender spot. I found out about it when I grabbed her. (Sometimes I couldn't resist grabbing her: she was so vulnerable.) I registered the soft squashy thing my fingers encountered under her school tunic.

I spoke to her after school.

"Rosemary." I should have asked her if she forgave us. She needed to think you had some intellectual appreciation of your aggressor relationship with her.

"Those funny things under your arms." This gave her as great a shock as touching her. She ran.

I caught her easily and twined my fingers in the loose of her tunic behind the right shoulder. She struggled, but with that hold I could control her easily.

She wouldn't cooperate, no matter what I said, so I took matters into my own hands and felt all round under her weak arms. I wasn't wrong. There it was under one arm, and under the other. Two soft squashy places. I pressed inward, she choked back her scream, in more terror, I think, of my imminent discovery than of the violence on her.

The feel of the thing was familiar. I grabbed her shoulder, turned her back to me, lifted one arm into the air and looked down her short sleeve. Sitting sleepily down there in her armpit was a small vulva. It smelled of sweat.

"Don't tell anyone," pleaded Rosemary, when she could speak.

"Very well, Rosemary," I said. "But don't be disobliging to me if I suddenly want something."

She cringed, but I was too involved in my discovery to feel the usual sleepy pride that I was the cause of her fear.

The Creeping Vulva

In the next few months Rosemary developed lumps under her arms, on her neck, on the lower side of her breast, on her heel, ankle and calf, and on the inner part of her buttock. The lumps rose, became scaly, then itchy, then flaked gradually off to show small, damp slits. The girl with the most sensitivity to touch had developed the creeping vulva.

Poor Rosemary. She had wanted to be a surgeon.

Some who failed took it as a blessing to have the uncertainty lifted, but not Rosemary. When later a remission occurred in her state, she lost all the creeping vulvas but those on calf and buttock; a fearful hope burdened her from that time on.

Growing Pains

My breasts have got a go on. They were small lumps for quite a few months, now they're really developing. Today, in Maths, they hurt. Once, when I bent down to pick up a fallen pen, my left breast brushed the desk, and it hurt like mad.

It's rather exciting to be able to say the word "breast" about my two.

I'm writing this at night, and I'm getting pains again. I go to put my hand up to ward off the pain; I remember in time and do not touch them. Last time I clapped my hands to them in pain I nearly screamed. Alethea Hunt screaming! I would never forgive myself.

This is the next day. Griselda Cadbury and Marie-Louise looked meaningfully at my new breasts as I entered the schoolgate.

International Nose Race of the Year Blot

I won lots of trophies for sport at Primary and began to do the same at high school. In Primary I won races up to four hundred meters; the long jump; our team won the area basketball competition; there were softball cups and tennis trophies. In high school there was still basketball and athletics and in addition music—I played the piano and went in local eisteddfods and began to learn wind instruments.

There were no prizes for schoolwork. If I wanted prizes it was no use me coming first in English, German, Science, Music, History—and sometimes Math—it didn't even show up in the half-yearly report. They weren't allowed to encourage one kid's excellence against another's. Equality forbade it. There were book prizes, though, from teachers who sneaked them to us privately.

I didn't like the system, naturally.

We all had the same opportunities, apart from our genes. The idea of patently unequal people being treated as if they were the same was repugnant to me. Why have no medals for schoolwork, and yet have prizes for track and field? Why no winner for what we learned, when there was always a winner in everything else?

> *Tinker, tailor, soldier, sailor,*
> *Rich man, poor man, beggarman, thief:*
> *All equal.*

Mucking Up on the Teacher

Monday morning, Mister Groundwater was trying to whip us into a frenzy of enthusiasm over intransitive verbs, when the kids received, from sources unknown, a burst of energy that started to show itself in smart remarks, jokes, tentative yelling, small quarrels between each other. Just as suddenly it focused on the teacher. I don't know how it happened but suddenly we surged forward round him and he was hitting at us, his blows bouncing off our resilient heads and chests and faces. We weren't hitting him, just crowding him backward to the wall. All pushing him back. The blackboard ledge received his old buttocks, his back against the chalky green of the board, our class a giant scrum; as football must have had such scrums hundreds of years ago when games traversed whole cities and the space between towns; before referees.

He was besieged, frightened, yelling at us.

He couldn't move. None of us did for a while. When he stopped making a noise and was trying to get his breath in the crush, the absence of his monotonous voice had a curious effect on us. Slowly the interest went out of it. Kids at the outside peeled off, soon as we were all back in our seats, and Mister Groundwater still against the wall, still panting, getting his breath. He didn't say a word. He was a relief teacher. We had five different English teachers that term.

When there were missiles flying round the room, I joined in. From father I learned the way to make paper pellets, folding them over into thin tubes, giving them a bend in the middle and hooking them on to the middle of a doubled rubber band held in two fingers of the forward hand, pulling the pellet back with the aiming hand and letting go. I was soon as accurate as the boys and added a refinement of my own. I used a hard, thick paper, and my pellets hurt.

Sometimes they hit the teacher. Mister Judson, our next English teacher, threw the duster once, and hit Stuart Regan. Stuart rose manfully in his place and threw it back. Mister Judson caught it on the chest.

It was a foolish business, being so young. I was a double fool: I had so much to look forward to. What did it matter if Frees and failures fooled and danced all the way to their lighthearted graves?

Blind Freddy

I never did it, but a gang of really rough girls in school did things to the blind kids. Not things to hurt them, but things.

We had kids blind and partly blind. They gave it a cheerful name, and instead of calling them partly blind called them partially sighted.

I guess the best of us is only partly sighted, at the best, compared to what a camera can see in one blink, or what a small insect sees, or a bird stationary in the sky.

"What do you see, Fred?" they'd ask him, because he always gave a strange answer. His name really was Fred.

"I see—seven pints." Maybe his parents didn't know he was going to be blind.

"What of?"

"Anything. Seven pints."

"Why pints?"

"I like pints. A good old word. Clean."

"How would you know what clean is?" one of the roughies said. She had huge thighs and no neck. The boys were afraid of her. She was afraid of nothing.

"Dirty is sort of rough and gritty," he said mildly. "A glass is clean. People are gritty. Except some parts."

I left then. I knew what he meant. Poor helpless Fred had his hand guided into certain places by the roughies, and at other times they held him while they investigated some of his physical properties. He never complained. They covered his tool and toolbag, as they called them, in boot polish one day. I guess his parents thought it was boys did it no matter what he told them.

The biggest of the roughies, Celia O'Donnell, had a puffy face that hid her eyes. In a fight with other girls, they could never get to her eyes with their fingernails. She had a husky voice. She whispered in Freddy's ear, and they took him round the corner. He would go home tired after they had amused themselves with him, but he never told tales as far as we knew. Parents were afraid of the girl gangs.

I don't think anyone liked Freddy. It was inhuman to take it all the time and never want to dish it out, even if you're blind.

I never watched what they did when they opened his trousers.

Franka Bultovic

She could never tell what I wanted with her. She thought of me as just another girl. She was tiny and pretty, like a flower with blue eyes.

But when I looked at her I was no girl: she was the girl. I felt like a mountain, a ponderous mountain descending to touch with granite fingers the barely warm flesh of something new born. She fascinated me.

It didn't last long, just a week or two. In that time startling things happened when I masturbated. Once Franka floated above me—in my imagination—so that I could touch her and be touched, and put my face into all sorts of places, and when I came space

216

opened in strips, and I heard the music of whales and tree stumps that were dead before we whites blundered ashore in the surf.

The World Record

Father and I saw Professor Henrietta D. Walden II at the shopping-town when we went bowling together. She had gone from Freedom From to Freedom To: the dynamic part of freedom, the positive, what it's all about.

Her voice was frayed. That world record must have meant a lot to her.

The Grizzle Game

For a few months the whole school picked up a game the boys played, called Grizzle. You kept a check on your friends, and if someone chose to do a certain thing, or have a certain thing, or do something a certain way, and after that grizzled about it, the penalty was: no one took any notice of the next two things you said.

If you grizzled twice, the next penalty was: no one took notice of the next four things you said. It doubled all the time: the next penalty was eight, then sixteen, and so on.

There were kids in the playground that couldn't expect to have any notice taken of them for years. When they went over a reasonable score—say two—they got impatient and wanted to change the rules or have the game banned, but their friends were implacable. They'd had to watch *they* didn't complain, so they were going to see no one else did.

Lifelong enmities that took weeks to dissolve were formed by the game. When little kids got to hear of a high score, they gave cheek from a distance, baiting the grizzler.

The Alternative Society

One of the woodwork teachers at school, Mister Adams, was at odds with society. He lived down our street. He was convinced that things around us, trees, flowers, bricks, bitumen, posts, fences, rubber, iron, were wrongly named. He went round booking everything he saw, entering its name in a notebook, sometimes hanging a ticket from it. He carried a box of bits of string ready for threading through the tickets and tying on to trees and fences. He had ticketed three suburbs, people said.

"We've only been here on earth five minutes," he said to my father. It was Sunday morning, and my father was apologetically mowing the grass with his machine. He was half-glad to turn the wretched thing off, and half-anxious about having to turn it on again. He didn't know much about machines.

"Yet we expect to be able to go ahead and name the fruits of the earth and the equipment God placed here for us," Mister Adams continued.

"I daresay it's a legitimate aim," my father said.

"What we've done is take the first names that came into our heads, without doing research on the whole problem," Mister Adams said.

"What's that, Mister Adams?" I asked, pointing to the two Eucalyptus Scoparia.

"Shardik," he said immediately.

"And that?" I pointed to the letterbox.

"Zoan."

"But I though Zoan was a tree," I said. My father looked at me, saying shush with his face.

"Is it?" said Mister Adams. He began searching through his book. He found the place. "There is a Zoan tree, yes. It's a tree shaped like a letterbox."

"And what about that?" A mauve hibiscus.

"An early-flowering Saldis," he said without consulting his writ.

"Is this just an alternative naming, alternative to what we've got?" father asked.

"It is an attempt to find the real names," the woodwork teacher said loudly.

"We could find all sorts of alternatives," I said, supporting father.

Mister Adams was gone, saying words like, "Real names, not the first ones ancient savages thought of. Nothing has its real name." His head was forward, well ahead of his body. He strode firmly, following it. He knew he was right.

He was hopeless in class. The kids gave him a terrible time.

Love of Home

When he took us out driving, father was always pointing out scenes and vistas that seemed to come round the corner at us, particularly when he was there. A road west, that bore on toward the deep blue of the mountains, often surprised us with a sudden corner lined with poplars or almonds and a further receding field lowering itself gently down toward the river, a post and wire fence staggering under the weight of the sun, rotten at the base; the corn speading on the river flat green or golden, tall or just poking up toward the height it wanted; a log-grey shack propped up by weeds; a wheel or two and the remains of a harrow; an old dog sitting up on a post; things you see out among the fields and paddocks.

"Beautiful, isn't it?" he said. Of course it was beautiful. So was the slow sag of the electric wires out in the street when you were in bed in the morning or just lying there on a wet day. So was the feel of the bedclothes, sheets cool and blanket rough and friendly as the hairs on father's forearm. So was the fire in the back of the pub in Lithgow where we stopped on a winter night. Everything was beautiful.

"Yep," I answered in a businesslike manner.

He looked across at me, said nothing.

It wasn't till I was older that I said those things first, without agreeing with what someone else told me. As if I fell more in love with the world the older I got.

He must have had much the same thing in mind when he took me to have photographs taken: "Look at the camera as if you see for the first time the wonder of the universe and are on the edge of understanding."

219

I don't know if that's what I did or not, but he was caught up in his own lyrical attitude and went on, "Every moment is a subject for infinite art." He made a natural pause after that, and went on thinking. Perhaps it was from a play he'd read.

I prefer to think it was his own thoughts.

My pause was respectful. He was saying something important, and wanted me to absorb it. I didn't want him ever to think I thought he wasn't as smart as he wanted me to think.

In the mountains the grey-green and hazy bush covered every rise and choked every valley. (Humans will live here for ages to come, but not after the word "green" disappears.) Down to the edge of the dams and rivers it spread, just as it went right to the water's edge in the harbors and on the coast.

I thought, looking at it with a pleased feeling that this was my country, that if the world from far away was round and smooth like a ball, what delightful fur this forestland was. I could feel myself smiling at it. I knew its rocks and mossed stones, its courageous twisted trees pouring themselves over rock ledges, its sudden pools of white sand on bush tracks, its valleys opening with tall straight gums marching downward toward creek beds and up again the other sides. I loved it.

I think it is the only real love I ever felt; except one that was special, and human, and brief.

Sucking to the Teacher

At school I was doodling during maths while the teacher was going on about sets and paradoxes.

" . . . Paradoxes have played a vital part in the development of logic and the philosophy of mathematics. There came a day when Russell asked himself:

> *"Is the class of classes*
> *That are not members of themselves*
> *A member of itself?*

220

> If it is: it isn't
> And if it isn't, it is."

He went on about self-reference, and whether it should be banned from significant speech. It was the sort of mind-stretching that gives you a workout but doesn't mean a thing in the syllabus. Educational, but not markable: our assessments wouldn't show its value. I doodled.

Here for you, my reader, is that doodle, preserved these few years as an extra dimension of me that you can approve or deplore:

> *Sometimes in the now when may is at an end*
> *And when will be tomorrow while but is at an end*
> *And and is in the wings though if is at an end –*
> *Then is is imminent for was is at an end.*

Belinda Lachman looked over my shoulder and was going to tell on me, but I moved my right leg in a swinging arc and scraped the edge of my sole down the shin of her right leg from near the knee to the big vein on her anklebone. I have good vision from the sides of my eyes so I was able to perform this feat (pardon me) without moving my head, and my leg was still and back in place before her awful gasping shriek. The first thing the class knew she was upon me, cursing and spitting and striking at me with her nails.

I shrugged off her attack and backed away in distaste, as if I was so absorbed in paradox that I hadn't had time to react properly.

Then I reacted. "Help!" I called, reasonably. Arms pulled her away. The teacher came up the aisle to discipline her, while I watched her with the horror that only an educated person can affect with any degree of believability.

In English I continued my whimsical mood, and wrote out something on the different meanings of words that had Mister Patel full of admiration and the other kids wrinkling up their mouths at me in disgust. Which gave me the opportunity to smile gently, and look like the only civilized person present.

> *"She tried to shy the flint at the fishpond*
> *Since there was no coconut shy handy,*
> *But it landed a few meters shy.*
> *Some said: she's a bit shy of hitting it.*
> *Others: It's the only time she's ever been shy."*

"Very good, Alex. You are being a very inventive girl," he beamed. He looked at peace with the world. I hoped I would never be. His brown unlined face and white teeth and yellow eye-whites glowed at me, they were something to see. He gave us a whole period to write two pages on a subject of our choice.

English Expression: River

River did not know where he came from. There was talk at the crosswaters and the meetings of subsidiary creeks, but the river you talked to one day had a different expression from yesterday's river. It seemed to River that he alone had a coherent self. He never changed, though others did.

River had always felt that wonderful things—strange, mysterious things—were going to happen. He was eager for the future, which he felt was going to bring him something better than he had ever known.

We called him Po River. He came from the western hills, and lost himself in the salt of the upper reaches of the harbor. But before he got near the salt the runoff from backyards and factories and institutions thickened him like a soup, a green soup. River didn't know we called him Po. Life had always been easy, yet if you talked to him you'd imagine he was the hardest-done-by river in existence.

The persistence of deep rivers that have worn away thousands of feet of rock and in old age are narrow watercourses had been told in stories rivers tell when they meet, and River knew them. His complacence was differently based. He in ages gone had worn down a valley many many kilometers wide, so his landscape was almost flat. His flow was often so sleepy that it couldn't be seen. He rushed only when the hysteria of flood got the better of him.

One day a young person came and looked at River and learned and listened. She looked and saw how he had flowed for only a short geological time and smiled at River's simplicity in thinking of himself as age-old. Then she remembered, and she remembered like this: Our time, our scale of the passing of moments, isn't geological time. Our time elevates even River's time to eternity, for River always flows. We can conceive of River being not-there, then with us, then gone; but can we conceive of the actions we ought to live by, in harmony with this conception of time?

When River says he flows past and is always present, he is suffering from a word-blindness that sees the object equivalent to a word that is not itself equal to the full description of River's being. For there are things we will never know.

Mister Patel gave me 18½ out of 20, and it counted toward my assessment. He omitted to ask me what my last paragraph meant. I knew what it meant when I wrote it, but I can't make it out at all, now.

The Impossible Game

We played it on the first school day of every month in the winter. The game was not student against student: it was student bodies against masonry.

There was a brick wall, a quirky wall put up to shield the fire hoses and spray nozzles for school security against fire down at the very lip of the creek, and the idea was to push it over. It looked like a very ordinary wall, and as such it should have been unable to resist several tons of human body straining against it, but it was not as ordinary as it seemed. Its brickwork had been rendered over with cement, and painted white. We did not know the bricks were those patent bricks with holes up through them and that reinforcing rods had been poked up them and bedded into the concrete foundations that went down half a meter under surface level.

We developed a war cry from this game:

> *Play the impossible game,*
> *Learn the impossible.*
> *Be impossible.*
> *It's possible.*
> *Try harder,*
> *Try now.*
> *Go!*

We huddled and punched our fists downward in time, until "It's possible." The next two phrases we punched upward, and for "go!" we punched both hands up into the air and jumped as high as we could. Then all backs bent to the task, pushing and straining.

It's still there.

Reverence for the Past

Under the moon at night the suburbs of the poor spread out flat for miles around like mud huts in the dark, populating a desert. If only the place was hilly, and there were avalanches.

The Carraways, searchers for Australia's past, came round from house to house asking, looking, photographing, noting, giving catalogue numbers to the relics of the past. Not much over two hundred years, yet to them it was precious.

Useless to talk to them of the ever-extending past that prehistorians were constantly uncovering: the Carraways were concerned only with traces of white civilization. Show them old Bibles with family names, fire irons, pots and kettles, smoothing irons, bridles and chains and bits, drays, mining equipment and so on, and they were in their element.

Mr. and Mrs. Carraway had a legion of helpers: young people converted to the religion of the country's past, older Australians dedicated to the idea that there might be something worth preserving, something the rest of us had overlooked, something hidden somewhere that would make sense of our being here and what we had done to the land.

My father joked about it. At school we were told to take it seriously, but his laughter stopped me from taking it the way the schoolteachers wanted.

The idea that the timber and fibro and brick veneer places spreading for miles around could have anything in them of value besides the people, was enough to get him going.

"Look at that," he said to me as we stood on the front patio. With his arm he indicated the sweep of dozens of suburbs down below us, and the thousands of lighted windows.

"In the morning we'll find it is an encampment of soldiers, and they'll wake with bugles and clashing of arms, a bit of gunnery practice and a few executions to keep morale high."

When my parents first got to our house and began a little gentle digging to get the ground in order for planting grass, he found a glass bottle stopper. It was in the days when bottle collecting was starting, an old Eno's bottle top from the century before, and the Carraways went mad over it. They sent collectors every week to try to get it off him, but they didn't win until they sent an old guy who talked and talked and wouldn't stop. My mother threw it at him.

Confession

It was shortly after I turned thirteen. Little Robert Haycock was left with me for a few minutes after an accident outside the Primary school. Three kids were injured when one of our seniors skidded his car the length of the gravel that lies on Fermi Street that T-joins Euclid Way at the school front gate. I comforted him as best I could with my presence. I put an arm around him, stooping, finally bending at the knees and crouching near him to take his attention from the blood. His legs were extremely thin and white and his school trousers large. Without thinking enough about it to want to stop myself, almost in the style of a mother checking up on the condition of her handiwork, I let my hand slip up the wide trouser bottoms and glide straight to his penis. I knew I couldn't have two tries—boys get very impatient when they're fiddled with. My hand encountered a tiny projection and a small round lump: the penis and scrotum of Robert Haycock. It was a cool day, and it seemed reasonable that both items were small and hard.

I had never had a small brother to explore. Only a tall father to go Ping! with my forefinger.

Robert didn't seem to notice. I didn't let my hand move in case it tickled him and his giggles drew attention, just let both stiff items lie in my palm. He looked at my face, but I was looking away, so I guess he thought I wasn't focusing on him. After a minute I took my hand out, and said sensible things to him, and took him up the Fermi Street hill a bit, for his house was that way.

I brushed my hand past my nose to see, but there was no odor.

I don't know *why* I did it, I just did. Normally I'd be dubious about brandishing such a private experience, but it happened, so I'm including it.

While I'm Confessing

While I'm confessing, I might as well tell about little Terry, my cousin on father's side. Their family was passing through on the way south to visit some of their relatives—on father's brother's wife's side. And since all our accommodation was taken little Terry was put in with me.

It was cold and he was soon asleep. When I got to bed I was peculiarly sleepless, and though I felt my breathing coming regularly and perhaps deeply, the way I felt sleep coming when it wasn't the usual head-on-pillow-fast-asleep drill, I didn't go to sleep as soon as I had expected. Instead, I amused myself by taking Terry's trousers down and sentimentally pressing him to my warm body. With an unusually dry mouth, I took off my pants and lifted my old-style nightie, which was the rage then. His little excrescence pressed against me. I tried to massage the short businesslike member to an interesting size, but it only came out a short way. On an impulse I widened my thighs and pressed his little thing in toward my wetter part, but only its tip touched and on the slidy surface. I rubbed it back and forth, as if it were a blotter. I couldn't stop. I rolled him on top of me and widened my legs more, and with my arm round behind his botty I pushed all his equipment into that place; I found that to get any contact at all I had to lift my knees in much the same way as women did when I'd seen them on the education films giving birth.

He came awake, I thought. I put him down and breathed regularly. My eyes were shut. My chest beat against the blanket. Guilt made me keep my hands off him. I stayed awake for many minutes, it seemed. My mouth was still dry. If only I had a little brother.

In the morning I chided him for having his pajamas undone and tied the cord myself in a nice bow.

Outlets

I could bring up my foot when I was little and put my big toe in my mouth. I wondered tonight if I'd grown too big to bend my head over like that anymore. I tried, sitting on my bed. My head reached only to a place level with my navel: I couldn't get my head down to, say, between my legs.

So it's no use thinking of that.

In the bath I was attracted by the look of the spout in which the streams of hot and cold water were married. I had an impulse to put my under parts in contact with that spout, but though I tried hard I could not manage it. Instead, I lay on my back, legs up against the wall on either side of the spout, and with the water adjusted to a nice warmth and a good strong flow, I let the torrent wash down on the crucial parts. The plug was out, the water ran down the drain, and the steady throbbing pressure on and around my clitoris brought me to a wonderfully satisfying and exciting climax.

A Naughty Thought

One very cold morning the neighborhood dogs were running about to warm themselves, and in their game they chased the small spaniel from the end of the street, where Rutherford Road crosses it, and as they passed our house their breath shot out before them in puffs. I thought how much more assistance it would have been to them if the jets of their breath discharged from the other end.

The End

The cicadas that spent years underground and came up in summer into the light and spent a month or so flying about and making a noise and mating, then were nothing, had nevertheless passed on the future of cicadas to others during their mating flight.

The future of humans was in me, in small part: it's no wonder I was oriented toward the future. Tomorrow was important, I was young still, tomorrow would be my day.

But when you sit down and think about it, tomorrow is different from that. Tomorrow is the time to be born. It's better not to be here now, rather to remain a possibility in the loins of the present, so that the eventual dissolution and the end of everything could be postponed. Is that what the Greeks meant by "Better never to be born"? To remain a possibility forever, to stay asleep in the seeds of the eternal present. For if the meaning of God is the state of death-union with the elements—then God is to be feared above all, and union with God a miserable end of everything.

End: a dreadful word. Before my own end, would I be able to do something heroic: something to distinguish myself?

Father's

Father was having a nap. It was a July Sunday, after lunch. The couch was in the sunroom, the window came down to the floor, and the room was bathed in light.

I had been reading to him from Ecclesiastes, which he said was his favorite poem, and was not very far into the last chapter when he dozed off. He didn't snore, but with his head slightly forward on the sun-couch he made a rumbling in the back of his nose that was very *like* a snore.

His sun-shorts were loose at the leg, and his thick thighs with the brown skin and shiny black hairs and the two small patches of broken purple thread-like veins just above the knee on the inside of the leg, were on view. Also the tip of a certain organ associated with Ping! in my younger days.

I went on reading about the silver bowl and put out a few fingers of my right hand to touch that tip. It had been many years since I had Ping!-ed it. It was less proper for a girl aged over five years, somehow.

I put my fingers on its broad spade-shaped head, still reading aloud, testing the feel of it, also the contrast between my temperature and its temperature. They were near enough to the same.

I put my whole hand round it, surprised by the weight in its head. It rolled over indolently in my fingers when I relaxed my grip, and the mouth, redder than the rather blue-pink head, looked straight at me as if it were an eye. The lips relaxed and parted, showing a dark pink gullet, smooth and shiny with the shine of flesh like the inside of your lip.

I wanted to grip it tightly and laugh about it, happily, with a comradely sense of togetherness, but I dared not. I kept talking, saying, "Remember now thy creator in the days of your youth, remember now your creator in the days of thy youth," over and over, because I didn't have the wit to go on, when he began to stir. He opened his eyes. My hands were back where they belonged.

"You said that. Why did you say that twice?"

I'd said it thirteen times.

Phew . . . close.

Lessons

Teachers weren't supposed to give you class positions, but we all compared marks. Three of us stayed at the top, each year. We were smart enough not to be contaminated by the antiwork ethic of

229

the blobs, knowing full well they'd never make it and we would, provided no changes came to us.

That didn't stop us pursuing the teachers that could be pursued, sensing their weakness and aiming at it every chance we got. The ones that got excited by their subject were the easiest marks. They forgot everything in the heat of history, or German, and we could do anything to them as long as when they turned to look at us we were attending. Like hunters we were, mastering our environment, just as in later years the salesmen among us would sense the vanity, the indecision, the awe, the greed, the desire for status in the "marks" that wandered into range, and would play upon those weaknesses and achieve success in terms of sales volume; or the public service politicians that would snake their way by any means until they achieved the desk they wanted, all the while using the invaluable lessons learned, though not knowingly taught, at dear old school.

Out in the open air some birds look mainly down, for meals; others look mainly up, in fear of the birds looking down.

What I learned at school was the ability to respond to hints and commands, or "stimulus," the desire to compete to do things better or arrive somewhere before others, the satisfaction of getting rewards, the horror of being among the blobs: I didn't know I was smart till I got to school and found out what a dill was.

I learned to read at home; my general knowledge came from home; my attitude to the future, to myself, to others, came from home; my personality, my love of independence, my social skills, my ability to talk easily with strangers and adults, all came from my home and my father. And mother too. At least she surrounded me with love for my first six years.

It occurs to me now that at school they tested us on what we learned at home.

Here's an old year seven report father made a fuss of; I remember it because he was so pleased. I did better at other times, but this one I still have.

Subject	Mark	Average	Remarks
English	96	75	An excellent result from a wholesome personality. Keep going, Alethea!
Mathematics	95	70	Alethea is a delight to teach —shows maturity in her approach to work.
Science	90	70	Alethea really works. Keep it up.
Social Sc.	94	74	An excellent result; Al is a capable and interested student.
Art	87	72	Excellent student. Always works extremely well.
Craft	90	63	Works well in practical class.
Language	98	76	Al's work is almost faultless. She has enormous language ability.
Speech, Drama	78	65	Top of the class.
Music	85	58	An excellent result. Alethea is a most talented student with great potential.
PE, Sport			Represents school in all sports.

And the Head's comment: Congratulations, etc.

After year seven they cut down on giving us marks, but we three were able to get them: not all the teachers agreed with the policy edicts imposed from above.

Father's Penis Revisited

Father was asleep and mother safely writing. He had spread his body along the black couch in the sunroom, and since it was a hot day he had his old shorts on and nothing else. I knelt by the couch and looked all round to see if someone was looking, but though

I felt I was being watched I was sure there was no one there. His feet were bare, and the tops were brown with the sun he so enjoyed. I ran my hands over the skin where it was smooth, on the fronts of his thighs where no doubt trousers wore off the hair.

Moisture in my throat seemed an obstacle: I swallowed it so it would not prevent me. Would he wake up? I watched and held my breath. He didn't move. I touched the penis, soft and limp and biscuit brown. If my existence was sacred to me then surely this sluggish lump of flesh was; through it I was introduced to my mother; or part of me was introduced, through my mother, to the remaining part. This body was therefore sacred too.

I leaned forward and bent my head over it, keeping my eyes open, and let my lips touch it, just the neck of it. It was the same temperature as my lips. The head was turned up into a fold of the shorts. I put a finger against the shorts and brought it against the hidden head, and gently eased it down out of its confinement. It fell the last bit, straightening lazily.

Suddenly his large body moved, and I was on my feet and at the door before his movement had settled. He had turned over. My heart beat quickly so that I was aware of it. I ran guiltily back to my room to read Jane Austen. What if that wasn't the origin of my life? Was it still wrong if he wasn't really my father? I had to force myself to look at the page before I could silence such thoughts.

> Oh, cried Elizabeth, I am excessively diverted. But
> it is so strange.

Cheats Never Prosper

I won the painting prize for the whole school in year eight. I used a lot of titanium white and a tube of glistening gold together with lots of colors and painted Jesus Christ as an Eastern mystic and teacher dying on a jewel-encrusted cross. I think they gave me the prize as much for the rather literary conception as for technique, though here I got right away from the impasto that was popular then and made the work as flat and traditional as a Dali. I cheated by drawing all the objects faintly in pencil first so I wouldn't lose sight of the details after I'd got all the background in.

I consider it cheating, anyway.

When I went up to collect the prize there were three great roars overhead, three formations of airplanes were organizing the air. The prize was a certificate, but the art teacher slipped me a personal gift of a black-covered edition of Baudelaire later.

Standing on the platform with the assistant Head, my destiny seemed to arch high above me; but was it honor, or threat?

Is the Verb to Orgas Or Orgase?

Marie-Louise wasn't bitter about her family. They were always out or busy or away, and she got practically no mothering. No fathering, either. Actually her parents weren't up to much, and it might have been for the best. She didn't complain. They had their life to live.

"When I get out of the machine, I'll have a smashing time," she said. Childhood was the machine.

"Buggar lessons," she said. She kept to around a middle mark in everything, her assessments were just short of good. The teachers used to get worked up about it, but couldn't make an impression.

"I'll tell you something if you promise to tell no one else," she said during the scripture period. I knew what that meant: half a dozen knew already, but she hadn't got around to telling everyone in the school.

"I've read books on it."

"On what, ML?"

"Sex. That's the key to everything once you get out of this shit."

I was younger than Marie-Louise. The nipple areas on her chest had started to swell, and the first bumpiness had appeared round them.

She practiced whenever she could—in class, on sports day, all weekend.

What was she practicing? Her orgasm.

"At home and weekends I hang around reading a book when wrinklies are talking, specially men, and they see me reading and don't hunt me away. You know what I found? Men like a woman that can come quick. The women think they're clever because they just lie there and criticize when the men can't do the second one quickly, or want to rest, but they're missing the point. All you have to do is please men, and they'll do anything for you. And you have to practice."

"Don't we all?" I said.

"You don't understand. I mean to do it quick and often. I'm trying for ten seconds."

"Ten seconds?" I squeaked, thinking of my laborious efforts, my aching finger, my spit. And the air about me pounding like a heartbeat.

The English Lesson

Mrs. Plumpton was taking us for English. Suddenly there was a loud gasp.

"I've done it!" ML burst out, and stood up all pink.

"Did what?" said Plumpton.

"Split the gerundial infinitive." And sat down.

"We don't do gerunds. How do you know what a gerund is? Have you been listening to your parents?"

"I want to do extra work, to keep ahead." That was a laugh.

"There'll be no questions on gerunds, Fienberg. You're wasting your time."

"I thought you'd say that. But my knowledge of grammar has nothing to do with English, Mrs. Plumpton. I find I have to learn *some* grammar," apologetically, "to understand the foreign language I'm doing." You could always beat the more conscientious teachers like that. They knew there were recurring times when you were allowed to learn grammar.

During recess we asked ML how.

"Sat still and worked the muscles."

"Did you really break ten seconds?"

"Course I did!"

We didn't believe her, but she didn't mind. I was never present, later, when she made love with males, but I knew even then that they wouldn't know if it was real or not. They had to take your word for it, you could fool them anytime. If you started out saying you weren't easily aroused, they went away very bushy-tailed if you came quickly.

After two years of high school ML had a collection of busts, plaster casts of famous historical heads. Ned Kelly, Beethoven, Einstein, Churchill, Stalin, Mozart. Criminals and artists. She used to say hello to them in the morning and kiss them goodnight when she went to bed.

Her father bought her busts of famous women. Sylvia Plath, Mary Wollstonecraft, Marie Curie, Marilyn Monroe—people like that. For company, no doubt.

She kissed them too.

After the English lesson, I watched Plumpton in the playground. I liked her because she was capable of liking ML.

She arrested one's eyes, walking with a slight lean forward, thrusting against the atmosphere, wanting to go faster and more powerfully than constraints would let her. Striding forward toward the science block—to see Miss Grundweise, though I didn't know this then—she had such a masculine walk that she was the focus of hundreds of female eyes. She had a face like a cantata—long and a funny shape.

However, since I had to do history just then, I decided to save up that feeling about her, and think about it later.

This Pen Has So Much More Story I Could Write

This time I was bolder. The drinking father had done had left him good-natured, but he went straight to the lounge, and almost immediately passed out. His head was propped forward as he lay on his back and began to snore. I carefully pulled away the cushions his

235

head rested on, managing his head with my left hand, and settled him down flat. That way, I didn't feel he was looking at me. Besides, being level stopped his snoring, and mother would have no reason to leave her work.

I undid the zipper down the front of his trousers, kneeling before him, searched for the slit in his underpants, and felt for the penis. This time there was no hurry or thumping heart, I was determined to learn as much about it as I could.

His hand made a movement and came over onto his front, touching mine. I didn't let go his penis, but neither did the contact disturb him. I moved my hand slightly away, then with my left hand gently lifted his and put it beside his thigh.

I pulled the penis out of the gap in his clothes. As I had known since I was a small girl he was circumcised, and the head was covered in tiny glistening wrinkles, no doubt for expansion.

A noise! I dropped it. It was only mother, shifting her chair in the other room. The penis had fallen back into a nest of underclothes, and it moved. I reached in and pulled up the entire scrotum gently so it was propped on the underpants' folds, and the head settled back on a bed of flesh and moved again. The head made small, slow movements forward, as if advancing, then stopped, and retracted. It was quite short and thick, the head was as long and as broad as the length of the rest of it. Wrinkles in the brown flesh behind the head were so plentiful it would be impossible to count them.

I wished I had my camera.

The head itself was a study. I pulled it out from its wrinkled bed and from the thin brown scar of his circumcision. It felt as if it was made of muscle, reminding me of the sheep's heart I had cut up at school, though it was not red. There were so many colors in it I despair of describing them. Round the base, where a sort of collar broadens out, it was a mauve or mauve-red; this shaded, getting narrower, into a pleasant pink, and it was pink all round its slit of a mouth. I lifted up the head and looked at the mouth. It seemed about a centimeter and a half long, and quite fallen together as

236

if asleep. But when I squeezed the mouth at both ends, it opened crazily so that when I looked at it sideways as you would a mouth, it wore a disapproving expression. I got both hands and put a finger lightly on both sides of the mouth and gently opened it. Every time I touched it I had a compulsion to be gentle that surprised me. The pink and wet and glistening surfaces of the inside of its mouth delighted me; when I let the lips come together there was a clearly defined round craterish part that was the mouth proper and at the other side a film of thin skin, on the underside, that looked as if it could tear apart. Were there two channels inside it? When I opened it and looked down its throat, it seemed so, and one channel went on the underside of the penis where the thinner membrane was. But I knew from school there was one channel only, for sperm and pee.

It slipped out of my fingers and went straight back to its bed of scrotum, which hollowed itself out slightly to receive its companion. Then it lengthened and retracted, this time shrinking back and at the same time turning on one side with the cuteness of a baby's movements. And when it shrank to its furthest—I had a stray idea that perhaps it might keep going—it stopped there for a little, then nosed forward again. Almost like breathing.

I had never properly seen the scrotum. I inserted the fingers of both hands under and around it, watching that the fine, soft skin was not pinched, and when I was under it and could feel the join with the rest of him I lifted and heaped it all above his underclothes, so that I could get at all of it.

It lay heaped there—heaped is the word—and I saw the long hairs, some brown, some white, and all with curl in them; they entered the bag itself at an acute angle, and I could see the hair under the skin as it approached its roots. There were veins branching just under the surface; I held it up and could feel two large oval things like large nuts, that slid around inside the bag; one of them had a softish appendage beneath it; and when I held the skin out with two hands I was fascinated by the thinness of this bag, the way it was round and wrinkled and compact at one time, and at another stretched and pink with red veins and slanting hairs, having lost the dull brown color it had when it was all together in a heap.

From the heap I lifted the penis and held it straight up, and the bag moved! The incredibly wrinkled skin on top of it, where the penis had rested, was crawling! It moved sideways, its lattice of structural wrinkles, and wrinkles due to its folded position, moving together a little way—very slowly—then moving back. It too breathed.

But why would it breathe? It was more like thinking. What an idea! That both of these two lowly, protected, abused, serviceable, talented organisms—beings?—persons?—were thinking. Alone, apparently unobserved, they thought. Of what? Of the destiny of nations, of the sine wave graph of human fortunes and endless change? Or were they thinking for the man whose apparent append-ages they were?

In which case perhaps he was the appendage to them.

Holding the penis erect like that, I saw the circumcision mark clearly. I turned it round and saw the collar thing shaping upward and pointing at the mouth via a narrow channel in the head. There was a limit to how far you could pull it upwards; though it was soft and stretchy, there was a limit. I could feel a gristly thing inside it that I had come to the end of. It was just over seventeen centimeters: I knew that because just over seventeen centimeters was the length of my hand from middle finger to base of thumb.

He was still deeply asleep. I knew from times he had been drinking that he would be asleep for at least three hours.

I began to give the thing a tickle, all of it; from the pile of scrotum skin to the columnar penis, just an idle thing to do, like a child's game, turning it round in my fingers and pressing and lengthening it, noting the long brownish raised line on the under side that led down and broadened toward the beginning of the scrotum and continued right on underneath, dividing the scrotum into two sides and the hairs that sprouted where that line began, hairs and pores that had been stained a purply brown, even several lumps on the skin of the scrotum itself. And going on in this way for some time, hardly thinking what I was doing, the thing began to straighten and thicken. I was making it erect! What would happen? Would he wake?

For some reason I felt a duty to it and could not or would not stop. With my fingers I traced the thickness and checked it from the head where it seemed to stop just short of the fleshy mouth itself, like a tense muscle, down to the inner parts of the scrotum and further than that—I checked with my fingers inside the underpants—into something like the center of the scrotum and down into his body! Right in him. It wasn't just something attached to the skin or to some outside shell of the body, it came from deep inside him!

It stood up without support. I ran my fingers down it and up again, seeing how the fine skin on the outside slipped along over the muscle inside, noting how the mouth stood open, how the green veins that were thick under the skin were more prominent and the thin reddish ones were still no different from what they had been except there were more of them and a big green vein I hadn't noticed before was down near the base, perhaps a quarter of the way up.

I bent over to—well, to smell it, I suppose. There was a slight smell of cigarettes, probably from the place he'd been drinking; there was a light soap smell; also a smell I could not place, never having met it before. I couldn't describe it: it was warm and wettish, and—but no, I had no word for it since I had never come across it.

It was so clean and fine, and he was so fast asleep, I put my mouth over it tentatively. There was no taste. Just for fun I tried my mouth over it as far as it would go. It went back into my throat, I felt it near that thing that hangs down, the uvula, and it nearly made me cough and sneeze at the same time. I tried it again, and made a point of breathing through my nose and it was all right.

I looked sideways at his face. All I could see was chin and nose and eyebrows. What would I do now if he woke? Say—"You never gave me a talk about things, so I was finding out for myself?" It was funny to see him so helpless.

I moved my mouth up and down on it, but nothing happened.

I took my mouth off it, got my handkerchief and wiped my spit off. Not long after I stopped touching it, it began to wilt. The head inclined, but instead of bending from up there near the top, it began to collapse from nearer the bottom and perhaps in the middle too. I replaced everything and did him up and went back to my book.

I was sorry to be getting near the end of Jane Austen.

Father on Irrationality

It was the same night. When he looked at me I tried not to blush or anything silly.

"Irrationality has a positive value. Think of our leaders. They wouldn't be leaders if they weren't technically insane. Who is it wants to lead a nation? Is there a preknown destination for a nation? If there's not, where is a leader taking us? Is the leader, or the hundred aspirants to leader, someone who thinks he's the best man to do it? How did he know? Did he find out? No, he didn't: he's convinced in the absence of evidence. If he says he found out, where did he find out? Who told him? The answer is: *he* told him. So he talks to himself and believes what he hears. But now you say—" (I hadn't said a thing.) "What about writers and composers and people who invent things? Ah, here is the value of being able to follow one's own direction in the absence of a preknown goal, in the absence of evidence that one can do the task. For these things are activities for which there can be no training. They can be trained in details, in the manner used by others, but for the whole task they're on their own. They must develop their own way of doing. So when a young person says: I will be a great painter—is that rational?"

He paused.

"It sounds reasonable," I said tentatively, looking away.

He clapped a hand to his forehead. "She's got me. Yes— reasonable. But not rational." He was sitting back against a corner of the lounge. The parts of him that I knew about were bunched under his trousers. I love you, father, I said in my head, and when he looked away from my face, I let my eyes rest down there, just to see them again.

"Me: ML"

Her budding breasts pointed like arrowheads at a distant enemy who would inevitably fall. They were sharp and stuck up under her tunic; it was impossible to tit clash her, they were so far apart, and small.

When she wrote verse for the English lesson, her stuff was always about herself. "Me: ML" was a sample title:

> Only yesterday she stood under
> A streetlight in a busy town;
> It drowned her in the gold of sodium.
> She groped, caught in darkness loud as thunder.
> Four walls she built round her mind
> But the twisted heart, the forgotten part of her
> Is unprotected, open to the sky.
> Her consciousness is a room clouded
> With smoke. Her sky concave,
> Beneath it she feels
> An inner greatness wrapped in distracting laughter.
> The calm she feels is paper-frail,
> Deep dangerous fluids swirl beneath,
> Which are no friends to her.
>
> Hot metal passes her face
> Arrows of acid, arrows of fire
> Rioting from her own brain
> Pouring from her,
> Returning,
> Aimed at only her.

"Do you like it?" she asked. "Not that I give a shit."

I didn't answer. I think she hadn't asked the right question. Plumpton liked it: that was enough to give ML the chance for a sneer.

> *"Oompah, oompah,*
> *Shove it up your joompah,"*

she said cheerfully when she got 19½ out of 20.

A Disease Called the Future

Kids hung out of the buses each afternoon, making the noises of hell for the driver. They yelled at people walking in the street, flicked lolly papers into the driving windows of cars, and tortured anonymous citizens with their laughter.

The only thing that could silence them was the sight of a long sleek car drawn up alongside the bus at the lights, a long car with expensive people in it, expensive young people. Pros, not proles.

When the wheeled money had drawn away ahead, the kids would sigh collectively; they knew there were two classes and the hope of riches was something that would recede further every year they lived. The years would stretch hope out thinner until one day they would fail the grading or their bodies would change and it would snap.

Today a long red car was there at the intersection and the kids shut up, watching full of envy as it hurtled ahead, subsiding in a communal sorrow when it was out of sight.

There was a glow in the sky as if the world had blood pressure. The clouds were crystallized sugar. When a miserable few drops of rain came, they were greasy like sweat, and looked as if they'd taste of salt. The sky coughed, its nose ran. The drops brought up the smell of the bitumen road, then evaporated on the warmth left by the sun. The road we were on was an artery of the world, and it was clogged with waste products, like us kids. We were not an organ of society: we were a danger to it. Parasites embedded in the walls of society.

A big storm came up that night, the wind picked at the locks, tried the doors for weakness, tried to knock them down. The roof beams groaned. But as I lay sweating in bed trying to emulate Marie-Louise I felt it wasn't the roof propping up the sky: it was me.

Next day I stopped at the top of the street after school and stood for about twenty minutes looking for signs of humanity on the faces of people who passed in cars and trucks and buses.

I gazed in at the windows of cars that had to stop at the crossing—and they hated stopping, it used their cars up—looking in at them, trying to say without speaking: Do you know me? Do you recognize me? As if, perhaps having seeds of future humanity in them, their recognition of me meant that I was part of the future too.

So much of our thought, so much of our desire is toward the future. As if the present is only a nuisance, an obstacle, to be got over, round, through as soon as possible. The end of the future is, individually, death. Yet if there had been a betting agency taking bets against death, the whole society would have invested.

Was I part of the future? Were they? And why were death and the future so much on my mind, so much a *part* of my mind? Thirteen years of age. Did mother know? And was that why she had retreated from the world? Was that why she dangled greatness in front of me? Or had she caused me to choose death and the future as companions *because* of that word?

I knew I was being unreasonable.

After yesterday's storm this is one of those days of bird's-egg sky and sharp-beaked birds. How changeable the world is from one day to the next!

Scaredy Cats

I had to stop playing hidings with the kids from along the street. When I was "in" I went after them, not cautiously but as if I were a hungry tiger, leaping through the middle of bushes and pouncing on them. I don't know what made me do it, but they got frightened and for a while they didn't know whether they liked the fright or wanted me elsewhere. After I leaped headfirst through a clump of hibiscus bushes three houses along Heisenberg Close, the grown-ups were against me too, and they told their children to come inside, which meant we had to move off to a frontyard represented by at least someone in the game. But the rest decided they didn't want me landing on them either and went inside, and next day they were nowhere to be seen.

I was left standing out the front near the eucalypts by myself, breathed on by a soft October wind with a mouthful of early summer flowers—but the taste of flowers was in the wind's mouth, not mine.

The Spare Room Was Full of Mother's Notes

Father bought a prefabricated shed and had it erected in our back-yard. The neighbors wondered if it was a toolshed, a playhouse, a supersize dog kennel. He said no to everything. He wasn't ashamed of my mother's notes, just careful of her right to keep making them in privacy.

The shed was called Proust, after the redoubtable Marcel, who also chronicled moments of conscious life. We assumed this was what mother did.

We moved mother's oldest notes to the furthest corners of the shed, over her protests. She wanted the most ancient things closest at hand, so her past would be easily accessible.

"OK," said my father. "Fair enough. So we put the latest things in first, at floor level."

"Will I be able to get at them easily?" asked my mother.

She could not visualize future events. She had no way of picturing where those notes would end up in relation to the things put in later.

"Naturally not."

"But I want them where I can look over them immediately."

"But you want the old ones where you can look over *them* immediately," said my father.

"Of course."

"But you can't have both."

"Don't be silly," she laughed. "Of course I can."

The removal bogged down until mother carried things out to the shed herself. She got the piles one deep round the walls, all were accessible easily. Then she went back inside to consult the volume of unplaced notes. There were still too many in the spare room for her to get at them easily. She added another row alternately on top of the first row in the shed, then inside the first row. Both ways were inconvenient.

"Would you like a dozen sheds in the yard so you can have one row round the inside of the walls in each shed?"

"Wonderful!" said my mother, clapping her hands.

"Don't be ridiculous," said my father in the only display of annoyance with her that I ever saw. She spent the rest of the day in deep depression at such savagery, and in furious notetaking activity.

I suggested shelves all round, so nothing had to be lifted to get at the rest. Father put the shelves in. Mother put her boxes on the shelves. The house settled down.

Harvey Comes Up Roses

Harvey Lowe was the boy I kept next to in optional woodwork class; he worked in his father's workshop at home and made chessmen on his father's lathe. He was the best boy at woodwork, and I determined I would be best girl. I watched every movement he made, and I could see the difference between us. He loved wood, and seemed to understand it. When he cut or hammered, it was if he said to it: This will do you good, you want to be this new shape, nothing's going to hurt you, you and I are working together.

But I, although I admired the grain and the shiny effects as you turned the planed wood against the light, I didn't love it. The smell was nice, no more. Harvey Lowe drank it in as if he was a baby snuggling against, and drinking in, the smell of his mother.

He had a Maria Callas rose growing under his right armpit. Only the flower: the stem was inside.

"I can't bud from it," he said sadly. "I went to the nursery, and they told me they need more stem. There's no stem, no stem at all. Still, there's a market for the blooms."

245

He got a dollar a rose. His armpit Maria Callas was famous, and researchers and curio collectors and sellers would have bid up the price, except they formed a ring and agreed to keep the price at a dollar. It was all a matter of being on the spot when the rose appeared as a bud and bloomed. It only took a day in summer, and sometimes in winter there were weeks between blooms.

It got in the way of his woodwork, but he looked after it well in the other classes. He wasn't in my class for anything else. I did top levels in everything: he was only good at woodwork.

"Still, there's a market for the blooms," he said when I asked to smell it, then wrinkled my nose and straightened up, looking down at his honest but none-too-bright face. He wore a protector to stop his bloom from being crushed. It smelled.

The Big G

In letters from friends, quiet asides from teachers, admiring comments from neighbors who didn't have kids around my age, and from relatives who by reason of circumstance were exempt from jealousy, came the same message: I was destined for big things.

Don't laugh. I wasn't a large, brutal, kneeing and elbow-jabbing basketball player in class; I was a diligent, clever student, sometimes attentive. I did some work at home, but I was lucky in that I seemed to understand the teachers the first time. That was a great advantage; it meant that all later learning was built on a base. The kids that didn't understand the first time were in a sweat trying to understand what went on three steps ago, and never caught up. I know the lessons weren't useful later, and knew then, but it instilled a confidence, a presence in the face of new situations, that stayed with me.

From what people had been saying for years, I began to aspire, all on my own, toward a glowing distant light called fame. Reputation was another name for it. There was yet another word, but I never said it to myself. I heard it from a friend at high school, a girl kept at high school by her brothers, though she couldn't easily afford the uniform. Somehow they managed to get the material and

246

have it made up by ladies who lived in proper houses. They lived in a tent in the bush. Her name was Lil Lutherburrow, the one who wrote the poem.

The shy word was greatness.

"Your name will live," Lil wrote to me in a holiday letter. "There is greatness in you. I can tell. I know it." (Why did I take notice of a Free?)

That word gave me the urge to push against its accompanying idea of death and the future, against the dissolution of self, against separation from others. Against the final relinquishing of life, to which I was now committed, and had been, for thirteen years.

Before conception all one's possibilities are intact: the possibility that one will be born some day; that one will be unlike all who have ever lived; the possibility of being so different and so special and so full of energy that one's existence might *be* greatness.

Yes, I am committed to the future, which is a rope coiled on the deck of a boat. Length by length it is taken up, and each length is a day; it is lowered over the side into deep water length by length, and on the end of it is an anchor. The future is used up length by length and thrown overboard, and when the anchor strikes the seabed there is no need for more.

It Looked As Drunk As He Was

I had waited, not really having planned anything, for father to come home Sunday morning. He'd been out all night; he rolled out of a taxi, singing, and slumped onto the sun lounge. Mother took one look and went gladly back to her desk. She wouldn't be interrupted all morning, not even with nuisance kisses on the back of her neck.

What I did was to get it out, raising it in the same way as before, and placing its head, or its mouth as I think of it, against the part of my unders where it obviously ought to go. I rubbed it back and forth against the soft flesh a number of times, but couldn't get it to make an impression on my little clitoral bump, but another thing happened. A quantity of moisture from my natural stock of such things seemed

247

to respond to the movement in those parts and descended to the area affected; no sooner there than the back and forth movement was abruptly stopped, for the mouth of his penis slipped in.

What should I do? My legs were spread one on each side of him, my thighs straining with the unaccustomed spread position. It was obvious I wouldn't be able to move much. Men pushed in and back, but if they were stationary the female would have to move up and down. What punishment on the muscles!

I decided to just let myself down to see what it felt like inside. Would I tear something? We'd have to see what happened. I let myself down slowly and felt a slight sensation round the entrance, no more. Was that all? Wasn't I a virgin? Where was the destruction of tissues? The blood? I looked under me: no blood. I gratefully allowed myself to rest on his body, with it in as far as its length would take it. There *was* something then, a sort of fullness; perhaps it was pushing against some organ or other.

I thought it might be indecent to go up and down, apart from the difficulty, so I got up until its mouth was only just in me, and ran my fingers lightly up and down it, using the moisture that I had left on it. I did this for quite a time.

When my thighs couldn't take it anymore, I got off. The penis chose that moment to erupt. Two spurts of whitish thick fluid went into the air, and more welled up and overflowed the end of it, running down the side rather like cornflour and water when it's halfway between being cooked and uncooked—part clear, part cloudy. I think I had expected the spurts to rise up like a volcano and shoot around everywhere: at least I knew now it didn't come in bucketsful. But maybe inside mother, the normal way, there would be more.

I didn't think it right to give myself an orgasm with my father, so I cleaned up his penis and wiped up round his underclothes and replaced everything.

Even when I'd wiped its mouth it lay there, head on one side, dribbling slowly. It looked as drunk as he was.

When I'd wiped it all up, I wished I'd spent more time looking at the semen itself. I should have examined it more closely. How could there be millions in that little lot?

Arnold Long, the jumping boy, had been at school for the partly sighted in his primary days. He'd always been hopping about on one leg or two before, but at High he began to show promise at the thing he became famous for. He looked very cute; even a dour fourteen-year-old girl could acknowledge *that;* hopping up and down, a grin on his face, his smooth downy cheeks decorated with a large pink spot on either side of the grin. His eyes never shone, though; the lids didn't open like other kids', and the sun didn't have a chance to catch the glint of liquid on his eyeball.

His pleasure in jumping was the most innocent thing in the whole school, I guess.

When he got away from the asphalt on to the grassed edge of the playing fields he bounced up from the balls of his feet and went high, high, touching easily the lower branches of the trees no one else could reach. One of the teachers suggested he try for the long jump. After school he had to be shown the white marker and learn to find it as he ran toward it. It was painful to watch but he kept at it.

One of the teachers told his parents, and arranged for him to be given practice after school.

I saw him jumping there and was startled to see him jump 5.8 meters. In year eight, and only partly seeing! I hurried home and marked out a run-up across the neighbors' front lawn, got father's mattock and dug a jumping pit, digging the sandy soil up so it no longer had lumps and sods. By the time father got home I had adjusted the jumping mark so that with a good jump I landed in the middle of the pit.

The car came round the curve in Heisenberg Close, slowed to turn right up our drive and as it climbed the twenty meter slope I took off. The car was stopped and I was flying through the air and father watched in amazement as I landed in the greyish sand and sent spurts of soil before me; I saw his eyes go to the run-up, the jumping mark, and again to the pit I had dug.

"Al! What have you done?" he said, with no great originality.

"Training for the broad jump."

"But you trained at school before," he said lamely.

"That meant I didn't train."

"But you won before, with no training."

"Not now. There's a kid at school can jump 5.8 meters."

"I can jump that," he countered. "At least I could."

"Get your gear off, father. And show me," I dared him.

"Did you dig the hole?"

"I dug the pit."

"Oh."

He went inside, kissed mother, ignored her irritation, changed into shorts and jogging shoes and came out to me.

By the time father had lined up for his first jump, some other kids had come by, and stood watching.

Father jumped, I jumped. I put the board so that a 5.8 meter jump would land me in the middle of the jumping pit. Father insisted on having first go, and failed. The audience made a murmur of sympathy. They were girls from year ten and nine, mostly living down in Boyle Avenue.

I went to the start of my run, shut my eyes for a second to rest them, relaxed all over as I stood there, breathed deeply, then took off, trying to judge my run-up so there were no uneven strides just before the jumping-off board. I flew, working my legs as I had seen Olympic athletes do 5.8 meters. I stood up, thinking with satisfaction of Arnold Long.

The audience made no sound. Father had another go, and failed again. I'm afraid I laughed.

"I beat you!" I rejoiced, but the watching girls sympathized with the loser. They couldn't have jumped it, either.

Perhaps I shouldn't have got him to compete with me. Perhaps he was tired. Adults *do* get tired at odd times during the day, as well as at night.

He smiled at me, his spirits up.

"Good jumping, darling," he said. "You're a winner. Men are definitely the weakest sex." We had a little understanding about the number of the sexes. He went inside.

I practiced until I could get to the 5.8 meter mark every time, and went in when I was satisfied I could match Arnold Long.

He was sitting at the dining room table.

"I can do it!" I said. "I can do it every time."

He didn't look at me, but said quietly, "I suppose it must be right, and we *are* the weak ones."

That's all he said, but an hour later when I'd finished my homework I came out ravenous, and he hadn't even started getting tea ready. He was still sitting there, looking out of the big back window, one elbow on the table and its hand with a thumb under his chin and forefinger resting below his nose, the other arm loose across his left knee. He didn't seem to notice me, and as I looked one of those small, harmless flies landed on his forehead, stopped to search about for goodies among his pores, trotted a few paces further on, scouted around, crossed its front legs busily with a washing motion, one over the other, then reversing the movement. It took off briefly, though father made no movement, then landed again, just above his right eye, did much the same things. Very friendly. It made a short flight, landed on the back of his hand, and did a difficult journey down his arm, awkwardly negotiating the long hairs, full of the high seriousness of small creatures. Neither of them noticed me. I went quietly away.

This Isn't Exactly a Dream

It's a mental picture I carry with me: a ring of adoring faces surrounds me, my mother, my teachers, various boys' faces, neighbors, relatives. They beam a message at me with their eyes and their smiles, and I reward them with a smile of my own which I can reproduce at will.

This almost-dream picture is liable to become visible to me at any time; on my way to school, dreaming during one of those interminable explanations of surds to the duller kids in the class, and unreal and imaginary numbers. Or in the middle of eating my tea at night, with a fork halfway to my mouth, with perhaps some underdone steak on it that I know I shouldn't like—because of certain intellectual objections to killing animals, which one may have if one wishes—I shouldn't like but I do.

This picture is most powerful, sensually, if I'm in bed at night and I've decided to masturbate. I do it with all those beaming, approving faces watching me, and when it comes the orgasm is shattering—an ecstasy of pleasure shot through and through with apprehension, a feeling of some mysterious pain which is something other than pain. This particular one starts up in my chest and descends on a thin thread of feeling that winds down below my navel, then strikes in deep with a warmth, a radiance that words can't take hold of.

Have You Had a Bleed?

They'd asked me so often, the kids at school, that it was with a great sense of relief that I felt the intimations and small miseries of my approaching initiation.

When it came it *would* be sports day. I was the only one of the regular basketball team that was out injured that day, so I sat and watched. My schoolbag was between my legs, I shifted it to one side of me, glad of the comfort of sitting down and containing within the solid block of my lower trunk parts the unease that had got into me and to have my legs together right from my ankles to the top of my thighs. I took out a pen and an exercise book and wrote a poem.

> *Mirror bordered by flesh-frame*
> *Reflecting, as it must,*
> *Blue sky between white,*
> *Floating chunks of edible mountain,*
> *Toothpick trees.*
> *Smash the mirror,*
> *Each long sliver of brittle flesh on the grass*
> *A piece of the jigsaw,*
> *Part of the sky-mirror,*
> *Bearing bits of brittle blood.*

It wasn't really a poem. Did I mean the mirror was the mind? Or the world was a dinner? Or the body was a mirror?

I gave up. It was a mess. I began watching the game again, while daylight fell in ribbons round me.

Friends For a Time

Shaziye Osman was coming from tennis when the bus dropped me back at school. I walked with her.

Shaziye was, courtesy of our biology class, called the Callistemon Queen, or Cancer Knobs. She had knobs on her arms like the cankers on a tree, or the seeds on an arm of bottlebrush.

"Hello, Cancer," I said ungraciously to her, but she was so glad to be walking with me she didn't mind. I was mainly hoping the pad was in place, and no leaks.

"It's not a cancer," she corrected me mildly. "It's just that some of the inside has surfaced."

"Have you got it on the rest of you?" I said. I didn't really care. The day of your first period ought to be special, but here I was talking with Cancer Knobs, and not feeling very special at all. What if the blood ran down your legs?

Her father had wheat stalks in his elbows. When the specialist referred him to the state agriculture department the verdict was that it was an old hardy type of wheat with heads not as full as more recently developed grain, but it would be handy for the genetic bank; he was to submit the full ears, when they came, to the scientists, and they would harvest him for the benefit of future stocks.

We talked about wheat and her father for the rest of the walk. She left me when I turned off into Heisenberg Close. She had another kilometer to go. She never took the bus because of her knobs: the kids pinched them and it hurt.

I saw her next day too, and we became friends for a week or two.

We told each other everything. She'd had her first bleed five months before.

We practiced together *how* to look attentive; our teacher was a magazine article on how to hypnotize males. We practiced our timing—*when* to look attentive. We practiced random and puzzling expressions calculated to put them off balance.

We devised small movements of hand, head, eyes to force them to look. We tried to work out verbal ploys to lead them on, to get them to say more; in short, to make them look like the fools we knew them to be.

We told each other everything.

One morning, before my second period, I suddenly thought: I'll be walking with that pill Shaziye again this morning. I'm sick of her.

I left home ten minutes early and never walked with her again.

It was the same week that the Park was pronounced dead: the one near Carpentaria Chemicals. They had to dig out all the soil to a depth of a meter, and bring fresh earth in.

Maria and Tony

Maria Attardi came from a school out toward the mountains; her father had moved to be near his relatives. She often sat up the front of my aisle in music, her legs out sideways and feet planted well back behind her. I tried to copy her position, but found it put weight on the lower parts of me, and it felt like something that would lead to masturbation. I liked to sit back and regard the teacher in a detached manner. Most of them thought I was being superior.

Maria used to wait on the newsagent's corner for a dark boy in a red car hung with tassels and with gold flashes on the side. Tony, she said his name was. Tony Sergio. His father worked in a gambling place.

She'd had periods since year seven. I watched her, her face, her actions, her words, to see if I could see why I was different from her. She was medium in English and terrible at maths. Why should I bother my head about her? However, she was in my class for English, and something about her kept me thinking of her, and looking. When Mister Patel had us for two periods and gave us the whole time for writing a story, I had Maria in mind, only I made her a child.

Maria's special friend was Annette Julian. Her older brother was Mario. He had always loved to make things. At that time he was making a girl he called Lisa. She grew out of him, feet first. His family, who came from the Mediterranean, had such pride that they kept him locked in his room because of his deformity. He didn't have a room to himself before, so this could be seen as an improvement in his station in life.

By the time two feet were out and it was clear this was a female of perhaps eighteen—he was sixteen—he knew every line of the feet, every hair, every toe-shape; the arches, the insteps, the pattern of prints on the soles. He fingered them constantly, and they wiggled slightly as if they liked the contact. He discovered what any mother knows, that we are born with all the wrinkles necessary to make the movements we need, without stretching and tearing the skin.

Soon there had to be a foot-rest for the new legs, for it was a great weight for the front of him, and soreness developed at the top of the extrusion where the skin stretched, and also beneath, where skin, common to him and his girl, folded up and was pressed together.

I dreamed that at night her unformed soul crawled out from her limbs and inspected him.

My Father Was Mother to the Woman of the Future

My father was my mother in all practical ways, such as cleaning up after me, washing the dishes I'd eaten from, also the cats' plates, doing the cooking for my unpredictable appetite, making my bed. Mother had turned aside from such futilities years before though she seemed happy enough that they continued to be done. She was her own woman: she certainly didn't belong to father or to me. We went our own way in the house, taking care not to disturb her. If you went up to her to say something, the aura round her gave you a little push while you were still several meters away, and if you came on despite that, and spoke to her while her pen was busy on the paper, it was most likely that you would get no reply. If she had finished her sentence she might look up and look at you as if she were listening, but her eyes seemed to penetrate your body like those cosmic rays the man put dry cleaning fluid down a hole to catch, and you knew she could see only a vague outline of you, and everything important was beyond.

Father was mother to the woman of the future, and the future extended before me like it did before mother; she had millions of bits of paper to write on in the future: I had millions of moments on which to write in large letters that word I was so shy of.

Father Is Sometimes Silent

Father is sometimes silent in what I think of as a real situation, and I know why. It's because he is afraid that he might go straight into the lines of some play he'd done, speaking lines instead of turning his attention painfully to what is actually happening.

I worry for him.

Several times I've been talking to him and being bright and so forth, and he's begun to look at me in a really loving fatherly way, then suddenly caught himself and said: "Shit! I did that on stage!"

Apologizing, blaming himself. I would have been content with the look as it was, wherever else he used it.

By a stroke of bad luck I hit his eye when he and I were having our weekly boxing. There's still a lump on the eyebrow. It wasn't my fault entirely: he put out his left hand just as I was coming forward and my right glove traveled over his forearm and elbow and shoulder and landed over his left eye. I was sorry for that, especially as I'd beaten him in jumping so recently. He was silent after my punch, too. It was exactly what he'd told me to do.

Sometimes When Father Had Been Drinking

Sometimes when father had been drinking, but not enough for passing out, he had peculiar moods: some miserable and dark, some querulous.

He once burst out to me, "Who am I? Am I my best part? Am I someone I have never discovered?"

He was under no illusion that I was too young to understand.

"Why haven't writers written a part for me, *me!*—myself—for my real self? Am I to die when my writer, the writer of *me,* is still a child? Unborn, even?"

He gazed into his steel pocket mirror and asked passionately and fearfully: "Who is it? Who am I? What am I?"

His distress was not painful for me: he was an adult. I was shaken by my own storms; his were not earthshaking to me, though his words opened a new door on the world of grown-ups.

"I've always had to feel others' emotions! Never mine. How am I to know after all this time whether mine are really mine? Am I too practiced in emotions, can I bring them too facilely to the surface, to know which contain me?"

"Is facilely a word?" I asked. This brutal remark brought him back to his accustomed pleasantly genial state.

"I do run on, don't I darling?" And he kept silent for a bit. Then, "No. I've never even felt those emotions I have to act. They're all practice. Windowdressing. Inside, I feel nothing. They say the pain of some of my professional emotions is terrible. But it's just pain. Not terrible: just pain. The pain is unreal, it's in the audience. I throw the words, the situation, the expression at them. They feel it all. I'm a dummy." He laughed, clearly wanting me to laugh. I smiled nicely.

I imagined him then, on his deathbed, still with the mirror, being different people, acting others' lives, and saying "Which one is dying? They all are. But which damned one is me?"

I didn't tell him my imaginings.

I don't think father ever spoke like that to mother. I daresay she would have taken no notice.

And yet, despite her ignoring us—I don't mean purposely, but in effect that is what she does—mother dominates us. She's not even there, she's in another room, yet she prescribes what we will do. I'm sure father does what he does because it is the way to please her and give her nothing to complain of.

There are times when I'd like to complain, but I'm afraid it will disturb her. I censor myself because of her. And I don't like it.

She didn't fall deep into one love like he did: she fell deep into herself and became a miner.

Time and Women

All the girls I knew turned every time they passed a window or a sheet of glass, even a shiny expanse of metal, and looked at themselves. The gesture could have been mistaken from a distance for a sporty toss of the head, one designed to have the hair fall in a windblown fashion over the forehead, or a curious look into a shop window, but it wasn't.

Not one man looked sideways into windows. Why not? If the behavior of the women was normal, why were the males lacking in this bit of display? Were they so caught up in their round of being active—even sprawling around they seemed to be thinking of distant objects and actions, rather than clothes and their hairdo—that they had no time for the slide into neutral gear that allowed the mind to slip from active pursuits and objects to interior matters of self-contemplation?

Did females live longer because of that interior life, so that of any hour they had a higher proportion of time devoted to their own interior concerns? Did they truly live within, in a manner allied to but different from Eastern contemplatives? Were the hairdo, the overall appearance, the face-color, the lottery of the future, the equivalent of navel, nirvana and mantra?

Did men have shorter lives because they did not allow themselves this time? Was that why women were often so unused, in the sense that they knew less of the world's objects, less of the world's motives? If so, how did they manage to age more quickly yet live longer? Or is that not a fair question?

Had they used themselves up less?

A longer life with less in it, or a shorter one with more—is that the choice?

The sun, which teaches us time, knows the answer, but which of us knows how to ask the right question?

Pale Robert

When there was rain the boys in senior school took us for rides in their cars. One of their favorite places was at the bottom of the gorge, where a road led down to a depression, then up out of it. The depression filled with about half a meter of water, and the boys got up speed and ran at the sheet of water and if they had enough speed they aquaplaned over to the other edge of the water then, when their tires hit solid ground they skidded, for the wheels, after aquaplaning, weren't straight forward.

The best was when Don Strong had his antique Beetle, with its flat plate underneath to give it flotation, filled with kids and the rest of us on the roof. There was no other traffic down there in the gorge, everyone knew it flooded after rain.

When everyone was there, a sort of nerviness rose from us—we all felt it—and we took it for energy and were pleased with ourselves.

Even Robert Gambling, who had a brown rabbit growing, came with the rest of us to enjoy the thrills of danger.

He had kept the rabbit secret until the very day that the whole crew on the roof of Donny Strong's car was thrown off when the car hit something under water, and stopped. Robert was under several others, under water, and swallowed lots, and when the others got up, he floated. We pulled him out and turned him upside down to get the water out, and his shirt fell open. There was the head of the rabbit. We gave it some grass. It took three months to grow out.

He had a rabbit get stuck once, and no one was able to help him. He was taken to the University, but since no one knew the mechanism by which the animal grew, they couldn't help him. The rabbit was agitated, and struggled, and its struggles exhausted Robert Gambling, who got weaker and weaker, all his strength going to the rabbit. I think they should have taken the risk and killed it, but they didn't. The rabbit was stronger than Pale Robert, and lived off him until Robert died. After which, of course, the rabbit's life was siphoned off by the power in Robert's death.

Some hours after tea on the day he was cremated I went outside and stood in the backyard looking up at the stars that seemed so

259

cold and naked in the blue-black sky. And yet, I thought, their reality—their existence—is burning, and they will be dead when their fire is out, and they will grow cold. All over the sky there are stars forming; burning; fading; cold.

Robert Gambling was now a gram or so of ash: and the rest gas. I stayed out a while longer, and found myself listening to the leaves unfold in October's spring, and drinking in the sweetness on the night air. I felt a little guilty for being diverted so easily from Robert's going—but not much.

There Has To Be a First Time

In all the enjoyment and excitement and playing around, the boys would try surreptitiously to touch us up—squeeze a breast or rest a hand on your bottom or manage to scrape their arm between your legs.

I didn't really have the softness that would allow me to let people do things to me when they felt like it. I was one who did things, not one of those to whom things were done, and I knew that if I expected to have any—or rather, enough—of the normal sex experiences I would need to overcome this fault.

I resolved that when the first presentable boy wanted me, I would be obliging, however tempted I was to attack him for presumption.

The First of the Month

It was after school, Friday the first of December.

He came up to me directly, then seemed to sheer off sideways, maintaining contact only with his eyes, which he let slide up and down my body. He moved forward, he moved back, getting different views. I looked him straight in the eyes, but he wouldn't do the same to me. Finally he stood still in front of me, but his eyes never met mine. He seemed to want me to feed on the interest his eyes showed in my human form, never mind mental contact.

His name was Roger Hardy. Don't laugh. He was two years above me, in year ten. When we packed into Don Strong's Beetle he was one of the kids under me. I guess touching me on the legs did something for him; it was no more to me than rubbing against a cat.

As he performed this primitive mating display in front of me, I remembered I should have hurried home. Sonya, the neighbors' Labrador, was due to have a litter, and I was to get whichever male pup I chose. Mother reminded me as I left the house.

"If you're late you might find they've all gone. Everyone wants males."

However, there was a male here who wanted me.

It had to happen sometime. I don't mean it was just a case of get it over with. Up to then the thing that all the older women had over us—even the hockey teacher—was that they'd had it, they knew what it was like. And most of us hadn't. Even the Scripture lady had it every night, we assured each other.

We'd had plenty of kissing, plenty of feeling, hands round our shoulders feeling a tit, or sliding off a knee down between the legs. They liked to touch us.

"You know it's got to be sometime. Well, this is it." He put his arm around me. We were the same height. We went over to the grass behind the Assembly Hall.

Roger told me very directly what he was going to do.

"What I'll do is this, I'll take your pants down or you can, and I'll put this little guy a little way in. Be sure to let's know if it hurts."

He said the last bit with emphasis, to get me thinking about that aspect of it and to take my mind off what was actually happening, like an insurance salesman gets you thinking of loved ones and protection and takes your mind off the essential part of *his* operation, which is the regular installments of cash from you to him forever.

He got me to lie down, pants off. I'd gone to the lavatory at lunchtime but I wish I'd had a wash. He said, "Hold these lucky coins for me."

He put one coin in each hand. They felt small, I had to clench my fist. Was he afraid I'd scratch if I had my hands free?

His thing was out stiff already, I could see it pushing out the front of his grey school pants. He unzipped, and it burst past his white underpants. It looked like a thick blunt arrow, not as thick as father's, or as brown.

His face came close to mine and he grabbed round me with one arm, while he held his thing and steadied it to push it in me. When it touched me down there the end of it wasn't hard, it was all soft. Like sponge rubber round the hard bonelike core.

He pushed against me, but his thing didn't find the entrance. He wiggled it about against the flat part that becomes the fold in your leg when you've got them together. But there was no way in there.

I wondered if I ought to say anything. Like, "If at first you don't," or something. I didn't want to laugh, but a small giggle wasn't out of the question.

I held the stupid coins and didn't say anything. Flat on my back. It resembled an operation: he was the doctor.

At last he got the idea to put his shoulder down on the ground beside my head, and leave his two hands free to work out the problem. I felt one hand at me, getting the hairs separated with a finger, searching for the lips. Labia major, the diagram said in the sex book. And labia minor.

Then with the other hand he grabbed his thing and worked the tip around where there was some moisture. It wasn't the moisture the book said was stimulated by this situation: it was sweat or the remnants of the pee I'd had after we were let out last period. Shortly he looked a bit less anxious and felt confident enough to bring one hand back to put it around my neck. I caught a familiar smell as the hand passed my face.

He pushed. His face screwed up, it was hurting him a bit. I still didn't like to say anything. Maybe it would put him off. I was supposed to just lie there and be sexy. I didn't know how to be that, I guess it meant just being a female. That's all they seem to need.

It slipped in suddenly, and he looked relieved.

"Did that hurt?"

I didn't know what to say.

"No."

"Have you been done before?" I felt he wanted me to say no.

"No."

"Do you ride horses?"

"Yes. Do you?"

"Got nothing to do with it if I ride horses. Only if you do."

"What difference does it make?"

"Shut up and let me get on with it."

"I'll pull away if you want to be like that."

"You won't. You haven't been fucked if you don't cop the spunk."

It didn't take long for his thing to yield results. He made several frantic grunts and one like a howl, that became joyful, then died away. He stopped, and breathed deeply, and eased back out of me a bit, but not right out. I couldn't feel much, but I felt *that* much. I did feel—when the convulsive movements had stopped—the sudden expansions they call throbs. I think. I stayed still, wondering what the correct behavior was. I hadn't noticed anything. I suppose I'd expected something burning hot in me, or something. I don't know what I'd expected, really. The girls that had had it would never tell you the details you really wanted to know.

Then I felt something wet dribbling down out of me, toward my bottom. I involuntarily turned a bit on one buttock, to have it run down more on the side. I don't know why I did that. Respect for the seed of life, maybe.

No. I wasn't thinking of the seed of life, I only had my handkerchief to wipe myself, and I guess I didn't want to wipe in there with it. There might be something left that would make a mess on my hanky.

He was still in, and he was still stiff.

"Still got your lucky coins?"

I opened my hands and showed him. His breath was not as neutral as father's.

He felt in my school tunic for anything in the way of breasts—there wasn't much—grunted and put both arms round me and did it all again.

I had to go back to a flat position. I felt the liquid drip down the crease of my bottom. I felt when it was on it. I didn't like it.

He pushed back and forward this time, a good deal harder and fiercer. He was more puffed at the end. Some of the time I felt his heart going. He made more noises. I don't know how to describe them—these were rather like the reckless yells of someone excitedly going into danger.

That made two, and his penis was still stiff. I heard a foot crunch on the edge of the bitumen path where it was crumbling into gravel. So did Roger Hardy. He must have thought it was one of the damn teachers. He twisted his body and wrenched away, stood up, zippered his school trousers, and ran.

I pushed my school skirt down and pretended to be taking a rest. No one appeared. Whoever it was must have turned away up the fork in the path toward the school gate.

Roger was gone. The intruder was gone. I remained, with a lucky coin in each hand. I put the coins in my schoolcase. I felt more wetness coming. I dabbed at it with my hanky, which was now quite sticky.

I ought to throw it away, there were no initials on it. I sniffed at it. Funny smell, rather interesting in fact, though how much was mine I couldn't tell. Their thing has to go past that part of you, so no wonder.

I set off for home. Outside the school gates the other kids rushed at me from behind trees.

"You sneaky bastards," I greeted them. They threw themselves about.

"Who fucked Al? Who fucked Al?" they chanted. "Spunky! Spunky!"

Semen ran down my leg again. I felt it.

When they'd calmed down, they asked why Roger Hardy ran off up the street.

"Did you bash him?" they asked. I didn't have to answer.

"Did you get two lucky coins?" asked Sharon Jameson. I said yes.

"He does that to everyone!" they roared. "They're just the first coins he comes across in his pocket. They're not lucky!"

I was going to put them away in my drawer, just the same.

When I'd crossed the bridge and lugged my schoolbag up to the Goughs' house on the corner, Robert Gough was already at his piano practice. He was playing Mozart. I stopped. There was a recording playing, and he was playing over the pianist on the recording. It was K 488, the end of the first movement, where the orchestral part sounds like a huge mechanical process winding down and coming to a precisely synchronized stop. Robert took up the solo part after an excruciatingly long pause. Then the sad liquid notes lifted themselves slowly, so slowly, into their song, and their song was like something sung after heavy tears have gone, but only after.

I pulled myself away from it. That pale, skinny little bastard! I would never be able to play like that. I was glad when I could hear it no longer.

"You missed seeing the puppy being born," mother said, when I got in the door.

"When did it come?"

"Twenty minutes ago."

"Oh no!" I complained. "Why did it have to be then!"

"If you'd come at the right time you'd have seen it all," she observed with calm. "I reminded you this morning."

But I didn't come at the right time.

I went next door to look at the puppy. I called him Creep. My hanky, when it dried, felt quite stiff. And had an interesting smell.

As mother was speaking to me critically about not being there for the birth, there were a few moments when we were still enough, both of us, for me to look straight into her eyes, and there, sideways on as she was to the light, I saw myself reflected in the shiny center of her eyes, a light and glittering figure on her pupils.

265

And yet, looking into those eyes, I was reminded of a mirror, a mirror with no eyes, a mirror that could not see me.

Next day in the playground Roger directed a penetrating look toward my thighs and the place where, if they were scissor blades, they would cut things.

One of the teachers saw this exchange and looked also. Others followed the eyes. I was some distance away, my back against the brick wall, standing in the sun outside the science block.

Gradually, more and more of the student population turned and looked at the space between my thighs that males are so interested in. I spread my legs, enjoying the attention.

After a minute I was tired of this and crossed my legs and went on talking to Marie-Louise.

Monday afternoon he did it again. The girls waited for me in the same place, little bitches.

He tried to give me two more coins.

"Hold these two lucky coins for me."

"You said that before."

"Did I?"

I'm surprised he remembered my face.

He unzippered. I watched, my pants in a neat ball stuffed down the front of my school tunic.

There it was, large as life. He had less trouble getting it in. He plunged to and fro smugly. I went home with another hanky stiffened up. Father didn't notice when he put the washing in the machine.

I thought at first I was abnormal when I didn't like it much. I don't mean I disliked it, there was hardly anything to dislike, unless you minded strange breath blowing in your face. I mean there was nothing in it that would make you jump up and down in one spot and clap your hands with delight. It was a very grey and indeterminate consolation to promise myself that I would persist until I got the taste for it.

But I had had it: that was the main thing. No one could laugh at me for being scared or reluctant or inexperienced.

That was the thing bothering me. I had invaginated a male, and I didn't feel a thing. I mean literally. I knew there are no nerve-ends in the vagina, but somehow I expected *something*. There should have been a tingling at least, or the game wasn't fair. All I had, and it wasn't all the time, was a feeling of fullness. And, of course, the more vigorous strokes when the male pubic bone struck mine, cushioned only by the soft flesh and the hair.

> *Pinch and a punch*
> *For the first of the month.*

Clotted Cream

Tuesday afternoon my greatest wish was to see some of it. I said as much to Roger.

"What?" he said aggressively. "This is what you'll see!" fishing for it.

I punched him in the side, where his lowest rib was.

"Don't get aggressive with me," I warned him. "Or I'll cut the stupid thing off!"

He seemed alarmed, as well he might.

"All I want to do is see it. I mean just some of it," I said reasonably. "What does it take to get it to come out?"

He relaxed, obviously glad we were talking of his precious penis.

"Well, you could rub up and down it," he said. "Specially if you have something a bit slippery."

I nodded, spat into my hands, and rubbed the sticky spit up and down. It elevated itself to its maximum, and from there on it was a minute or two and more spit than I had—he had to contribute—until he seemed to twist his body, bring his legs together somewhat, and said, "Ooooh. Now . . !"

Next second it was a well spurting. It wasn't terribly pleasant having it in my hands, but science is science. It was clotted. Not a

267

consistent clotting: an uneven one. And the color white, but not a thick white, rather transparent in parts. Along with the clotted part there was a fine clear liquid, that felt much more slippery than the other material. It was the same as father's, except there was more, and it spurted higher.

I'd have saved myself all this trouble if I'd been with the other girls when they did it to little half-blind Fred.

Somehow, after the first time, everyone seemed to know. I saw people glance at me on the way to school, even teachers at school, with that look in their eye, a knowing mixture of respect and slight contempt. How clever of them to manage it!

I didn't see the boys, or girls either, going round telling others, but more and more seemed to know. As if I carried a mark on me that identified me as someone who'd had it and therefore was in the running to be had.

Sale Time

After school resumed, and I was in year nine, Leonard Digges bought me off Roger Hardy. He gave forty dollars for me. Only forty!

Leonard was a bigger boy, in year twelve. Perhaps that had something to do with such a cheap rate.

"I don't mind," Roger said. "It's all cop. I got you for nought. And when I'm in sixth I'll have to pay younger kids to break 'em in for me." And he went off looking for a first year kid. It was the time for sales of this kind, and other girls were offering themselves like obliging animals to boys they thought they might like. They weren't always allowed to transfer.

"I'm no animal," Rosemary said when I asked her whose she was.

When Leonard had me in his car, I was worried about people looking in, and let my school tunic fall down over me, which annoyed him. He liked us both to be able to see it going in and out.

When he got in I watched his face for any sign that he thought I was satisfactory or otherwise. His expression told me nothing, and when he'd finished he said nothing, just took it out and wiped it on his handkerchief.

I was glad when Hugh Holland bought me. He was a small rich kid and paid a hundred dollars for me. Leonard tried to lean on him and get more, but Hugh had the money in crisp twenties and went to put them back in his pocket and turn away, and that was too much for Leonard.

It sounds disgraceful, I know, but I took the view that it was their private transaction. For me it was a passport to experience.

With both Leonard and Hugh there was again, when they came, a wild assortment of groans and cries and short, piggy gruntings. Did they feel a great deal of pleasure? Much more than we females? Did one need a great deal of experience before one caught the essence of it? Or were their cries and drastic facial expressions at *the* moment just another manifestation of male heartiness?

I knew some girls shrieked and moaned, but I always suspected them. I hadn't felt anything to be particularly bucked about—certainly nothing as wildly pleasurable as when I masturbated. But of course at those times I had to keep very quiet.

Anger, Even

Hugh Holland's first go with me was a failure. I think my physical strength and the reputation I had from sports rather put him in the shade. (I think too, I grabbed their wrists or other things with more power than I intended, and that set them back on their heels, rather.)

It was in the car, and we got naked with the car rug handy in case of police or peepers, and I thought he was being more excited than the occasion warranted. It wasn't as if he'd never done it before in a female.

By the time he was in position and moving his thing towards the patch of hair we wanted him to penetrate, he seemed to convulse, his hand clenched over it as if he could stop it coming, but I think the extra pressure probably helped it come.

It came, all right, several spurts of semen on my stomach, on the top of my left thigh, and one into the thicket, where it's so awkward to wipe away.

I knew it was called premature ejaculation, and it wasn't serious. I found it funny, and laughed. He thought I was smiling at him. Males often think you're smiling at them when you're really laughing at them. Though there was a sort of excitement at the back of my throat, of all places, before the event, that, not being satisfied, could, I felt, turn quickly to irritation. Anger, even.

Peeknik

There were picnics and strip barbecues and dirty affairs like peekniks. And we had a number of all of them, and since I had disposed of the burden of my childhood, and been de-virginated, I was invited to more and more.

It became a joke that we always had to take Don Kershaw, whatever party we had, for he issued paper, like tissue, from a slit under his shirt.

"Wipe, wipe, wipe yourself," we sang in the cars on the way to the clearings in Duffy's Forest that we used for group affairs, "Wipe yourself on Don's," to the tune of "Row your boat."

The influence on his cells of the image of outside objects had made him productive of something that benefited his fellows, and we valued him for it.

(A peeknik was where each pair that did it had all the others standing round watching. The male that couldn't do it publicly couldn't turn up to the next peeknik.)

Organs

It was at a sort of barbecue-houseparty at the Fienbergs (the parents were away) that I had another squeeze of Acker Campbell's organs. He had stomach organs that craved the light so greatly that they grew outside him. (Did they crave to be seen?) The one I squeezed was a length of tubing that had an opalescent whitish skin and appeared to be a darker, pinker color inside. At the party he had several more red things protruding, and one beginning.

The first edge of red had formed outside, and he showed me, on certain conditions, the way it seemed to ooze outside of him, in a stringy sort of way, as if it came separately through his pores in strands, then re-formed outside. And it did look like that.

"What will you do when you're hollow?" I asked him.

"You're hollow. What do you do?" he said.

"Hollow?" Then his hand came up my leg, which wasn't at all sensitive, so I didn't bother about it. When his fingers were at the gate I realized what he meant by hollow but it was too late. The hand up my crotch had worked my automatic defenses, and by the time I had any more thoughts at all, Acker was on his back on the carpet. My arm had swept round and had taken him under the jaw and he had fallen under the blow.

Poor Acker. Later I let him fiddle with me, but only for a few seconds. I didn't like it much. It felt as if his hand was fiddling around in a bag of marbles and really didn't have any clear aim.

Later I relented and allowed one finger in while I played with his organs, those that had come out seeking the light. He didn't feel it at the time, anyway, when I squeezed one containing food or gunk in the process. It aroused a research impulse in me: I wanted a knife to see what was inside.

Mutual Masturbation

When we were together, boys and girls alike, what was it but mutual masturbation? I did it to them, they did it to me, but each of us, I and they, had to specify what we wanted in order to get the most satisfaction out of the others' actions. That's what I mean by masturbation: we already knew what we wanted done. We knew, from doing it ourselves, what we wanted, then merely got another to fill in for us. Instead of my hand, it was a boy's, but I had to tell him the place and the frequency and all the rest, in order for his actions to get as close as possible to my own, which, of course, satisfied me most exactly.

Some Word I Have Never Known

In social science I got into trouble for arguing with the teacher.

"It is *not* an affluent society!" I was practically shouting. They got a good wage for turning up at school, and some of them weren't bad teachers, but there was no excuse for raising your voice and losing your cool. I'd never had to raise my voice before to stir a teach.

"We will stand by the popularly accepted definition of this society as an affluent society," she answered. She was tired, she'd had a filthy weekend. I mean lousy.

The other kids looked at me in mid-yawn, which was the nearest they got to startled attention.

It was Monday. I'd been listening to visitors at home on the weekend, moaning and complaining about this and that.

I lowered my voice. "Let's be calm about this, Mrs. Winz. I look around me—*at the society I live in*—" (underlining each word) "and what do I see? I see cheap building, with less rooms than in the old houses and less space in those rooms. I see things built that are only just strong enough to stand up, yet I see old terraces in the city built over a hundred years ago that haven't got a crack in the brickwork. The staircases and doors in the old places are of Tasmanian redwood and cedar: these days they sell what they call pine and it's not, they sell what they call maple and it's—Ah! I forget the name, but it's no good. Goods can't be produced cheaply any more. Mortgages of forty-five years are common. Young people starting out can't get a house. Schools have to show kids what caterpillars are, and flowers, and cows and horses, instead of the kids being able to see all these things for themselves in the bush or in parks. No, Mrs. Winz, this is a poor society."

I had quoted fairly well some of the grown-ups' complaints. I'd forgotten "hemlock."

"The affluence of a society," said Mrs. Winz, "does not rest upon a few areas of complaint by consumers as to quality of individual items. It rests upon the general availability of a large range of consumer goods, the credit to pay for them, the standing of the country as to its gold reserves, the—"

Mrs. Winz went on for a long time, long after I'd forgotten what I'd said, telling me more about economics than I wanted to know just then.

While she droned on I wondered, thanks to all the times I'd heard these things discussed at home when we had visitors, what had happened to the ideals of past political agitators who wanted to make life long, easier and comfortable for the least fortunate. For now the least fortunate were a larger class than ever before, or at least larger than for several hundred years. The only thing that could mitigate their failure was the undeniable fact that this large lower class of society was as equal in opportunity and in treatment as could humanly be expected.

Next period was history, with Mister Saussere in Room 26. He went on about Australia.

"This," he said, "is a proletarian country. I don't wish to say something too hard, but in your country you make a virtue of plainness—plain speaking—where older cultures might prefer a decent evasion. Older cultures like the European, the Asian. You see, even your rich talk like louts. I have heard them, with my own ears."

"You mix with the top people, Mister Saussere?" asked Griselda, with innocence.

"I am invited along to receptions because of my family history," said Mister Saussere. "It is another indication of your country's—ah—youth. But to get on, your land has no dream, not even a dream that has existed for a while then misfired, like others who started out with good cheerfulness. I must add that the people of this country appear to me to possess no—how do you call it?—guts? No determination?

"I speak to you, because you will be the future citizens, of whatever class. Where is your sense of achievement? Where is your sense of responsibility? You act as if you must work because penalties await you if you don't, you speak as if today was unbearable and tomorrow will, hopefully, not exist. You have no dream, just a national sleep."

He was really knocking us, but we knew how to take criticism: we were Australians; we'd knocked ourselves for two hundred years.

It was that time of the month, the thought of it weighed heavy in my head. Walking home with my heavy schoolcase, my blood weighed like lead between my hips, pulling me down. With a disability like this, how could I ever expect to be capable of heroism? Yet poor old Boof had been a hero, once, and he was just a dog buried up the backyard where the leaves were fresh and damp on dewy mornings.

(Some word I have never known is struggling to be said. When will I hold it in my mouth?)

Dream of the Tiger

I became a boy in the dream. I loved fishing, and while throwing my baited line down into the water, making sure to keep it clear of the oystered rocks—incongruously in a freshwater bush creek—the lean tiger walked up to me along the thin bush track and knocked me over. Just swished his paw at me and whack! I was on the ground.

I say the lean tiger, because the tiger I saw at Taronga was alarmingly poor-looking. His sides sank in. I was dizzy when he knocked me over and didn't resist when his teeth sank into my waist. I wasn't naked, but where his teeth sank into my side the flesh was bare. The realization that I was being eaten roused me to resist. I pushed out my hands toward his face, trying to hurt his eyes.

He took two bites to bite my fingers off. I don't remember if he chewed them. (Often I've got back into the dream to see if he chewed my fingers, but I could never tell for sure.)

His claws sank into my side, into both sides. The clothing magically disappeared from the places in the instant his claws touched my skin. My skin is very smooth there, and went in steeply round each claw point, before the skin broke.

He bit both my arms off. He didn't chew them up. He never did that, anytime I dreamed the tiger.

My arms lay there, arranged gracefully enough, not even getting sand on to the torn flesh, mainly because the ground was turning into rather comfortable rock. Clean, but not terribly hard.

Unfortunately, at that point his jaws closed over my head and he bit my head off. It lay there, resting on its side, not rocking or knocking, and the wretched beast began to chew at my ribs, which are my tenderest spot.

I stood there, clothed and unharmed, looking at my remains. It was the funniest feeling watching him chew at my pubic region, relishing the soft pink of my genital area and getting the hairs stuck in his mouth. And watching him chew my bottom.

I've since had feelings like that with some males, watching them act out their fantasies on my disposable body, from the slight eminence of a pillow.

Secret Thoughts

I had the feeling that any of the people I knew could have led me toward greatness: if only I could decipher the thing about them that could have pointed the way. Was mother's whole life a lesson to me that I would shortly understand?

Was there really something about me to correspond to what my well-meaning relatives saw in me? Perhaps what they said *had* been prompted by an intuition and wasn't just a dutiful impulse, a mere loyalty to the family stock.

Alongside my growing belief in my future was another feeling—an amusement at myself: I was so ready to believe and apply to myself the *greatness* thing they said, without altogether believing *them*.

The Mercy of Alethea Hunt

I went to the Opera House with Greg Melrose, a boy in year eleven, simply because he wasn't in the usual game of Pantzaroff and Inboys. Greg called for me, was respectful to father and didn't seem to notice that mother mumbled and didn't look up.

After he had parked and we walked along the timbered walkway with the sea sparkling on the left, I thought to myself—since he left large patches of silence—that there was an imbalance between the behavior of boy and girl. At least between this sort of boy and girl. I'm sure he was behaving more carefully with me than he did elsewhere. He was tender, solicitous, protective, imaginative, and his whole being turned inward constantly to our circle of two. And I? I was the same as usual.

He didn't try to touch me up, just awarded me a respectful kiss at the end of the evening. Was he always like that? Was it just acting? It was altogether different from being with the other boys. I wasn't sure I liked it.

We saw *Lower Depths;* it was set for English. The audience laughed a lot, it was a great success, the best comedy in years.

Outside, people had sprayed messages on the rock wall; others answered. As if people wanted conversation, at a distance. One series was:

> GOD NEVER SLEEPS.
> POOR OLD BUGGER
> TRY MAKING IT LAST THING
> GET FULL EVERY NIGHT, IT WORKS FOR ME.
> ME TOO
> COUNT THE LAMBS OF HEAVEN
> TRY WORKING HARD ALL DAY
> TRY GETTING WORK.

Coming back in the car, Greg drove through the city streets. In Elizabeth Street, I saw something funny, and we pulled over to watch.

A bedraggled man with a crazy mouth was taking cartons and stuff from a pile outside the Carlton Arcade, taking them up the Prudential steps, ratting them methodically by tearing open each parcel of rubbish, taking what he wanted and putting it all back where he got it, in smaller bits. Another old tattered man of the night was entering the Martin Place opening in the wall outside the Prudential, making his way to several green plastic bags. He was taller, he could bend over into them and extract the goodies the affluent workers had discarded.

Greg watched my amusement and said something about our very own lower depths. Then we drove home to Church Hill, where no one walked the streets after dark.

I wanted him to ask, but he didn't. Shyness crippled him, or he was respectful of me, or his morals prevented him: some disability. I didn't bother to force the issue, just accepted the kiss and went inside.

Dear, gentle Australia! Land where leaves fall unwillingly, but people are felled to the earth by the lightest of blows!

Little Me

Friday morning I lay in bed just at the moment when you realize you're awake and, without thinking, suddenly leap out of bed.

I saw her. One of her. It was me. I couldn't make out if she was a hundred meters away through the wall of the house, or a centimeter high crawling over the hinge on the door of my wardrobe, between the door and the frame. She crawled out of the crack and stood on the hinge. At first she didn't seem to see me, but when I moved my head she was watching me.

I looked away, then back, and she was gone.

In the bathroom, the first thing I saw was a little Alethea climbing up out of the sinkhole. Another ran round the rim of the bath; one stood on the window sill sunning herself.

At school one greeted me on the gatepost, another came up out of the hole that was used for an inkwell in the old days when kids used ink.

Could they see me? They waved, sometimes.

Perhaps I was bigger than this world. I looked round me to check. No, the other kids seemed much the same size as I was.

Perhaps they saw the world like this and were afraid to tell, wondering if they were alone in their dismay. Perhaps they too saw tiny versions of themselves.

That night something woke me. I was tied hand and foot. Six captors—one black, one yellow, one coffee-colored, three white—watched as crowds of little Aletheas escaped from my body. No orifice was spared: ears, eyes, nose, mouth, bladder, anus, vagina—all poured with duplicates. They were scooped up by my captors but they couldn't hold them. Hosts of Aletheas fell to the ground and were wasted. There were so many. When I was empty they unbound me. Each went away with only one of me, which they clutched like a sample from a fair or a lucky-dip prize.

ENGLISH EXPRESSION: POEM AGAINST DOOM

The plagues, the floods, the ice, the endless wars,
Don't you remember?
In your blood is there not an echo
Is there not some red stain transported
From what once was home?
Muscles grew big in later generations
As in the first: the nerves as steady; the will
To fight, survive.
What makes you think emergencies of now
Are greater than the past's? More dire?
Why do you think it impossible to survive?
Or, pared to a few, to rise again?
Animals, birds, fish, insects
Often all-but-destroyed:
They rise again.
It would not be the first time the world knew
A precious few, nor bowed before the onslaught
Of determined men and gave way, made room,
Backed off, until that few
Niched themselves in to a defended place.

I ended it there, because the English period ended. I wanted to remind Australians of their heritage; I wanted to tell them they were not separate, or even remote from, their past. I wanted to go on to tell them how I conceived of humanity as a force of nature, equal to natural catastrophies in our effect on the planet.

I felt passionately about this theme at the time, and our year nine English teacher, Miss Heaton, who was actually the English master, was enthusiastic. But from what she said she was only happy to have someone good at English and didn't feel my message with any urgency at all. It could have been about tenth century tapestry. She wanted us to love words, but didn't care much what they meant.

Poor Maria

When we got back from the May holidays we were horrified to find that Maria Attardi's father was in jail for killing Maria. His explanation to the court was that Maria had been "opened."

We discussed this news during breaks and were unanimous that what Maria did with herself was nothing to do with her father. We tried to see the sense behind the father's dreadful action, for there was a chance that he really believed something bad had happened to Maria, but we could not grasp the attitude, common enough in history books, of the father being so concerned that his child had had sexual intercourse. We couldn't understand.

I asked my father, and all he could say was that some old-fashioned people thought she might be spoiled for marriage by being had before then, but he couldn't see why. None of the kids at school had a clue why he should be so upset, not even the boys, or perhaps specially not the boys. It was a mystery.

Poor Maria. Every time I remember her name I think of her sitting in class, looking obediently forward, her rather shapeless ankles pushed out to either side of her chair and a little back so that her heels rose off the ground. Her long hair was very dark brown and she had thick eyebrows. She had turned fifteen last November: my birthday was ten days ago.

Nothing happened to Tony Sergio. He went to a high school out near Cheapley.

279

When I got home Creep was lying stretched out on the ground, content with the earth. Sometimes he would look up, when he heard a leaf move.

A Digression: The Landscape Is Never Finished

Does history really move in a circle? Is any given moment simply a dot on the circle?

I think of human history as having a wave motion; the successive waves of history. You know how, when you look back on the things history people have written in their books, a wave of ideas just grows, then gets hold of people; one truth prevails for a while, and it's called reason, then it's balanced by a wave of opposition and heresy, called unreason, and that climbs over everyone; there's the odd violence which builds up to a peak, there's disorder in the name of order and disorder just for the fun of it, conflict comes to be the usual thing. Plans, panaceas and solutions are announced, tried, have no effect on the thing they're aimed at but a lot of unforeseen effects on lots of other things. Until a new wave of "truth" takes over. The truth will be different from the previous one and the burning issues will be dropped as if they never mattered.

I think of humans as living on a sort of cosmic coral reef, the waves of time, of truth or circumstance breaking over the reef, and humans as tiny additions to the whole reef.

Once upon a time, it said in our history, humans lived—like polyps on a reef—an apparently hopeless life, getting food, some shelter, and little more. Then the idea of heaven grew, tacked on to a hopeless life. They carried on like that for a bit. Then some clever people got the idea there was no heaven to go to, so humans had better make this life better. But they didn't make this life any better, no matter how they tried: it stayed hopeless, full of misery, loneliness, suffering and much too quickly over, since that's how humans are. And they upset the heaven-believers into the bargain. The odd poet or artist or philosopher speculated on heaven, the something-after-death idea that keeps coming to the surface, but

280

after so much disappointment and uncertainty the bulk of coral polyps gave the heaven idea away and acted as if this was the only reef, the only reef ever.

Successive waves of history beat over the cosmic coral reef, bringing new seeds, algae, dead fish, debris; and the polyps stolidly added to their numbers and built the reef higher. Sometimes catastrophe blew the whole thing away, but polyps came and did what polyps do, and built it all up again.

The ground where our house is was once a black tribe's territory; whites pushed them west to perish.

Much of our coastal land, where harvests once were, is now full of kitchens; the harvests are pushed west as the first Australians were.

And will a new wave push us west?

I like to think that when that happens we will be as the seeds of flowers and trees and living things in the desert, waiting for something more than accidents and sudden storms to bring on our next flowering; something more deliberate.

My Tits

They were now a respectable size. I called the left one Cassie, after Cassandra, since she seemed to me to have a slight droop. Perhaps I was being a little hard on myself, but she was slightly smaller in the mirror and from my view of her she *did* seem not so firm and spunky as Helen, the right one. I hope it wasn't the beginnings of tit-drop.

I pictured to myself the original Helen as not being a strapping great female like some of the statues show Greek women—the sleeping Ariadne, for instance, with mighty legs, a round stomach sitting up, big workmanlike breast, heroic arms—rather I saw Helen as on the small side, bright and quick witted, with a flashing smile, a sudden dirty temper, and a small but virile body on which her breasts stood up with pride. I wanted my right breast to be like her.

Sometimes, waking in the morning, glimpsing Helen under the edge of my pajama top as she rounded inward toward the middle of my chest, I thought of the sea's edge and a quiet beach, and this pale curved arm of sand. I wonder if anyone will ever think they're beautiful.

Day Dream

A band tune that heralded the national news became my tune. With that tune in my head, taking me over, I ascended a flight of stairs that led out on to a platform high over a vast sloping plain that contained millions of people and those millions of people had to wait for me, and the tune was ever playing and never coming to a finish and as I mounted the steps, slowing the whole process imaginatively so that the tune was playing but didn't get further forward, I ascended, higher and higher, till in view of the furthest reaches of my audience, then more, and closer, then to the top step and beginning to walk across the platform where I could see them all and they me. I never finished the moment, always wanting the ultimate moment to be better than all before, to be the sum of all: to be more. And I never got that previous moment up to the pitch where I thought that only a step further would be as much as I wanted. I was walking forward, getting no closer to the place where I was to stop, and speak, and be applauded with frenzied devotion. I wanted it to be perfect, and I was never satisfied.

I daresay for the purpose of my fantasy I might just as well have been looking down on millions of dead packed in a vast, choking cemetery, like sardines side by side.

Approach of the Assistant Sportsmaster

His approach was rather to the mind. It was interesting to find him giving me sentences that contained a number of baits, usually one more or less political, one sort of shabby-philosophical, one personal.

"If the country gets through this fuss about higher intakes through the grading gate, whether or not the result is an enlightened one bearing in mind the possible distress to cases of borderline intelligence, will this have any effect on your family and your emphasis on assessable subjects for the gateway examinations?"

Try saying it. Then imagine being a girl watching the approach of this tall, athletic, not very good-looking young man that you expect to say, "How about it?" straight away.

I watched his face as it approached closer to me. He gradually let his eyelids fall shut. He was feeling romantic. I might have said "Good luck," but by that time his mouth was fastened on mine.

Personally, I find it absurd that at one moment they have a limp, sausage-like thing that under suitable stimulus erects itself, empties, then resumes its flaccid state: helpless, stupid, obtuse; and we are completely ready at any time, waiting only on their lordships' convenience. There's something not quite fair here, specially considering that they are the ones trying continually to impregnate females, while we don't mind at all if we put it off indefinitely. I'm surprised we females don't use our power more ruthlessly.

He made no attempt to stimulate me; I was just a receptable, a bag or a box for him to put his penis into and to withdraw from as soon as he had made his deposit. I expected more from an older man.

Saturdays at the Quarry

When they took us to the old quarry, I was as big as most of the boys and this gave me a freedom I relished.

We were playing around, not exactly throwing anyone into the deep quarry hole covered with green slime, but playing pretty rough. I was beginning to be very strong. If I had two boys, one grabbing an arm each, I could bring my arms together in front of me, and the boys would swish round and collide. I always felt bad if they were a bit smaller than me and their heads smacked.

A man was there: Mister Jonson. He didn't approach me like the boys did, he was slow and kept his eyes on my face, and he waited till the horseplay had died down a bit and the other kids were starting to get together with each other. Marie-Louise and I were alone, and she was beginning to get that look of concentrating.

"Sit on the log and do it," I advised her. Her accomplishment was praiseworthy, but I never tried to copy her.

Mister Jonson approached me very slowly, and for some reason I found myself going backwards, until I no longer wanted to look at the different colors that showed in the stone where the quarry workers had split the stone in steep cliffs and made cracks down the face of rock. And I no longer looked at Marie-Louise. The other kids had stripped and were running around; some sat, squatted or lay draped over clean sandstone, and everything was pretty. Even the kids turned toward me and squatting looked pretty with their little patch of dark between the legs. To my eyes it was the first time fucking had been beautiful.

He went past me. I wondered if he had a wife. I wondered idly if he'd met her down here in the quarry, and if so, whether the sandstone had looked as it did now.

I felt him behind me. I felt two warm dry hands on my hip bones. The large brown fingers pointed forward. The hands tickled as I felt pressure from the thumbs behind. And those fingers were going in. I had to bend.

I looked down at the hands. His face may have been the face of an old adventurer raiding a younger age group, but the hands were the hands of a navvy. Though not work-stained, or cracked.

The tobacco breath round my neck and into my face was new. And the silence was new and the breathlessness. The slow hands were another new thing. He nudged my legs apart with his knees. I was watching the four veined, contrasting feet as he entered me.

He kept me with him for a long time, long after the other kids had changed partners, long after everyone else had had a swim in the cool pool—the clean one—down the slope of colored sand that spilled straight from the level place where the quarry men worked their stone. The sand was powdery, friendly.

He put my bottom on his shoulder and carried me along the track away from the sunny stone to his car, where he worked in a different way. He took time, his hands going round everywhere, everything stretched out tight and sensitive. My feet in the car straps, his face slightly rough with silvery stubble and his lips and tongue wet with his spit and various moistures. Everything in contact with everything, he said. I came three times. It was the first time I'd had an orgasm with someone else, the first time it had been anything like the frenzy I reached when I did it myself. Usually other hands don't go to the right places, or if they do it's only to leave too soon. I didn't want Mister Jonson to stop, so I didn't tell him when it happened first. Toward the second it was getting unbearable, but I bore it. It was even more unbearable the third time, and something else happened. He said not to worry, and didn't mind it going over his hands, and even his face. The floor of the car was wet.

He must have been working himself up to it for a long time, because I was dripping for a long time after. My smell was all over him.

He seemed far more pleased afterward than the boys; perhaps they were too young to know how to express pleasure. I really felt, with Mister Jonson, that I'd given him something, and he liked it.

I was an Australian adolescent, a healthy girl-plant growing in the sun. What could be more natural to such a plant than generosity? I had things others wanted: why shouldn't I give? Whether or not I gave to make others happy, whatever reason I gave or had—they would be happy if they got what they wanted.

I looked into the whirling, mysterious future and could see myself giving, giving, and others happy, pleased, and still others, coming and occupying the place the first ones had; so many that I couldn't get rid of them. They began to own me (in my future imagination), and the world began to close in around me.

It isn't comfortable to be owned. I threw off such thoughts.

I walked home, refusing lifts. The day was dry. Watt Boulevard was cool with its many trees nearly touching overhead; Malthus Parade was alive with traffic; Euclid Way, past the primary school, dipped steeply down toward the bridge. It was a day for thinking.

I had comfort, and bounding health and beauty. I wanted for nothing, yet I wanted everything, for I wanted the thing that is most difficult to come by, the thing that cannot be demanded, nor enforced by strength or wealth or beauty: I wanted love.

To be loved, I mean. I was convinced I was incapable of loving.

Perhaps there is no one with so rigorous a definition of what it is to be loved as one who cannot herself love. (Or himself, for all I know. But perhaps I shouldn't add that: I have never considered that men love. Men want: love is female.)

There was one other thing I wanted, and I blame my mother for it.

285

I thought of females. Females entered my head and danced around my mind. Is that what thinking is? Do the objects actually enter one? Females talking, chewing (most people you see eating in the street are female), females walking slowly and being cursed by males in a hurry, females upset when they're in the wrong and lashing out, females looking in mirrors, making mirrors out of passing windows and shiny steel sheets, checking, always checking, on appearances.

I thought of females in love.

Don't you think it's funny? Along comes some guy, and he's active, always doing something, never still, and he has the idea that there's love in him—that he loves—and he says so. And what happens? If she likes him, it won't be long before *she* loves. But this is what gets me: it's not before. Only in cases of crushes does the female get on the love-trail before the male. But after he loves, she begins to. As if his action is the trigger. I wonder if that's accurate.

Who wouldn't be suspicious of that order in a process? When do the males check up on the sort of love that only comes to the surface when their interest is already assured and declared? But perhaps males never know. Or care. Perhaps if they love at all their own love is a skin-deep thing, transferable with their alighting glances. Perhaps their self-love protects them from such thoughts.

I was still dripping as I got home. Daddy was in the bathroom drying himself after a shower. He was rubbing his face. I leaned in at the door and pulled his one. It was thick, like Mister Jonson's.

"Ow!" he said, and saw it was me. "Help, Mara!"

Mother smiled as she wrote. She didn't look around. I think father was just a little startled: I hadn't done that for years.

I went to the toilet and got rid of the rest of Mister Jonson. I washed my red pants myself—the ones with the white flowers—and hung them out with the rest of the washing.

It was like an amusing secret, being the only one to know about those red pants. Teatime wasn't far off; I walked on our wide front lawn, looking down the valley toward the reserve. The border of night was visible among the tall trees.

Creep came out to meet me. I think he admires me.

Once, Mister Jonson went through all the motions I had come to expect, and when it was over I found there was nothing to wipe away to keep my little pant clean. I mean dry. (I use the word "pant" for the singular of pants; as far as I know only Marie-Louise and I refer to them in this way.)

"That was a clean one," I said.

He was suspicious immediately.

"What? What do you mean?" he said sharply.

I swiftly aimed my hand at his face, to remind him. I had got over my slight awkwardness at being with an older person. He ducked.

"Don't you get sharp with me," I said in a blend of fierceness and coldness. He said nothing, only watched my face warily.

'Clean,' I prompted him, showing him the dry handkerchief.

"Oh," and his face was full of concealment. "It all inside. In your tubes." He tried to smile, and partly succeeded.

It was something else, I knew.

I didn't find out till later that some of them can mimic the spasms of ejaculation, and produce nothing. "Dry-blowing," it's called.

On one of our afternoons at the quarry a boy from year seven was left with me to give him his first.

"The swallows," he said. "The swallows!"

He was poking his little thing—so much thinner than the other males' that I felt motherly and stroked his hand—into the right place, when he began again.

"Swallows! Swallows!" he yelped, and looked behind him. I thought he needed help and grabbed him under the arms and pushed and pulled him back and forwards in case he hadn't got the idea, but it wasn't that. He went limp and it took me at least two minutes of shaking and pulling to understand that he'd had it almost as soon as it got in; I knew because by that time he made distressed sounds, and besides I felt the tiny thing slip out and the liquid run down on my anus.

"Swallows be stuffed," he said. And when I didn't understand, he told me. "They said that when it happened I'd feel as if swallows were flying out of my arsehole. You didn't see any, did you?"

"Beat it, shorty."

He was glad to get away. The way he looked you'd think I'd been rasping his little childish thing with sandpaper.

He was only twelve, and I'd felt motherly. It was a nice feeling.

Observation

It's not fair, I suppose, but at school we could be cheekier and more independent than the boys, more confident in our ability to get away with little departures from the rules, and the reason was plain: they were visited with more punishments than we were for much the same little sins.

At the same time, we didn't *have* to be naughty. If we chose to, we could be. The boys, though, seemed to break out independently whether they made a decision: it was as if something inside them had control and when it said: do this, they did it. And watched, helpless and amazed, when authority caught up with them. As if they didn't know what they were about.

As well, we were more game than they in standing up to authority. But if our consciences ever bothered us, it wasn't apparent. I didn't find any of the other girls who worried about it. It was sneaky, in a way: paltry. Like the rich accepting privilege without demur.

The Sock Exchange

Mister Jonson took to picking me up on the corner of Newton Crescent and Euclid Way. He took me to an unattended tip adjoining the bush, where he settled into a routine of touching me up, then when I'd had it, he entered me. Sometimes it was in his car, sometimes out on the ground in the shadow of the cliff of rubbish. The rubbish was being added during working hours all through the week, and the tip would eventually blossom into a new playing field. It wasn't smelly rubbish, just bits of timber, scrap building materials, tins, glass, bricks, soil filling.

I composed a poem on the subject, to impress the English master. I showed in words the filling of a woman and the filling

288

of the tip. I showed how the tip produced a grassed oval and the woman produced new players to play on it. The next area was then filled, and the next women, and the filled women were producing new players for the next patch of civilized space. Miss Heaton showed it to the other teachers, but stopped short of reading it to the class.

Mister Jonson ran a sock exchange. He was a scientist who would supply new pairs of socks in return for socks worn for a number of hours. People who produced a sick certificate and guaranteed to have worn their socks for three days got two free pairs. He reached the tiny flakes of skin and bacteria that lived in them.

One day he brought another girl with him. She had a large bottom and above it a tiny waist and rather long trunk leading up to thin shoulders. Below the bottom were two stumpy, hairy legs. I christened her the Centaur. She was deeply religious, imprisoned at the bottom of a fundamentalist well, with a single view of the heavens.

Her religious cast of mind took the form of honesty, a comforting trait in other people. In case the withholding of information could be thought to be lying, she told everyone everything that happened to her. Without religion she could have been an ordinary gossip. She kept a list of everyone she knew, and when she got pregnant to Mister Jonson she told all the kids in the district, just as she'd told them every detail of every time Mister Jonson had done her.

Mister Jonson thought the smiles of all the kids and the familiar cry of 'Hullo, Mister Jonson,' were a tribute to the popularity of his sock exchange and the PR job he'd done for science.

Mister Jonson began to come out into the world, and although the way of his coming out seemed unusual to those close to him, and distressing to Mister Jonson himself, since it meant he was no longer a scientist, it was very little worry to the public at large. (It was interesting to see how news had importance and seriousness close to its source, and progressively less further away, until at a distance of a few kilometers it became a joke.)

The organs of Mister Jonson had grown tired of the darkness inside his body cavities and took it on themselves to come out into the light.

He'd always been an active man, but now he had to look out for his lungs and take care of his kidneys. Special moisturizing containers had to be put over them so they didn't dry out in the predatory air. His case wasn't unique, and he therefore didn't benefit from his value as a curiosity.

The last time I saw him he told me of his change. As he was talking I saw in each of his eyes a huge unshed tear, and I was sorry for him.

Not Long for the Machine

Mary Madeleine Murphy was not the most brutal girl in school, but she was the loudest, the most vulgar, the dirtiest. If you wanted to find the girl who could spit furthest from the window of a schoolbus, who could get a car driver's hand on the wheel at a level sixty kilometers in calm conditions; if you wanted to find the girl who most terrorized the younger kids in the lavatories, bashing on the door or pushing it open while the kids were having a pee or just finding somewhere to change clothes on sports day; if you wanted to find the ringleader of the chi-acking on speech day or the source of the yells of distress among pockets of lower class kids in the playground—look no further.

There's no doubt she must have noticed it first, but I'd be close to second. We were at Blacktown High, changing for basketball in the long change rooms. She had her left foot up on the brown wooden slats while she put on her team socks. Somehow her left elbow swished her skirt up past her dark regulation pants, and I saw it. It was a bluey-pink round thing—made of flesh—and it seemed to be growing out of her waist. The glimpse was gone.

"Say, MM," I said. "That thing?"

"What thing, you big pile of It?" Everyone allowed her to talk roughly to them, even me, and I could have knocked her silly. The point was, you could have bashed her and she'd still do it next time.

290

There's a certain respect you owe to people like that. You can't destroy their personality.

"That thing at the side of you. Sort of a pink thing, like the head of a dick."

Her eyes rimmed wide, and she stared hatred at me.

"Shut your mouth about that, you stupid smelly slut," she said. I backhanded her calmly—for the "smelly"—a little blood trickled from her mouth where her lip caught on the teeth at the side of her mouth. Her incisors stuck out a bit.

"Well, darling? What is it?"

"Shove your head up it," she replied, undaunted. I shrugged.

"I'll spread it round."

But she wouldn't say a word. I didn't tell anyone. She even played well.

Ezekiel M'Aksombe

I met him at the quarry. His line was direct.

"Feel this," he said and in the same movement put my hand on his spout, which was, of course, black.

What did he want me to feel? It was the same as any other. But he kept my hand pressed there, and pressed harder. Presently I felt the push of firmness in it as it swelled, filling out with blood.

I began to laugh. It was not the first time it had hit me as ludicrous that something like a sausage skin full of blood was going to be inserted into me. Of course there was no question of minding, but the—well—the temporary nature of the male apparatus got my funny bone. Soon it would be in me in the flush of its natural rhythm. All too soon it would be emptied of its blood as the male who was on the end of it would be emptied of his desire, and his ability.

He was too caught up in his male assurance and self-importance to be affected by my amusement. Very likely he translated it as delight. My body was built for me by father and mother, but Ezekiel, like other males, thought that when he was in it, it was inhabited by a god.

291

I had him several times. He was healthy enough, but in his eyes a vacancy would sometimes swim to the surface and look out at me.

My Theory

My theory, dating from that time, is that basically males found us uninteresting. They were interested in our bodies, piece by piece; they lit up when they saw our assembled components approaching.

But us: no.

The person inside was a hinderance, an obtrusion, an edge they wanted smoothed away. No matter what we said, it connected in their minds with nakedness, cavities, moisture, semen, warmth, comfort and relief. And if they could not make that connection, they didn't—*did not*—want to hear our voices. Uninteresting and useless: that was their verdict. Nothing we said, nothing we did, nothing we thought or wanted, was of the slightest interest.

As long as it didn't cost them and if they could not have our bodies, we might as well be outside the universe, for all males cared.

Males

But it was maddening that they had so many ideas. Some of them were all the time coming up with something new. I comforted myself that these weren't the smart boys, but the lively ones; the smart ones drily excelled, while the lively ones seemed almost to ignore the smart ones and their excellences: they put energy into continually new things. It was as if they manipulated the words used to describe objects and ways of handling them, then altered the words to arrive at new verbal descriptions for such handling, then simply used the new description as a new method.

Where's an example?

Yes. Now say one of them was talking of the difficulties with some new method of transferring power from the engine of a vehicle to the wheels to the road, one of that sort would re-arrange the words in the sentence and come out with a suggestion for transferring power from the road to the wheels or to some other intermediary piece of equipment to the engine. And he would add to his new formula in such a way that it made sense. He would be playing with the words, but also using words as if they were close to being objects.

Why are we so different? Is it that we females talk so much and with so much enjoyment that we talk out all our springs, our inventiveness, our seriousness, where they keep their mouths shut and the lid on, raise some internal pressure tending toward action, force themselves onward, force out of themselves a kind of distillation of their lives expressed in ideas and new arrangements of existing objects? Is it that we live now, where they save themselves up and live, in a way, for tomorrow? And for others?

I envy them that.

Consciousness of Absent Objects

Science began to be interesting.

"The whole organism, besides being larger than the smaller parts, is larger than the sum of the parts. And in addition, is qualitatively different from the sum of its parts," said Miss Cruickshank, the science teacher. "Viewed as disassembled bits, lying around," she added.

"Does this mean that pure orange juice is just the same if it comes from a tree or a chemical plant?" asked Alastair Crombie, who transferred from another school in year ten.

"Certainly—not," she hesitated.

"What do you mean the whole is larger than the parts?" I said.

"Isn't it obvious?" she said.

"In a way. But does it matter?"

"What are you getting at?" She was nice, treating my idiot questions seriously. I'd only asked a question because I felt uncomfortable and wanted to be forced to think of something else.

"Well, it seems to me that the whole thing *is* the same or does the same because the parts are as they are."

"What?"

"I think of it as starting at the atomic level, then the focus widening to cellular scale, then on up to the whole as seen by the eye at usual size. All straight through: the final thing being what it is because the whole lot scales down to atomic level."

"I'm sorry, Hunt. I don't follow. The connection—"

"You know how one race of ants or people is wary or hostile to another. Yet some, of the same kind, join together. Like in the electron micrographs. Well, the same with atoms, or cells. Like to like, unlike repel. The immuno reaction. The body recognizes intruders and begins to isolate them and destroy biologically. So," as the class yawned, "so philosophy arises from the cells, it all goes back to the attraction and repulsion of atoms and molecules . . ."

"Shut up," the class grated at me.

"You'll feel better in a while, dear," said Cruickshank.

I didn't, though. I don't know why I felt uncomfortable—I just did. I decided to cut off from the class, deliberately un-hearing Cruickshank.

A thought came into my head: how can you be conscious of something that isn't present?

I do it a lot of the time. I can see in my mind's eye my father's face, our front lawn, the twin eucalypts, anything I want to recall; the question is: how do I do it? I know I do it accurately, because I check my mental picture with the actual. I mean: how can our minds do it? And since to be conscious usually carries with it a meaning of sensing things, what sense is it that detects or resurrects objects in their physical absence, or when they are hidden from sight?

Perhaps I would find out after high school, when I got through the grading gate and went to university.

Old Mother Hubbard

On the way home from school I kept feeling the feelings that were, so to speak, under the skin of my mind, and was opening my free hand to look at the palm, turning it over to compare it from memory

294

with the hands of males, when the old man in the corner house, old Mister Huddart, called out to me in a girl's voice.

"Miss!"

I'd been told not to take notice of Old Mother Hubbard as he had been known at his workplace, a factory that made doorknobs of plastic and metal. His brain, during the last few years of his working life, was being taken over by a young girl's. It showed itself in his liking for sudden giggles, pretty lollies, boxes of chocolates.

Old Mother Hubbard played with his shrubs, cutting them into nice shapes. He wore a frilly apron, yet he fought with his wife, and after fighting, asked permission to do the most ordinary things around the house, such as having a piece of cake or going to bed.

He had begun to wet the bed, the neighbors said; and often he had been observed milking his sad-faced dog.

"Miss!"

"Oh shut up, Nancy!" I yelled at him.

He looked puzzled, then began to sing in a falsetto voice, standing quite still:

> "*Pretty little ducky ducky*
> *Come and be killed,*
> *Pretty little pussy pussy*
> *come and be killed*
> *pretty little kiddie kiddie*
> *come and be killed*
> *pretty little daddy daddy*
> *come and be killed*
> *pretty little mummy mummy*
> *come and be killed*
> *pretty little neighbor neighbor*
> *come and be killed*
> *pretty little . . . . . ."*

and as I walked on and up our front steps the clear, hopeless voice faded into the mysterious space that began a little way from our house.

As I sat down to tea two dogs were discussing some matter loudly within our space. Perhaps they were discussing their nightly prayer that their masters would stay well and well-off: or pets wouldn't eat. They were still discussing when I crawled into bed. Dogs' voices don't disturb me.

The slice of sky I see from my window, decorated round the year with a different pattern of stars, told me of explosions, deadly rays, unimaginable heat and the violence of utter cold; it was never far from my science-taught head that the atmosphere that protected me and made the stars twinkle and the sunsets glow, was only a temporary shield from the destruction that waits.

And yet, even a teenage girl knew that she ought to carry on as if life was forever; the facts of the cosmic situation must have little or no emotional impact on me if I was to stay mentally healthy.

John Mabbe

His approach was social.

"Let's go to the Shellback," he said enthusiastically.

I guess after all the direct sexual attempts I had weathered recently I thought there was a devious flavor about this method, but after we were on our way to the place I began to feel there was a certain comfort about it; the sex bit didn't have to be right away. And once there, with the life and energy and packed nature of the Shellback, it was pleasant.

He began to drink quickly. I signed to him with my eyes, but he took no notice. If I was going to get anything at all it would have to be while he was sober, so I got him outside after an hour and made him come good in the car. I didn't explain when he grumbled, merely said, "Shut up."

"What's wrong with later? At my place."

I waited until I had placed him in, then a little more until he had got the idea well enough not to pull out, and said mildly, "Pig's arse to your place. You'll be no good to me by then. Have you noticed the way you're pouring them into you?"

"I'm OK drunk," he said, slightly injured in tone.

"Not for me, you aren't. I want a maximum effort."

He raised his face a little, to make sure I got his injured expression, then went at it like a steam hammer.

I led him back inside afterwards, well satisfied with myself.

It had been some time before I realized that males did not notice my subtle changes of expression. I had signed to them, as to females, since I was about nine, with my face, and with small hints about my eyes and sudden stillness and a lift of eyebrows—I am still unable to raise only one eyebrow—and at no time did they notice a single thing or take the faintest hint. They did not notice the subtlety of my changes of expression.

Yet I detected them in the mirror quite easily.

Food, Glorious Food

John Mabbe had me for a longish time while I was fifteen, but John Schanke wanted me. John Mabbe was aggressive, and long after he no longer wanted to inhabit my body he hung on to me so John Schanke couldn't have me. And John Schanke really liked me. I don't mean just to get my pants down or rub his hands over my tits and wiggle them about: he liked the me inside. Often he would be watching over the fence when we were all playing at the quarry as if something in him was feeding on the sight.

On school excursions he seemed to find a place near me on the ferry or the bus. He would never let an arm or a leg touch me. Once when his sleeve brushed my arm he drew it away as if the material of his school blazer had nerve-endings.

John Mabbe began to accuse me of having it with John Schanke. I didn't hit him or abuse him, though he was afraid I might shame him in front of the other kids.

I didn't bother to answer. There was something in the reluctance of Schanke to touch me that stirred something in me. Perhaps that's a wrong way of saying it: perhaps it stirred something in me that had never awakened. Anyone who touched me, I imagined, had either touched me because he wanted to, or it was accidental.

297

But to know someone wanted to touch, yet didn't: that caused the stirring. I began to look for the feeling, began to get near him, just to have him take himself away out of range. When the sleeve of my blazer was near the sleeve of his I felt a tingle up the arm. When the sleeves touched, the tingle was vibrant and became warm. It stayed like that for ages, until it felt hot. He moved his arm away, and the tingle died. My arm felt immediately empty of blood, hollow and cold.

I caught sight of my hand, hanging like a piece of meat on the end of my arm. There was a mark, an ink mark on my thumb. I was only a schoolgirl, after all. What a lot of fuss to be making about a boy.

I didn't necessarily want to go with John Mabbe to the quarry, but that week it was the only way to be fairly sure that John Schanke would be somewhere around. (Since he wouldn't let any of him touch me I could hardly get him on the phone. Well, of course I could have, but the thing he was awakening told me I wasn't supposed to.)

"Where's that gig?" Mabbe said. I didn't let him in me, I was just holding it as he liked me to. "Where's he at, the dickhead?" He looked round, his penis pulled against my hand. I gave it a sharp jerk at the base that brought him to heel.

"Cut it out!" he squealed. "If you break it off I'll take you to court. You'll be bound over to keep the peace!" He doubled over, laughing. I caught sight of John Schanke's ear showing round a tree. I had an idea. I would be curious about him, ask him things. I would show I was careless of his feelings, I would look at him in a pitying way, yet take an interest in him. Perhaps . . .

Perhaps John Schanke had had enough of looking round corners. He came from behind his tree on the edge of the cleared quarry floor, walking toward us. He saw Mabbe's thing poking out from my fist and disappearing back down into his jeans. He looked away from my face and from me, and fixed his eyes on Mabbe. Mabbe got to his feet in a hurry, tried to put it back in, couldn't, and finally did the top button up before the fight began.

They gave each other a few hits with closed fists. A small amount of blood appeared on both their faces, and Mabbe's erection began to go down. He seemed to fight better for a while, but eventually Schanke's fury told, and he bore Mabbe toward the water. At the foot of the old rock cliff was the quarry pool, the water dark and slimy and never making ripples. And cold, cold and deep, so deep it never warmed up, they said.

Schanke had him going, but as Mabbe overbalanced his hand caught Schanke's arm and pulled him in too.

They were filthy. They continued the fight in the water, and again when they both climbed out. His little shrunken dick was still out, taking the air.

I didn't bother to wait. I didn't care who won. I certainly didn't consider they were fighting over me, the filthy things. Their eyes pressed my back as I left.

On the way home I felt in a poetic mood. I would talk to father and get him to tell me of his early years in the theatre. I walked on, my eyes on the concrete paving slabs, stepping on each crack for luck.

My head was not suited to thinking that day, particularly walking along; the pleasant movement of my legs and my body above them induced a feeling of such sleepiness that it was as if I slept as I walked. The sun, the scent of spring flowers, the green shoots budding out from the grey bark of trees. How was it, in the midst of this beauty, this spiritual blessing of the recurring seasons, that into my head there came pictures of possible dinners that father might make for us that evening: a roast; his special pork and peaches; a carefully tender steak, with my favorite vegetables not quite cooked?

Near home there was a new dog, part cattle-dog, with a funny pinky color, that had a look about him as if he'd like a taste of human. Just a little bit, but I was the morsel he had in his mind's eye. I shoved him off, with loud noises.

At home father was cooking, surrounded by food. The sun filled the kitchen like affection.

"Do you know what you look like?" said Miss Footlow today.

I waited. What did she mean look like? Of course I knew what I looked like.

"From the back you have a slouching walk," she said.

Still I said nothing. Why was she attacking me? Had I missed some jocular note I should respond to? Had I been absent when the subject had come up with other kids?

"Like a horse," she explained.

I smiled. I liked the comparison.

"Or a cat. Or—have you seen greyhounds being walked?"

"Certainly."

"Like the back legs of a greyhound. When it's walking, mind, not when it's running."

I must have looked puzzled. I was trying to see where the criticism lay in this mysterious communication. I didn't know. Was she jealous of me? She walked on over toward the staff room. She waddled. Wherever she walked she probably drove every lizard back under its rock.

John Schanke's Approach and Four Questions

It surprised me. He'd always made a point of not touching me, of shying away.

I daresay some would have called it an insulting approach, but to me the result was what counted. I was prepared to turn him away at any time, even after penetration; content to wait and see how I felt, adding up the plusses and minuses, and ready to decide on that basis.

He said, "Let me see your right breast!" standing in front of me in the primitive masculine salesman-hunter's attitude of cutting off my escape. I could feel the power of this confrontation even though I knew it was only an emotional power that held me, and a step back and a half-turn was all that was necessary to be rid of it.

What would he do then? Why shouldn't I?

I pulled the fabric to one side and Helen, my right breast, popped out, hanging slightly over the hem. Why hadn't I shown him Cassie, instead of the breast he asked for?

His triumph was concealed behind a frowning examination of her. Helen's nipple pointed slightly upward, toward his left shoulder. Cassandra waited, she knew her turn was coming.

John Schanke and I had a thing going for a while after that, but I never felt the same as I did when we were almost touching but not quite.

Schanke blamed Mabbe for spoiling things, and they were enemies forever.

(Did the hatred that makes enemies amount to a deformity that would make him a Free? And if that was so, was love a change? And going on from there, did no Servant of Society love?

Was that why I seemed to have no love in me?)

The Predator Behind My Eyes

Something about the trees in the bushland reserve occupied me today. It is November, and the thin bark, last year's growth, is peeling from the eucalypts, leaving the cool, green-cream new flesh facing north and the sun: brown bark still adheres on the southern sides.

There was a warning bell sounding faintly in my body somewhere, some part of me I had never used before.

Warning bell? Perhaps an awakening bell.

What was it saying to me?

I stood still, watching the trees with wide eyes and open mouth, the way I concentrate (mother calls it dreaming), and in my eyes the trees crowded together until they were many; there was movement among them; I was running; other creatures ran.

The others ran before me, they were running away; I was running after them! My heart wanted to beat faster to match the speed of my body, but the dreaming me stood still; my heart beat slowly to suit a standing girl. But behind my eyes I was running faster, and the creatures in front of me were getting closer and running for their lives. Running from me, for their lives. I was a predator. When I caught them I would kill, carry them up into a tree and eat their bodies.

The trees emptied from my mind and became again the few dozen that usually stood on the edge of the reserve. A Saturday dog that noticed my stillness approached me, it was that pinky-brown cattle dog, and was about to bark, standing so he could run away immediately. I noticed him, and turned, both arms stretching out toward him as if to seize him violently. He fled, with anxious yelps. I walked home, wondering.

The Terrible Suburbs Where No One Speaks the Truth

A few streets away there's a boy called Brian Lethbridge, known for his habit of being curious.

Every day on the way to school and coming back, you can see him listening to the grey metal cabinet standing in a superior fashion some distance from the traffic lights, controlling them with clicks and mutterings.

Girls giggle and hit him as they go past. Boys glance at him and look away. Everyone's frightened of looking as if they don't know something, as if when you're young you could be anything other than ignorant.

I often yell at the girls and say, "Get and listen with him! You stupid cruds might learn something."

That makes them get the shits with me, but they're too scared to give me a back answer. They do it again next time they see him. And he always does it. He looks over fences, pats electricity poles, listens underneath the transformers, runs his hand over brickwork and wrought iron he passes, looks closely at dogs. There's an Airedale, Simba, down at the bend in Euclid Way, and he sneaks up to the nearest place he can see it from and watches it when it doesn't know.

Father predicts a strong future for him if he gets graded.

When his teachers get him working on a project, they find themselves inundated with material. He gets his parents out on weekends going to places like foundries and steelworks and dairy product factories and so forth, and winds up getting a limit set on the size of his project. On steel, he went to the south coast in the holidays and came back with samples, biographies, process diagrams, photographs and project books full. The teachers couldn't get through it, there were seven books full and a briefcase.

"We need a Brian Lethbridge Hall in this school, just to exhibit a single one of your projects," Mister Khaled told him. "In future, just one project book." And when his father objected, "Well, two at the most." He hopes to go to university when the time comes.

He refuses to do it with me. Perhaps in a year or two I'll ask him again. I thought I was doing him a favor; he's two years younger than I am: where's his curiosity?

I might begin by telling him of the bright birds with wings of lead that flap over those terrible suburbs where no one speaks the truth.

Creep's

One afternoon during the week, I was finding it hard to get down to my homework, and filled to overflowing with vague restlessness. I had a drink of water. It was too flat. I tried a cordial; it was insipid. I climbed the climbing tree that I'd spent so many hours in when I was a child: it bored me to be on show to any neighbor that chanced to look. I ran around the yard, through the side gate and did a circuit of the front lawn: there was no taste in running, though I made every fourth stride a hop, step or jump.

I hadn't masturbated: perhaps I was uneasy because of that. At least when you do, you don't have to wait for someone else.

Creep stirred himself, barked, and followed me, and when he got to where I was in the front of the house, stood like a sentinel and barked at nothing, and everyone.

I cuddled him, bending down, and he let his hindquarters sink down and his back legs lie sideways, standing only on his front paws. His head extended upward, nuzzling at me, finding the channel between my thighs, his nose buried upward, towards my pubic region. My eyes found his lower parts; his penis with its long-haired sheath. The pink tip of it stuck out perhaps a millimeter. As I stroked him harder, pushing his head down toward his body, more than the tip of it protruded from that hairy sheath. It was wetly pink, very shiny, like the inside of a mouth.

I stooped and touched it. It retracted a little; his head stayed up. I was still stooping, and held it in my hand. I was a little—shy? embarrassed? ashamed?—I don't know which, and it was a minute before I could squat beside him and look into his warm brown eyes, holding it in my hand.

The Head's Message to Us on Speech Day

"Young people are known for the way they bravely face the world, but at the same time the world is facing them, confronting them. There are a number of wars in different parts of the world, as there usually are, and the question I want you all to face is: What are you prepared to kill or be killed for in war today? I ask further the general question: What are you prepared to die for?

"That is all. I want that question to be on your mind, in the background of your thoughts. Sooner or later you—the essential you, inside—will compose an answer to it out of your experience of life and out of your developing natures.

"What are you prepared to die for?"

When it was all over I was able to miss the crush and get out of the hall behind the stage and carry my prizes to the car, where I waited for father, who was besieged as usual. I saw him way back inside the doors of the Assembly Hall. Darkness surrounded me; I rested my loot on the car roof. Mother was missing, perhaps crouched in a corner, fearful of her thoughts being disturbed.

Poor mother. Perhaps at some time she lifted more than she could carry—or carried more than she could bear.

Benjamin Allan Lawson Lee Swanson

A person approached me. It was an old man with linen face and paper hands. When he was middle-aged they called him The Cone; he was built on solid lines near the ground, and in those days had eyes like stoves, though now his hair was raffia. A mouthwreck for years, he had steel wool eyebrows; in his prime his bottom was like the back of a bus. His complexion was rather Great Dividing Range conglomerate. Can you see him? When he was young they called him Balls. His father saw to that.

In old age the good people, Free citizens and voters of our district, looked on him as harmless, and the main reasons for this were a benign desire to keep him out of institutions, and his habit of reciting his name in full, followed by his initials, together with the child-names his folks dreamed up for him.

Little bonny Benny, tiny funny bunny, pretty sunny Benny, and Balls.

Benjamin boy, Allan me lad, Lawson me gurgler, Lee me little soldier, Swanson me diver, and Balls.

Repetition never wearied him.

I tripped him when I was twelve, in the grounds of the high school on a similar speech night, for putting his hand up my tunic in the crowd. He fell in a lump, hurting some ladies. Toothbrushes fell out of his clothes, about a hundred; all used. He did it to all of us, but there were times we didn't want to be touched, however old or harmless the person was.

Waiting for father I elbowed him now at fifteen for the same offense. I wasn't about to let some bastard do anything I didn't want him to do.

My elbow went right in where his ribs should have been.

It was dark in the parking area, I was glad no one saw me. He didn't grunt, which was strange. I put my hand inside his chest; it went right in between the buttons. It was empty.

I reached down and around and with resentment came upon a group of quite greasy—knackers, the boys call them—hanging down inside the front of his trousers. Up higher, a softish bladder hung suspended. I squeezed it, and wet came through on the front of him. I put my other hand in, squeezed the bladder and held his dick; I could feel the liquid coursing through it. The pool spread round his feet. I had to jump clear. Higher, a repulsive liver brushed the back of my wrist. A heart writhed and clenched frighteningly.

There was no one around. Parents and kids outside the Assembly Hall, in and out among the young trees, were frozen in attitudes of talk and listening.

I pulled the coat entrance apart with both hands, like enormous cloth lips, and got in. He *was* a cone, there was a ton of room, it was like a cathedral in there. Could I expect a conversation?

A dim light spread upward from niches in this edifice. I ran up a flight of steps to look out of the eyes—which was strange since I was as tall as Balls—but through his eyes the world was full of sharp hurtful things, spines and prickles, sharp edges, blades and dangers.

A thin dilapidated music sounded, persisting, growing and clanging; I began to swing like an ape on a growth inside the throat, knocking against heart and lungs, stretching the growth till my feet touched bottom. I scaled the ribs hand over hand, like a kid gone mad in a playscene. I ascended the spine like a native up a coconut tree. Fronds with the heads of blindworms reached for me.

I shinnied down, got off at the fly, grabbed his thing with both hands and swung down to the ground, leaving him standing with it out. On firmer ground I walked in a ladylike way over to my father, who had disengaged himself from admirers and was looking anxiously round for mother.

Mrs. Ellerslie and Mrs. Besanko said, "Naughty man! Put that away!" And told everyone in loud voices what a dirty old devil he was. Hundreds of us there had felt the old man's hands for years, and we knew it wasn't terribly dirty, but we kept quiet.

Being Your Own Person

The head was a bare pink plain reaching over from front to back, a broad tongue of shining tough skin poking into the skirting mangroves, coming down at the back into a loop of vegetation.

Tufts at the side stood up with quixotic belligerence above the ears, only to go down fighting farther back.

306

Below the collar there was such a mass of cloudy tendrils, swirls of fine hairs, that you wanted to get his head between you and the light, to see the wonder of it, and the poetry, like a tree on a spring afternoon. The hairs here and there frizzed out aimlessly. There were split ends.

As he bent his head sideways, the skin folds of that side of his face crumpled like a concertina. Old Balls was up to his knees in death.

On the way home in the car my father talked about being authentic, belonging to yourself.

"To be your own person, to act from your own center, that's being an authentic person." His voice hardly carried above the noise of the engine and the wind padding the car's edges and surfaces. His voice was soft, the ride was soft, wind soft. Mother looked out of the window at the passing lights.

"The air does rush past," she said poetically.

"Like the lights, the air is stationary," I informed her. "We humans move. You could come back in ten years and stand in the same patch of air."

"You're not serious!" she exclaimed.

At least she wasn't writing notes.

There Is No Usual

Old Mister Cowan still worked on his coffin. He lined it with lead, took the lining out, painted the timber many times, had pictures put in it, an oxygen bottle, food—in case he was buried alive, though that was unlikely since postmortems were general—relined it, clad the outside in stainless steel, stripped the whole thing down to the bare essential shape, scraped off the paint, and started again.

It was a permanent hobby. His wife didn't object, though she made no move to have one of her own in the garage.

When people spoke of it they seemed to resent his behavior as being different, as if they thought their own was in line with the usual. But I watched, I looked around at all the people I knew,

I listened to stories, and as far as I could see there was no usual, not anywhere.

Perspective

As an assignment for Art, I used a small square of pressed chipboard (that once, in another form, stood vertical in the Huon district of Tasmania), and mixed sand with paint to give a suitably primitive background. When the mixture of ochre and sand was dry, I scratched the figures into it. The foreground was a darkened cave, made by mixing black mud into another mixture of paint, and when it was almost dry, spreading black dirt over it. In this blackness the silhouette of a cave-dweller sat looking out into the sandy glare of day. The profiles of small ancient buildings sat nearby on the lowest horizon; behind them larger buildings, up to three or four storeys; and behind these the usual big-city skyscrapers. But behind the jagged tracery of skyscrapers and elegant, sometimes monstrous towers with their bulbs on top, the newest building spread across the sky and rose toward the stars, blotting out all distance and all height, and with millions of windows, rising to cut off any view of the sky from the dark cave.

I had the city history of man in my painting. I got a rave assessment from Miss Barwon, who predicted that I would go far: she liked me. Not like Footlow, our regular art teacher. Footlow was jealous of me.

A Social Illusion

Yesterday the man from the river came for the last time. This time mammals and lifelike children grew from his pockets and he paraded around the empty streets leading them like a family, or tribe.

At the end when he had assembled them all on the oval he unwound a belt-like thing from his waist and held it at arm's length. He marched round the perimeter of the oval holding it out, calling, "These are the last days! These are the last days!" We could hear his words as far away as Heisenberg Close.

News broadcasts told the human inhabitants of the metropolitan area that the man had been seen in fourteen suburban locations, holding out the unwound belt and proclaiming the last days.

The last thing the man from the river did was to hold out the belt-like thing and ceremoniously take from the end of it a small plug. He began to collapse where he stood, sagging at the top and the middle first, then falling in a heap. When he was flat, the mammals and children gradually deflated until all were level with the grass.

The whole lot blew away by morning.

A Wojan of the Future

This approach was a beauty, believe me. He was, irritatingly, absorbed in my face. You know how it is; a girl knows her face, knows it well. The deficiencies seem sometimes to be signposted, provided even with audio-visual equipment saying "Get a load of this mess!" and all one wants to do is get attention away from a bottom lip that's not full enough, or from eyes that don't open as wide as some of the dreamy dears that snap up males like besotted flies with their gooey great eyes practically running with liquid and probably catching all the dust around.

My eyes are, unfortunately, not very big in the sense that the top lid doesn't open in an almost circular way, rather it is inclined to be narrow. Intelligent, you must grant me, but narrow. Not slits, though.

All he would do was examine me. Waiting for me to crack.

Not altogether comfortable with this I remarked, "Well, shitface, what's on your mind?"

He looked at my eyes in anger and as if with that look he could make threats of thunder shake the air. He drew back the left side of his body and quickly punched at me with his left fist. Mindful of the karate kicks I had seen—but never executed—I doubled my body over sideways, also to the left, and pushed out my right foot toward his middle. I was only playing. Unfortunately for him, I hit, and he missed. I should have just punched him, like I did father.

When he felt better I asked why he tried to punch me.

"Because of the way you spoke to me," he said.

"It was only words."

"It's not only words to me," he explained. "You see, when someone speaks like that to a male, it's on. I mean, it's too late for more talk, it's the signal for: let's shut up and get stuck into it and see who comes out on top. Fists, boots, what the thing is. But with a wojan, you're not supposed to hit them. They're equal, but you're not supposed to. So the guy has already lost face being talked to like that, and the only way to save it is with the old aggro. But he can't. He knows this, so he won't argue in public with a woman. You can't win with a wojan, in a man's terms, by all he's learned, all the rules he's lived by since he was five or six years old, out in the street with the kids nearby and in the playground with the kids at school and the teacher to be reported to."

"Well, you struck at me first," I said. "What's a wojan?"

"Just a word for females."

"And all this aggro theory?"

"I'm a verbal behavior and situation perception adviser. Sounds a lot, but it's just prole stuff."

He began to walk away.

"What's your name?" I called after him.

"Claudio Matuzelski."

"Come back, Claudio."

In his car he insisted I undress myself. After that, all he wanted to do was look at it and poke it with a finger. Nothing more. Enraged, I pulled my things on and left him, still with his trousers on.

I called out, "Shit for brains, Claudio!"

He didn't attempt to fight with me again.

Under Fire at School

I came under fire at school yesterday for saying that man's been on the planet much longer than anyone is prepared to guess, and that the extinction of the dinosaurs saw his rise; that man was first dark and that the light-skinned ones are new; that it will be wonderful when most of the continents join up again as once they were, though this time at the opposite end of the globe.

Miss Brockman said no good purpose was served by such speculation, which contained an element of irresponsibility; on the other hand Mister Pollard thought the exercise of such ideas was mind-expanding, and one of the steps in the practice of creativity.

Which is right? And aren't we coming closer to Asia every year?

In school today I was punished for saying that the Chinese are the Teutons of Asia. The punishment was an essay of apology. I hate apologizing.

I got my own back, though, on Mister Saussere in an argument in class on European culture. He had said that European culture could not "take," in Australia, implying a lack in us. I pointed out that it had not "taken" in the United States, Canada or South Africa either—the main colonies of Europe—except to some extent in the main cities. Then I let him have it.

"European culture, as you call it, is a metropolitan thing, a product of the cities of Europe; it has never even penetrated the villages and backwoods of Europe. No wonder it didn't travel to such distant backwoods as we have," I said. He went on to speak of the lust for ownership and the spirit of materialism having become the dominant values in Australia; he didn't want to admit I was right, in front of the class.

Karen Gott

She ate like a pig, blew her nose on her fingers, and didn't care what she said or did. She was magnificently coarse.

She had the reputation of being very hard on males. They said she would get their things out and compel them to erect, then hit it, or twist it round sideways, or sucker them into putting it into her mouth, then bite. That part of them is very sensitive to pain.

Once, they said, she got one of her men drunk and stapled the loose skin of his testicle bag to a wooden spectator bench at the oval.

When she detected any type of lovesick behavior among the younger girls, she would get them into a corner, shake them, and say, "OK you. Go round and say to fifty kids, I love you. Sincerely. That'll get the loveshit out of you."

Usually it worked. She stood over them until they had completed the fifty, and some of those girls got as hard as she was.

Karen had transferred from a city high school at the request of that school; the authorities thought a quiet area like ours might have a steadying influence on her. What happened was that she teamed up with the brutal bunch and vied with the five leaders of the bunch to be top leader.

For the teachers, having Karen Gott in their classes turned the weather grey as ashes.

We weren't supposed to have real contests in our boxing class—just training lessons—but Karen challenged me, and I didn't feel like backing off. It wasn't my fault—she turned it into a fight; I would have sparred all the time. She hadn't done the training, just thought she could fight because she was tough. When she started hitting to hurt, I punched her hard and broke her nose.

We weren't allowed after that to do more than spar, with the sportsmaster present to supervise.

I Am Sixteen

I am sixteen, and in my dreams the thing that calls to me is the most unreasonable thing of all: that I am different, unique, beyond compare. That I am on the edge of something big and don't know what it is. Will I last long enough to know it?

Is it someone I have yet to meet?

Is it a guess? An insight?

Is it something I will do? Something I am?

Will I be a martyr in a cause I do not approve? A leader? What?

It's such a torment, being held fast by this prophecy of mother's. How did I let it take such a grip on me? Yet how can I ask this question, since my view on the world is from inside this state of mind? I can't get out and examine it, nor can I get out and walk away from it.

The trouble is, all my life I have felt it *is* reasonable. When my mother said her "Some day . . ." to me, I could see myself wrapped in the greatness she predicted. Not in detail, or clearly, but I could see it.

Surely I should have had a hint of what it is, by now.

The Dream of the Greatest Woman in the World
When would I begin, when would I feel it, when would it be apparent to others?

I woke in the night to dreams of greatness. The precise form it took always eluded me. I woke at night to the long dream moments before the applause of an immense audience spread out below me, whose clapping and shouting I could feel before they began, whose sudden roar of recognition was like a natural phenomenon and carried me high above them to a place where I was supported on nothing more solid than the upswelling force of their emotion.

Time and again I reached the top step of the platform on which I had four paces to go to put my hands out and touch the ranks of microphones at a little above waist height, the place where I would stop and begin to speak.

Speak? Of course speak. It had something to do with speaking to a multitude. But telling them what?

Before I opened my mouth the noise of their earthquaking response to the greatness I represented took my breath away, then filled my chest with an emotion that was lighter than air and had far more lift than any air. I breathed deeply, let it fill me, and began to ascend. As the noise died down I spoke and my voice rose above the noises of the world, and the world grew silent, bound by the spell I cast over them like a net, like a gas. They were listening, receiving; I was raping their minds.

When I woke the hands of the woman of the future were wet with sweat.

Son of Cannon

The man with the cannon growing from him—who was now rather suspended from the end of it than growing it—had a son, Mark, who did the usual things boys do in Australia; playing games, stealing, by turns being a good boy and a little bastard, until he began to solidify at the age of fourteen, just as puberty came over him like a bad joke.

The sort of orebody he began to be allowed him in a moment of anxiety to arrange things so that his penis became solid when it was extended. He had a naive belief that this foolishness would wear off—and who among the free citizens of the world is without a touch of this saving hope?—so that when his flesh relaxed again into the supple, familiar smoothness, softness, flexibility, he wouldn't have lost the opportunity for growth in the member that means so much to males.

Mark, son of Cannon, gradually settled into a weighted existence, and after a painful three weeks, did not move again. His eyes were the last things to be immobilized, though after this scientists detected brain life through electrodes placed on his surface, and some claimed to have got an ECG. The thing was that the electrodes could be placed anywhere—movement in his interior had to be detectable everywhere on him since he was solid, brittle and coherent throughout. His surface was still smooth, since he was a sort of bronzy, aluminum, nickel-iron amalgam. This was inferred from surface color and spectroscopic analysis; his parents refused to allow bits to be chipped off: they thought he might bleed when he resumed his proper shape later.

He has not changed so far. They keep him in the hall as a statue.

Fucked by a Tree

Oliver Morris had the attitude that any female was going to be overwhelmed by the magnitude of his experience.

I admit there is a certain attraction about the idea of a business-like approach in which all the clumsiness and drollery of extreme youth is excluded, but something is missing nevertheless. I daresay it is my continual secret complaint: that love has never touched me.

(I wonder do males complain as much? I mean to themselves. If they don't, but go just from one defeat or unsatisfying experience to another, hardly thinking about it, blearily through life like unreflective zombies—then it's no wonder a female counts herself lucky she's not male.)

Oliver prevailed on me to allow his penis to plunge back and forwards within the slithery halls, and I didn't mind. He had branches of willow growing from his feet, arms, legs and the middle of his abdomen, just above the hairy triangle.

In his first high school year the teachers got him to break off bits, and they planted them in two lines on either side of the creek down past the rifle range, to form an avenue in the bush. Strangely a stream appeared soon after, bigger and stronger than the old creek; it flowed all the way along the valley where before it sometimes ducked out of sight under a day creek bed.

He kept his growths trimmed, his parents were reimbursed for cuttings they sent round the country.

Well, maybe not a tree: fucked by a sapling.

He kept me there, demonstrating that, as he boasted, he could get "eight off the one stick." I didn't tell him how many I could have had during the time it took him to achieve the first one, if I put my mind to it. And I must confess that I don't really know if he was simulating any or all or most of the eight. I think the only way to check such a statement would be to withdraw each time and for a witness to check that there was an ejaculation each time. With at least *some* sperm content. I don't think dry-blowing should be counted.

At the end he looked drained as the sweat dried on his face and neck and front.

One of the creek willows had its bank partly removed by little kids digging for treasure; the exposed tree roots crossed over each other like arms.

315

Perhaps I Would Be

Perhaps I would be an explorer of the human condition, an enlarger of the mind of man, the age of man; move men to action, inject a vision into their lives; give them a foretaste of experiences that would seduce them from their present lifelessness, enlarge their grasp of the world. I might help my fellow human fix his position in the universe he inhabits, even in the body he inhabits. Perhaps help others create their own unique world.

I might perhaps even create a world that never existed before.

On the other hand I might, at twenty, be sleek and self-contained, remembering best the brittle winters of other lands; the times I went with men to cabins in the snow and stayed a fortnight loving and being loved, exploring only the borders of another human whose essential being, behind the skin, would be forever hidden under bland and sudden lust. Decaying in pretty colors.

The Possessor of Lisa

Mario Julian by now had grown his girl-product to the extent of her legs; the buttocks were out and the long-awaited pussy there. His friends came to see him, hearing an incautious word from his young brothers; held his hands to keep him powerless, and used her.

He was shocked, and gasped out to them: "You're doing *me!* You're doing *me!*" And they left.

He touched her constantly. His parents marveled that he regarded her as part of himself; the way he protected her, the way he fingered her and knew her and thought of her all the time.

"He really loves that girl," his mother said.

"KKKKnnnnnnncccccccccK!" his father snorted.

Both Feet Firmly on a Cloud

I was sitting in Science, it was Monday; outside the science block and in the street leading to the school I saw a person rise up out of the drain underneath the lip of the gutter, a person with a number of heads and on each head a different hairdo. A lady gardener, with not much to do till her family came home, struck at the person with a garden spade so that the top of one of the heads was split down the center and blood ran out.

Some of the other heads turned to look at her, and several mouths opened and shut, talking to her and commenting on her actions. While they were attending to her the wounded head joined back together and the blood stopped. The lady with the spade turned away, annoyed, and resumed pottering in the garden.

The person with the heads turned toward the school, and when it got to the wire gate stopped and looked toward me. I narrowed my eyes and tried to see the various words it had growing on its various heads. Yes, growing. Not just printed.

What I did was to ascend out of the school window into the air above the school playground and step onto a small cloud. I planted my school shoes firmly on that cloud and watched down on the many-headed person with satisfaction as it writhed and twisted its heads and made little leaps up off the asphalt as if it wanted to ascend with me. I folded my arms and gazed down on the miserable cowering thing benignly. The power in my eyes, and the concentration behind them that I mobilized so easily, worked on it like a judgment. The heads one by one wilted and hung limply down on the end of their long necks. The body shrank and grew thin. Very soon it was small and groundfast and was glad to become a shrub.

I started up the cloud and drove over to the window I'd come from. I flew in, sat at my desk, and packed the cloud in my schoolcase. It folded up into a square no bigger than my white hanky. In fact it was my white hanky.

In the playground I was thoughtful. Kids said, "Look at Hunt. Thinks she's Jessica Christ. Won't speak to anyone."

They didn't have visions. Major visions.

That Word

That word that has followed me all my life (because I have not allowed it to cut loose) was it only a casual word mother spoke?

It couldn't be casual: she said it so often.

Was it a habit?

Was she repeating something she'd heard might be good for little kids to hear?

Was she repeating something she'd heard when she too was young?

Had she been joking—admittedly an adult joke—and I simply not capable of appreciating it?

Yet it had to be more than that, or why did I respond to it so readily and so completely? (But people can respond to things other people don't intend . . .)

No, it had to be more than a casual, accidental joke.

I wonder if mother even remembers. How can she, when she acts as if we—father and I—were dead and she doesn't visit our graves?

Little Things

There was a great demand for our bodies. We girls didn't put all that much value on what our bodies represented: they did that. We simply went along with it. We were necessary; it brought advantages. Little things, it's true, but little things were all that males could give.

In truth, those little things—the dinners, the sights, the money, the drives, the gifts, the sexual exercise—were all they had to give. Their sperm ran out again, and was flushed away.

Later, once the males got the idea that our bodies were to us no more than theirs were to them, our value would vanish. They would say we weren't attractive.

Those of us who cared least for our toilet, the boys rejected first. But in general, by the time we showed this casual disregard for the magic they saw in our bodies—which we had never understood—we would be middle-aged, tied down by children we had borne and supported.

And to us their bodies held precious little of the magic ours did for them.

They never cared for their nails or toenails, they didn't build up their faces, study their ears and noses, align their hair carefully in the mirror, put softening cream on the points of their elbows, brush their hair for five minutes or two hundred strokes at night, make mouths into the mirror, practicing their "I love you" or their "No-to-mean-yes." Well, not all of them.

Lil Lutherburrow

I rescued her one day at school from fifth form boys. She had wandered into their territory around on the lower side of the Assembly Hall, and they had taken her prisoner. By their rules, she had to report back to them every playbreak and lunchtime, until they decided to release her.

They did things to Lil. When I saw what was going on, I charged into their area and grabbed her. They got on to me and tried to hold me, but I had no vulnerable points, and they had.

"Lil!" I yelled at her. "You come round back to our area. Right now."

She could see I was trying to help her, and responded. She came.

"Isn't it against the rules, to leave without being released?"

She was that simple.

"Rules, what rules? They make the rules up! Take no notice of boys' stupid rules!" I was shouting at her.

"I'm sorry," she said quietly. "Thanks for helping me. I didn't know when I'd get free." That was all she said, but she was my friend for life.

It's easily said, but it was true. Lil was the steadiest friend I had. Maybe the only real friend. And she didn't even get around with our group. I never bothered to keep the friendship in good order, but she always remembered, always wrote. I never once wrote back.

The boys got her after school, and she hadn't wanted to be got. She wasn't like the rest of our knot of hardened girls. It was one thing to go looking for trouble, it was quite another to have it forced on you. I shot my mouth off, and next thing there were police at the school.

Lil had those kids in the palm of her hand, but she was too nice a person. In the end she claimed she was willing. That let the boys off the hook.

Lil threw her reputation away and saved the boys from nice long sentences and the savagery of a sedentary judge.

"I give up, Lil," I told her.

"They're only boys. You can't punish them for being boys," she said.

In return they got her down by the river, near Little Coogee. Kids were in canoes on the mucky water, and the boys from school were in Lil on the bank.

Lil's Car-Eater

Lil left school early. She got a job as office assistant in a tire retread business where she made out work orders and kept records of work and hours and overtime.

She admired one of the mechanics there. He wasn't really a mechanic, since he had no qualifications, but he helped take off and put back on the wheels of cars, and wielded his rubber hammer and rolled car wheels along the concrete floor with abandon.

As a hobby he was eating a car. After work each day he went home and broke bits off the bomb in his backyard and ate them. He'd polished off the front fenders and the front and rear bumpers; he still had a way to go. The other men at the retread place used to accompany him to the lavatory to hear him shit. His name was Gavin May. The car was an old FJ Holden. Lil wrote me about him. I'd never had much to do with her, but she considered she was my friend.

Dear Alex, You know I got this job at Booker's, well there's a guy there eats cars. No, honestly. I don't go out with him, though maybe I would if he asked me. Just to see what he's like. I only know him at work. How's your father's act? Does he still have to go to

Sydney to die each day? Anyway, this guy Gavin counts the bits as they go through him in the natural way, I guess he wants to get into the record books though I haven't asked him this yet. And is your mother OK? Those people that keep trying to get us to shift out of the bush are still trying, we have to keep moving. The dogs give us good warning when anyone comes though. I'd like to ask Gavin how he's going to prove to the record books that he's eaten the bits that come out of him, but I think he'd think I was rude. I wouldn't want that, it's just that I want to see him get what he wants and into the record books if that's what he wants and I can't stand to think he might not be able to prove it. The people might laugh at him and not believe him and I wouldn't want to see him disappointed. I think I might ask him some question about it and maybe if he thinks I'm not laughing at him and if he sees I don't really understand so he can explain it to me, he might take me out. I know you're busy so don't worry about answering this, it's a pleasure to know a person like you and to write to you and feel that you're still my friend, because I'm still yours,

Lil.

Encounters with Nothing

Like cats we were, straying near the source of food. Asleep, scratching, playing, washing, playing at sex, returning to the source of food, never leaving, but for short prowls near other animals.

The little rules and laws we lived by were our prejudices, crystalized for a time to give the impression of permanence. Then a new batch of kids came on the scene and lived by a slightly altered set of prejudices.

Our responses to questions put to us by our surroundings were a selection from the feelings we had at the time. We dramatized each truth, each feeling for our own benefit, as if we were trying on new clothes; tasting each new truth, each hypothesis, each new outfit.

Judgment is a duty of every person, we were told. Judge yourself, pronounce sentence, execute the sentence: that was learning to be an adult.

The pursuit of ourselves was expected to occupy our youth. It was supposed that we would approach the goodness and simplicity of the ideal, Citizen Christ, as a form of selfhood in action. We were engaged in doing things that formed a search for our identity.

What made us not know? Why were we uncertain of our identity? Surely other races, other times, other people were born knowing exactly what they were and where they fitted in. Maybe we had too much time. There was nothing we *had* to do each day to survive. Everything was so free it seemed we did as we liked.

And when we found our identities, what we found was that we were trivial. I don't mean what we did was trivial, though it was. I mean *we* were, in ourselves. So trivial and unimportant that it didn't matter if we found an identity or not. It didn't matter if we had one. It never had mattered. We were just here for a space, then not here. Like pet animals, cockroaches, leopards in a zoo.

We had chosen idleness, and pleasing ourselves. We looked into the distance for the dreams and colored visions that might be the future, but what we saw was distance. Admittedly distance too was a drug.

We accepted the regular meals, the rightful shelter, the protection of custom, the nourishment of entertainment, like laboratory mice.

On an excursion once I saw in a laboratory a nude mouse. It scampered about and sometimes stopped and watched me. Its eyes were bright, and, I thought, knowing. But later, when its head had been snipped off with the secateurs and its braincase opened, the rest of its head looked at me with just the same expression it had when it was alive. It had known nothing.

Of all the young I knew, I think I was most convinced of my ability to get through the grading gate into the minority, and of the rightness of this happening.

My comfort was internal. Perhaps that was why I hungered for harshness, danger, risks, complications, enemies.

Instead, what I had at sixteen, was dream after dream of violent action, fighting and shouting, and an awakening to nothing each morning. There was school and sport and the joy and vigor of competition, but once I'd accepted this order, it was easy. It was unsubstantial; there was really nothing to fight. Every breath, it seemed, was part of a lifelong fight against nothingness, and the effort of the fight, the essential assertiveness of the fighter, was what held us together. For though there was nothing to fight, the fight must continue, or we would fall to pieces.

Without this fight we are ghosts merely, phantoms, inhabitants of a dream dreamed by some shadowy consciousness—(once in ten times it dreams of us and we have existence).

But I would be no ghost: I would fight: I would make the effort: I would hold together.

I wrote a sort of poem about it, but I didn't show it to anyone. It looked too much like a poem about war and the devices of war.

Blooms appear where no green is
and there is hate, a deep flower.
Children in bronze rooms
wear it as more than charms.

The black rain screams and sings
into the prepared soil. The hour
is expectant, dizzy, and becomes
choked in its need of flames.

Hearing a man's thunder begin
beasts and the kings of beasts cower;
a red shield covers shames,
and crosses – men's names.

The young are weary of things
lacking violence. The world is sour.
The wheel turns and comes
back on those it tames.

We will be rid of all silences
but those that cluster within the flower

whose unimaginable blooms
shall purge us from all harms.

Note Made After Friday's Science Period

It could only be pointless to address you, inheritors of the next universe. When our universe shrinks finally, explodes, and after desolate ages inconceivable as a mental picture to humankind, forms new systems and stranger galaxies, the particles of these pages will be not only dispersed, but may not even exist as atoms of the same elements, for who knows in what way the next set of elementary particles may re-form after the next universal explosion?

If only there was a way of leaving decipherable traces of our works and what it meant to be us, for the inheritors of the next cycle of life. Assuming curiosity has a value then. But we, in our compartment of the ages, are shut off from the next cycle as finally as from the life of the cycle before us, and that is a boundary nothing can cross but perhaps some of the elements of which we— the universe—are made.

The Painting Class

I caused a sensation—admittedly only a sensation at our school, but school was a world—by doing a painting of the cruxifixion.

It was a painting of a painting, for the crucifixion in my canvas was posed. It was real enough, and blood flowed, and a human sacrifice made, but the artists capturing it at the foot of the cross were artists first, prepared to sacrifice one man so that their painting had reality. There they were, canvases stretched on easels, brushes poised, spaddling on palettes or busy brushing; a whole class of outdoor painters while the figure on the cross writhed and gradually ceased moaning and began to faint away for longer periods, until immobility and the upright position and loss of blood and shock took consciousness away for good. Then only drying blood was left.

The painting class worked like demons. Their part-finished paintings showed on their canvases, and all were different!

The painting class won first prize in our school art competition—art was made attractive for potential Frees—and attracted notice from local painters.

The Crucifixion as an Artwork, commented the local throwaway paper. Portrait of the Artist as a Young God, said a metropolitan daily, sourly.

How delightful it is to be good at things!

Inspiration, Ambition?

Her head was down, her body had a forward lean. Determination was printed on her T-shirt, pig-headedness on her face.

"A woman's gotta do what a woman's gotta do," she grated through clenched dentures. (Sorry, I don't know that they were.)

Mrs. Footlow, our art teacher, was inspired, it seemed. She had, I think, been spurred by my small success to try her hand at something ambitious. She was working on a panel to illustrate the emotional aspects of the magic square totaling thirty-four. She was trying to combine hard-edge expressionism and post-industrial apocalyptic. Styles swirled under her hand as no doubt they did in her teaching brain. We watched as we went past the art room on the way to lunch.

In the playground I made a remark about Footloose Footlow trampling down the plants in the garden of styles with the Wellington boots of coarse ambition.

"Love thy neighbor," MM said, unhelpfully. Which was all very well for MM, but Footlow had said to me a week before, "You have no desert spaces, no untamed wilderness in you." And she meant it to hurt.

Oh, haven't I? I've got as many as Australia has.

Rose Hearts and Pomegranate

The image persisted in my mind of the rubbish tip spreading down from the completed sports oval. In its shadow we parked our cars.

Each time we came, more filling had pushed us further away and raised a cliff of rubbish to shade us from the houses a few hundred meters away. By summer a second oval was done—over the places where we played—and another being filled down into the slope of the bush.

Others played there too. Grown-ups. I think of a shabby pair: she an outcast, wearing an overcoat in all weathers; he with that sockless look and unpressed clothes that were not the uniform of the unpressed young.

Perhaps they were building a kid to play on the next oval but one.

In summer we put the rubber on the bitumen and played on beaches. Once, when I just felt like sitting on a rock, I wrote this:

> Look *at us running to swim in a vintage sea*
> *Pink flesh and white bone*
> *White bellies and sudden pink petals of mouth*
> *Other petals of thick rose mushroom, sly pink*
> *Opening their mouths against the blush purple soft head*
> *Concealing its bone hardness*
> *Towering over rising brown foliage.*
> *That pink bulb will push apart my brown nest of hairs.*
> *His arm throws itself over my head, his hand white after long swimming,*
> *Cold blue fingers pull open my brown bud*
> *Finding the glistening petals, pink*
> *Of the heart of my rose.*
> *And further, down the cone-shaped-like-a-whirlpool*
> *To the pinkish pomegranate pieces that will yield and open,*
> *Flesh teeth glistening in a circle: moist.*

I put it in at school for English Expression. Mister Khoury said I was developing an interest in poetry, and I was intelligent. I suppose he meant it as a pat on the back. Was he serious? I hope he didn't think I was fool enough to want to be a poet, lonely in a cold society.

In a sense we were free to do anything and go anywhere, certain of nothing but that our energy would take us somewhere. But then certainty wasn't the point.

Freedom from and Freedom to

I longed to leave the machine of childhood which wanted to teach me the virtues of community. (In case I became a Free.)

I wanted the luxuries of privacy, my individual freedom; anonymity among the elite of the Serving Class.

When I was free of the machine, my freedom could be translated into the dynamics of action. The free act, as an ideal, floated tantalizingly before my mental eyes. Freedom to steer myself on the waves of the sea of society, rather than loll on the sea bed. Free of entailments, free from the drag of the sea anchor of conscience. The unmotivated act.

What a freedom it seemed! To achieve a life of unmotivated acts, a life as free as breathing, as free as the workings of the circulation, as free from direction as the involuntary nervous system.

I thought then that nothing could be so inspiring as to shake off these humans that were all round me, and to go alone into the class of people where I would feel at home. The world seemed to ring with meaning more resoundingly every day, and I responded with the energy and imagination that I felt growing within me.

I must admit I often felt, thinking of the other kids, most of whom would never make it, rather like the vines and creepers on the fence and round the trees: night and day they grew, reaching for something.

Something to strangle. Certainly, the social system was unfair, but that's not felt keenly by those on top.

Fame

Acker Campbell was now practically hollow. They kept him at home for fear of his organs being punctured by some inquisitive or malicious member of the public. He would no longer let others squeeze his liver or his lungs, or feel the processes in his guts with their bare hands. He had to be sponged constantly, like the dolphins and other sea creatures that were moved over land. They didn't let me close to him, they kept him behind a glass screen.

"It's not funny anymore, is it?" he said to me plaintively.

"Are you really hollow?" I said. There wasn't much to say.

For answer he lifted some of his organs aside and fisted himself on the chest. It gave out a lovely hollow boom.

"At least I haven't got a live body growing out of me," he said with something like satisfaction, meaning Mario Julian.

I didn't see him again, only pictures of him, in science articles and on television. In a funny way he had made it, despite his change. As I went home I wondered at his lack of resentment, and at his ability, even in his condition, to look down on someone else.

A Lovely Day

The morning I got Lil's next letter I was sleeping so soundly and wanted so much to stay in bed for the rest of time that I was really offended when the devil in the clock smashed the silence of my room. I took it personally and got up grumpy and wouldn't look at father as he handed me my breakfast. Nor did I ask him "How's mother?" as he returned from her room after giving her hers.

By the time I'd got out of the frontyard onto the footpath by the special step father put in so I wouldn't tramp down the rockery since I wouldn't go the long way round the letterbox down the front drive, I'd forgotten everything except what a lovely day it was and didn't even remember being grumpy.

On the way to school the houses growing out of the hill opposite looked pretty, and I passed a one-legged peewit and a kookaburra that cocked her head at the ground from her branch with a look of disappointment. In the yard of the old corner house near the bridge a large patch of violets was busy subduing all the grass around it by cutting off their sunlight with a dense cover of leaves, from which the delicate violet stalks and petals looked up demurely.

The weather was hot. I knew that when I came home from school at three I would see high birds looking, looking for the reflection of water.

Lil's Next Letter

Dearest Al,

Please excuse me writing to you again. I hear of you often from Jimmy and Maurie, my little brothers. They're in year seven and eight. I've been home today to look after Mum, I hope they won't dock me for the day. It's been raining and where we are now in the bush the trees are thick and very tall, since we're down near the bottom of the valley. Sometimes when it's raining I imagine I hear the trees saying, We'll bend our crowns over to make a roof for Lil's family. And their trunks are thick, just like the blocks of rock those primitive men put up at that place Stonehedge that we learned about in sixth class. I guess those people in olden times were pretty well stumped for a way of getting a roof over it. But I guess if they'd built roofs over them there'd have been no way for reverence to come in. I like the idea of a church open to the sky and God. Did I tell you my guy's old man got divorced and had to leave the kids? Even if he hadn't got divorced he'd've had to go—there was no room for him anymore. The things he left behind they split up. As if he was dead. You wouldn't know his mother, my guy's mother I mean. I'm not knocking her, she'll live till she's a hundred and after all she's my guy's mother, but I can't help feeling sorry for the father. He's gone to live in the city, you know, where it's cheap. One room he lives in. He can't afford to come and see the little kids. I went and told them it seemed a bit wrong for him to be put out like that, put out sort of to die. They threw me out. I was just saying what I thought. I was in there to that city a little while ago, it was cold, the wind was fierce trying to blow the sky away. There were so many people they had no name, just like drops of rain. The old buildings, well, even the fire escapes looked lonely. Poor man. As for the neons, trying to put some brightness over it all to cover the dark and dirt. Maybe in the future people won't need to be

329

virtuous and do the right thing, maybe the system will make sure everyone gets justice. I did what he wanted when I visited him and now my guy's very mad with me. But it was just sort of sympathy. It didn't mean anything. I hope you and your family are well. I kiss our school photo every day to kiss you.

Your friend, Lil.

There'd Been a Party

Next morning father sat in the comfortable chair with the bright green upholstery, his head in his hands. Still connected at the neck, of course.

"Oh God. Oh God," he was saying.

I grabbed his hair and pulled up his head to look at his face. Tears patched the skin under his eyes, messing the remains of his eye make-up. He didn't always remove it completely when he came from the theatre.

He stared at me with sorrow.

"Dead, dead, dead," he moaned.

"Everyday." He put out a hand to grab me, but some unsympathy made me knock the wrist aside. He didn't care, or didn't show it.

"Can you know what it is to die every day of your life and knowing that at the end you'll never wake to play again?"

"You mean it's not the story of the play that's done this to you?" I said. "Just your part, having to die before the end?"

He didn't answer.

"What about the others that die? What about the ultimate change that the play's all about?"

"But me! That doesn't help me. If only I was still in my mother. Better still, if only I was still a spermal possibility. Then I'd never know I existed, flushed down some lavatory, dying on a handkerchief, or washed out of someone's underclothes. At least the infinite possibility would be there. What a blessed state. To have it all to come. Instead of which, once the egg is fertilized, it's the beginning of the end. Life, birth, living, just a brief final flowering

330

before the real end. And I mean E-N-D. No more possibility. Cast the seed of my own life, much comfort that is, then curl up and die. Wither. Back to elements. Never come again. All possibility gone. Exhausted."

I made breakfast for him. You can't expect a father overwhelmed by the sorrow of existence to make breakfast for himself.

"Do you want something for your head?" I asked.

I mean, he was older than I; he'd survived this long: why not longer? I fetched him tablets for his head, and a glass of water and left him to his sorrow.

Separate

A thing that bothered mother was my coming home into the house after sport or music practice just on time for tea and walking up to father, putting both hands on the sides of his face and saying sweetly, and outrageously, "This is the man of all men that I have intercourse with!"

"Alethea!" she trumpeted when I first did it. "This is your father!"

"Is he?" I said.

"To think you can speak of your father like that!"

"Mother, it pleases and grieves me; pleases that you are for once talking to me, though I'm quite tough and could last forever without response from you; grieves that you think I can't speak to father in any fashion I like after all these years of only speaking to father and not you, of telling him, not you, about my periods and telling him about the boys that touch me up and telling him about the men I screw and telling him about my coming greatness and telling him about the changes I see in the world about me and that I never see in you."

This was not strictly a logical discourse, nor was it meant to be. I didn't tell him any of those things, and she often spoke to me. Well, fairly often.

Father made a pacifying gesture, his hands came up near his face, then out toward me, and one remained vaguely pointing in my direction while the other wavered over toward mother; as if both arms performed some sort of linking of the two females in his life who happened to share the house.

But there was no such link. Not between him and us, or between any of us then, for I was separate, and though I would probably be part of him and of them tomorrow, I was myself then. Just at the moment that I was proclaiming he was the man I had intercourse with!

I could do that *because* I was separate.

I wasn't the same all the time. When I got a letter from Lil and smiled at her way of living her life—why didn't she get away from that family?—or lifted an elbow into someone's ribs at basketball, or stayed awake at night thinking of poems, refusing one of the kids at the quarry for no reason at all, or moralizing in an essay about the conduct of politicians and powerful corporations, I was being a different person. One person in one place, and a stranger to that person in another.

Which one was I? Was it natural to be all those different people? Or was it a deep fault in me that I had so many faces?

I dreamed waking and sleeping, of greatness, whatever that might be; and I knew I had to do, to perform, to act. My life was cut up between two options: action and dreams.

Was it part of my trouble that I had inside me another person who was reacting to and countering what I did and thought, so that by doing the complementary thing at each step she was effectively nullifying all I did and wanted?

You Can Admire the Old

Today I think of death. Not in the same way as when I was three or four, but as a terrible certainty. Myself, my flesh, my hands, my face, my legs, my new breasts, all are going to perish. Perhaps today, tomorrow, but if I live to be a hundred, it will be certain some day.

I look around. All those much older are just as game as always, doing the same things, smiling the same smiles, yet they're getting old. I can't look more fearful than they look, for in the natural course they will drop before I do. And there they are, walking into obliteration with their eyes open.

It's one thing about the old that you can admire.

I've even seen old people out at night gazing up in wonder and enjoyment at the high-sailing clouds and bright moonlight leaking through: and it's all going to be there after them as it was before them. Yet they don't seem to resent the facts.

I wonder if father and mother do.

When I think of death I think always of them, and always I feel just a bit weepy. Dear parents—you, too, mother—may dreams always guard your sleep and stand like sentinels over your sanity and health!

LITANY OF SUCCESS, SUNG BY CHORUS OF TEACHERS

> *Your father will be here later,*
> *I've asked him here specially.*
> *You'll achieve.*
> *She's an achiever,*
> *She's bright*
> *She's aggressive*
> *She's strong*
> *She's the best we've ever had*
>
> *No apparent disabilities*
> *No sign of inherited weakness*
> *No lack of spirit*
> *No absence of self-esteem*
> *No lack of any quality necessary*
> *One day*
> *You will remember us*
> *And remember that we said*
> *You will achieve far beyond*
> *Any other product of this school*

And any product of your own family
Or ancestry
You will remember
One day
We join together in being proud of you
And promising that we will do
Everything we can do
To help you
Succeed.

Xmas Holiday

The girl was lifted gently from a car, and seated on a patch of white bush sand at the side of the Mona Vale Road. The bag over her head was ventilated. She sat there while the car drove calmly away past Terrey Hills, her knees drawn up under her long skirt, her hands together in a muff-like loop of material.

The first rescuers to decide she wasn't a bomb tried to get her to her feet. When they stood her up—and she stood in a curiously crouched way—she fell over. Falling, she put out both arms to save herself, as if handcuffed.

When they abandoned impatience and embraced investigation, they found her hands had grown together at the palms, her feet sole to sole. The graft scars were fresh.

Medical students had held her in a weekender over the six-week Christmas break, had immobilized her, fed her, kept her quiet, and performed the surgery necessary to graft together her hands and feet. They did it as a holiday exercise, and anonymously wrote a teaser report on the work, hoping to interest the newspapers in parting with large sums of money for a fuller report. The deal stayed at that stage, for the relatives of the linked girl made it hot for press and police, threatening to have the perpetrators and anyone who cooperated with them. The relatives even argued that she should not be separated right away, they wanted the public to be aroused against the privileged Servants of Society by exposure to her misery.

She was Mary Pogson, of Popper Way, and before the holiday she had been in year ten. Her best friend was Mercedes Facciuola, and she went out with Challenger Lutherburrow.

Fourteen Minutes and Fourteen Seconds

Father had this mad idea to get some fresh cold air, and Blackheath wasn't far on a Sunday if you got up before the other million cars.

"Let's walk from the highway," I urged the authorities. If you didn't speak quickly they'd ride all the way to their air, get out, sniff, and get back in the car. My father drove on a bit with his father look and finally consented to park.

We walked along a road that said Evans Lookout. My father lost his resigned look after a while and made creaky jokes about lookout for Evans, and my mother loyally made notes. I don't *know* that she wrote about what he said: I'm guessing. Maybe she wrote about liquidambars and pines.

Another road became a bush track over on our left, so we walked across and took that one. I picked up a silvered grey stick to ward off snakes. Downhill we walked, sniffing the cold air gratefully, and at a dammed pool we got on to a narrow path that said Braeside Walk, where we had to go single file.

I led the way. Alternate breaths of cooler and not so cool air blew in our faces, and we exclaimed about them. Ahead, the creek that ran alongside the path, only two or three meters away, showed as a spear of silver, straight and broader in the distance.

Where the reasonably flat bed of the creek broadened near the path to about four or five meters, I could see that it was not merely a creek bed; it was the top stratum of the whole mountain of rock that supported our small valley. We'd been walking down the slight slope of what appeared to be a valley; now it appeared that the valley was merely a ripple on top of a huge ridge, and the creek bed went another twenty meters, then was no more. It cut off sharply, the water disappeared, and the next thing in view where the creek should have continued was a valley floor covered with the blobby, conical tops of trees a hundred meters below.

I walked along the red brown creek bed and sat on a rock, looking down. My father muttered and wanted to shout; my mother said nothing. (I don't think she took in the fact that the chocolate brown rock stopped as if a cake knife had cut it.)

The water proceeded at the same pace to the sharp edge, then casually went over. It didn't seem to realize it had such a long fall.

I sat. Father watched anxiously, leaning against a large concrete thing that might once have been a barrier or a sign. Perhaps they had so many people jumping over that removing the sign gave suicides no clue it was such a handy place.

I looked down. It was a good place to think. There was nothing to stop a person from just walking to the edge and I trembled, but not so the water. Water doesn't bruise. It was the freedom to do it that fascinated me. But the thought of the pile of rocks below, broken slabs of fallen cliff face, leaving this perpendicular face of rock smooth and regular. And how sharp the rocks looked. No, I didn't get to my feet and jump. But the thought of it tugged at my feet. And thinking of that fall made pains in my legs.

Freedom to jump. Freedom to not jump. I was beyond reach of my father's hand. I didn't want the freedom to jump, I wanted the bread of living. With all its unfreedoms. When you're free the answer seems to be that you have nothing else but freedom. It's like owning a hole in the ground. Hole is a noun, and you think that because other nouns are objects you can do things with a hole, but just try moving it.

"You're sure you're safe there?" father asked. Some words were questions in that sentence, others were statements, as if he was asking me was I safe and assuring himself and me that I was safe, only to say the very next word with a question in his voice. You'd have to hear it to get it, you can't really describe it in words.

If I did walk out to that edge, and put one foot over, would some magic or miracle save me? Would the act be irrevocable? Would there be a ledge below to save me, or a frail tree to grip while my father rescued me? No, I knew the cliff was sheer from top to bottom.

If miracles could happen, who could say that all sorts of odd things wouldn't happen without warning in the future? I'd be a slave to freaky slips in the system of cause and effect, time-slips, memory reconstructions. They sounded fine, but to happen without me calling them down, made me a slave to accidents.

The wide valleys ended where ridges remained. It looked as if the ridges were there first and the rest had sunk or fallen down and got washed away. You could look round from one ridge with its exposed sheer sides to another one a kilometer away, and see how the top stratum of rock kept a level line to its neighbor. Its lower edge was defined by green things growing, then beneath that another stratum of rock, not so deep though, could be seen to be the brother of the second top stratum way over on the right, and over here on the left. The time it must have taken. And there was I, sitting on a rock that would one day get bowled over when the creek bed was full of flood rains; I lived and breathed and could see the rocks and cliffs and strata, and would die shortly. The rock would go on for practically ever, and it couldn't even see.

That was the thing that reconciled me to living, with all its disadvantages; being able to do things: to see, to know, to move.

Alternate breaths of warm and cold air came up from the lip of the drop. The ages-old fallen rocks overgrown with green and covered by earth and vegetation bowed dumbly under the large sky. Those trees and grasses were wide open to the rest of the universe, with only an atmosphere in the way. Somehow, with all the pictures of the earth, I'd never thought of the natural features of the earth as being so open to the universe, so that if there was anyone to see, they could.

Feeling the scale of it I could no longer believe that humans bowed down to anything of wood or rock. No wonder people began to worship the Out There.

But I, a large schoolgirl sitting on a rock above Govett's un-signposted leap, I needed no one to worship. I needed no one to keep me in order, to keep my conscience. I didn't want to be part of a human ant-heap, though I was attached to it. I didn't mind taking responsibility for what I did; I was insignificant enough beside the wreck of this rocky plain now broken down in parts to valleys and ridges: how could I hope to oppose its alleged Maker Spirit? Freedom seemed to be freedom to choose, and the mountains couldn't choose. The water couldn't.

I could. I got to my feet and walked back to father. Mother had climbed to another lookout and was standing at the edge of another hundred meter drop, writing.

"That was fourteen minutes and fourteen seconds," he said, relieved.

"In the wilderness," I added.

"Have you been thinking of fame and reputation, time and death?"

"The precariousness of life," I answered. "The insignificance of humans."

"The precariousness of all life?"

"No, just mine." I looked again at the concrete blocks. They had holes in them. There had been a bridge, and signs, once. Now there was nothing to tell you were even approaching the top of the falls. It must have had quite an attraction, that drop.

On the way back in the car I listened to a religious story on the car radio of a great man who attained everything. At the pinnacle of his success, or greatness—I still couldn't separate them—he became aware of a younger rival, and he considered this young rival better than he was.

He called the younger person, offering to stand down in his favor.

"No," the young person said. "I'd be given it on a plate, I would have no chance to achieve greatness myself."

I thought about it.

Was greatness more in the work done?

The radio man went on to an informal analysis of the Great Man. He was two-sided, a compound of Jekyll and Hyde, but in an apparently agreeable blend. At the end of a major stage in his life he finds he has to choose between one and the other. The broadcaster didn't say if he had to choose for image purposes, or for his own spiritual satisfaction. I took it as the latter.

He also found his life had little meaning.

In the story the great man chose Jekyll, and his young friend chose Hyde. They seemed to be of equal strength, but since in this world good is less powerful than evil, the only way they could seem to be of equal strength was in the consideration that there were adverse social indications for evil, consequences of evil, which trimmed the balance.

Evil and good were evenly matched.

And, in fact, that was how I thought of them.

Where did Alethea Hunt stand in all this? The trees flying past seemed to say: A.H. has something missing. What is it? Is it knowing what I should do? Is it knowing where this supposed and far-off greatness might lie?

Or is it—terrible thought—that the thing in me is lacking that would push this hint of what I am and should do up into view?

It was going on in my head when I got home.

I guess I was quiet, sitting down at teatime, for father raised a glass of tomato juice to me and said, "Here's to my big little girl," as a toast. I raised my own glass after a small hesitation and silently clinked glasses. As the glass chimed, I said within myself, somewhere near my liver, it seemed, "Greatness and the whys."

I felt a glow of spiritual energy, but it faded after the fourth mouthful of father's steak with wine sauce.

"I'd marry you, you know," I said to him. "If you weren't past it."

"For my cooking, I hope," he said.

"Of course your cooking."

A moment later, after the thought of what else he'd meant but not said had faded, I remembered my spiritual energy burst.

Drink the toast to greatness, yes. Say the words, yes. But do nothing, nothing to bring the wish about. Greatness was as far away as its definition.

Greatness could come from the greatness of a cause. But in my youthful and empty cynicism there was no room for causes: there were none. As for any cause being great—that belonged to the past. But why? Wasn't it a matter of searching, in any age, for causes that must be possible?

I returned to the ancient domestic wisdom I had taken in from I knew not where: greatness is within, be great there.

Going to bed, after finishing an essay for social science on the rate of human sign learning in chimpanzees, there still returned to my mind the thought: push the search to the end and live with the consequences.

Even if in my tiredness at the end of the day I reverted lazily to the conventional domestic wisdom of the interior existence of goals and virtue and greatness, the urge toward action still remained.

I fell asleep dreaming of two young chimps combining three signs into the action-sentence: "Gimme more drink." If I hadn't been so sleepy I would have flushed with embarrassment at the parallel: three stupid mammals stumbling over combinations of words.

My Car

Tomorrow is my birthday, and father is getting me a car. It's only small, but I don't mind. The party will be at Strathallen, so mother won't be disturbed. Besides, the kids drink a lot and make a noise, and noise is unpopular round our streets.

I had a win at school today. They wouldn't let girls start up a weight-lifting class in the gym after school, so I brought some women's organizations into the argument, and today we were told in assembly that the school had decided to start a class for girls at the sportsmaster's suggestion, and if the parents' association would put in half the money the school would get the rest.

Celia O'Donnell and her gang are all going to be in the class when it gets going. They want to get stronger for their forays, on late shopping nights, into shoppingtowns where other gangs go.

It will be good to be mobile and go where I like when I like.

340

The day after my birthday party we played Bankstown.

I was last to finish dressing after the game, but with a car, who cared?

Little noises in the wall of the change rooms at the stadium turned out on investigation—I thought it was a rat—to be a friend of the caretaker. He was fascinatingly dirty, so filthy that he was lovely. Washed-out eyes observed me from his wine dark face. I wanted that dirty thing in me.

"Contemplation of the worthlessness of thought or action is the only thing worth doing," he said, settling back on the pile of matting where he had enthroned himself, and insisted that I impale myself on him and do all the work.

I felt a little wave of viciousness toward him as it passed into me, as if I was adding to the mess he was in. Dirtying him, I mean. (Why did I feel that?) It was streaked with grime, and on the back of it—when it was up, the part I could see, the under part—the dirt was so ingrained it was studded with blackheads like black-currants in a cake. At the roots, where it joined his body, the crease was dark brown, even slightly purple brown, and shiny with sweat. The smell of that part of him was so awful that it had a sweetness at the back of it, like an aftertaste.

"Do you come here often?" I asked. I didn't mean it. I continued to ride up and down.

"I live here. I go for a walk when events are on."

"What about training at nights?"

"I'm asleep then, in the storeroom." His teeth were stained to the gums, and there was something horrible about the bright pink inside his mouth. I wanted to get in there, with all of me, and revel in the mess. His throat made me think of a sewer.

"I enjoyed that," I said when I'd finished and he'd finished.

He lay back on the matting after I'd raised myself off him, his thing wilting slowly and the stuff running down it, bits clotted on it near its collar, and the watery part running down the inside of his leg toward his bottom, and over the wrinkled and hanging old purse with long hairs growing sparsely on it.

He didn't mind. Spider webs like grey scum clung near the ceiling.

A noise on the concrete floor, and behind us stood a child of about thirteen with gorgeous grey-green-cobalt eyes, skin looking so fine it might split to the touch, and hair golden at the front and on top and lightening to not-much-more-gold-than-blonde at the nape of his neck. His lips were darker than pink, with another shade that troubled me. His lips he carried apart, under a fine slim nose. Something inside me turned over. I could feel those more-than-pink lips with the bright wetness traveling in an angel's caress all over my parts. I thought I saw his delicate white penis rise from a hairless place into the air until it was surrounded by three pink surfaces and those surfaces belonged to me. I swallowed with a dry mouth, and licked my lips with my tongue.

"Gets to you, doesn't he?" said my filthy companion, lying there with waves of aromatic human gusting from him. The air shook.

I pulled myself together as I dressed and thought soberly of greatness.

But what was that shade: darker than pink?

Why were we here on earth? What should we be? What should we do? Did greatness have a part? What was the purpose of greatness?

Perhaps its purpose was to give every generation an example of something necessary to humanity, something necessary but practically unconscious on the part of ordinary humans. Was this slight consciousness given to me as a trust, as to someone who could make use of it?

It didn't seem that many of those around me were concerned with finding out why they were here. Or did they have thoughts they never made known?

What a lot of questions.

I stood up before the baffled beautiful eyes of the first year boy, and the beautiful filth of the caretaker's friend.

The boy and the man both provoked in me feelings I didn't usually have even when I was tearing into one of father's steaks.

342

A blob of semen slid down my upper leg and stopped. Perhaps it was caught on a few of the hairs on the inside of my thigh. I wiped it carelessly, pulled on my tight pants, picked up my heavy schoolcase and with dignity went out. I don't know what happened in there after I left.

Perhaps the whole of life was searching; going, but not arriving; simply going toward, never reaching. The journey is the whole of life.

But that couldn't be so. I was left with the same questions to answer: What should we be, what should we do?

When I got to the street, I looked behind because I felt eyes on me. It was the beautiful first year boy. All the way home I wanted to go back, lift him in my arms and crush him to me. Would I eventually have a male as beautiful as that boy? Had father looked like that once? His boyhood pictures in the album showed a handsome boy's face, but not a beautiful one. What would it be like to own a toy as pretty as that?

The Female Flying Dutchman

I held my legs wide for the moon, which beamed right up over the sill to light up my bed; I was a spider trapping the light.

The light caught the silhouettes of the short hairs on the tops of my thighs, and made mountains of my upturned breasts.

Outside the window, high against the moon in the jeweled dark, a black spider hung down from her thick webline suspended from our phone wires.

I imagined I was dying, naked and sensitive to light, which felt like hands and touched me with interest; I was breathing hard, I was dying, the spider spun its thick strong wheel and waited, shifting a little every few minutes; I felt moist. A globe of moisture came out of me, came out like a spider to the sticky part of its web, and waited, then dropping slightly through the jungle and leaving its sticky trace, forming a film round some hairs. It gradually changed shape and formed a perfect tear, and dropped into the hand of a man whose face I could not see.

1. He sealed it in a locket and wore it forever round his neck, round his waist, dangling near his sinister, powerful prick and its display of fierce hair with its back-up of silent inscrutable scrotum full of testicles, puffed and overflowing. He treasured it.

2. He never washed that hand. That hand did nothing ever after, he kept it clenched to retain till he died, my moisture, my sticky trap . . .

3. I changed my dream. He rubbed it over his face and body, it glowed so that I might recognize him . . .

4. He put it on the tip of his tongue, then on four limbs he came looking for me, climbing over the sill, along my bed, between my legs, looking for the taste he had on his tongue, his tongue . . . for the essence that has become part of him . . .

I went to sleep and woke before dawn, legs no longer apart. And cold. The moon was gone, the sky bare. I found my pajamas and put them on, going to sleep, too sleepy to regret the one who had me as an essence inside him and could not forget, but would be marked by me forever.

I woke again at six. The sun was up.

It took only the mental picture of the top of his shoulders to make the feelings come. By the top of his shoulders I mean the silhouette of his head, including the way he shaped his hair, the curve down to his neck, the way his neck curved outward to the beginning of the wide part of his shoulders, and the shape of the top of them down perhaps a few centimeters . . .

I could picture the long muscles of his upper arm showing, one after the other, as his arms moved; showing under the skin and under the slight thickness, the slight softness between the skin and the muscles they covered.

And the feelings that came! They were the important thing! They were the things that lifted me from my picture of where I usually was in the world to a picture that I could never see clearly, but could exactly feel. As if feeling were the location.

And the picture of where I was ordinarily? Why, it was a picture of a mass of millions of people standing shoulder to shoulder on level ground, and the mass stretched for so far into the distance that the horizon consisted of the heads of people like grains of sand. And to the east, the south, the west . . .

It was the thought of that special part of him that made me feel those feelings in my arms, along the inside of the softer skin of my arms. When I touched it with my own hand, there was next to nothing. But if I touched it—in the dark—in a way that was almost not a touch! And when there was no touch at all but so close to touching, that's when I felt a tingle along all my surfaces, echoed on the sides of my tongue and downward where it was rooted to my throat.

I lay there, feeling I was perhaps condemned to sail the seas of emotion for ever, never to land or stop, never to become one with the magic mountain of feeling – everything – all – at – once – forever – and – never – stopping.

Would I be condemned to pay with my soul for whatever of this magic eternity of moments I managed to get hold of? And when I got a better hold on these moments, what would I do with them? Would they really be as evanescent as people said? Was there something I could do to ensure that they did not slip through my fingers?

Love and Sweat

I have mixed feelings about one's partner sweating down on one. I mean on me. Every woman knows how it is, the male with the penis inserted and pointing slightly upward, the arms, or at least one arm around one's neck so that the downward pressure of the arm and the upward bend of the penis make the latter something of a hook, down past which one's body cannot go; and if the day is warm or if the effort is a little beyond the male's physical readiness the drops of sweat come from his chest and neck and face and drip round past the base of his ears, and drop on one's body and breasts and face. One's face! And sometimes so much that it seems both have been rubbed generously with oil.

If only I had experienced love. If only I'd had a man that I could feel deeply for. Then I could learn to love, perhaps, his excretions. And smile, and brush aside his apologies and make him feel entirely welcome. Yes.

If only I could have one who was entirely welcome!

Art Assignment: St. Francis Curing the Leopards
The saint was not preaching with arms upraised gracefully from his lonely, set-apart figure to a meek and rather ludicrous quantity of winged creatures: he was standing astride one leopard which lay on her back, paws raised straight up and a trusting, even a rather humorous look on her great jaws. The little saint was examining the leopard's body, apparently feeling for lumps, and the two forepaws enclosed his slight robed figure in a friendly manner.

The other leopards were lying around on their sides, tongues lolling. And the whole thing was in a cave lit by rays of the sun outside; a village was some distance from the cave, down a long slope; behind the village was the rather modest skyline of a small city; behind that, rising to the height of the old skyscrapers, was a vast metropolis of buildings of all shapes and sizes, but large. As a backdrop there was one single building that extended from one side of the horizon to the other and lost itself in the sky so that there was no blue at the top of the picture; windows for miles up and miles across, as if that building was the rest of the world in that direction.

I was unconscious of what I had done until Footlow pounced.

"You've done that before, Hunt! Exactly the same."

"Leopards?" I said, not understanding.

"No, no. That cave perspective. The city with buildings that get bigger the further away they are."

Of course. Why had I repeated that particular image? For a time I felt guilty about it, until I realized that if it was so much in my mind, *that* fact was the important thing. And forgave myself immediately.

Parent Assessment: My Father

I think he had at the bottom of his mind, as a sort of mental sludge left from the time and the fashions when he was young, an implicit view of how social and political change is achieved. In those days it was revolution, attacking and destroying the power bases of society itself. The bastions of power were the large private and public bureaucracies, insulated against popular persuasion, which listen to no voice but violence and the threat of violence. He had been conditioned to despise reformers, or fear them and remove himself from anything that was not wholesale destruction and overturning. Out of the old the new may rise.

Yet, at the same time, he fervently desired a better world; more peace, cooperation, contentment: less alienation, less bigotry. And his temperament was in line with these fine sentiments; he was a man inwardly at ease with himself.

He had an inward stabilizer that righted him after any sort of disturbance. Even if he had lost his mental battle and didn't know where to go, he was able to dismiss the problem, clear it off his mental desk and put it away for some other time. Unsolved matters, unfinished thought, all went down into the drawer marked "Later," and he got on with the routine of living. Perhaps there was a sort of health in it.

Despite the fervors of his youth, he didn't go into politics, or even business—to rebel against the revolutionary way of thinking. He valued neither money nor power. He was a cooperative man rather than competitive: independent, democratic. But his democracy was internal, he was free within himself, and would have been free under any flag.

Yet he said to me once he was not certain who had led his life.

Creative Social Science: Sunset in the Suburbs

Sunset in the suburbs, and the emptiness of the continent drifts in, like the emptiness of the moment after "Gooday" has been spoken by an Australian to a stranger. This Australian has no ties with any other Australian in the form of words; he has no recognition

347

signals apart from the absence of words. He has no ties except the emptiness and the silence. It is a continent of dreams we inhabit, a waiting continent. All who have set foot in its bush, its lonely places, know that silence. The continent is dreaming. We have felt it and been afraid, and turned to trivial things, and retired to the outer rim as if ready to depart. Everyday the quiet tides of darkness roll over us from the menacing interior.

The Australians, not yet the damned of the earth, get a certain comfort from the sunset. After all, one breathes. Though it's better to breathe audibly once or twice or even that assurance wobbles. A bout of heavy breathing can let the darkness come down more lightly, and mitigate its threat. This is the collective sigh you can hear across the wide brown land just after the gold edge of the sun has gone.

Creative Social Science: The Strangest Continent
By Gabriel Sentongo

The country itself is so new that the people transplanted there suffer a curious eye trouble. The sun is something they have not yet assimilated. It illuminates, and the last thing they want is to see their landscape; it dazzles the eyes, and they have a great resistance to being dazzled.

The land itself tries everything to keep them away from its sacred inner self. It floods them, drowning everything under vast tracts of callous water; it denies them water; it burns them from their bland fields which have laid waste the original and proper soul of the country.

They take refuge in tight settlements on the least inhospitable edge of the continent. The interior remains unsubdued and empty because they don't know what to fill it with; they have neither the energy nor the fierceness to subdue it.

It was two hundred years before the inhabitants knew the land they walked on had a history. And by that time the majority needed special assistance to see any distance beyond the Media Average

Satisfactory Sight; that is, the distance one could hold a newspaper, read what it said, and view television.

Of any person standing on that continent, looking into the distance, you may be sure he sees nothing. His sight is not equal to emptiness. He is resting. He is idling.

Gabriel was always knocking Australia, but we didn't mind. He and his family—what was left of it—were refugees. Their village had been dispersed; the people lived in the bush for a long time before daring to go back. They stayed for a bit, then had to run again when a different lot of soldiers came. Finally they got on a refugee boat and landed on the west coast of our country. We let them in. Gabriel was only tiny when the troubles started; he got here when he was nine. He is full of imagination.

I wrote a poem about being a refugee, as far as I could imagine it. I may put it in with my next assignment, if I get the chance.

> *At first we came back very slowly*
> *unwilling, I suppose, to see a home*
> *in this half-forgotten assortment of hill, tree*
> *and winding road at evening.*
> *But the tiny houses were obviously snuggling closer*
> *in the waning light*
> *and in the end we were glad to bed down there.*
>
> *It is years since then*
> *but mornings continue to startle us*
> *the sun pushing too fast into the sky*
> *callous light inflaming the heavy face in the mirror*
> *stripping the world bare far too suddenly.*
>
> *We have brought home with us the house inside our hearts*
> *built during the hunger and the running away.*
> *It is ourselves we die of.*

Despite the Glorious Dreams

Despite the glorious dreams that I waited for eagerly every night—dreams of sensual riches—no one among the boys at school and the casual males at parties could arouse me, since Mister Jonson's purely physical success. No matter what lead-up they performed, no matter how much time I had with them, or they with me—no one.

Once or twice I felt the shivery beginning of the at-home-on-my-bed feelings, but they seemed to be independent of the company I was in. When I say independent I mean they didn't coincide with the times I was with them; the feeling might be starting, then they would interrupt; they might have been with me, and have "done" me—(their word)—when the feeling would start, and go on through their leave taking, and persist after they had gone, but it was something that had arisen of itself. Because of some trigger in me, or simply because it was time. They hadn't done it.

The place in me where this response lived, was untouched.

Willie Kemp

I was laughing at him and confused him: he thought I was smiling at him. Their egos are immense. However, I let things proceed.

"What do you do for a crust?" I asked Willie as he and his approached my body.

"I'm at Business Sensitivity School," he answered in capitals. He kept trying to get in at all sorts of points where there was no hole, and one where there was, but not the right one. He got in, settled forward on his favorite elbow—they usually settle down to the position they always take—and explained.

"Basically it's the smelling out of profit. Training in feeling for the profit situation."

"How do they make you sensitive?"

"Same as they make you sensitive to anything. Surround you with it, surround you with the lack of it, rub you up against it, deprive you; most of all, talk about it and see examples of it in figures, buildings, products, balance sheets, ads, all that sort of thing."

"The elusive profit," I said. Business had no interest for me, it seemed so simple and uninteresting.

"That's it!" he said with animation. "Treat it like you're a hunter! Go after it, smell it out, then bang! Bring it down and bag it."

When his physiological processes currently on-going climaxed, it was not with a bang at the end of a steep reckless out-of-control hill, but a pathetic whimper.

"Oooohhh," he said, giving himself to me. And subsided like an emptying bag of air.

"Well," I said brightly. "It wasn't a cannon, but there *was* a recoil."

He hadn't the energy to reply.

He gave himself to me. I gave myself to none of them. I don't know what that "myself" means, but it's something inside that I've never seen, maybe that no one has ever seen.

When he'd returned to a semblance of life in a minute or two, he said, "I don't know anyone like you. I guess I haven't had that much experience, but I haven't heard of anyone like you either. Past or present. No one."

I heard him in silence and waited while he got it up. He certainly needed a long recovery time for a boy with an almost silent bombardment. At the crucial moment he coiled up, almost as if he was hurting, then fired and let the spasms shake him. His interior jerked him about. Not the tail wagging the dog, but the dog's guts wagging both tail and dog. Quite unlike the kids that ride like cowboys and keep going long after it's all out and running everywhere.

Something about him annoyed me. He was too observant of me. He deferred to my wishes in the tiniest things, never taking it on himself to be definite, to insist, to contradict. The question is: could I ever stand to be worshipped?

I tolerated him several times, then let him go.

Dried Husks of Insects

How sad it was when the fuck was ended, particularly if there was nothing in it for me and I was merely waiting. The male eased away, withdrew, and the emptiness of the whole barren continent flooded the place where he had been, and this emptiness it was that overwhelmed the slight, shadowy soul of the male.

I felt pity for them. Not sympathy: pity. They were light as leaves, a breath of wind would blow them away, out of the sight of humans, of females. A whisper of human breath could do it: a word from the mouth of a skilled female.

Wwhhhhhhhhh! They were gone. They ceased to exist.

What a Funny Race Men Are

To think that opening your legs is in any way giving them access to you. As if this hole: dull, unfeeling, so expandable, was a health and wealth-giving prize to them, and an advantage given up and lost by us!

They have *had* us, they say. Had be damned! They've been in contact with a few dozen square centimeters of mucous surface, coated with a lubricant which prevents actual contact with the internal flesh. They have never reached beyond the surface. Yet, when they open their arms to us, their vitals are exposed.

If all qualities ever manifest in mankind are latent in all mankind, how can they be looking for, how can they find, anything important and unusual in a continual reconnoitering of our various surfaces? What keeps them going? Are they primed daily, in a mechanical way, so they cannot help themselves?

To men, ours was a sub-world where duty, honor, truth and honesty were mere words. Dishonesty in women wasn't much to blame, in fact we were incurably dishonest, nothing we said could be taken at its face value unless it was favorable; sin to a woman was being caught.

How ridiculous men are.

You can see them in public positions, issuing curt commands with asperity. "Get the morning tea immediately!" The managers of offices peopled by bowed sheep, with jaw muscles standing out, standing rigidly on legs loosely hairy and hidden by the trouser; how ridiculous they are.

And in a personal crisis, what is their remedy for doubt, indecision, fear, and the nameless dread of loneliness? Why, they look for a tunnel into the problem and push a shaft in and make little explosions in it, hoping to blow up the world. But after every calamity and orgasm and the death of part of their world, their problems still remain. They simply do not know what to do with us.

They look back, each one of them, on a time when they were children and their families provided bounds for them and their mothers gave them law and affection in equal parts and the world was simple and there was no need to trouble themselves with the enormous effort to give affection to, or be interested in, or spend their precious egos on others. Their personal sadness is that they ever had to leave their little ballgames and paddling in water or mud or snow or trying to catch innocent fish, and at every chance they go back to what gives them greatest pleasure, they go back to what they think the world is all about. For to men, the world is a toy, and life consists in playing with it, manipulating it, prodding it to make it move, and finally destroying it, just as they did with their first caterpillar or ladybird or puppy or lone ranger cap gun. Children almighty, in charge of the universe, their bottoms wiped by mother.

And what to do with women? They don't know. They try to use her, like they used good old Mum, then want her out of the way, to have no regulatory power over their self-destructive activities.

They are children.

They are afraid of us.

Love

I don't really think that humans mean little to me, it's just that the feelings people give me seem to be—not dissociated—but to have a slightly loose fit with the things that give me those feelings.

I *know* touches to my skin electrify me; I've found that touches I give myself are so wonderful, so far beyond what others' casual or even intended touches mean to me, it's no wonder touch is the thing I wait for; the touch of love certainly, but love's touch as a physical thing on my skin.

What I need is someone to touch me with love.

A Dirty Dose

The older family members and clergymen didn't know the significance of the place, but we held the marriage of Sandra Noonan and Ollie Hartigan in the old quarry. The kids all sat around, draped on the big rocks, lying on the flat shelves of sandstone just like they did on regular Saturdays while the officiator and parents and friends arranged themselves round Ollie and Sandra.

After the service most of us went up to the lake to have a party in the open, with barbecue things, and not long after I drank something I began to feel a change coming in me. A spell of dreaming, feeling that all normal restraints had lifted from me, that the trees around were fantastic people, that I had unbalanced something in my head and would feel peculiar until it got back into position. I wandered away from the party to give my head a chance to clear.

I said hullo to a tall person who turned out to be a tree, and must have misjudged his distance, for he knocked me down with a blow to the side of the face. This was a different Alethea Hunt; the girl who was knocked over by no one and who hit back harder for every hit she got.

I was next lying in a grassy scrubby place and hardly noticed two males, my absorption in my interior state was so complete. I know that I was half naked and barefoot, I never found my shoes; scratched by the sharp ends of native bushes, on my back in the grass and stunted shrubs. Tears fell from my eyes, and the whole earth and heavens were sad. Above me, between the crowns of trees, the sky was endless, so that my mind tried to follow the endlessness across and back, then deeper into the unresisting but impenetrable blue. The endless sky, the earth spinning dizzily, the endless sky and the deep deep sun burning and spinning above me. The sun burned and slowed all my thoughts to a crawl, my thoughts crawled on the inside of my mental barrel. Chewing some grass seemed a reasonable thing to do, as bits of white cloud softly passed over my head. I reached up and touched a cottonwool cloud, which burst softly with a musical note.

My hands were damp. I touched myself with them, and they felt as if hands were a foreign piece of matter, rather like soft wood. The rest of me was damp too, like a sweat that comes when the body feels the approach of death through sickness.

Pains through me seemed to have been there all my life. My head felt as if the left hand of death was gripping the case of my brain. I rolled from side to side, trying to roll from under the pain. I pinched my skin and heard a yell. Immediately I felt more pain, this time closer to the surface. I clasped my stomach down low. I scratched myself with nails I had chewed into sharp points and succeeded in cutting the skin. Cold sweat poured from me, down my sides in channels, making pools of liquid on the earth beside me.

I screamed to myself: "Think! Think of a world with no pain, where everything is happy; all pain is unnecessary, therefore there is peace and painlessness everywhere, and no tears."

"Look at the sun! Kiss the sun! The sun is so kind and good, he kisses all the children of the earth. He's also lazy, a golden flower. He's a fiery spider with webs of heat and flame. He is the mouth of a flame-thrower held in the hands of an enemy."

A soft white cloud above was spinning. I'd had no food for many days, yet I wasn't hungry. What was making my body arch and stretch and tremble? In tears, my legs were apart for the sun to touch me there; my mouth was open for the sun to come in and bless the interior of my mouth. My breasts were bare to the touch of the sun; I squeezed them so that the little mouth in each nipple would open and receive the sun.

Still in pain, but able to get up, I pulled flowers, grass. Still pain. Several dandelion spheres came up with the grass, I held up the dandelions and blew them higher than my head. Tiny seeds fell and drifted and sailed away to earth, the air was white with downy parachutes; dandelions were descending to conquer the earth and the other plants. The soil would be carpeted with dandelions and flat spiky green leaves out of which soft hollow stalks would rise and throw their armies high into the air again.

The pain will not go.

Some abandoned parachutes drifted near men's trousers. I was down again, and the pain worse and I craned up to see the party and catch the smell of the blessed meat and the virgin yearling beef and the bread-filled sausages and screaming fat.

Perhaps I would be pregnant later. I would become a dandelion and be golden like the sun for a while, then burst, and seeds would come out, and I could sleep on them like a pillow, walk on them like a white carpet.

Those two males had finished their sport with me. The trousers left off being on the ground, and went away. White gobs of semen dripped down between my legs and colorless liquid, which ran faster, carried it down onto Australian earth. The semen showed a nice reluctance to drip off the soft inside flesh of my legs. In the sky another cloud in the shape of panties hung on a black snaky cloud the shape of a tree. It was, in fact, rapidly changing into a bush, a wild currant bush. I could see the eating party clearly, they were eating and dancing. Vapors from the flames surrounded them, and they danced within the flames and vapors like sprites in a log fire.

Walking through the bushes toward the distant party I was bent double. The pain. The wet on my face told me I'd been crying. I tried, but I couldn't weep anymore.

People passed by through the bushes, and I spoke to them, but they were too busy to answer. They couldn't have known I was Alethea Hunt.

I gathered strength and ran down and jeered at the wedding party and the eaters. I was pinched and grabbed but I did not retaliate. The bride's parents (she'd been bride to every kid in the school) rode at the head of a band of professional hunters mounted on trail bikes. I was chased off, and peered at them from within bushes, and round the trunks of trees. They chased me, I was flying over the twiggy ground, falling and stumbling and knocking things. When I fell I wriggled like a snake until my wits came back enough for me to stand and run. I ran far.

I ran straight into three men. I was glad it was a long way from the party, glad that my pursuers had disappeared. I would be ashamed to let others see my legs dragged apart. The men were silent, like dogs. When my hair was grabbed, I shut my eyes. I felt one man tread on my hair, the other watching, while the third fucked away.

I felt each one tremble as he came to get into my helpless body. I lay flat, crucified, the nails entering the middle of me rather than my hands and feet, as women who have been crucified long before Christ was; as they continued to be crucified with the sexual nail.

As they fucked forwards and backwards, pushing in, pulling back, the same movement all the convulsive time, they became lighter, their faces became the faces, their forms the forms, of angels. Their happiness, temporary though it might be, roughly though it might be grasped, was more important than my pain. As each one finished for a while, he went back to being unhappy, miserable. Each then looked as if he wanted to kick me. Imagine angels kicking!

They looked at each other as if they could read, as angels, what the other felt as his penis rubbed back and away along the inside of my vagina.

Others came past, looked at the angels and at me, and were sick, then went away to drink more. My angels looked as innocent as white clouds high in the sky and parachuting dandelion seeds falling on the fertile earth.

Perhaps Australia

I didn't know who brought me home. It was father who woke me, asking gently if I wanted dinner. I think he thought I had been drinking, or taking things. I lay on my bed for a little time, thinking.

Who was I?

I had grown from the soil of Australia; its promise of greatness was my own; it was unique, as I was; in a sense it too was an outcast, like I feel I am; it is alone in the world in a special way, as I am alone; it has a strength which has not yet been tested, not yet been developed;

357

it is young, like me; it has resources in its body; like me, it doesn't quite fit with the world as it is, though it may yet do; it waits, gathering its strength, which is its enormous silence, about it like a coat, waiting for an ideal friend, a lover, a spouse—who does not come.

The country is a virgin, as I feel I am, essentially. The hidden place in me has not been touched; my trivial adventures have not touched it. Besides, in a larger sense I am not the person who did those things: I am different.

Am I perhaps Australia?

Letter From Lil

Dear Alethea,

Remember young Sarah Sarau at school, who left after third year to get a job in Coles, well she's in a sort of rest home where they bar the windows. I went there to visit when I heard, but they wouldn't let me see her unless they searched me first, which I didn't mind, but the man took me into the changing room and asked me about Sarah. I had to say I was very close to her in order to get to see her, so I had to do what he wanted or he was going to report me and see that they heard about it at the tire place and I thought, well, it's pretty funny, and wouldn't he get into trouble too, but I thought well, better I don't get into any trouble and get to see poor Sarah or things might get tough for her. All he wanted was to take my pants down and bend me forward across his desk. It was better not having to put my front against him; that way I didn't feel it was quite like doing it. My guy couldn't say much if I didn't see the man's face.

I made it up to my guy that night, I told him I'd gone crazy and he was the man with crystal balls and I felt them to find my fortune and he was real tickled, with me pretending they were talking to me. I even held them when he was in, and you'll be glad to know that I felt better when I made him do me all sorts of ways, including bent over his sink so no one would have had me any way he hadn't. I felt so good, I pretended he was that Captain Ahab that Miss Manassa gave us in first year, and he

358

was chasing this big white whale (me) ready to harpoon her on sight. Believe me I was so happy it had happened the same as with that man at the place that I was only dying to have his boat overturn and make him drown in me. I really felt like a whale or the sea.

He made some money out of being on show with eating cars, and he's gone on the stock market, he says the market rises and falls faster than women's skirts but just as sure. At the rest home some visitors were tormenting the old folks, who looked a bit savage. And when a man blew a whistle a lot of people came out and began to comb the grass with real combs.

I like it best with my guy when he pins me and we're face to face and I'm helpless. I nearly drown in my own mind when I can't even move, and I pray that it will last forever.

Your loyal friend, Lil.

His Touch

Aysha Kemal's parents gave a party for year twelve in the grounds of their ranch-style house off Marconi Highway, and again I had some sort of blackout. I tried, while it was beginning to affect me, to remember who was at the party who might also have been at the quarry wedding, thinking I might come up with the name of someone who would want to put me out. I couldn't match names at all. The drug took effect so soon. It blinded me.

I didn't panic. I just took a little longer to walk places, and made a show of looking around me when someone was talking, so they wouldn't pick up the fact that I couldn't see their eyes.

The rougher ones at the party, apparently in the secret and knowing I couldn't see them, led me down away from the house on a slope that went further down into the valley toward the old rifle range.

What I mean is, I had to be led. It was only a bit later that they took me away from the rest and got me against the fence. Somehow they hooked my arms back to that fence.

When they'd all shot their bolt, they left me. All but one. He unhooked my arms, and it was the touch of his hand on my left wrist, then my right, that stopped me lashing out at him. Instead, I stood still and waited. I could feel the places on my wrists where his hands touched me.

"Are you all right?" he said. His voice was like a kiss. Not the rough male kiss you first think of, not the wet thing they put on you when they think they're being romantic and sexy like women want. His voice was a feather-light kiss, yet firm. It said we were strangers, yet there might be a world of something ahead.

As I stood there still, hoping I didn't have to speak (fearing that if I did my voice would sound harsh and shrieky) he touched my face. I still couldn't see. I guess he touched my face so that if I *could* see I'd have a chance to rear back and show that I could. His skin was so fine it would have rippled in the wind.

He touched my face.

That touch! His hand wasn't hot, yet it was like a fire through me. I staggered.

He only meant to catch me. I know that. But when I staggered he put his arms out and caught me. My knees felt loose. It was if his judgment was so perfect and he was so strong that he not only adjusted to my sudden stagger, but as well he judged when and where to grab me so exactly that there was no sudden clutch, no scraping fingernails, no squeezing of the soft inner part of my arms, no jarring. I knew then what it must be like to be caught strongly yet with such comfort that one's own muscles were completely free to perform, like a trapeze artist caught by a partner.

In that moment I could see a little. And he saw that I could see. A second he waited, while I tried to adjust to the cloudy sight of him. Then, before I properly could, he turned and walked up the slope of grass toward the back of the house and the tennis court and barbecue pit. Then he was gone.

Colors came quickly back. The grass was a brilliant green that looked liquid. I was so bursting with feeling that I forgot the eager young animals that had been at me, and walked ecstatically toward the party over the blend of couch and summer grass that they probably called a lawn, with here and there a plant of trigger grass and the beginning of a paspalum infestation. My feet inside my silly white shoes, the pair with the straps, felt like fairy floss. I couldn't feel the ground.

The touch of his hands! How I wished I'd seen them, seen their exact shape, the way the fingers joined the palm, the color of the backs of his fingers, the glint of afternoon sun on the crisp hairs on the back of his hand and on that part where the wrist leaves off and the arm begins.

But I had nearly seen his face just as he turned away to go. His walk, well ahead of me, was light yet firm. I imagined him carrying me . . .

Back at the party I gave none of them the slightest sign that I recognized them—which indeed I didn't—nor the smallest hint of a suspicious look. I treated everyone as if we were all members of the party, and it didn't hurt me to know there were eight of them that knew very well what the inside of my vagina felt like to their sexual probes.

He touched me. I was blind, and he touched me.

Not even a kiss. No casual jostling of a breast, no accidental elbow brushing my stomach and coming to a full stop outside my equatorial triangle.

Was he only a boy?

I was dancing with anyone that asked me, enjoying the movements of the dances and looking for him all the time. My gentle man-child, I murmured, Are you married, a plasterer by trade, a knight of the Southern Cross, a football coach? I know nothing about you. Are you gentle because you hold your power in reserve, do you have that holding-back that gives the impression of great power in potential? Is potential closely related to potent? Have you been held in reserve all your life, always patient? If you let loose would we all have to worry? Are you boastful, vicious, full of lies?

The colors of the dance, the mercifully ever-changing pattern of dancing movement, soothed me by their excitement.

To eat or drink, I accepted nothing offered: I followed others to the buffet and picked up near where someone else had picked up.

Another girl standing often alone, attracted me. She too, glancing through the window glass at the neighboring lights, would allow her gaze to become steady, then fixed; she would be interrupted well-meaningly every time by males, and each time her face would straighten out into an expression containing less interest than she displayed looking into the heart of the night.

I asked after him. How was I to describe him? The soft boy, the boy who came up last from the gully?

They didn't know. Some told me he had gone away. To harden in the sun, one said. His name was Colin. Or did I christen him with that innocuous name? The name of my favorite boy doll when I was a small child.

He had left the party.

Ah, my gentle man-child, my boy, my man—how I tried to recapture every detail I had darkly glimpsed of you, how I tried to reconstruct you from insufficient data now that you had gone! If only I had been quicker, and followed you more closely up the slope.

I was left holding my wrists, with his touch still imprinted on them. Once I put a hand to my face, but took it away, in case I disturbed the place where his fingers had been.

Bodies All Over the House

Still at the party. Much later. Drunk. No sign of my one who touched me and left his touch. This was merely a pick-up, it didn't interfere with thinking of my boy who was gone.

A map of lower Italy on his jaw spread black stubble down his throat to the chest. By contrast, the alleys of East London persisted on his face through three generations. The glob of phlegm at the tip of his throat, was the tip of a London fog that he constantly swallowed. When he opened his mouth wider, in speaking, I could almost hear the glob drop down his uvula and gum it temporarily to the base of his tongue.

He was warm against me. His face was warm, looking at me. And close. When, in shifting, he moved away, I saw he grew cold; his face bones showed, he was lonely. I was sorry for him, I could see he felt lost. I knew that when he moved, he moved in cold airs he carried about with him, and from within his cold he desired me. He turned, and turned again, aimlessly. I wanted to guide him, but I could only do that if I was near, and I could only be near if he came to me.

When he came close he would be warm in my circle of warm. And when his face was toward me he would be warmed and desirable and interesting. He would light up. He would desire me.

He would be happy, desiring me. He would be excited, seeing he could have me. He would be exhilarated, having me. And having had me, he would be sad again.

Oh well.

In the dark. When I felt it, put my hand round it and found it was firm and warm and adequate, I said in relief, "Thank God you've got something there."

My gentle man-child, where were you? Who were you? What was your name? Where did you lay your head to sleep? Did you breathe so quietly, when you were asleep, that I would have to bend close, closer, to be sure you were alive?

My boy, my man. Some day I'll find you.

My dark-jawed Londoner enjoyed me. It was gratifying to feel his enjoyment. Better than masturbation.

We slept where we fell. There were bodies all over the house. The darkness of night was private to us all.

When I woke I found he'd done me in my sleep. At least he'd had the consideration to put a handkerchief up between my legs when he'd finished, to save the drips.

Why is it some men seem to have a larger collar—flange is the word in the books—and when they pull out they seem to drag half the semen with them? Others must do it differently.

But I think I know. When you've been done from behind, their penis comes out with very little on it. Perhaps the top lip of the flange is cleaned by the thin skin on the more rearward end of the vagina. They all say it feels such a lot different, but as for me I prefer to have them in front. Where I can touch them and do some kissing, if I like them, or just plain see what they're up to. And every woman must get *some* amusement from their facial contortions.

But you, my boy who touched me, who woke me from the sleep of childhood, how it could be with you! You could do everything, if only you would. I would be there, helping you in every action: helping you do me, helping you love me. My smell would reach into your every pore and bathe you, and you couldn't get rid of the thought of me.

Components of Greatness

I spent the whole of next day in a sort of daze. My thoughts played round with the meaning, the source, the possible effects of my new condition. Something else came with it: a steering of my thought toward the idea of love.

I couldn't get away from it. Love, love. What was it?

Colin's touch sounded through me like a bell the moment I thought of him, with more effect even than I'd felt before. I was a bell with many mouths. The echoes of his touch sounded throughout my body. A bell with many mouths, his touch sounding in them all.

I was dry with a thirst to find love. No sooner did that come as words into mental view than I recognized the truth of it. The rest of me relaxed with an invisible sigh. I was bones inside a loose skin. I slumped. I was filled, gradually, like a large wineskin, with a feeling of joy that I cannot express.

One touch to my flesh had drawn me toward love.

Perhaps finding love would be my greatness. What did it mean, to find love? Would I find it in me? In others?

Never once did I think I might be a great lover, only that I might be greatly loved. Where was the greatness in that? Where was the strength, the goodness, the beauty, originality, dignity; the judgment?

In the meantime my nipples ached for him, for the touch of his hands, for the pressure of his body. They wanted so much . . .

Nipples can be very demanding.

The Transfer of Ideas Unit

I tried to take my mind from my absent boy; I tried to think, in spite of my boiling thoughts, of the future.

What the world accepts as greatness must have some power the future respects. Perhaps it implies power over the future, bringing the future about.

An idea—it can be a re-arrangement of the words used to describe a state of affairs—sometimes has power to seize men's minds, alter their direction, suggest, even prescribe their actions. And the sum of their actions is the future.

Which ideas will be transferred into the future? Answer: those presented to humans with the ability to make them actions.

A special unit of ideas people could be formed to push, to help the transfer of their ideas, of others' ideas, perhaps even to Proles. A Transfer of Ideas Unit. No one knows the future, but with a Transfer of Ideas Unit, I would help cause the future that actually happens. Power is a component of greatness.

Perhaps my Transfer of Ideas Unit would grow out of me in the way Mario Julian's girl grew out of him.

For she was now out, and walking round. She could not speak, she knew nothing. All she did was respond to a quiet voice, and cling with her arms. She had no ovaries, no periods, she understood nothing: was completely dependent on anyone who had her ... And she had wandered off, and Mario was searching for his lost female self to rescue her body—for his own, of course—and whoever had her was not letting go nor letting on.

My Transfer of Ideas Unit was to be an underground organization that would get ideas that had been thought deeply about—in their effects and possible disadvantages and all that—from their source, before business people could arrange to patent them and keep them from the world—or to keep the world at bay until a fee was paid—and transfer them to those who would use them.

Its aim would be a changed society, in which its members had a new relation to property. The corollary was an enforcement unit, which would attend to those who attempted to copyright and patent. Not so radical as to seek to change the distribution of citizens between the classes, but it *was* something.

This was far more attractive to me than the program of the New Dreamers of the Absolute, with their microdets the size of heart pacemakers, and their destructive acts. It seemed a better thing to plant ideas than detonators and plastique. The New Dreamers had already been around the high schools, looking for suitable new members among those of us who might make it through the grading gate. They were at all universities, waiting to recruit their intellectual commandos, waiting for the numbers they needed and working to perfect their organization, which they modeled on the great criminal secret societies.

The New Dreamers of the Absolute

They said: there is no foundation in the individual on which democracy can be built.

They said: the series of events in the mind cannot be understood as a coherent pattern, only as observed, separate, even fragmented parts of a jumble. You cannot say: This inventory can be totaled and has such and such a meaning; all you can say is: it is there.

They stood for imagination: guard the imagination, preserve it, feed it, glorify it, and it will save you.

They said: Each time of change can be a beginning. This is—in general terms—still a beginning. In the beginning was the imagination, and the imagination was fed by the word.

They said: Humanity has reached another starting line, and does not know.

They said again: The light of freedom shines on monsters.

They said further: All humans are brothers and sisters; the only aliens are the State and its servants.

A Picture of Christ Kissing the World

Christ Giving the World a Big Sloppy Kiss, I titled it. Christ was huge, standing in space; the world was a beachball, its colors radiant. Christ's lips covered the belly of Australia.

It was originally meant to be the forty days and forty nights of rain and arklife, then when I thought further the forty days of Christ's desert experience seemed a good link, so Christ had to replace Noah. He had to be loving something, and what better than the world?

And if the temptations took three days, what of the thirty-seven remaining? I had that number of panels arranged as a border round the painting, showing the Son of God in various desert activities, such as catching the odd insect and lizard, straining dew from leaves in the mornings, hiding from bandits and wild animals, performing natural functions, just lying on the heavenly shoulder-blades contemplating, or asleep.

The teachers praised it, but with the things I had on my mind, my heart wasn't listening to them.

Even my weightlifting victories—bench press, squat and dead lift—in my first championship, could not satisfy that part in me that was empty.

English Expression: The Great Man

There is now among us a brain, a sensibility compared to which the rest of us are idiot children. This brain and sensibility is housed in a male body, yet apart from outward signs he is neither, and both.

I have seen him and there is nothing in him. Only those who do not know him like him, and it is impossible to know him. There is nothing in him to like, but, further, there is nothing *in* him. Yet he is a great man.

I have talked to him, and he has nothing to say, yet when he writes the world comes alive.

He does not care to live or die, yet what he does now will live by the spirit that he uses. That spirit is not in him; there is no sign of it in his eyes, his gestures, his way of living. He pulls it out of the air, perhaps, or—and this is a thought I have often—it uses him.

He shows neither sorrow nor joy, regret nor fear, desire nor hatred, yet he knows the bounds of all of them.

He combines words in fantastic, prophetic, heroic and profound ways; he is a performer using a keyboard, yet that keyboard is within him.

He has experienced nothing, and everything. A lion or a trout is familiar to him as a stone, and he sees a universe in that stone and builds it in words.

One person is as another to him, as a bird is, yet all are precious.

He cannot love. Because he knows.

The English teacher was a little worried by this.

"It's all very well using imagination, but you can't rely on some jaded teacher marking your exam paper up on something entirely new to him."

I began to feel that Mr. Ramadan thought he knew better than I did what was in my mind. But the most annoying thing was, he thought everything I did was pointed toward the examinations. I knew perfectly well what to do in examinations: I knew exactly what they wanted.

A White Woman Of a Man

It was only the natural growth of a talented boy into a maturing and brilliant pianist, but I was impressed. Robert Gough had been a pale insipid kid at Primary, and had grown into a pale insipid youth.

In an August recital father took me to, he played Chopin at the Opera House. His hair was cut short, his tails long, and from this replica of the younger piano masters came music that took me and floated me up among the sound reflectors, some way above the pianist on his stage.

It was music that sounded *with* you—how can I say it?—with the inner parts, of you in such a way that they were in time with a music in the blood, as if the notes had always been there, but you had forgotten.

I sat back. The notes hung in the air, unwilling to fall; within a phrase they stepped forward, slowed in mid-stride. Mid-stride? In mid-air. Or were cast out over the surface of silence, like flies for fishes, and drawn back gently. We were an audience of fish with open mouths—to breathe with no noise and not break the silence.

The prunus that grew brown-leaved and flowered pink at the corner of the Goughs' backyard rustled into my mind; I remembered afternoons when I came back from a sweaty, messy root in the playground after school, and the notes of Mozart cascading up out of the window where he played, flirting with the electric wires on their poles and dazzling round my head their mocking clarity. Tears came to my eyes listening to the elegant misery of Chopin, as once or twice they did as I bowed my head at my own strength and sloppiness as the semen of boys leaked down my legs.

I was glad of Chopin's half-tones of tears, and didn't bother wiping my face.

In our snailed, sailed, shelled cathedral of reverence for sound and the movement of sound, Robert Gough bowed, thinking over the keys. He played mazurkas, études, waltzes; cerebral dances, studies of aristocratic sorrow. The stylized frenzy of the performer was held in an easy, cold control that matched the coldness at the heart of Chopin.

I could no longer see the individuals of the audience, only a tear-blurred mass of lumps, and those lumps were human heads.

Robert Gough knew what revolutionary war was, through the master whose fingers wrote the study he played, and in following that other man's notes, he knew what war should be and how his notes should advance, like soldiers with their arms. Always advance, always triumphant.

The polonaises followed. The pianist crouched, an ugly manikin over his helpless instrument, and battled to control the rising tide of sound. But the composer had won that battle over a century before. I began to think of the twin problems laid out before me, of Colin's touch of love and whether I would get through the grading gate toward greatness.

I disliked the polonaises. My thoughts made the memory of the cheerful afternoon street outside the Goughs' house vanish. I sat back, estranged from this crowd, and alien; thinking somewhere within the triangle bounded by genius, glory, and genitals.

I Am Beginning To Be Afraid of Where I Have To Go

My life was unsatisfying. The expectation of something wonderful somewhere in the future had lifted me up for so long that if I began to fall down, I felt I would keep on falling. It could not be possible that an ordinary life was all there was for me. My mother's prophecy accorded too well with my own feelings about the possibilities within me, to let it all go.

I had had every chance. I had every ability necessary. What did I lack? A task? Then it was imagination at fault.

Was I looking in the wrong place?

Did I lack courage to choose? Did I have too much imagination, seeing n possibilities, then multiplying each n by n.

Was I too much caught up with the idea of power?

Was I too proud to fasten on one thing alone?

Was it my too great reverence for my self that had pushed aside my possibilities?

Was it simply that I could not bear to choose?

Was it that I wanted love now, as well as the wonderful future all my childhood years seemed to promise, and these two things were pulling me in different directions?

Yet love had always been impossible to me. How can I say that the power of the touch that haunted me was love or could have led to love? I had never experienced love. To say that love was a reciprocal feeling aroused in me by another's desire, was that to talk about love?

I Wrote This Poem

I wrote this poem about it, but left out all my doubts.

The waves are hungry for the bay
and fast as great wild horses race across

the deep green dangerous kingdoms of the drowned;
the sea is hungry for its love
and so am I.

The cliff is yearning for the sky
and straining upward while it wears away
and bears the marks of blows about its base;
the earth is waiting for its love
and so am I.

The night is restless for the day
and all those cold white stars could tell you why
pointing with stiff fingers without sound
the night's impatient for its love
and so am I.

Letter From Lil

Dear Alex,

I know you know I'm not brilliant like you are, but I know you would always want to be a great person some day and if I was a praying sort I'd have prayed for it to be. As for me all I'm fit for is to look after Kevin, my old man. Did I tell you Gavin left me, and I'm living with Kevin. About the time I left Booker's to work at the hospital, it was. He drinks a lot and that keeps him away from the place a lot and he can hardly raise the effort to do me. One of his kids, Ray, is sitting on a flagpole to raise money for new equipment for the crippled kids' school, I like to have them do things for others, otherwise they get to think they're the only ones on earth. One of our chooks died Saturday and I and Kevin's kids made a coffin for it and tied it up with a ribbon. When they filled the grave in they put a cross made up of two sticks and a bit of string. Kev went crook when he got home from work, he got home early not drunk, that was one time they wished he'd stayed at the pub longer. His own old man used to stay with us, he's not as healthy as my father, I sort of

371

knew he was going to die, he sat on our veranda, listening to the weather. He was cautious like an oyster, didn't say much, not like my father who runs practically instead of walking and talks the hind leg off a donkey. He had trees to look at, the iron-bark that always catches the breeze in its leaves no matter how small a breeze, and the coral tree with red flowers. The day he died the moon was white and flew like a kids kite among the little clouds, and the concrete of the old patio was warm with the sun soaking into it all day, and warm far into the night, long after we called the doctor and lifted him inside onto a bed. He lay on the concrete, it made me think of an old house in sort of ruins, and the tenant gone. I knew he was dead before I got to him.

The day we went to the funeral the sky was like a sea made of grey, bits fell down and we called them drops because they dropped on us. Don't mind me talking like this, funerals make me feel sort of loose, as if bits of me might come off anytime. I was standing there with the two youngest, holding a hand each and no hand left over for my hanky, and I saw something move from the corner of my eye, standing there at the graveside, and you know what it was? One petal of a flower had just opened from its bud, it sort of opened with a click, a click that made no click if you get me, like if you said k softly, and I was so happy I saw that flower open, it was only a freesia, that I cried more, but the kids don't understand if you suddenly take your hand away so I had to stand there with tears down me. They argued before he was buried about where to have the wake, they said not at our place because we had no way to keep the beer from getting warm.

So now I'm writing to you, dearest Al, using this nice silver colored pen that was gifted to me, not given but gifted if you don't mind me twisting English around, and the sun is coming in the door like a, like a what? I guess it's not *like* anything, it just is. Just light. And here's me telling you things like this. Don't mind me, dear Al. I'm sitting here writing this to you and the thought that comes into my head is that nothing ever stops. What happened before, goes on. I don't know why I thought that thought. I guess my duty in life is to bring up the kids and love them and keep on loving my old man no matter what.

I send my love to you too, dearest Al. Please be happy,

Your Lil.

Homework

This winter has been clear and sun-filled. The August winds were late, coming early in September when spring should have started; the weather has turned cold and wet and windy, it is going to be a spring of changes: now hot, now cold; we'll have rain and winds and probably a wet November.

As I watched the world over my homework from my window, a blast of thunder shook the glass in its frame. A storm was on the suburbs. Large raindrops fell, almost sadly, then quicker drops, then lancing spears, drifts of rain, columns of spears coming across the road, kicking up the little bits of splash I used to think of as the cats and dogs it was raining.

Thinking again of that touch, as I do so often, it seems to me that the feeling it gave me, and still gives me in my memory of it, is the nearest thing to the feeling I give myself when I can no longer resist the urge to do it and when it is a really elaborate one with all the subtle touches I like to feel. I can't help it. Perhaps others feel the same way. But what a thought it is—that the best you can think of that you can compare such a magic touch with, and what may follow from that electric touch—is your own masturbation!

Signs of Age

The years since I was a small child have passed like a dream. When I look at myself for signs—at my mirror or my hands—there is nothing fresh to notice. No new lines on my palm; perhaps several on the backs of my hands. Where the thumb meets the body of the hand there's a crease that looks sharper when I waggle my thumb than it was: sharper and deeper, and the skin folding up. As for

373

my face—there's nothing; nothing to tell I'm older and in despair that I might never reach anything at all, let alone achieve. There is, perhaps, something. The fold over my eyes which leads down to my eyelids, seems to be not so full and plumped out as it was: it seems the curve is almost there but some slight amount of flesh underneath has gone.

Imagination is busy, looking for signs.

When the exams are over, I've resolved to spend some time with my parents instead of either working or being out all the time enjoying myself or competing in things.

Thoughts of Colin

How does he do the things he has to do, with such small hands?

Why is his skin so fine and so soft?

Are men's necks meant to be places so desirable to kiss?

Are they meant for a woman's lips to linger on, to camp there?

How can a man's foot be attractive to a female?

Do other women hear music and singing at the movement of a man's wrist?

Is a man's palm meant to be fine and strong, pink and soft, all at the same time?

When he talks to me he touches each word, and each word touches me.

When I am near him his smell, the smell of his skin, starts a thin thread of feeling that travels right down from my chest to my clitoris.

Have other women kissed the ground where a man has trod?

His kiss is sometimes chaste and open, but always golden. On the bed it begins by seeming white, but as his body penetrates mine, his kiss turns transparent gold. At each approach and part withdrawal, his kiss goes through this change—turning white, then golden and transparent as he comes further into me.

He, not just his body, penetrates *me,* not just my body.

My beautiful young man, talk in your dreams to me.

I think about him. I wish I knew who he is, and where to find him. Sometimes I feel so empty, thinking about him, that the world looks bare and has no color. I feel so lonely. I can't stop thinking about him; he fills my head.

Tonight I sat up and wrote a poem to him.

> Gentle invader of my heart and ways
> leave me some neutral space unconquered
> for myself. Since you remain a depth
> I may not fathom, you must rest content
> to know that tangled uninviting thickets
> mined areas, precipices, exist
> in this no-man's-land it would be foolish to enter.
> Better we both respect the boundaries
> we find than try to stumble on the hidden
> final mystery that separates
> you from me and me from what is mine.
> And to this careful, fearful skirmishing
> and reverent warfare, bring the love you are.

Actually, I didn't mean all that. I'd be satisfied if I could find him, then have him near me—his flesh and bones and voice—every time I wanted him to be.

My Tunnel of Inertia

The examinations passed in a blur. I know I did well. After the years of wondering, it seems absurd that I was ever not completely confident. All that is needed now is to wait.

If only my heart didn't feel so dry and empty. The touch that boy gave me, the response in me that had been waiting for it, my helplessness to resist the feelings that flooded up inside me, have given me a new direction; my eyes are no longer entirely on living up to others' expectations. But nothing is strong enough to drive me to action.

My tunnel of inertia is filled with blobs of half-heavy things that move up and down and obstruct each other, defying me and the laws of gravity, and these are evasions and excuses and paranoias.

(All my life I have had a feeling that I am not wholly real, not complete; that I am waiting for something to be added to me. But is that thing my ambition—or is it love?)

Mother's Monument

Today I found what mother was writing. I had come across a list of her sexual intercourse occasions, with descriptions, written up in diaries labeled S. There was one diary for each year since she had started to fuck at fifteen. There were no blank days; when she missed her exercise, as she called it in the diaries, she explained why and how it came about and what she thought of it and him and the situation, the feelings she had expected to have, wanted to have and had been denied, those she would have if she were denied again.

The main discovery was that in the piles of notebooks, all the paper tied and clipped and sewn, the subject was her life and feelings before my conception. At the stage she had reached, she had only just decided to think around the question of whether she would decide to have a baby. There were some notes, though, to be added later, on the subject of my conception. They confirmed what I overheard when I was so very young. All the words, the emotions, summed her anticipations.

There were descriptions of the appearance and the personality of a baby she might have, if she had one. There were a number of differences in these descriptions, but the central unwavering opinion she had was that, when it came, it would be special. *It* meant me. One passage ran: "Even though I have been screwed four thousand one hundred and seventeen times, or rather, on that number of occasions, I know that my baby will be an amazing child."

What sort of mother would she become when she realized I was here? I shouldn't say that, because she loved me. It was all there in the notes.

Though she had never liked or even noticed kids, the first sight of me had done it: she had loved me from that moment, the feeling fading as I got older and moved around more, finally leaving her when I was able to go out unsupervised.

The movement of her love and her feelings was mostly a paper movement.

I saw only the papers available to me there on the table, the most recent ones, and all I read accounted for her feelings as she was preparing to decide about me. I had one look into the older notes. She was a girl of eleven then, searching for an answer to the question: Who am I? Now, at forty-three she was still looking for the answer.

Yet it was a monument of love, though made of paper. I was all there, in anticipation.

What a pity I have no way of knowing her. Yet what good would that do? I would probably be more sorry for her than I am now.

I can see her, bent over her papers—this is a little after nine—always bending over that desk, always concentrating. I feel like writing something about her.

MOTHER

She is a little tired tonight; the slight
of the long-dead whisper re-forms; no storms
forget their original targets, regrets
never fail to return; the trail
of the lightning leads inevitably
back to the first scar.

Those prone—there is no shelter from those shafts—
retire. Their glory was illusion; there is no shame
attaching to certain defeat. Clashing
the broken pieces—shards, tears
brittle as sharp glass—
in the hand, the blood remembers.

And remembers the bright mornings that never were,
nor ever
should be; the comforts invisible, the light intense
that seeks a surface anywhere, in places
always elsewhere. Fall content,
who wake up bruised from dreams
and dream you still sleep.

(Why is it that when I try to write a poem the thing comes out more like poems I've read and less like the truth of what I'm writing about? I don't really think and speak like that. When I think, I'm in a state of—innocence, perhaps—about the world, and all is fresh and new and strange.)

Why didn't I ask more questions? I wish I knew more about her; why she shut herself in. Was there a change neither father nor she told me of?

The Book Burners

I went with my father to watch the late shopping at the shoppingtown.

An artist held a large audience while he painted black branches on gaunt trees and stippled willow leaves over a creek with an old shaving brush. The roughnut Frees, men and women, stood enthralled. The prices scaled from fifty to two hundred, but the glib eighteenth-century beauty he placed on the canvas was too rich and meaningful for them.

Shopping people led round vegetables on leads of leather, raffia; books walked and waddled round on the tiled mosaic floor; old people towed lighted stoves to keep them warm if they felt a moment's chill; a wealthy woman had a man in tow to hold her array of books so that when she felt like it she could stop and have him hold them up and she could read a few sentences and walk on.

Books without visible means of support were corralled in a corner of shoppingtown and burned at the end of every month.

The lust of the public for fire and destruction took a particular lift from the burning of books, symbols of their personal failings and defeats while in the machine of childhood.

Near the Tiki Bar I saw them chained, having fallen from the tables of disgrace where they sold three for a dollar.

Surfers late from the beach, still with their boards leaning against shopfronts, helped make a fire in a waste tin, and threw copies of Marx and Frank Harris on the flames. The fire was no good, though, and some books easily jumped out, springing up fiercely from the ground, and biting at the surfers' pinkly-blue shins. (It had got cold.)

"The only way!" shouted a helper, a thick Dutch person. "The only way! They must be clubbed! Club them to death!" And he laid about him with a wrench of antique design.

Several vagrant books loitered further and further away from the battle, trying to sidle round the corner toward the stair exit to the basement parking area. Copies of William Burroughs and Hemingway, in chains, propped themselves dejectedly by a door.

"Get the porn!" shouted an elderly shopper. "Hard porn, leather porn, plastic porn, steel porn, fashion porn, electronic porn, medical porn—get the lot!"

Surfers, shoppers, secretaries, onlookers, librarians, failed motorists, cripples selling cheap pens, mothers, tourists, trippers, travelers attracted by the violence, came and bashed the books. Admittedly some of the books had been disorderly and drunk, shouting bad things in the public ear, some had been anaesthetized by years of careless thinking, some were abusive, some dishonest, disloyal, some badly written, some with blurred photographs, some with nothing between the covers but photographs.

Jane Austen, with the help of a book of do-it-yourself porn, made a run for it and got under the swing doors of the Tiki Bar and escaped.

My father, always on the alert for the genuine, had something to say about book burners.

"You can see those idiots aren't used to burning books. Look at them," he said disparagingly.

"The way they use the wrist, see? No flexibility, no grace. The way they stand. Stance is one of the features of the judging for competitors in any book burning. The head should be high, but slightly inclined. The aim should never be perfect—that shows less passion than enough. The expression should not be complete joy or unwavering ferocity, but an alternating play of the two, together with a resigned, almost saintly expression. The real *aficionados* build a conical fire, do the correct training, take exercises and the recommended diet, as do those in international competition. At the last Olympics I saw the fires, in rows, all burning at once. Thrilling. They hold that event at night, for crowd purposes, and photograph it for judging at leisure. The only thing that detracted from it was that they took account of each competitor's attitude and contribution to the event as a spectacle. I favor the idea of the competitor as an individual; he should not even notice the presence of other book burners."

Those who smiled and approved book burning were a pitiful sight: they were the failures and the grotesques of our society, the members of Tea Drinkers clubs, rubberites, Footwear Associations, Pedestrian clubs, Anti-Trouser people, Cystitis clubs, Street Decor unions, Park watchers, Open Space Rangers, the neighborhood Tax forces, Alternative Accountants, Shadow Solicitors, amateur architects, noise investigators, professors of flower arrangement, cane products consultants, pore closers and lymph drainers, brick cleaners, personal cleanliness commissioners, and the Changelings.

To me the most pathetic sight was the oldest books, second-hand, dog-eared and faded, going to their death without a sound.

> And the firelight danced
> In the eyes of the free.

As we were leaving I caught sight of a small red glow—a campfire—and half a circle of black people sitting round the fire, clutching spears. The other half of the circular group must have existed somewhere in another dimension of the Aquarium Supplies and Powdered Fish shop. As I stopped to watch, part of a shower of rain descended through the Acousti-Damper ceiling and wet the black backs, but did not seem to cause the fire to sputter, merely to glow brighter.

You Can't Plant All the Forest at Once

I was quiet on the way home after the suburban thrills of shopping. My father must have thought I was upset in some way by the burning—as if in my years on earth I had not adjusted to the events around me.

"Existing is thrusting and violence," he said heavily, yet there was a tenderness in his voice. "The myriad sperm that darted and wriggled in your mother's vagina were conquered and elbowed aside by the sperm that started you. You won. They lost. You are a person; they long since expired on the cold ceramic of the lavatory or in the sewer pipes or the gut of a fish, but most likely in the sewer processing tanks, in a sea of shit. Even the action of your mother in cutting her husband out of the herd to be her servant for life, wasn't that violent? Wasn't that thrusting and competition and eventual winning what her desires then wanted?"

"Yes, father," I said drily.

"Life is a dangerous weapon. By your life you condemn others to oblivion. What you eat cannot be eaten by the hungry of other lands. Remember Clayton Emmet dying because of the need of another to breathe, and so his lungs were pierced." Emmet was a character in one of his plays, I believe.

"To be is to act. To grow is to impose on the world. Humility can only be an addition, it is not evidenced in any reluctance on the part of humans to enter the world. None can be passive while breathing. Dying itself is an action; you cannot be detached from the world. One's dying can harm others, as well as benefit them."

What was he getting round to?

I waited.

"You can't blame yourself for the separation of Frees from Servers, nor for your being so different from those people we've been watching. You can't be blamed for going down the road that's ahead of you."

381

Dear old Dad. He thought I felt badly about the Frees. I suppose I do, in a way. We might as well be divided into classes by a lottery as by merit: merit's just as much a matter of chance.

In my bedroom I lay thinking about my country and how our society had developed in the way it had; how my father and my teachers had ingrained in me the lesson that nothing could be done with the old system. It dug itself in over so many generations, it put out roots, planted stays deep down till nothing could be removed without pulling everything out.

The choice was: pull the lot at once, destroy it, or leave it and add where you could. Since they could not, in Stendhal's phrase, plant all the forest at once, they added, bit by bit.

The people were too quiet, too patient, some said too cowardly and lazy, to have a revolution. Nothing was worth the effort, they felt their very lives to be trivial.

They had no big ideas, no fantastic enthusiasms; they lacked optimism, generosity of spirit, imagination, and that courage that throws open the window of imagination. The division of Society had happened with no opposition: the Free citizens believed in and embraced their inferiority.

Backed against the wall by the expansion of other nations, they seemed introverted, defensive, cramped in every respect.

If the land could be opened! If the people could expand and flex brain and muscle. If they could shake their minds free of the past, free of barbarism, free of slavery; break chains and ties.

Every night I will repeat my hope, that a new enlightenment of my country may redeem two centuries of darkness.

Open Up! Release your energy that you have saved so long!

I excited myself so much with all this unaccustomed concern for others that I found it hard to go to sleep.

It Was My First Sickness

It was a swimming pool party. Little boys with slippery, rubbery skin writhed in the water. Adults who trod on them lost their footing; some struck arms, heads, on tiled edges and were hurt.

382

On the grass people ate, talked, touched each other. I was alone, sitting on the pool edge, my legs in clear water. The smell of chlorine rose up from the wavelets.

Jesus bids us shine when the water covers our bodies in the heavy sunlight.

I sat motionless; people all round me, noisy, exuberant, perhaps happy. I was alone, separate from others. My thoughts flew to Colin, wherever he was.

If I could only see him. Just once. How I wanted to be near him! And if near, what could stop me touching him—touching that skin so fine it rippled in the wind.

If I could be near him, touching him, looking at his face, feeling his eyes on me. And when he'd looked at my face he'd want to look at my arms, my legs, my neck, the palms of my hands, the inner fold of my elbows, my shoulders, the shape of my feet. And I would tear away the fabric of my dress in my haste to have him devour my breasts with his eyes, and touch them and tell me about them. He would touch the curve of my waist with the fingers of his left hand, while his right hand held the nipple over my heart, and he would lean forward and touch it with his lips, then kiss that breast; some kisses passionate and fierce and some so delicate I would have to listen hard to feel them. And I would lean against him so everything was within easy reach for him, and my hand would rest on his shoulder and touch his back and drop until it rested on his thigh, where it would slip a little and cover the warm center of him with his beautiful penis underneath. And his face would come up, and he would look at my eyes, each in turn and from one to the other deciding which he loved best and telling me about the color and the tiny flecks of light and dark radiating from the deep pupil, and I would see the changes on his face and feel inside me the expression of his eyes as they looked at every detail of my body and finally found their way back to mine. And I would lock his gaze onto me, onto my eyes, into me. And the depths in my eyes would draw his soul into me, and I would hold that soul with every strength in me, and holding that, his body would be mine, and he would love me. Me.

I sat letting my thoughts wash over me, then recede till my mind was empty.

. I looked round at the trivial occupations of the other guests. I was alone. There was no Colin here.

I felt tired, as if all my insides had gone out of me. I didn't mind if I slipped off the edge and sank to the floor of the pool. I loved him.

How I loved him! It was such a violent feeling that I could have smashed a few heads together and screamed it out to everyone. But there was no energy left in me.

It was my first sickness. The animal within had decided to fail.

All My Yesterdays Crowding Round

I dragged myself home. Our house was only a few hundred meters away. On the corner of Heisenberg Close, Old Mother Hubbard pulled his coat round him as if against cold rain, but the sun was hot: this rain was in his bones. He said something after me, but I heard nothing.

At home I could see in my father's face that he thought my tiredness, which probably sagged my features, was a mood. Mother didn't look up, she was busy loving me on paper.

I put a knee on my bed and allowed myself to fall on my face. It was a relief.

I thought: I have been logical in my attitude to the world, but the world is not logical. I've learned when I was supposed to learn. I've developed my abilities as best I could. How can I be sick? I've never been sick. I've done nothing to deserve sickness. I thought the irrational was just a frill, a fantastic decoration edging the solid border of the world, but it is an integral, essential part of the world. It has caught up with me because I neither understand it nor respect it. It could destroy me.

Is that unreasonable?

I fell asleep and dreamed. I dreamed of brothers and sisters I'd never had, of dogs speaking to me on footpaths, of costume balls, of women's dresses walking along uninhabited except by full breasts, of men in checks and dirty shoes, of witches holding out for me my costume so that I might be dressed for a ball. (It was a light green jacket, with scarlet bows over the pockets.)

I took train journeys in trains that turned over, scattering debris and dead over a large area. I flew, beating my arms with one strong stroke to clear the traffic, and with four or five strokes rising above housetops. I glided slowly over the lives of the fantastic people that make up the population of my life.

I swam again at that pool party. There was hardly enough water, in fact there was a sucking mud on the pool bottom. Musicians dressed as gypsies abused us with their songs as we struggled in the deepening mud.

Even my dreams felt sick.

It was late afternoon when I woke. I got on my feet, looking hopelessly about for something to potter with.

The old chest of drawers was something.

In the top drawer were things I'd used recently, but it wasn't far underneath to the layers of the past. And in the back corner of the top drawer I found the old apple I stole when I was eight.

Wrinkled, very tiny and dry, it was hardly a red color at all now. It was soft and wrinkled like an old person's skin. Wryly I remembered thinking extraordinary people have the right to transgress with impunity. This withered apple was the evidence. (If I could wake tomorrow and be a little girl again.)

What was the matter with me? I had never felt weak before, or even tired, except for a minute or two after a game or a race. I had done well in the examinations, I would be in the top few percent through the grading gate. I belonged in the Serving Class, not among the Frees, where you expect weakness of all kinds.

Was it the forked path under my feet that even now was tearing me in two directions, that had induced this deplorable, embarrassing weakness? In one direction fame, ambition, greatness perhaps: and the new direction called love.

Why did these things take me in different ways; why couldn't they both point in the same direction? What was the meaning contained in this violent difference between the two?

I felt my pulse. It punched up at my finger strongly. I could feel that pulse all over me: feet, backs of knees; I saw my front throbbing, just above my stomach. When I touched the table, the doorhandle, they throbbed in time with me. They had my pulse. Anything I touched at that moment contained a rhythm directly traceable back to my pulse, my blood, my rhythm.

My heart was struggling at my ribs not in weakness but strength, like a large animal in a too-small burrow. I didn't feel at all sick.

Nor did I feel weak. And I certainly wasn't tired. In that moment I felt as I did just as I was lifting a weight, just as I was taking off from the board on a long jump—I felt marvelous!

A few minutes later I felt so relaxed that I lay flat out on my bed, as easy and boneless as a cat.

A Fabulous Monster

At the table father said: "Darling, your eyes!"

And turned to mother. "See her eyes. Don't you think they're changing? Not grey. More green, but a lot of yellow."

Mother glanced up briefly. "She's probably tired." Her head went down over her plate, and she went on feeding.

"Are they really?" I said. I must have looked alarmed. He quickly reassured me.

"Of course not. Just caught a golden glint. You turned your head, and the light glanced off your eyes with a different color."

I ate ravenously. My father didn't mention my eyes again, but now and then I felt his head turn toward me, watching. What had he really seen? Were they becoming yellow?

Instead of tormenting myself with love and achievement I kept my mind on my food. As I ate, there came into my head a vision of a field of grass as wide as the world, it seemed. I saw rivers and lakes; the waving grasses, bending before light breezes, beckoned to me. I felt caught up in a community of living things that were being called by these watered plains. I stayed with the vision, but rising higher and higher above it until the plains were so far below and the coasts bordering them were in sight, so high that at last Australia was the iris of a great eye, and the coasts its thin border.

I was so cold, so far above the world, in a profound emptiness lashed by a terrible wind. I looked more closely with my changing eyes: the wind was caused by people rushing into existence and living and dying so quickly they couldn't be seen, and it's thousands of years into the future and no desert left in the world, no desert at all.

Time rushed by, roared and whistled, there was a perfume such as I've never smelled before, the smell of spring after spring after spring, all running into one another and rich with living things and everything that grows.

I followed the dream further; it slowed; soon I would see, at the very end, what will be.

Father touched my forehead.

"Darling, you're out in a cold sweat. What's the matter? Something I can do to help?"

I jumped at his touch, my arm came up involuntarily and my nails scratched his arm.

"Sorry," I said, and my voice was peculiar, more like a guttural cough than a girl's voice.

I began, that night, to collect all my pieces of paper, my souvenirs from childhood, fantasies, school compositions; anything that might give someone the clue as to what I was and what I became, and why. On mother's paper I began to write everything I could recall.

I did not know what was happening, except that I was changing. I was never going to be the same again. The animal within hadn't failed: it was asserting itself, it was taking over.

Was I a fabulous monster, a mythical beast that would be a symbol for future females, an archetype for the future?

Whatever words I used I could not conceal from myself that I was now a failure in ordinary terms: I was one with the guilt and grief borne by all other failures and changelings. I shared the punishment visited on the majority: I was free. The responsibility for society rested with others: I would never share it now.

All the time I thought it was youth I was gradually leaving, but it's life as others know it that's going!

Night accepted me as it had never done before, as it must have accepted all those before me who contributed to my inheritance; I felt welcome and borne upwards. I slept like a curled lump. Toward dawn I had a dream: I dreamed that all the words in the world are necessary to make up one soul, and I had blank, numb spaces in me where I had lost many words but no way of knowing which words were gone.

A Straw to Clutch At

I wonder if fame is a kind of greatness. Perhaps I may have fame some day because people will know I believed in a future for mankind. So many, without quite knowing it, never really believe the world will last long after their own demise. That's the next step: the ability to think of the future of the race.

But what was my future?

If only I had been able to love. But now, with this unknowable change coming, the possibility of love was behind me.

Will my change be a kind of death? If it is, the way to face it and stay on an even keel, is to take what I can of it day by day, and enjoy it; holding each moment in front of my face like an absorbing book so I cannot see the rest of the universe or know fear of death. Perhaps this is what animals do.

Will my change be my greatness? (Sometimes I wish I had never heard the word. Or that mother had kept her mouth shut instead of filling my head with such thoughts.)

Dread fills me. Yet I'm not cold about the heart: the reverse rather. When I change, will I remember the dear voice of my father? And mother's too? All they'll have is scraps of schoolpapers, photos, exercise books, prizes, to remember me. But they will live on.

I don't want to give any part of myself to death; I hope this is something other than death. Perhaps I won't be dead at all, but ready to be born again. (Of course I won't be dead: I'll be changed—and free.)

Black Tears

December is nearly gone, and I have got down on paper as much as I can remember. For the rest, the old notebooks and scraps of diaries are interleaved more or less in order in the pile of paper I shall soon bundle up and tie with string. If I find more I will include them.

My skin has changed, and I have father bring my meals to my room. He is terribly worried, poor dear human father.

I have times when I know my voice is not going to work properly, and I write a note for him. Mother is immersed in her work, as usual. My handwriting is unsteady. My grip on the pen has become clumsy.

I stay by myself in my room. The thing in me that is changing me from the inside makes me weep, and the tears are black. But they are not abject: ferocious rather, as if a terrible strength is building in me; and uncertain, for I don't know in what way this strength is to be used, or in what way it will use me.

All I know is that as a human I am some sort of Ugly Duckling: what the swan-equivalent will be I do not know.

The Fear of Alethea Hunt

Everything I thought I was is wrong. The tall girl who seemed to succeed at everything she touched—so healthy and intelligent—contained all the time the seeds of failure and shame. The person who seemed certain to step through the grading gate to become one with the responsible, hard-working Servants of Society, was becoming something other than human.

What am I?

Whatever I become, will I be able to stay sane? Sanity surely is a cushion against reality. No facts, no matter how dire, can have great emotional impact on a sane mind, since sanity depends on a consistent denial of so much of reality: one's deepest instinct is to go on.

If I can take each day as it comes, each change as it comes, and not panic!

Already my time-sense has changed: more movement, more events, seem to fit into each second.

Each night when darkness comes I go outside the house. Although I make no sound as my feet touch the grass, Creep whimpers from his kennel up under the peppermint gum. The sound makes something feel large and free and pleased and brutal in my body—somewhere between my shoulderblades and down as far as my stomach—and I can feel my eyes opening wider, and a brightness forms on the surface of my eyeballs. On the nape of my neck hairs rise. I am answering that in me that is a hunter.

Once, when father didn't know I'd gone out, he heard Creep's fear and came out with a torch. I turned as he pressed the button, and the light shone full on my face.

"What is it?" he gasped, retreating.

"Only me," my deep cough of a voice said. The light shone on my clothes, and he knew it was me.

"Your eyes," he said. And "Oh God!" pressing his hand to his head in theatrical despair. "They reflect the light. Like a—!"

He stopped. I stopped. I signed gently with my hand for him to go in first. He wasn't to look at me.

He did as I wanted.

The Light of Freedom Shines on Monsters

My thumb is retreating. It's hard to grip a pen. There is fur between my fingers. How I have managed this far I do not know.

Even with hands changing and eyes different, my body hairs getting thicker and standing up stiffly, my freedom to walk the streets gone, there is still something in me that has the will to do what I set out to do, and the will to be free to do it.

Ill Would Change Be at Whiles
Were It Not for the Change Beyond the Change.

I will go as soon as this shape becomes too awkward for me to be in a house. I hope I will be able to drive.

In my mind's eye I see a vast lake a thousand kilometers long and half a thousand wide. At the edge of it are towns, and quite near the towns the grass starts and a bit further back the first line of trees, then a patchwork of forests interspersed with grazing land and cultivated land. And a network of water channels bringing life.

I see a vast natural tract of wilderness where the rocks and stones are too thick for anything but trees and wild game.

Ah! my lake. I see its edge, I see the sun rising on it in the morning and setting in a red blaze before the dark wheel of night returns the sky to its deepest blue.

Last Letter From Lil

Dearest Al,

Here I am and there's nothing in the house but washed pots and peas. Something has come over me, I feel as if I've been hanging in a closet all day and they take me down at night, I guess I mean I feel as if I don't exist. When I go out and walk on the street, all I meet is eyes, hardly any people. Do you ever feel like this? And all the time waiting, waiting to go nowhere, waiting for someone with enough money to buy up my hunger. Did you ever think that birds and even poor moths have a better view of this world than we do? I often think that. I wonder if me feeling like this means someone close to me is in a bad way and I don't know. When I go to the town to get money for my pension check—I get extra now my guy's gone, but I need it for his kids and the new one coming: my one—I look up at the bank in the way people used to look up at cathedrals. Do you ever have the feeling, when you're in the middle of an emotion, that you want to keep it, maybe in your mouth, for if you let it go through you it will melt when it gets to your heart and you've lost it? I do.

I read in the magazine section of the Sunday paper that bits of skin are coming off all of us all the time and they get circulated round about, in the air and things—well, the germs and mites on the skinflakes must get to be brothers with everyone else's, mustn't they? I like little thoughts like that. I'm sorry to be nattering on about my worries, I'd hate anyone to think I was looking for sympathy. Did you know our flowers turned black in the garden? I thought at first it was the kids, but it was something in the plants.

When I was in the doctor's waiting room looking at the fish tank, waiting for them to blink, I dreamed I saw the doc's face through the tank, he beckoned me into the surgery, put me on the bed, and approached me slowly like a boat trying to make it to the shore when the tide won't let it and the current strong. But then he picked up my dress at the hem and cut it with his knife and it began to bleed. Isn't that a crazy dream? I hope some day you get the joy of passing on life, even though I don't want you to have to sacrifice yourself in any way. Love to my friend always,

Lil.

Last Words

The future is somehow . . .
somewhere in the despised and neglected desert,
the belly of the country
not the coastal rind.
The secret is in the emptiness.
The message is the thing we have feared,
the thing we have avoided
that we have looked at and skirted.
The secret will transform us
and give us the heart to transform emptiness.
If we go there
If we go there and listen
We will hear the voice of the eternal.
The eternal says that we are at the beginning of time.

Alethea Hunt, with 490 marks out of a possible 500 in the final High School examinations, was placed second in the State to a male student with 491.

She was at her family home when notification of this result was received from the Education authorities.

Several days later, she left with food supplies in her small car and drove toward the mountains, apparently headed past them toward the western plains. Civil authorities broadcast appeals to the public not to shoot at animals of unfamiliar or exotic species. To the date of publication of this book the car has not been found, nor has Alethea Hunt been sighted. In addition, there have been no complaints from farmers, graziers or cattlemen in regard to depredations on flocks, herds or poultry.

Mr. Hunt has offered a reward of one hundred thousand dollars if Alethea Hunt, or a female leopard, is captured painlessly and without injury.

Text Classics

The Commandant
Jessica Anderson
Introduced by Carmen Callil

Homesickness
Murray Bail
Introduced by Peter Conrad

Sydney Bridge Upside Down
David Ballantyne
Introduced by Kate De Goldi

Bush Studies
Barbara Baynton
Introduced by Helen Garner

A Difficult Young Man
Martin Boyd
Introduced by Sonya Hartnett

The Cardboard Crown
Martin Boyd
Introduced by Brenda Niall

The Australian Ugliness
Robin Boyd
Introduced by Christos Tsiolkas

All the Green Year
Don Charlwood
Introduced by Michael McGirr

The Even More Complete
Book of Australian Verse
John Clarke
Introduced by John Clarke

Diary of a Bad Year
J. M. Coetzee
Introduced by Peter Goldsworthy

Wake in Fright
Kenneth Cook
Introduced by Peter Temple

The Dying Trade
Peter Corris
Introduced by Charles Waterstreet

They're a Weird Mob
Nino Culotta
Introduced by Jacinta Tynan

The Songs of a Sentimental Bloke
C. J. Dennis
Introduced by Jack Thompson

Careful, He Might Hear You
Sumner Locke Elliott
Introduced by Robyn Nevin

Terra Australis
Matthew Flinders
Introduced by Tim Flannery

My Brilliant Career
Miles Franklin
Introduced by Jennifer Byrne

The Fringe Dwellers
Nene Gare
Introduced by Melissa Lucashenko

Cosmo Cosmolino
Helen Garner
Introduced by Ramona Koval

Dark Places
Kate Grenville
Introduced by Louise Adler

The Long Prospect
Elizabeth Harrower
Introduced by Fiona McGregor

The Watch Tower
Elizabeth Harrower
Introduced by Joan London